Fortune Falls

Book 1

Lou Vane

Cover designed by MiblArt
Edited by Heidi Spear

ISBN: 978-0-6452100-0-2

www.louvane.com

*I'm haunted by the memory of a girl. A girl who loved and was
loved, who dreamed of building a better world and being part of it.
I'm haunted by the memory of the girl we sacrificed.
That girl was me.*

CHAPTER 1

I lose count of the number of times I fall as I skid my way down the muddy track, hurrying to catch up. As the bank drops steeply in front of me, I hesitate, then grab hold of a branch, using it to slow my descent until my feet wedge safely against a tree root.

I let go of the branch and take another step. Both feet immediately slide in front of me, throwing me off balance. My arms flail and I overcompensate, throwing myself backwards and land heavily on the ground with a thud ... again.

This is ridiculous! I kick at an exposed tree root. *We aren't really going to continue in this weather, are we?*

I look further down the slope and see him waiting for me. His face turned away as he strains to hear the others, who I can just make out through the trees near the top of the waterfall. They're yelling to him, but I can't hear what they're saying. Their voices drowned out by the river echoing off the gorge walls and the rain pounding on the hood of my jacket.

Suddenly they begin to run toward us.

"What's going on?" I yell above the roar of the river, now so loud I can feel it.

He spins around, eyes wide with panic. "Run!" he screams as he scrambles back up the slope toward me. "Jess! RUN!"

His panic spurs me into action. I roll onto my knees so I'm now facing uphill, frantically grabbing at branches and tree roots, anything that will help to pull myself up. Finally, I'm standing, but my feet can't get traction as the earth slides beneath me. The roar continues to increase until it's deafening—terrifying. I *am* terrified, but I have no idea what of. All I know is that I need to get away from whatever it is they're running from.

The ground shakes, making the mud flow faster, the thunder in my ears reaching a crescendo as I make agonisingly slow progress back up the slope.

And then, almost as quickly as it starts, it stops. The ground stops shaking, the noise returning to the low rumble of the river.

I collapse to the ground, panting, and roll over to look back down the slope, expecting to see the others coming up the trail behind me. But the shock of what I see takes my breath away.

They're gone, all of them.

But not *just* them—*everything* is gone. The trees, the trail, the hillside we'd just been walking on. It's all gone.

My hands begin to shake, then my whole body. But this time it isn't the ground that's shaking, it's all me. I try to slow my breathing, to push down the panic. Willing myself to keep it under control.

Come on brain, stay with me. Don't abandon me now.

I shuffle to a nearby tree, clinging to it for protection in the hope that it will stop me from disappearing too. I remove my backpack and take the coil of rope slung across my shoulder and loop it around the tree. My hands fumble as I tie the rope in place and then attach it to my climbing harness. Only then can I breathe.

You're okay. You can't fall now.

I slump against the tree, blinking back tears as I stare at the spot where I'd been standing moments earlier. My entire body shudders as I realise what has happened.

The whole hillside has given way, crashing through the gorge below. The force of its power gouging away rock, so that the river that once flowed over the cliff in a waterfall has now been rerouted around it as well.

This can't be real. This can't be happening.

My lungs draw ragged breaths as I lower myself onto my stomach and begin to crawl down what's left of the slope. I let the rope out slowly, making sure it stays taut in case the ground crumples out from beneath me. I force myself to go as far as I can until I reach the edge.

I scan the chasm, searching for signs of my friends, hoping they've somehow survived and are waiting to be rescued. But I can't see anyone. There's nothing but mud and broken trees and rocks and more mud.

"No, no, no, no, no, no, no …"

I feel the panic begin to rise again. I try to hold it down but I can't, my body shaking uncontrollably.

They're all gone.

CHAPTER 2

Two weeks earlier

I look back at the man grumbling impatiently behind me, then to the queue of people that's formed behind him. Anxious heads search for the source of the noise growing in intensity somewhere out of sight. Everyone's on edge. Trapped with no means of escape. They know what's coming. We all do. And we're powerless to stop it.

No one can stop a crying baby.

I hear an exasperated huff and switch my gaze back to the man again. He's staring—no, he's glowering at me. *Seriously?* I frown at him. *What's your problem? It's not as if your seat's going anywhere.*

I glance down at his empty hands—there's not a bag in sight. He's still glaring at me when I look back up at his sour face. *I guess you carry your baggage on the inside, don't you, pal?* I shake my head, then return my attention to the young man, still hunched over his phone in the aisle seat.

"Excuse me," I repeat, adding a gentle tap on his shoulder this time.

Finally, he looks up, taking off his headphones, and I realise he's younger than I thought. Probably not much older than me.

"Hi. Sorry. I've got the window seat."

"Oh, sure," he says, undoing his seatbelt.

As the boy begins to stand, Mr. Impatient decides he can't possibly wait fifteen more seconds and tries to push past, rudely thrusting me forward. I fling out my hands to stop myself from falling, but my hands shoot straight over the headrest and I fall … chest first … into the boy's upturned face.

"Oh my god!" I yelp as he lets out a smothered grunt, trying to push me off him.

I flounder against him, struggling to untangle myself. I'm completely mortified, certain *nothing* could be more embarrassing— but I couldn't be *more* wrong. Because as we part, so does my blouse, opening all the way to my waist.

"Oh my god!" I shriek even louder, frantically doing up the buttons. "I'm so sorry!"

"It's fine, really." He laughs as he steps out into the aisle. "You don't need to apologise, seriously."

I cringe an embarrassed half smile, too mortified to make eye contact, and slide past him to my seat. From the corner of my eye, I see him watching me, but I'm still too flustered to look back, and begin rummaging in my bag for my phone.

Calm down, Jess, it's fine. You don't know him. He'll go back to looking at his phone in a second and you can just forget this ever happened.

I pull out my headphones, wishing they're noise-cancelling ones, as the child's wailing grows louder, and look up to see a frazzled woman carrying three bags and a toddler. I forget my embarrassment as I watch her strained face shuffle slowly toward me, grimacing apologetically as she makes her way down the plane. She pauses at the row in front of me and I hold my breath, willing her to keep going, then let out a loud sigh when she begins to usher her children into the seats. *Dammit!*

"Hi, I'm Matt." I almost don't hear him over the ear-splitting screams.

I look over at the boy I smothered, and he immediately stretches his hand across the empty middle seat. His brown eyes twinkle cheekily as he grins at me and then yells above the crying, "I figure we should at least be on a first name basis after that."

"It's nice to meet you, Matt," I yell back, shaking his hand. "I'm Jess."

"Nice to meet you too, Jess," he shouts as the wailing suddenly stops. Heads whip around to look in our direction and we both burst out laughing as Matt grimaces and tries to shrink out of sight. The air hostess standing at the row in front of us, pauses to give us a wary look before returning to her conversation with the mother.

"You can't be serious!" The mother's voice rises in distress. "We *confirmed* it would be okay for one of the twins to sit on my lap when we made the booking. I've got *three* kids and there's only one of me. What are you suggesting I do?"

Matt and I exchange a baffled look, then watch the air hostess wave to one of her colleagues further up the plane. As the colleague begins to walk down the aisle, Matt leans forward to get the mother's attention. "I'd be happy to help if I can. There's a spare seat right here beside me. We'd be happy to help, wouldn't we?"

Are you completely insane?

I manage to close my gaping mouth before he turns to look at me. He nods enthusiastically at me with smiley eyes and my head automatically starts to nod back … and before I can stop myself, my mouth opens and I say, "Yeah sure, if you think one of them would be okay to sit with us?"

Oh my god, Jess! What are you doing!?

The mother speaks to the child sitting beside her, then turns to look at us. "That would be wonderful, thank you," she says, lifting the boy into the aisle and leading him around to us. "This is Charlie."

"Hi, Charlie. I'm Matt, and this is Jess. Would you like to come and sit with us?"

Charlie gives a nod, his face breaking into a smile. Matt lifts him to stand on the seat between us, where he plops down with a giggle.

"How old are you Charlie?" Matt asks as he puts on Charlie's seat belt.

"Four and a half. How old are you?"

"Oh, I'm ancient. I'm seventeen and a half." He nods seriously.

Knew he was my age.

As Charlie wriggles excitedly in his seat, I begin to wonder how we're going to keep him entertained for the next couple of hours when Matt pulls out his phone and starts showing Charlie a game. Charlie immediately quietens and begins swiping at the screen, and I feel my apprehension easing as Matt patiently teaches him how to play.

"You're really good with kids," I say as Matt helps Charlie put on his headphones.

"I've just had a lot of practice, I guess. I come from a pretty big family." He shrugs. "There's six of us, and I'm the oldest. My youngest sister isn't much older than Charlie here."

"Wow, that *is* a big family. Your parents aren't Catholic by any chance?"

"Woah, stereotype much! But yeah." He rolls his eyes at me. "I guess you'd call them non-practicing."

"Non-practicing … contraception? 'Cos obviously they've been practicing the sex part just fine." I grin at him.

His face contorts. "You *do* realise that's my parents you're talking about?"

Heat instantly rushes to my face, humiliated at my failed attempt to be witty. *How could I say that to someone I've only just met?*

"Sorry, I didn't mean to offend." I look at him apologetically, then notice his eyes crinkling at the corners.

"Lucky for you, it takes a bit more than that to offend me. Like trying to smother me with your bosom, for instance. But hey, you've already done that and I'm still talking to you." He chuckles.

"Bosom!" Now it's my turn to . *Who uses that word?* I feel my face heating again and decide a change of subject is urgently needed. "It must be nice having so many brothers and sisters."

"Yeah, most of the time. But being the eldest isn't always that great though. I have to spend a lot of time helping out with the younger ones. Sometimes I wish I could just do my own thing like my friends do. What about you? Do you have any brothers or sisters?"

"No, it's just me. I've always wanted a sister, though. Maybe you could share one of yours?"

"How about a brother? I'm kinda fond of my sisters." He grins.

"I've got two children's meals and a vegetarian meal," the air hostess interrupts.

"The vegetarian meal is mine," Matt says, taking the meal. "And obviously the children's meals are for these two kids."

I screw up my nose at him and lower Charlie's tray table for Matt to place the meal on.

"Let's see what you've got to eat." Matt takes the cover off Charlie's food, clearly in the habit of taking care of his brothers and sisters.

I find myself smiling at him, impressed by his kindness toward this little boy and his mother when it hadn't even crossed my mind to help them. *I wonder how many guys our age would do this? Maybe they would, and it's just me who's selfish.* I feel embarrassed as I realise there's probably a big difference between me and people like Matt, and the sudden insight doesn't sit comfortably.

"I can help Charlie while you eat your meal if you like? You can enjoy not having to look after someone else for a change."

"Are you sure?" Matt raises his eyebrows at me as I nod. "Well, you know where I am if you need me. Good luck."

I give him a quizzical look. *What does that mean?*

"What do you want to eat first, Charlie?" I lift the edge of the bread to see what's inside. "Looks like you've got a ham and cheese sandwich."

"Don't like cheese."

"Oh, that's okay. We can just take the cheese out and then it's a ham sandwich," I say perkily. *No big deal, I've got this.*

"Don't like ham."

Are you kidding me? I glimpse Matt watching me out of the corner of my eye.

"Okay … how about we take the ham out too? You like bread don't you?"

"Mm-hmm. Bread's okay."

"Great, well, here's a yummy *bread* sandwich for you."

Matt snorts into his drink, then begins to cough.

"You okay?" I give Matt a sideways look.

"Yeah, I'm fine," he says between coughs.

I pick up a container of strawberry yogurt as Matt returns to his food. "I bet you like yogurt though, don't you?"

"You've got to be careful—" Matt starts to warn as I pull back the lid of the yogurt and it explodes out of the container. Charlie erupts into laughter.

"Why would they serve something that would explode!?" I sputter, looking down at my shirt, now covered in splotches of pink yogurt.

"Entertainment value?" Matt holds out a paper napkin to me.

I take the napkin and daub the yogurt from my face and top, feeling like a complete idiot. I feel like I've done nothing but embarrass myself since I met Matt. It's just been one blunder after another. And although I know I'll probably never see him again, I like this handsome, smiley boy and I want him to like me too. But at this rate, he's going to think I'm a complete clown.

Matt takes over looking after Charlie so I can eat, and I'm relieved to have a few moments where I'm not falling or spilling food or saying something stupid. By the time Charlie's mother hands back a small bag of toys for Charlie to play with, I'm determined to show Matt that I'm actually capable of doing something without making an idiot of myself. And yes, maybe it's because I want Matt to like me, but it's *also* because I want to prove to myself that I'm not as selfish as I suspect I am.

I offer to play with Charlie as he pulls toy cars from the bag, but it isn't long before I realise it isn't helping to dispel my goofball image. I try not to feel self-conscious as Matt grins at me, fumbling my way through Charlie's games, vrooming the cars over his table and mine. That is, until Charlie performs a supersized crash and flings his car directly into the side of my face. My hand jerks protectively to my cheek as I try not to react, not wanting to let on how much it hurts.

"Bet you never realised a four-year-old could be so dangerous," Matt says.

I gingerly touch my cheek bone and feel a hot raised welt and realise the final remnants of dignity I'd been hoping to salvage are now completely in tatters.

"Yeah, that's going to leave a bruise," Matt says sympathetically.

Great. Why today of all days? This is not the first impression I want to be making.

Matt continues to play with Charlie for the rest of the flight, keeping him occupied. He often looks up at me and smiles as they talk, making sure I'm included. Usually, I wouldn't have cared less if I'm included in a conversation with a four-year-old, but Matt makes me want to be a part of it.

"Thank you so much for taking such good care of Charlie." His mother leans over the back of her seat when the seatbelt sign turns off.

"You don't need to thank us. We've had a great time, haven't we, Charlie?" Matt ruffles Charlie's hair, then steps into the aisle and opens the overhead compartment. As he hands down the last bag to the mother, he smiles over at me, catching me watching him, and I feel a tingle of excitement run up my spine.

Come on, Jess, you like him. Why don't you give him your number? You know you want to.

...But maybe he's not interested. He'd ask for it, if he wanted it, wouldn't he?

"Let me give you a hand with those." Matt takes some of the mother's bags as she joins the queue, moving down the aisle.

Oh. He's going? I can't believe he's leaving without even saying goodbye.

At the last second, Matt calls back over his shoulder to me, "Catch you later, Jess."

I swallow my disappointment and force a smile. "Yeah, sure. Catch you later, Matt." Then he disappears out of sight.

After the aisle clears, I make my way into the airport and scan the busy terminal, hoping to see Matt. But there's no sign of him, so I head to the toilets to check out the damage.

I sigh at my reflection. *No wonder he didn't want your number. You look a mess!* Not only do I have a welt on my cheek, my hair and shirt are spattered with yogurt. Leaning over the sink, I use the tap to rinse the ends of my hair, then dry them with the hand-dryer. I change into a fresh t-shirt from my bag and take one last look in the mirror. It'll have to do.

I make my way through the bustling airport, following the signs to the baggage claim where I'm supposed to be met by someone from the Institute. My disappointment about Matt begins to disappear, replaced by a growing feeling of anticipation as I get closer to the meeting place. I've been looking forward to today since I received my acceptance letter from the Youth Leadership Programme three months ago, and now it's finally here.

I know that in the next few hours I'm going to meet people who will change my life forever. This programme isn't just about teaching us how to become better leaders, it's about making friendships and connections that will last a lifetime in the hope that we'll work together to make the world a better place.

"Naïve idealism," my dad had said to me when I told him I got accepted into the programme. I was floored by his response. He knew how much getting into this course had meant to me. He knew that I lay awake at night worrying about the kind of future that's in store for us. Yet he still didn't understand why I felt the need to do something, to be part of the solution.

"I can't sit back and watch as our world continues to be let down by its leaders," I replied. "Change needs to happen now, and at this rate, it's going to be up to my generation to do it. I want to be a part of that."

"I agree, honey, and I'm proud of you for wanting to be part of it." Mum hugged me. "And maybe it is naïve idealism." She gave my dad a pointed look. "But that's exactly what makes the potential for change possible."

I find myself smiling at the memory of Mum's words as I ride the escalator to the baggage claim. I scan the line of people holding placards at the bottom until I get to a man holding two signs, one saying 'Priya Amin' and another saying 'Jessica Maddox'.

I step off the escalator and walk over to the man, fixing the most confident smile I can muster, and hold out my hand. "Hi, I'm Jess."

"Hi, Jess, I'm Marley. How was your flight?" He shakes my hand, returning my smile.

"Surprisingly good, actually!"

He gives me a strange look, as though my response was unusual. I guess it was a little strange, but meeting Matt *had* made it a surprisingly good flight. Not that I can tell him that though.

"The um, view, it was incredible. I've never seen such huge mountains before. They're amazing."

Marley nods. "They certainly are. I prefer to see my mountains from the ground though. I'm not really a fan of flying myself."

"Yeah, I know what you mean. Can make your arms tired. Better to let the plane do it."

Marley doesn't seem to appreciate my joke, but at least someone does, as laughter bursts out behind me. I turn to see who it is and my stomach cartwheels.

CHAPTER 3

"Hey! I thought you'd left already."

"No, not yet, just getting my bag." Matt looks down at the small wheelie bag at his side.

"I'm so glad to catch you. I didn't think I was going to get the chance to say goodbye properly. I was thinking … I don't know if you're interested, but I was wondering if you—"

"Looks like you two already know each other?" Marley interrupts.

"Oh, yeah, we go way back. We're *bosom* buddies, aren't we, Jess?" His eyes twinkle mischievously.

Laughter explodes out of me, taking us both by surprise. "Yeah, we're *breast* mates," I manage to reply between fits of giggles.

"Oh, nice one!" Matt slaps me on the back, laughing.

Marley is looking at us like we're completely mad.

"We met on the flight," Matt explains as we try to stop laughing. "Bit of a long story."

"So, you're on the leadership camp too?" I ask.

"Yeah, small world, huh? It was a surprise to me when I saw your name, too." He looks toward the signs Marley's holding.

Marley spreads them out in a fan and I see there's a third one that I hadn't noticed before saying 'Matthew Davidson'.

"What were you saying before?" Matt asks. "Something you

thought I might be interested in?"

You can't exactly give him your number now that you're on the camp together, can you?

"Hi, I'm Priya. You must be from the Institute."

I turn to see a girl holding out her hand toward Marley as she introduces herself.

Oh, thank god for Priya!

"Hi, Priya, I'm Marley. This is Jess and Matt. They're also students on the course."

"Hi." She gives us a friendly wave.

"Hi." I smile back, immediately feeling inadequate. She's average height, but that's where our similarities end. Her mahogany hair is so long it reaches the middle of her back and is gorgeous, like everything else about her. I can't fault anything, and I'm trying hard to find a fault. But she's picture perfect—her clothes, her body, her skin, her teeth. I catch the subtle scent of jasmine as she flicks her hair over her shoulder. She even smells great.

I look down at my jeans and pull self-consciously at my t-shirt, feeling frumpy and boring in comparison. I push my hair away from my face, wishing I hadn't just had to dry it in a hand-dryer, cringing as I get a waft of strawberry yogurt.

"Hi, Priya. Nice to meet you." Matt's face lights up with the same warm smile I saw on the plane. I swallow as I realise either Matt does this with everyone, or he thinks Priya is just as beautiful as I do.

"Now that we're all here, we can get going. Have you all got your bags?" Marley asks.

"I checked in mine." Priya looks uncomfortably at my backpack as I nod in reply, then gives a nervous laugh. "I know we were told we'd be given everything we need, but I brought some extra things, just in case."

"No problem. Let's go get it then." Marley turns toward the baggage carousels.

We watch the bags as they come past on the conveyor belt, waiting for Priya's to arrive. My mouth drops open when she heaves an enormous hard-shell suitcase off the conveyor, then laughs nervously as she turns to see our stunned faces. "I wasn't sure what I'd need."

Her face radiates embarrassment and I feel a surge of joy at knowing she has an imperfection after all. I begin to think of something sarcastic to say and then realise I'm just being nasty for no reason … other than that she makes *me* feel insecure. But it's painfully obvious that Priya is feeling pretty insecure herself right now. "Well, you'll definitely be prepared for any eventuality."

Relief flickers in Priya's eyes, and she gives me a shy smile before turning to follow Marley to the exit. Marley leads us to a white van in the carpark, and as soon he lifts the back door open, Matt offers to help Priya with her suitcase.

"Thanks, Matt. I feel a bit embarrassed that I brought such a big bag." She stands back to let Matt take it.

I have to stop myself from laughing as Matt grunts in surprise as he lifts it into the back of the van. "Don't worry about it. Happy to help." He looks down at her and I swear his cheeks look flushed.

Probably just exertion from lifting the suitcase.

"You okay, Matt? You look like you might have pulled something." I grin as I climb into the van beside Priya, moving over to make room for him on the seat beside me.

Matt ignores me and shuts the door.

"I guess not then," I say under my breath and watch him get into the front seat beside Marley instead.

Marley calls back over his shoulder as he drives, "Our base is in Falls River. It's about an hour's drive from here. That's where we'll meet the others. You guys are the last to get here—the rest of the students arrived this morning."

"How many students are there?" I ask.

"There were supposed to be twelve in your group, but we received a couple of last-minute cancellations this morning due to illness, so there's only going to be ten of you."

"Oh, I thought there'd be more students doing the programme," Priya says.

"There are. We're running three courses back-to-back this summer. You're the second group, and there's one more after you. You'll get to meet the students from the other camps later in the year at the leadership conference."

Matt and Marley continue talking to each other, but it's hard to hear in the back, so I stop trying to listen and move my gaze toward the side window. As I do, I catch Priya looking at me.

"I don't mean to pry," she says shyly. "But I can see that your cheek is looking bruised." When I don't answer her immediately, she continues, "I'm sorry. I should just mind my own business."

"No, it's okay. I just got hit by a kid playing with a toy car on the flight. It's nothing."

"I know this is probably hard to believe given how small my bag is." She smiles wryly. "But I've got some concealer if you want to use it to cover the bruise."

"Really? That'd be great, thank you."

Priya reaches into a small bag on her lap and rummages through her things, then holds out a tube of concealer and a compact.

"Thanks," I say, taking them, and begin to apply the concealer. "Lucky for me you brought a few extra things."

"I feel so embarrassed about my bag." Priya gives me an uncomfortable smile. "My mum bought it as soon as she heard that my school wanted to nominate me for the leadership programme. She was so excited—so sure my application would be accepted. She wanted to surprise me. It was too late to return it by the time we got the information pack saying what we need to bring. I didn't want to disappoint her. She said it was the nicest bag she'd ever had. So, we packed it with pretty much everything I own."

"Everything?"

"Seriously, my wardrobe is almost empty." She laughs.

"My mum was pretty excited about my nomination too. My Dad, not so much. He thinks this is a waste of time and I should be 'using my summer more productively'."

"Really? What could be more productive than going on a leadership development camp?"

"Summer school."

"You go to school over the summer?"

"Usually. He thinks it will give me a better chance at getting accepted into Ashley. He's got his heart set on me going there. But I couldn't do it because of this camp."

"Oh, you're going to go to Ashley?" Priya looks impressed.

"That's where my dad *wants* me to go, but I doubt I'll even get in. My pick would be Spurrier."

"Me too! How awesome would it be if we ended up going to

Spurrier together? Maybe we could be roommates?"

"Maybe." I can't help but smile at Priya's enthusiasm.

"I can't wait to go to college," Priya gushes. "I love my mum, but she can be a little suffocating sometimes." She cringes guiltily.

So, even someone as nice as Priya feels this way. Maybe we aren't so different after all.

"I know what you mean. For me, it's my dad though. He has this master plan for me. He doesn't think I'm mature enough to know what I want." I shake my head. "If it wasn't for my mum, I wouldn't be doing this programme at all. But she said if she'd done what her parents had wanted her to do, she would never have become a lawyer. She'd be married to her high school boyfriend and working as a receptionist at her dad's old accounting firm."

"I guess it's hard for some parents to let their babies go."

"Yeah, but that's the problem. We aren't babies anymore."

We continue our journey for nearly an hour, slowing only as we reach a sign saying 'Welcome to Falls River'. We enter a small town with a wide main street, continuing until we pull off the road just as we're about to leave the town limits on the other side. We turn onto a short gravel driveway and pull into a car park in front of a building emblazoned with the words 'Falls River Guides' above the entrance.

Marley turns off the engine and looks at us in the rearview mirror. "This is it, guys. Grab your bags and let's head inside to meet the others."

"I'll give you a hand with your suitcase," Matt says to Priya as we climb out.

I reach into the back of the van to get my backpack, and Matt puts his hand out to stop me. "Allow me. It might be *booby* trapped."

"Oh, ho, ho." I laugh sarcastically. "They just keep on coming, don't they."

"I was planning that the whole ride here," he says proudly. "I've got more, you know."

"I don't doubt it. Maybe save some for later." I shake my head, laughing.

"Oh, come on, there's just one more I need to get off my *chest* …" He cracks up, slapping his leg as I give him an evil look. "I'm done, seriously. There's no more." He reaches into the van and hands me my bag, wiping a tear from the corner of his eye, then heaves Priya's suitcase out and drags it across the gravel to the front door.

We enter a large noisy room filled with people and bags, the walls on one side hidden by racks and blue bins. Most of the students are sitting on bench seats around an enormous wooden table off to one side of the room, but there are others looking at items on the racks.

We add our bags to the pile already in the corner and turn around, aware that the noise in the room has quietened as everyone stops talking to check out the new arrivals. The three of us stand awkwardly, unsure what to do.

Marley walks over to us and hands us each a sticker with our name on it. "Why don't you grab a seat at the table?"

We make our way over to the table and I smile at no-one in particular as I sit beside Priya at one end and Matt takes a seat across from us.

"Hi, I'm Lily." A girl with shoulder-length blonde hair introduces herself.

"Hi, I'm Jess and this is Priya." I lean back a little so Lily and Priya can see each other more easily. "And that's Matt," I say, looking across the table toward Matt, who's already talking to a boy with a sticker saying 'Dean' on it.

"Can I have everyone's attention?" The room falls silent as we all turn to face Marley standing at the front of the room. "Can everyone take a seat at the table, please?" He waits a moment while the rest of the students join us.

"Oh my!" Lily says, and I follow her gaze back to the front of the room where Marley has been joined by three other people. It takes me a moment to work out what she's reacted to as I look along the line of new faces.

Standing next to Marley are two sporty looking women wearing red polo tops with an emblem of a river cutting through mountain peaks and it says 'Falls River Guides' underneath. But Lily's eyes are fixed on the man on the other side of them, another of the guides, who is laughing at something they've said.

He stands half a head taller than either of the women next to him, with dark brown hair poking teasingly out beneath his cap. His physique is muscular, but not in a weight-lifting kind of way. It looks like it's as a result of doing his job—in addition to some very good genes. He looks like he doesn't care about his appearance, which makes me wonder if it's deliberate. Maybe he doesn't know how good he looks, or maybe he knows, but doesn't care. Either way, Lily's reaction isn't *completely* unjustified.

"Welcome to Falls River, everyone, and to the first module of the Youth Leadership Programme. I think I've managed to meet most of you by now, but just in case we haven't met, I'm Marley. I'm a Professor of Psychology at Spurrier University and I'm also an associate with The Global Leadership Institute. This is Spurrier's first year working with T.G.L.I. and we completed our first camp a couple of days ago. You'll be relieved to know it went extremely well. We had a lot of fun, with only a few minor injuries and broken bones."

There's a spatter of uncomfortable laughter around the table, none of us certain whether he's joking or not. Marley sees his joke has fallen flat and raises his hands as if to placate an unhappy crowd. "I'm kidding. Of course, there weren't any injuries. A few bruised egos maybe, but no broken bones." He smiles reassuringly. "So, as I was saying, this is going to be a great experience for you all. But I want to give this reminder at the outset. This is not a holiday. It is going to be hard work. We're going to push you to your limits with the intention of helping you to learn about yourselves, to grow, and eventually become better leaders. But we *will* have a lot of fun along the way too.

"And once we've finished getting you out of your comfort zone in the great outdoors, we'll return here where we'll spend a couple of days challenging your thinking about what it is to be effective leaders," Marley continues.

"So, to ensure we safely complete the wilderness adventure component of the programme, we have the very capable team from Falls River Guides accompanying us." He turns toward the guides standing beside him. "This is Emily." A woman with blonde hair in a ponytail smiles and waves to the group. "Skye." The dark-haired woman standing next to her nods and smiles. "And Ethan."

Ethan, the man Lily still hasn't taken her eyes from, takes off his cap and jokingly bends his head in a small bow to the group. "Pleased to meet you," he says, grinning.

The other guides laugh at his formal greeting, and Skye ruffles his hair affectionately when he straightens. His hair sticks up everywhere afterwards, but he doesn't seem to mind and doesn't put his cap back on, instead holding it in his hand as he continues to smile.

He knows he has everyone's attention—his eyes take in each of us, skimming from Priya to me, then on to Lily and continuing around the table. I glance at Lily and she's actually blushing, as though this is all for her benefit, and I realise I'm cringing. I know I shouldn't judge him before I've met him, but I've met guys like him before. They're always arrogant jerks with over-inflated egos.

How could you possibly be any different? Shallow, vain, thinking you're the GOAT. And fine, maybe you are the Greatest Of All Time and I'm just jealous because I'm not. But to me, you're just a regular goat ... A very hot regular goat.

CHAPTER 4

"I know you're keen to meet the rest of the students," Emily says. "But before we do that, we need to get our gear ready for tomorrow. We'll be leaving straight after breakfast. Here's a list of all the equipment you're going to need for our trip." She places a pile of paper on the table in front of Priya. "Once you've got everything, place it all together with any personal items you want to include. But remember, you have to carry everything you take, so be selective about what you choose. If you have questions, ask any of the guides. We're all here to help."

I take one of the equipment lists and hang back to see where everyone goes. Ethan stands by the large blue bins and is quickly surrounded by a group of students. The rest have spread out along the racks, so I make my way there and begin collecting items from the list.

I collect a backpack, waterproof jacket, and pants, all with the logo of Falls River Guides on them, polypropylene tops, socks, and gloves. I shove everything into the pack as I go.

"Why do we need all this cold weather gear at this time of year?" I ask Emily, who is making sure we get the right sizes.

"It gets pretty cold up at the Lodge at night, even in summer. And the weather can change with little warning any time of year up there, so we need to be prepared just in case."

"Good to know," I say, putting an extra pair of woollen socks in my pack.

Once I've collected everything from the racks, I head over to the bins. Ethan is talking to Lily and a girl with long ebony hair called Holly, and I feel relieved that his attention is taken by them. The girls burst into laughter at something he says, Lily laughing so hard she reaches out to touch Ethan's arm, needing to steady herself. He looks pleased at their response, clearly enjoying their attention.

Ethan is still talking to the girls as I quickly add the last items to my already full arms. I figure I'm home and clear, and quietly begin to slink away.

"Hi, we haven't met. I'm Ethan."

I freeze, then slowly turn to look up at him. "Hi."

"And you are?" He tilts his head, raising his eyebrows. His entire face asking the question.

"I'm Jess." It sounds robotic, unfriendly, so I smile awkwardly as a kind of afterthought.

"Is there anything I can help with? Do you think you've got everything?"

I look down at my armload of bags and equipment. "I think I have everything." I look back up at his handsome face and his eyes are focused intently on mine. I feel my ability to speak fading. *Remember he's a goat, he's just a goat!*

"I'm all goat thanks."

His eyebrows shoot up in surprise, a grin spreading across his face, and I'm instantly mortified. My cheeks flood with heat, so hot it overflows down my neck. I want to disappear, but I have nowhere to hide.

"Good, I mean I'm all good thanks." I laugh uncomfortably, shaking my head.

"You like goats?"

"Not particularly … Just *kidding* around?" I screw up my nose, grimacing at my joke.

Ethan doesn't react for a moment and then lets out a loud bark of laughter. I manage a small laugh, relieved that he thinks I'm just trying to be funny, as Lily and Holly's heads whip around to see what's going on. I don't stick around to see their reaction and quickly escape to join the rest of the group sitting spaced out on the floor with their belongings in front of them.

I pick a spot near Priya and empty the bags from my arms onto the floor and unpack everything I've stashed in the backpack. My eyes widen as I discover a very sharp-looking hunting knife in a sheath inside one of the packs from the bins. *What the heck are we going to need this for?*

"For the next week, you'll be sleeping in tents." Marley begins to read names off a piece of paper in his hand. Priya nudges me with her elbow, grinning at me when our names are called out together. I smile back, glad that I'm going to be with her too.

"Come and get a tent," Emily says, standing beside a pile of tent bags on the floor. "Once you're packed, we'll have some dinner and then it's an early night. Wake-up call will be at six tomorrow. We want to be on the road by seven."

I grab a tent from the pile and push it into the bottom of my backpack. It takes up half the pack, but I manage to squeeze everything else in and attach the sleeping mat to the outside.

"Right," Emily calls out. "If everyone's ready, please bring your bags and follow me."

We follow Emily through a door at the back of the room into a windowless passageway, past two doors with signs indicating they're bathrooms. She opens the door at the opposite end of the passage to reveal a large bunkroom with two-tiered bunks lining the walls of the room. "This is your room for tonight. Pick a bed and leave your packs in here, then head back to the common room. Pizza should be here any second."

I head to the bunk furthest away from the door and pull my sleeping bag out of my pack, laying it out on the top bunk.

"I'm so glad you chose the top bed," Priya says as she lays her sleeping bag on the bunkbed beneath mine. "I never sleep well on the top bunk. I always worry I might fall off in my sleep."

"I've done that," Dean says from the bunk next to us. "Not sure what hurt more, my shoulder or my pride."

"Maybe you should take the bottom bunk, Jess," Matt calls after me as I walk toward the bunkroom door. "Your pride couldn't take much more today, could it?"

"My pride is doing just fine, thank you very much," I reply haughtily over my shoulder as I head through the doorway, pleased he can't see the grin on my face.

The mouthwatering smell of pizza greets me as soon as I enter the common room. Emily and Marley are sitting at one end of the table and I assume that's where all the team leaders will go, so I sit next to a boy with large black-rimmed glasses at the other end. We introduce ourselves while we wait for everyone else to be seated. His name is Kalen.

Dean plonks himself onto the bench beside me and Priya sits on his other side. The rest of the spaces quickly begin to fill and I cast my gaze along the faces sitting opposite, making my way up to our end of the table. I look up as a figure steps over the bench to sit opposite me. I swallow in surprise, and return Ethan's smile.

Before he has a chance to say anything, Matt appears out of nowhere and begins to squeeze himself into some imagined space between Ethan and the girl sitting beside him, forcing them both to move apart to make room for him. And now *he* is the one sitting directly opposite. He doesn't look up until he opens the lid of the pizza box on the table in front of him and holds it out to me. "Ladies first."

"Should probably offer it to Dean then." I shrug.

Ethan bursts into laughter as Matt raises his eyebrows in surprise.

"Finally, someone shows me the respect I deserve!" Dean reaches into the box and lifts out an enormous piece of pepperoni pizza. He takes a huge bite, then continues to speak with his mouth full, spitting food as he talks. "My parents raised me to be a lady. Thank you for noticing, Jess. Truly, thank you."

"Any chance you could make room for us?" Lily and Holly are standing at the end of the table, smiling down at Ethan and Kalen. "You guys don't mind scooching down a bit, do you?" Lily bats her long lashes at them.

"Sure." Kalen grins back with a smile so big I wonder if his face might break and shuffles toward me until I'm wedged between him and Dean, who hasn't budged an inch.

"Do I smell or something?" Priya mutters, looking at the big gap beside her.

I look along the table past Dean and Priya and see there's a large space where Lily and Holly could have easily sat, but instead they've chosen to insert themselves at the end of the table next to Ethan and Kalen.

Dean leans closer to Priya and sniffs. "Hmm … you're not *that* bad."

"Oh my god, seriously?" Priya looks horrified as she tries to sniff the armpit of her shirt and when that passes the test, she sniffs her hair, trying to find the source.

Dean throws his head back, laughing.

"He's joking, Priya." I say. "You smell great—really great, like jasmine."

Dean's head swivels to look at me, eyebrows raised. "Jasmine, huh?" He nods as if making a mental note.

I glance across the table at Lily, who's now sitting comfortably next to Ethan, looking up at him like the cat that caught the canary as he holds out a box of pizza to her.

"Come on, guys, can you scooch down just a little further?" Holly asks impatiently, not yet able to fit beside Kalen.

"You could always sit on my knee?" Kalen offers, semi-hopeful.

I raise my eyebrows at Dean and Priya. "What do you think?"

"I guess we're … *scooching*," Dean says demurely, and the three of us shuffle along to give Holly the room she needs.

Everyone adds pizza to their plates, devouring the contents of the boxes in front of us, but I notice Matt hasn't taken any and realise why. I stand and walk down the table to where there are still a couple of unopened boxes and ask Emily if she can see what kind of pizza they contain.

"Do you mind if I take this one?"

Emily hands it up to me and I carry it back to my seat. Before I sit, I hold the box out to Matt with one hand and wave my other in a flourish. "I think this might be what you're waiting for, m'lord."

He opens the box and looks up at me in surprise. "How'd you know?"

"You had the vegetarian meal on the flight."

"Thanks!" He looks impressed that I'd remembered, then takes an enormous bite. "Mmm, this is really good." Matt's words are barely intelligible, his mouth stuffed full of food. "I was so hungry I was about to start gnawing on Ethan."

"Would've made the whole vegetarian thing a bit of a wasted effort though, wouldn't it?" Kalen retorts.

"Come on guys, Ethan's not a piece of meat, you know." Dean shakes his head in mock disapproval.

"Looks pretty tasty to me." Lily smiles at Ethan.

I hastily cover my mouth with my hand, trying to prevent my mouthful of food ejecting all over the table as I begin to laugh—then start to cough, choking on a crumb I manage to inhale in the process. Dean bats me on the back with the flat of his hand as I continue to cough, my face turning beetroot from a mixture of embarrassment and the effort of coughing. Finally, it subsides after Matt hands me a glass of water.

Lily gives me a contemptuous glare as I chug back its contents before she angrily looks away. And for the briefest of moments, I feel something close to pity for the goat as I watch him squirm uncomfortably in his seat.

CHAPTER 5

"Has everyone checked they've got everything from the bunkroom?" Skye calls out.

"Yes," a few people reply. Then it dawns on me that I've left my sleeping bag on my bed.

I'd woken in the dark, an hour before the wake-up call, and decided to get up and have a shower. Not wanting to risk waking anyone, I'd only taken my backpack with me and intended to return for my sleeping bag later, then completely forgotten about it.

I don't say anything and go straight to the bunkroom where I hastily pull the sleeping bag down from the bed and start stuffing it into its bag.

"I was wondering who left that," Skye says from the doorway.

"Ah, yeah, thanks. I was trying to be quiet when I got up this morning."

"You need to make sure you look after your kit. *You're* responsible for your stuff here. We aren't your parents."

I feel like I'm being told off. "Yeah, absolutely. I meant to come back for it, I just forgot. Thanks for reminding me."

I feel embarrassed as I return to the common room, aware that I'm the only one who left something behind. And it wasn't as if it was something insignificant either. *It was your sleeping bag, for god's sake. You would've been screwed without it.*

"Heads up, everyone," Emily calls out. "If you are *not* carrying a tent, you need to come and collect a food bag. And when you're finished doing that, it's time to take your backpacks to the vehicles."

I wait for Priya to grab one of the food bags, then we join the others outside. There's a Falls River guide standing by each of the three jeeps. Priya and I head over to Emily, who helps lift our packs onto the roof rack, then we climb into the vehicle. We make our way to the two seats at the back of the jeep, and Dean and Matt take the row of seats in front of us.

A few minutes later, Emily jumps into the driver's seat next to Marley and leans around to look back at us. "Everyone buckled up?"

She receives a chorus of yeses and starts the engine. We're the first vehicle to depart. I look behind us as we pull out of the carpark to see the other vehicles following.

We exit the driveway onto the road and head away from the Falls River township, quickly getting up to speed on the open road. Marley turns his head and calls back, "We've got a four-hour drive ahead of us. If anyone needs to stop, just yell out. Other than that, settle back and enjoy the view."

And that's what we do. Other than Marley and Emily talking in the front, the rest of us sit back and watch the scenery unfolding out the windows.

Green pastures soon give way to dense forest as the road winds its way into a gorge with a river snaking far below us. Marley points out the front window and we lean forward to catch a glimpse of lofty waterfalls cascading over bluffs.

Once we exit the gorge, the land flattens into a plateau, a welcome mat for the mountain range looming ahead. It feels like we're the only ones stupid enough to be out of our beds this early, the road completely empty of traffic other than an occasional farm vehicle. I figure there probably isn't much out here other than farms, but then realise there must be a military base somewhere nearby as a convoy of army trucks streams past us, heading in the opposite direction. I glance out the back window as we turn onto a side road and count seven trucks before the other jeeps following behind us block my view.

A few minutes later we veer off the side road onto a narrow dirt track that branches up the hillside on the right. At first, we're able to look down upon the farmland below, but it isn't long before the road enters the tree line and we can only catch glimpses of the valley beneath. Then the forest becomes so dense that we can't see it at all.

The track is pitted with potholes and Emily's able to avoid many of them at first. But before long she has to slow to a crawl as she navigates the dips and bumps on the road and tries to evade the crevice gouged like a centreline. Now I see why we're in these jeeps; there's no way a van could get up here. We continue our painfully slow pace up and down steep hills, fording rivers in the ravines in between, until we emerge from the surrounding forest onto a large treeless scar. The remnant of a landslide from years ago.

"It's not much farther until the end of the road," Emily calls back to us as she pulls over. "But this is the only opportunity to see the view down the valley, so we'll have a quick break here for lunch. Don't get too close to the edge, okay guys?"

I understand her warning as soon as I get out of the jeep and see how steeply the mountainside drops off beside us. There'd be no surviving a fall down there. We'd been driving in the trees for so long I hadn't realised how high we'd actually climbed, and I have to strain my eyes to make out the handful of tiny farmhouses hidden amongst the patchwork of fields far below. The valley continues into the distance, narrowing until it finally ends at a wall of mountains that runs from north to south. The mountain range forming a natural border with Morrison County hidden on its western flank. I pull my phone from my pocket to take a photo and notice some of the others doing the same.

"Has anyone got any signal?" Priya calls out, lifting her phone above her head and shading her eyes to look at the screen from below.

I glance down at the bars on mine and I've got nothing. I chime in with the others, calling out that I don't, when Skye interrupts, "There's no cell phone coverage up here. We're going to be offline for the next week. No calls, no messages, no social media, no access to the internet." Skye smirks as an unhappy murmur grumbles through the group.

It isn't long before we're told to get back in the jeeps and we're continuing along the road in the trees again. But we've only been driving another few minutes when the jeep slows and then stops for the final time.

Emily turns and smiles. "This is the end of the road, folks. Now we walk."

We spill out of the jeeps, eager to begin our trek as the drivers pass our packs down from the roof racks. I haven't even finished putting on my backpack when two of the guides suddenly jump into their jeeps and drive back down the road.

"They're taking the jeeps?" I ask.

"Yeah. We leave one vehicle here in case of an emergency, but the others are returning to Base Camp for another guiding trip we've got booked," Emily replies. "They'll come back and pick us up at the end of camp."

"Let's get moving," Skye calls over her shoulder as she walks into the trees. "We've got a four-hour hike ahead of us and we want to get to the Lodge before dark."

Emily gives me a smile and gestures for me to follow. We enter the trees at the end of the road and walk single file along the track in the shade of the high canopy. After a few minutes, I understand why the road ended where it did. The trees open to a ravine, much wider and deeper than the ones we'd forded earlier, the bank dropping steeply to a river raging over rapids below. The only way across is via a narrow swing bridge suspended across the gorge.

Not long after crossing the bridge, we enter a small meadow with a stream lining one side. We cross the clearing and follow the stream, making our way along its shingle bank, occasionally passing small piles of stones as we walk. Emily explains that they're called *cairns* and are used to mark the path so we know we're still on the right track. Eventually we re-enter the trees at an entrance marked by a red and yellow striped wooden stake.

"We've been doing a lot of work on these paths over the last few years, trying to improve the access to the Lodge since we started bringing groups up here," Emily explains.

"Isn't this the national park?" I ask, wondering why a private company is maintaining the track.

"No, this is privately owned land. The owners built the Lodge over fifty years ago, but ended up settling in the valley. About ten years ago, they agreed to hire it out to us so we could bring climbing groups up here, and after we started running camps with the Leadership Institute, they gave us exclusive use of it."

"Do you spend a lot of time up here?" I ask.

"We usually have one week on, one week off, depending on the length of the bookings. And when we're not working, all the guides are on call with Search and Rescue. We try to make the most of the work over the summer months. There's not a lot of work here over the winter."

"What do you do during the winter then?"

"Ethan and some of the other guides are students, so they only do this as a summer job. I originally came here for a single summer, but that was over four years ago. After Skye and I got together, we decided we wanted to stay here year-round, so we instruct at one of the ski resorts and work with Search and Rescue over the winter."

"You teach skiing too?" I ask, amazed. "Is there anything you can't do?"

"Ha, you give me too much credit. Skye's the one who can do anything. She trained as a paramedic. She's the first medical responder on Search and Rescue ops. You should see her—no matter how dire the situation, she has this incredible calmness about her. She always knows what to do."

"I don't think I could be like that," I say.

"Sure, you could. You just need the right training."

"No, I mean, I don't think I have the right temperament. I'm not a very calm person. I'm more of a 'Panic! Panic!' kind of person."

"Yeah, sometimes it does just come down to personality. But I think a lot of the time, panic comes from not knowing what to do. Training can help with that. The more you're exposed to certain situations, the more prepared you are to deal with them. One thing's for sure though—panic just makes everything worse. It shuts your brain down so you can't function. It never helps."

Until now, I hadn't really understood how coming into the wilderness could teach us anything about leadership. But this clicked with me. How can you lead if you're panicking?

I follow behind Ethan, Dean, and Priya at the front of the group as we continue along the narrow trail for the next few hours. I've nearly had enough, my shoulders aching from carrying a heavy pack for so long, when I notice the path lightening ahead, and then we exit the trees into an enormous clearing. Standing proudly in the middle of that clearing, bathed in the late afternoon sun, is a large log cabin.

Ethan turns to face us. "Welcome to the Lodge!"

CHAPTER 6

There are whoops and cheers as everyone exits the trees, realising we've arrived at our destination. I drop my backpack to the ground and sigh with relief as I stretch my arms and neck, trying to release the tension in my shoulders. I hear groans as others follow suit. Lying on the grass with their arms outstretched, faces basking in the warm sun.

The Lodge sits in the middle of a rectangular-shaped clearing, bordered by trees on all sides. A river emerges from the forest at the top corner of the clearing where it is split in two by a raised embankment. One branch of the river continues along the right side of the clearing and disappears into the trees in the direction we've just come. The second runs along the top end of the clearing opposite us. Trees line the bank on the other side of the stream but don't extend far, ending abruptly at the base of rocky bluffs rising steeply behind them.

"I know you're all tired," Emily calls out. "But there are a couple of things we need to do before we can put our feet up for the day."

Her announcement is met with a chorus of loud groans.

"I'm going to show you where the toilets are and then you need to pitch your tents and get them ready for tonight before it gets dark. Come on."

The guides appear amused at how tired we look as we drag

ourselves to our feet. I try to hide how sore I am. I figure they're watching us to see how we cope, and I don't want them to think I can't keep up. I'd considered myself to be pretty fit before coming here, but my body just isn't used to carrying a heavy load for so long.

"Hey Jess, give us a hand, will you?"

I turn to see Matt and Dean lying on the ground behind me. "You look like you've still got lots of energy," Matt says, holding his hand up toward me.

"What do you think, Priya?" I tilt my head, as if weighing up whether or not to help them. "Maybe we should just leave them here?"

"Come on, Priya, don't abandon us," Dean pleads.

Priya laughs, reaching down to take Dean's upstretched hand. "How could I possibly refuse a face like that?"

I take Matt's hand, letting out an exaggerated groan as I lean back to pull him up … which turns out to be surprisingly hard to do. He's much heavier than I expected.

The four of us run to catch up with the others. Emily shows us where the two eco toilets are located in a small hut further back near the trees behind the Lodge. She then explains that a rain-water tank feeds the taps in the Lodge and is safe to drink.

"The Lodge has solar panels and a small battery." Emily points to the roof of the Lodge. "It's enough to provide power for lights and for the radio, but not much else. There's an outlet you can use to charge your phones, but use it during the day."

She leads us around to the front of the Lodge. "One last thing before you can relax. You need to get on with setting up your tents for the night. You need to work it out on your own. No help from the guides."

Priya and I pick up our packs and head over to a spot about halfway between the Lodge and a clump of trees and get to work setting up the tent. I look around when we finish securing the fly and notice that we're the first to get ours up. We've all chosen to pitch our tents close together—safety in numbers, I guess—but Matt and Dean's is closest to ours.

"I suppose we need to take this to the Lodge." Priya lifts the bag of food out of her pack.

We head over to the Lodge and climb the stairs to the deck where

Marley is leaning against the wooden railing, watching everyone.

"Well done on being the first to finish," he says. "You can take the food inside. Emily will tell you where to put it."

We open the door and enter a large rustic room where everything is made of wood—the floors, the walls, the ceiling, the enormous rectangular table dominating its centre. There's a collection of sofas and armchairs nestled cosily around the open fireplace at one end of room, a blazing fire already crackling in welcome. Emily, Skye, and Ethan are preparing food at the kitchen bench on the opposite side of the room.

"Hi," Priya calls out as we walk in.

Ethan turns and gives us a big smile. "Aha. You owe me ten bucks." He nudges Skye with his elbow.

Skye grumbles back at him, then looks over at us. "You can put the food on the floor in the storeroom."

We make our way past an open bunkroom door to the storeroom directly behind the kitchen and enter a small room lined with shelves stacked with food and equipment. Priya places our bag of food on the floor and we head back out.

"Is there anything we can help with?" Priya asks.

"You get to put your feet up tonight," Emily replies with a smile. "We'll get you to work tomorrow."

We both say thanks, then head outside to join Marley, who's watching the other students still wrestling with their tents. Slowly they join us on the deck as they finish and we remain outside chatting until Emily appears at the door, announcing dinner's ready.

My mouth waters as soon as we enter the Lodge, the smell of cooked garlic and onions heavy in the air along with other scents I can't distinguish other than being, well … food. The table is already lined with steaming bowls of stew, and I realise I'm absolutely ravenous. Talk is quickly replaced by eating and murmurs of appreciation as we thank the cooks, and hardly another word is spoken until all the bowls have been scraped clean.

After dinner we make our way to the seats by the fire where Marley is already waiting, standing in front of the fireplace, holding a cup of steaming hot chocolate in his hands.

"First, I wanted to congratulate you all on completing your first day of camp. I'm pleased to see we didn't lose anyone on our way here, which is always a relief." He chuckles. "I've got one housekeeping item I need to cover tonight, and then you're free for the rest of the evening. From tomorrow morning, you'll be responsible for meals, cleaning, and fire lighting. I've made up a roster for the next week. Make sure you check it. It's *your* responsibility to know what shift you're on and to turn up on time." He smiles and clasps his hands in front of him. "That's all I wanted to cover tonight. We'll get started with group activities first thing after breakfast tomorrow. Ethan, I think you wanted to suggest an activity for tonight though?"

"Yeah, I do." Ethan walks over from the kitchen. "There's a hot spring not far from here and it's a great way to end the day after a hike. Does anyone want to come?"

Without fail, every one of us raises our hand.

"Great," he says. "Get your headtorches and towels and we'll meet outside in five minutes."

The tiredness I'd been feeling a few minutes earlier vanishes, completely replaced by excitement at the idea of going for a swim in a hot spring in the middle of nowhere. It only takes a few minutes for everyone to get ready and meet back at the steps of the Lodge. We're all going except Emily and Skye, who decide to stay behind.

It's a clear evening and the moon, although not quite full, is bright enough to make out shapes in the distance once my eyes have the chance to adjust to the dark. Ethan leads the way and we follow behind, using our headlamps to help see the ground more clearly.

At first, I think I'm imagining things when I see lights in the distance. But they aren't hallucinations, their source revealed when we reach a small wooden bridge at the edge of the clearing. The bridge is lit by solar lights at both ends and the lights continue every few metres along a path on the other side of the stream.

The lights twinkle like fireflies through the branches—a magical fairy trail enticing us to follow. We talk in whispers as we walk, afraid anything louder will break the spell. The path diverts to follow a small side stream that climbs steeply until it reaches a stone weir. Water cascades down its sides as it overflows from the large pool that has formed behind it.

The pool is gently lit by solar lights placed amongst the rocks that line the edges. Dense steam rises from the pool, wafting over the lights in the cold air, obscuring them and blunting details, making everything soft and blurry.

"Wow," I exhale when I see the pool.

"I second that wow," Matt stops beside me.

We hurriedly strip down to our swimsuits, no need to feel self-conscious, the dim light providing a cloak of darkness. I tentatively dip my foot into the water. At first it's almost too hot as my cold feet adjust to the warmth, but after a few seconds of sitting on the edge, I'm able to lower myself in.

I wade to the other side of the pool and discover a rock ledge the perfect height to sit on, leaving my shoulders out of the water. I've never experienced anything like this before. It feels eerie, surreal. The steam swirls whenever someone moves, giving it an almost solid appearance, so dense it wets my face. I lay my head back to rest on the rocks behind me and look up at the sky. Through wafting steam, I make out the black sky covered in millions of stars. I'd been too busy looking at the ground as we walked here to pay much attention to the sky, but now I'm awestruck.

"It's impressive, isn't it?"

I lift my head and wave my hand through the steam to see who's talking. The air clears momentarily and it's Ethan. He's looking up at the stars too.

I wonder if he knows who he's talking to?

"I almost forgot I wasn't alone for a moment," I say. "I mean, obviously I know I'm not alone, but I just kinda did, if you know what I mean." I feel so inarticulate, unable to find the words to express myself.

"I know what you mean. It's easy to get lost in your own thoughts up here."

"I hadn't realised how big the sky is," I blurt, then wish I hadn't. It sounded so stupid as soon as I said it out loud.

"Makes you feel pretty insignificant, doesn't it? It's one of the things I miss the most when I leave here."

"You miss feeling insignificant?" I joke.

"Kind of, I guess." Ethan chuckles. "I mean, I miss how much more you can see when you're away from the city lights. Everything is so much clearer up here, and I don't just mean the sky. You get this perspective of how tiny we are in the scheme of things, and it's easy to forget that when you can't see this … to get bogged down in the petty day-to-day stuff that shouldn't really matter."

And now I feel even more inarticulate. "Emily said you're a student?"

"Yeah, I'm studying to be an environmental engineer. I start my third year at Ashley in a few weeks' time."

"Oh wow, you're at AIT! Good school."

"Yeah, I got lucky."

"You're being modest. Ashley's really competitive—you're obviously smarter than you look."

"Ha, likewise."

"You can't have thought I looked that stupid. You did bet on Priya and me to get the tent up first."

"What makes you think I bet on you to be first?"

"Because you won the bet against Skye."

"Oh." He laughs. "Not exactly. We weren't betting on who would be first. Skye bet you two wouldn't be able to work out how to pitch the tent without help, and I told her I reckon she was underestimating you girls and you'd be able to work it out just fine."

I'm glad he can't see me as I screw up my face. *Well, that's insulting. How could she think I wouldn't be able to work out how to pitch a simple tent?*

"I get the feeling Skye doesn't like me very much."

"I don't think Skye has any feelings about you one way or the other. She just thought you two looked like a couple of city princesses who'd never put up a tent before."

"Ouch, that's a bit harsh. I guess I have something to prove then."

"Don't we all."

****

"I can't believe they have hot pools up here," Priya says as we lie in our sleeping bags.

"I know! I've heard of places like this in Iceland and New Zealand where you can hike to natural hot pools, but I never thought I'd get to go to one myself."

"I saw a documentary about monkeys in Japan that sit in hot springs to keep warm in winter."

"Oh yeah, I've seen that too," I say. "That would be so cool. Could you imagine doing that in winter surrounded by snow? I wish I could do that sometime.”

“Be careful what you wish for. If it starts snowing up here tomorrow, I’m blaming you.” Priya laughs.

“We’ll blame you too!” Dean yells out from his tent.

“Hey, this is a private conversation,” I reply.

“But you’re so much more interesting than Matt,” Dean calls back.

“Well, that’s plain rude,” Matt says sleepily. “I’m just too talk to tired tonight.”

“Night-night then sleepyhead,” Priya calls out.

A chorus of ‘goodnight’ chimes out across all the tents, followed by laughter as we realise that everyone can hear.

CHAPTER 7

The morning starts out cool and crisp, but as our bonds grow with each new team building activity, so does the ferocity of the sun. Despite the rising temperature, we continue with challenge after challenge until Marley, as if noticing the heat for the first time, pauses mid-sentence to scan our sweat drenched faces, and finally tells us to take a break.

We collapse onto the cool grass in the shade of the trees near our tents, guzzling tepid water from our drink bottles. We chat easily, relaxed in each other's company, and I realise this morning's activities had clearly achieved what was intended. Before today, I'd really only talked to Matt, Dean, and Priya. But now I feel like I'm getting to know the others too.

I glance at Kalen, sitting next to me, reading a book. I noticed him reading it at breakfast this morning too.

"What are you reading?" I ask, leaning closer.

He glances up from his book and closes it to show me the cover. *"One Hundred Years of Solitude."*

"Oh. I haven't read that one," I say, not wanting to let on that I haven't even heard of it.

"I've just started it. It's supposed to be one of the greatest novels ever written."

"Oh yeah, I've heard of it." Matt leans across me to take a closer look. "Isn't it one of the top one hundred novels of all time or something?"

"Yeah, that's right." Kalen flashes a smile. "That's exactly what it is. My dad was reading an article about the best books ever written last year and we started going through the list together to see how many of them we've read. And although we'd read a few of them, we were really shocked to realise that we hadn't read many of them at all. So, we decided to work our way through the list, starting at the top."

"What number's this one?" I ask.

"There are loads of different lists," Kalen says, pulling a folded sheet of paper he's been using as a bookmark from between the pages. "But the one we're using has it at number nineteen. Number twenty is *The Great Gatsby* and I've already read that one, so it's straight onto number twenty-one after this. Still got a long way to go though." His voice fades off shyly as he finishes, swallowing awkwardly as though he thinks he's been talking too long. "You probably think it's pretty stupid."

"Not at all," Matt says immediately. "I think it's great that you're doing something like this with your dad. I'd love to do something like this with mine, but I doubt he'd ever do it, to be honest." He shrugs his shoulders. "But you've inspired me, Kalen. I think I might start doing it myself when I get home."

"Yeah, me too." I smile and Kalen visibly relaxes.

"We've got one more activity planned for today," Marley calls out. "But this one's an individual challenge rather than a team effort. Get your water bottles and a towel. We're going for a walk."

It's exactly what we want to hear. None of us wants to do any more running around in this heat, and the directive to bring a towel hints strongly at the promise of a swim.

"Should we change into swimsuits?" Lily asks.

"No, just come as you are," Marley replies.

Lily looks as disappointed as I feel. *I guess we aren't going for a swim after all.*

Ethan leads the way and we follow him across the clearing to where the river emerges from the surrounding forest. We enter the trees, grateful to be back under their protective canopy, permitting only dappled sunlight to reach the world beneath. The air immediately feels cooler, and the smell of damp earth greets us as we disturb the ground with our footsteps.

The path follows alongside the river, sometimes right beside it and at other times moving back into the trees, undulating over small rises, but overall climbing toward the cliffs looming behind. The river widens, disappearing around a sleepy bend where the bank rises above it, and Ethan diverts off the path to scramble to the top.

We climb after him and join Ethan near the edge. The river snakes in a large C around the rocky outcrop where we're standing, unable to carve its way through the hard rock beneath. The river has formed a deep pool directly below us. Its stony bottom disappearing beneath the dark blue water where the river has tried to gouge its way through, instead only digging deeper where the rock has stubbornly resisted its force.

"You've probably worked out what the challenge is already." Ethan holds his hand out as if introducing us to the river. "Yep, you've got to jump … from here." He bends and takes off his boots, then turns to face us. "It's pretty simple. Cross your arms in front of you like this and hold on to your shoulders. Then jump straight out, feet first. There's nothing to worry about as long as you jump straight, no hidden rocks beneath, and I'll be in the water when you get down. Emily will let you know when it's safe to jump."

He doesn't wait for anyone to say anything, smiles, and then casually steps off the ledge, landing cleanly in the water with a small splash. I lean forward and see his head pop back into view, waving up at everyone and calling out, "Ready!"

"No way," a tall boy called Jackson mutters beneath his breath. "I'm not doing that."

"You don't have to," Marley replies. "This is a personal challenge. It's up to each of you to decide if you want to do it or not."

I move back from the edge and we're all looking at each other, wondering who's going to go first. Then I notice Holly taking off her boots. She doesn't say anything, deliberately trying not to draw attention to herself, and quietly walks over to the jumping point. I nudge Priya and tip my head toward Holly. Some of the others notice too. Holly jumps. I hear a splash and rush back to the edge to see if she's okay. Her head emerges and she yells out, "Yeah!"

We start cheering. I can't believe how fearless she is. I'm terrified at the thought of jumping.

"Come on, guys, you'll love it," Holly calls up to us. "It's really deep. I couldn't touch the bottom."

I watch as Ethan swims over to Holly. She wraps her arm around his neck and they swim to the shallows at the side.

Kalen is the next surprise. He takes off his glasses and hands them to Marley before stepping closer to the edge, then jumps, yelling, "Holy shiiiit!" the entire way down.

And then there's a queue. I don't want anyone to think I'm afraid, so I take off my boots and get in line behind Matt. Each person has their own style—some scream, others are silent. Matt yells like he's attacking something as he leaps, a kind of war cry.

When it's my turn, I don't hesitate. I know if I think about it I won't jump. I just have to do it. It is terrifying and I scream for a second as I jump, but then quickly clamp my mouth shut, clenching my teeth together in anticipation of the impact.

I'm surprised how hard the water feels as I hit it, grateful I'd come down straight, my feet breaking my entry. The water feels icy, but euphoria quickly replaces the shock of the cold when I reach the surface.

I push my hair from my face and am greeted by Ethan grinning at me.

"Nice jump." He takes hold of my arm and helps tow me to the side.

"That was awesome!" I say as soon as my feet make contact with the stony bottom, and without thinking I grab Ethan into a hug. I feel self-conscious as soon as I do it and quickly pull away to face the others on the bank. Throwing my arms in the air as I bounce up and down in the water and yell, "Woohoo!"

I join the others watching from the bank and sit next to Oliver, a stocky boy about my height, with an aversion to porridge if his reaction to this morning's breakfast is anything to go by.

We watch as everyone takes their turn to jump until finally, Jackson stands at the edge. He looks down at us, then turns to say something to Marley. We wait, wondering whether he'll do it or chicken out. He turns back to face us and begins to scream, then jumps, continuing to scream the entire way down, torpedoing into the water—and he's still screaming seconds later when he emerges.

We laugh, cheering and clapping, and he's obviously pumped at overcoming his fear, his face triumphant as he thrusts his hands into the air and then submerges out of sight. Ethan quickly swims over to him and pulls him to the surface, then drags him coughing to the edge.

"You crazy idiot. Why didn't you tell us you can't swim?" Ethan says.

"I *can* swim a little bit … I'm just better if I can touch the bottom," Jackson gasps as he crawls out of the water to sit on the bank next to Oliver.

"Yeah, nah, that's called walking, mate, not swimming," Oliver replies.

"Even if it's in the water?" Jackson raises his eyebrows.

"Still walking." Oliver shakes his head, laughing.

"So, was it the jump you were worried about or the water?" I ask.

"The drowning mainly," he says, giving me a wry smile.

The next time I jump, I decide to go to a ledge further down the bank, closer to the water. I don't feel the need to do it from the highest point again, once is enough for me. The water is freezing, so after my second jump I sit on the rocks at the river's edge with Jackson and watch. Holly surprises us all by jumping again and again from the top ledge. And I find myself envious of her fearlessness.

"I think this is pretty genius actually," Oliver says, joining us. "We're bathing *and* washing our clothes at the same time. I think I might start bathing with my clothes on when I get home to save time."

"*Or* you could just use a washing machine," Jackson replies. "You know, the old-fashioned way."

"Wouldn't know about that," Oliver says. "I just chuck my clothes on the floor and they appear folded in my drawer the next day. The washing fairies do it while I'm at school."

"You can't be serious?" I say.

"Oh, Jess. Of course I'm not serious. I know fairies don't do the washing—they do the *dishes*. It's the *elves* that do the washing." He winks as he pokes me hard in the side making me yelp.

"I mean, your parents don't seriously still do your washing for you, do they?"

"Don't be ridiculous, of course they don't. That's what the housekeeper's for."

CHAPTER 8

"Ethan and I are going to see if we can catch some fish for dinner if anyone wants to join us," Emily announces after our final survival skills lesson for the day. A day that had started with learning how to build a shelter and safely light and maintain a fire and ended with Skye instructing us on the basics of first aid. Teaching us everything from CPR, to dealing with fractures and burns, to treating head injuries and hypothermia.

"What do you feel like doing?" Priya turns to me.

"I was thinking I might go fishing," I reply. "I've never been before. What about you? Do you want to come too?"

"Ugh, no thanks, can't think of anything worse." She pulls a face.

"Hey, girls." Dean walks over to us. "Matt and I are going to join the fishing group. Are you keen to come too?"

"I'm keen but Priya—"

"Is super keen," Priya interrupts, nudging me as she smiles at Dean. "Jess and I were just saying that we wanted to check out the fishing. Weren't we, Jess?"

"Ah, yeah, I … we were just talking about going fishing." I try not to laugh as Matt looks at me as though I'm a complete idiot.

"Great! That's great! Isn't it, Matt?" Dean says excitedly.

"Yeah, great," Matt grunts unenthusiastically.

"I've done a bit of fishing with my dad and uncle, but I doubt we're going to be using a rod up here. Should be fun," Dean says to Priya as they walk out of the Lodge together.

"There's a good fishing spot about half an hour back down the main track," Emily says.

Emily and Holly lead the way, with Dean and Priya following, chatting animatedly to each other as they walk. I've noticed they seem to naturally find each other wherever we go, and often sit beside each other at mealtime and group activities. Matt hangs back and walks with me.

"I've never been fishing before," he says. "I'm not sure if it's my thing really, never been a fan of killing animals for sport."

"Not surprising given the whole vegetarian thing," I reply. "I think hunting for sport is horrible too, but this isn't for sport though. We're going to eat it, aren't we?"

"Of course we're going to eat it," Ethan calls out behind us. I didn't realise he was listening. I thought he was talking to Lily. "We'll only take enough for dinner. Anything else we'll let go."

"Good to know," Matt says flatly, sounding a bit annoyed. I look over at him and he's focused intently on the path in front of us.

"My mum is a vegetarian." I lower my voice so Ethan and Lily can't overhear. "She doesn't eat meat for ethical reasons. So, I don't usually eat much either. Is that why you're a vegetarian?"

"I'm vegan actually, and it's for a lot of reasons. I don't like the idea of farming and killing animals for the purpose of feeding us when there are other things we can eat instead. It's also for environmental reasons. And I can't stand the taste of it either, to be honest."

"Why did you want to come fishing then?"

"I didn't really. I wasn't keen on the fishing part—I was just more interested in hanging out with you guys." He avoids making eye contact.

"Hmm."

"Hmm, what?" He glances at me.

"I didn't realise I had the power to entice someone to abandon their ideals so easily." I nudge him with my shoulder as we walk.

"Who says it was *you* I wanted to spend time with? Maybe it was Priya … or Ethan." He gives me a smile.

"Did I hear my name?" Ethan asks.

"Of course you did," Matt mutters, shaking his head.

"Matt was just saying how he was looking forward to you teaching him how to fish, Ethan," I reply over my shoulder.

"No pressure then," Ethan says. "I just hope we manage to catch something."

"You look like you're a pretty good catch … I mean … good at catching fish." Lily giggles at her joke.

I roll my eyes at Matt. Ethan must be loving it. *I bet his ego is as big as his biceps.*

We follow the river until we reach a fallen tree lying across it like a bridge from one bank to the other. The river isn't deep, but there are deeper patches close to the bank and a few large rocks near the middle, breaking the smooth flow of water where they poke through the surface.

"This is our special fishing spot, aye, Ethan," Emily says.

"Sure is, almost guaranteed to catch something here."

They empty their backpacks on the ground, producing fishing line, hooks, and sinkers, then Emily instructs us to find sticks to use as fishing rods. After we've collected our sticks, Ethan helps attach lengths of fishing wire to a hook and sinker, then we tie it on to complete our rod.

"You should try to keep as still as possible," he says. "The fish are startled by noise or movement, even shadows. You want to focus on areas where the fish have some cover, like the tree or bank overhanging, or by those rocks sticking out of the water."

As everyone vies for position around the fallen tree, I decide to head downstream to the rocks and cast my line toward the closest one.

"You might want to try the downstream side," Ethan says, joining me.

"Okay, thanks." I move the line to reposition the hook. I stand watching the water, expecting Ethan to leave, but he doesn't. The silence feels awkward, and I wish he would say something, or leave. "I suppose you've been fishing since you were a kid?" I ask to break the silence.

"Pretty much. I was seven the first time my dad took me fishing. Dad used to work up here as a guide actually."

"Does he still work as a guide?"

"No. Dad died in a climbing accident a while back."

"Oh, I'm really sorry to hear that."

"Yeah, well, it's one of the risks of the job, I guess. But he loved it, and he used to bring me up here every chance he could. When I got older, I was able to join him on some of his guiding trips." He pauses. "It's part of the reason I became a guide. I guess I spent so much of my childhood up here it feels like he's still here in a way."

"But you don't plan on being a guide forever by the sounds of it?"

"I love guiding, but I want to do something to help protect all this and I figure becoming an environmental engineer might be a way to help do that. So, this is just a holiday job for me."

Ethan puts his finger to his lips and whispers, "Did you see that?"

I shake my head. I didn't see anything.

"There." He points again and I see a shadow moving in the water near the rock. Then I feel a small tug on the line, tiny at first, and then a bigger tug.

I give the stick a quick jerk and feel the line tighten. "I think I've got something."

"Let's take a look. Wind the line in using the stick."

I start rotating the stick in my hands and then there's splashing near the rock. "Oh my god, I've caught one!"

I slowly pull the line in, towing the thrashing fish toward the bank where Ethan scoops it into a net.

"Hey, well done," Ethan says. "It's a good size."

He pulls his knife out, then hesitates. "Do you want to do it?"

I freeze, unsure what to do. I'd been so excited about catching the fish, I hadn't thought about the fact that it now had to be killed.

"I … I'm … I don't think I want to do it. I'm sorry." *How could I not have thought this through?*

"No, it's fine, I'll do it." He lays the flapping fish on a rock and quickly pushes the knife into its head.

I feel sick. "I know I probably should have done it. I'm sorry I couldn't."

"You don't need to apologise. I didn't want to kill my first fish either."

"Yeah, but you were seven," I reply. "No one would expect a seven-year-old to kill a fish."

"My dad did."

"He made you kill it?"

"Yep. Made me fillet it too. I cried the whole time."

The fish lying on the rock suddenly starts to twitch.

"It's still alive!" I shriek. I wait for Ethan to do something, but he doesn't move, and I'm horrified at the thought of it suffering. I grab the knife and stab the fish in the head … and then again. Finally, it stops moving. I realise I'm going to be sick and run toward the trees and vomit.

I can't bring myself to face Ethan, embarrassed at how I reacted, and sit on the ground, taking deep breaths to calm myself.

"You okay?" He walks up behind me.

I take a deep breath. "Yeah, I just need a second."

He hands me my water bottle and I take a drink.

"You know, I threw up after I killed my first fish too."

"Great. So, I've got the resilience of a seven-year-old."

He laughs and holds out his hand, helping me stand. "The first time is the hardest."

"I don't think I want to find out it gets easier." I shake my head.

"Lucky for you, you don't have to."

I look upriver to see what the others are doing, and Matt quickly looks away. I can only imagine how awful he thinks I am for stabbing the fish like that.

"That fish *was* dead, you know," Ethan says. "Sometimes they keep twitching after they're dead. Even when their head is cut off and they've been gutted, they can still move."

"Seriously? How is that even possible?"

"Its nerves are still working, I guess," Ethan replies. "It can even happen when it's chopped into pieces, especially when you add something salty. It's pretty freaky to watch. It scared the crap out of me the first time I saw it."

Ethan picks up the fish and we head back upstream to the others. Lily, Dean, and Holly have each caught a fish too. Priya and Matt are sitting together away from everyone else, chatting. Neither of them has attempted to catch anything. They stand and begin to walk down the track toward the Lodge before we reach them, and I wonder if they're trying to avoid us.

When we reach the Lodge, I find Priya and Lily in the kitchen with Kai, Lily's tent buddy. I head across the room to join them, glad that *they* at least remembered we're on dinner duty tonight. Kai looks as though she's already been here a while, standing with a knife in hand beside a chopping board piled with diced vegetables.

I glance from Kai to Lily and it occurs to me that they couldn't be two peas from more *different* pods. Where Lily is tall and athletic with light blue eyes and long blonde hair, Kai is petite with dark eyes that match her blacker than black pixie cut, giving her fine features an almost doll-like appearance. But although Kai *looks* cute and playful, her personality is anything but. She's all business. Always the first to raise her hand, the first to volunteer to lead a team, the first to take charge in a group activity. She doesn't join in on the jokes or banter, and most definitely wouldn't dream of flirting with one of our instructors.

Dean and Ethan arrive with the fish and offer to help us when they realise we have absolutely no idea how to cook it. After filleting the fish, Ethan whispers something to Dean, then goes into the storeroom, returning a few seconds later with aluminium foil and some herbs and salt.

After lying the fillets on the foil, Ethan asks Lily to sprinkle some salt on them. He's grinning from ear to ear and immediately I know what he hopes will happen. Dean's clearly in on it too, watching with a mischievous look on his face.

I hold my breath as Lily sprinkles salt on the fillets, waiting to see what will happen. But nothing does, and I *actually* feel disappointed. And then they begin to twitch. Lily leaps back from the bench and she, Priya, and Kai let out a scream.

"It's alive!!!!" Dean bellows as Ethan and I burst out laughing, and the girls' heads whip around to glare at us.

"That's not funny," Priya says angrily, finally getting over her initial shock.

"Oh, come on … it's a *little* funny." Dean takes a deep breath in an attempt to calm his laughter and tries to put his arm around her.

"Ugh, you stink of fish." She ducks out of his reach.

"Yeah, you really do stink, guys." Kai screws up her nose.

"Maybe we need a trip to the hot pool after dinner," Ethan says. "How about you, Dean? You scrub my back, I'll scrub yours?"

"Sounds good to me. How about it, girls? Can we persuade you to join us? Promise not to bring any fish. Don't we, Ethan?" Dean directs his comment to Priya, who's still glaring at him. "Oh, come on. Please forgive us."

****

Matt is quieter than usual at dinner and it feels like he's avoiding me, choosing to sit at the other end of the table. I'm sure he saw me stab the fish earlier and I can only imagine how callous it must've looked. He wouldn't have known why I did it, only that I was attacking that poor fish like some murderous wild woman, and I'm sure that's the reason he's keeping his distance.

I look for Matt as we leave the Lodge, hoping to talk to him on the way to the hot pool and see that he's already walking ahead with some of the others.

"Matt!" I call out.

He turns and waits for me to catch up. "Hi." He gives me a small smile when I reach him.

"Hey," I reply, suddenly not sure what I'm going to say.

"Did you enjoy the fishing today?" he asks.

"Not particularly. I hadn't really thought through the fact that I would have to kill the fish if I caught it. I threw up afterwards."

"I wondered if that was what happened. I saw you run off into the trees. I was a bit worried actually—but it looked like Ethan was looking after you, so I figured you'd be okay."

"Oh, that's nice of you to worry. I actually thought you were upset with me."

"Why would you think that?"

"You just seemed really quiet at dinner. I thought maybe it was to do with me killing the fish."

"No, I wasn't upset with you. Not at all! I guess I was just feeling a bit introspective after going fishing with you guys. It's not something I've ever been a part of before. Even though I didn't actually catch the fish myself, I was just feeling a bit … I dunno if guilty is the right word … but something like that." He pauses. "You probably think I'm pathetic for being bothered by it."

"Of course not! I think it's great that you care so much." I can't see his face as we walk along the dimly lit track, but maybe that's a good thing, making it easier to talk. "I think it's brave to take a stand about something you feel strongly about. Not many guys our age would. I actually think it's the opposite of pathetic, it's … it's … anti-pathetic," I say and we both burst out laughing.

"Thanks, Jess." Matt puts his arm around my shoulder and gives me a gentle squeeze as we walk.

Everyone's already in the water by the time we get there. The steam is just as thick as last time and it looks beautiful wafting in front of the solar lights, casting shadowy outlines of anyone sitting nearby. But unlike the eerie quietness of the first night, tonight the air is full of laughter and loud voices. Dean and Ethan's voices louder than the rest as they joke about scrubbing backs.

Matt and I strip down to our swimsuits, leaving our clothes at the edge of the pool. Matt steps in first and turns, holding out his hand to help me in, then we swim over to join the others.

"Isn't this the best way to finish the day?" Holly says as I sit beside her.

More laughter comes from across the pool. Dean is now trying to sell Ethan's back washing services to the others. Lily takes up the offer and begins giggling, saying he's tickling, not scrubbing.

"Ethan and Dean are such good fun, aren't they?" Holly laughs as she listens to their antics.

"Yeah, they sure are," I reply. "I think we've been really lucky with our group. Everyone seems to get on so well."

"I know! Everyone's so fun and easy to get along with. Some certainly seem to get on a little better than others though," she says as we hear Priya now laughing and squealing while Dean tells her he's going to scrub her back. Priya scoots over to sit by Holly, still laughing.

"We were just saying how much fun Dean and Ethan are," Holly says to her.

"They are, aren't they?" I can hear the smile in her voice.

"Dean's a great guy." Holly nudges me in the side.

"Yeah, really great. Don't you think so, Priya?" I take the hint.

"Mm hmm."

"Oh, come on," I say, exasperated. "That's all you have to say, mm hmm?"

"Of course I think Dean is great. He *is* great, obviously."

"You two seem to get on really well," Holly hints.

"I think I get on pretty well with you guys too," Priya replies with a laugh.

"Yeah, but I don't think we touch each other as much as you two do," I say, and Holly bursts out laughing.

"What do you mean? We don't touch each other!"

"Are you kidding me? You guys don't *stop* touching each other." Holly says. "I don't think you're even aware of it."

"I don't know what you're talking about."

"There's nothing to be embarrassed about. It's really cute. Obviously Dean likes you and you like him," I say.

"I honestly don't know what you're talking about. We're just friends."

"Yeah, of course you're friends, but Dean definitely likes you more than *just* friends," Holly continues. "I mean, he hasn't tried to scrub anyone else's back here tonight."

"That's just because I was sitting next to him, that's all."

"And that's because he *always* chooses to sit next to you, to walk with you, to talk to you." I'm not sure if she's playing dumb or really has no idea. "Come on, Priya, seriously, you haven't noticed?"

"No, not really," Priya says quietly. "I just thought he was probably like that with everyone."

Holly leans closer to Priya so she can speak more quietly. "He's not, Priya. I mean, he's friendly to everyone, but he pays *special* attention to *you*."

"Oh … are you sure? I'm so bad at reading these things, I can never tell if a guy is interested in me or not."

"Trust me," Holly replies. "He is definitely, one hundred percent, undeniably, interested in *you*! So, the question is, are *you* interested in *him*?"

There's a long pause. "Yeah, I guess I am. I just didn't think he'd be interested in me. He's so good looking and tall and smart and funny … and … just so everything. Why would he be interested in me? Are you really sure?"

"Yes!" Holly and I yell far too loudly as everyone falls silent.

"Nothing to see here," I call out. "You can go about your business, move along."

I hear Oliver laugh from the shadows as the others continue with their conversations.

"Seriously, Priya, are you just fishing for compliments or do you really not know what a catch you are?" I lower my voice.

"Priya, you're gorgeous, you're kind, everyone likes you, you're scary smart—" Holly says.

"You do have a tendency to over-pack though," I interrupt, and Priya bursts out laughing. "But seriously, you shouldn't doubt yourself. Dean is really into you. You just need to look at the signs. It's obvious to everyone except you."

"Speaking of signs." Holly nudges me and I see Ethan emerging from the mist.

For the briefest second, I wonder if she means this is a sign Ethan is interested in me. But my confusion disappears when he begins to speak to Holly. Embarrassed at my stupidity, I lower myself further into the water, gratefully hiding my crimson face in the darkness.

"What secret things are you girls talking about over here?" Ethan says to Holly. Holly starts to giggle.

"Seriously, what is with everyone giggling anytime Ethan starts talking to them?" I whisper to Priya.

"I know, right? Lily, Kai, Holly, you. You all do it every time you talk to him," she whispers back.

"I DO NOT!" I say forcefully, then lower my voice. "I do *not* giggle when I talk to him. Come on, you're joking, right?"

"Hahaha! You should see your face right now. You're horrified at the thought that you're a giggler just like the others."

"Yeah, I *am* actually. I'd be mortified if I behaved that way around him."

"I'm just kidding, Jess," she says quietly. "You don't. I'm just messing with you."

"Ugh, that's just plain mean, Priya. Don't do that. I'd never be able to look Ethan, or anyone else for that matter, in the eyes again if I thought I did that whole giggling thing when I talk to him."

"I just wanted a bit of payback after you girls gave me the third degree about Dean."

I see Dean emerging from the mist, and elbow Priya as he heads straight toward us. "Hey, I was wondering where you two had got to."

Priya lets out a ridiculous giggle, completely putting it on and doing it far too convincingly. Laughter explodes out of me, and I can't stop as Priya then bursts out laughing too.

"Well, who knew I was so funny?" Dean looks a bit taken aback.

I laugh until my face hurts and tears run down my cheeks. Slowly, I get the laughter under control, taking a few deep breaths to calm myself.

"I wasn't sure if you were laughing or crying for a moment." Ethan suddenly appears in front of me.

Without warning, he reaches his hand out and wipes a tear off my cheek, leaving dripping water in its place. The gesture is so utterly unexpected, the bubbles of laughter I'd been struggling to control instantly vaporise, leaving me in open mouthed shock.

Priya, Dean, and Holly have stopped talking and are watching us in silence too.

"Laughing, definitely laughing," I somehow manage to reply, breaking the silence.

"Well, I'm turning into a prune," Ethan says, oblivious to the stunned reaction of the rest of us. "I think it's probably time to head back to camp."

"Yeah, good idea," I say as he swims away.

I look at Priya and she says slowly, "What. Was. That?"

I go to speak but have no idea what to say and just shake my head slowly in disbelief.

What was *that?*

"Signs, ladies," Holly says. "You just need to look for them."

CHAPTER 9

"So, what was with you and Ethan last night?" Dean calls out from the kitchen.

Thankfully I have my back turned as I pick up a pile of bowls from the bottom shelf in the storeroom. *I can't believe he's asking me this—and in front of Matt and Priya too!* I stall for time, pretending I can't find what I'm looking for, then when I can't delay any longer, I turn to go back into the kitchen. Dean is standing in the doorway with a huge grin on his face, blocking my exit. I look past him and see Matt staring at me in the background.

"I'm not sure what you mean?" I try to sound unruffled. "Excuse me." I step closer, forcing him to step back and make room for me to pass.

I walk straight to the table, focusing my attention on the bowls in my hands, anything to avoid eye contact with Matt, who's now stirring the pot on the stove with great intensity.

"So, how'd you boys sleep last night?" Priya intercepts Dean as he starts to follow me.

"Ugh, it's like sleeping on concrete," Dean groans, and I let out a small sigh of relief, grateful for Priya's help to distract him. "I seriously don't think those sleeping mats make a difference."

Kai and Oliver arrive seconds later, then the door to the bunkroom opens, and Emily, Ethan, and Skye walk out. Skye's smug face seems to be permanently decorated with a smirk when she's around me. Ethan avoids eye contact with everyone, and I can't be sure, but he looks uncomfortable, embarrassed even.

Great, thanks, Dean.

Ethan sits about as far away from me as humanly possible at breakfast. If he could've taken his breakfast outside without drawing attention to himself, I'm sure he would have. Matt won't look at me either. Skye, however, doesn't *stop* looking at me. Every time I glance in Ethan's direction, she's looking back, smirking, giving me the distinct impression that she thinks I'm a just a big joke. A big city princess joke.

****

"Who's up for a new challenge?" Marley says energetically as we gather around the fireplace after breakfast.

His question is met with a mixture of groans, silence, and a single, "Yeah!" from Oliver.

"That's the attitude, Oliver!" Marley says.

"You know that means you've just volunteered to go first whatever it is we're doing, don't you, mate?" Jackson says, patting Oliver's back.

"So, what am I up for?" Oliver shrugs, unconcerned.

Emily lifts a helmet and a harness. "You lucky ducks get to go rock climbing today!" she announces excitedly.

"Yes!" Holly shouts, throwing her hands in the air.

"Why didn't I keep my big mouth shut?" Oliver groans, covering his face with his hands.

"'Cos you're just a big suck up, and you can't help yourself," Jackson says. "You'll be fine, buddy. I'll catch you."

After being fitted with helmets and climbing harnesses, we follow the guides over the small bridge at the end of the clearing, then continue along the path on the other side. But instead of turning up to the hot pool as we've done every other time, we cross the small creek and continue along the path, which eventually leads us to a large rockface rising high above the trees.

The cliff looks smooth and slippery from a distance, but as we get closer, I can see cracks and indentations covering its pitted surface and I'm relieved to see that it isn't completely vertical. The face gently sloping back as it rises above us.

55

We put on our climbing harnesses and then Emily demonstrates how to use the carabiner and belay device. She shows us how the device automatically brakes when there's tension on it to stop the rope feeding through, preventing the climber from falling if they slip.

"Heads up," Skye's voice calls from above, her face peering over the top of the cliff face.

"How did she get up there?" Kalen asks.

"There's a track around the side," Emily answers as Skye drops a length of rope down the rockface. A few seconds later, another lowers further along the wall.

We watch as Emily ties the rope to her harness, then Ethan loads the rope into the belay device and attaches it to his.

"Climbing," Emily says.

"Climb on," Ethan replies, and she begins to climb. We watch in silence as she ascends the wall, feeling for ridges and cracks in the rock with her fingers and feet, then pulling herself up the rockface. Ethan doesn't take his eyes off her, completely focused as he draws the slack down through the belay and keeps tension on the rope.

About halfway up the rockface Emily yells, "Falling" and appears to deliberately let go.

I hear gasps as she lets go, but Ethan pulls down with his brake hand and absorbs the weight of Emily's fall. She barely drops at all.

She shifts her weight forward onto the wall, and waves at us to show us it's all part of the demonstration, before resuming her climb. When Emily reaches the top, she looks back over her shoulder. "You can lower."

Ethan adjusts his grip and calls back, "Lowering."

Emily leans back perpendicular to the wall, only her feet now making contact with the rock, and begins walking backwards, reaching the bottom with a grin.

"Ollie, I think you volunteered to go first earlier?" Emily holds the rope out to him as he sighs, reluctantly nodding his head.

We watch from the base of the rockface, belaying the other students while we wait for our turn to climb. I've just finished belaying Priya when Lily and Matt take to the wall. I'm pretty sure Lily will be a natural at it because she's so sporty, however I'm not sure how Matt will go. But he surprises me.

Matt climbs with ease, and I realise he has the right physique for it. He's tall and strong, but not as bulky as Dean and Jackson, so he's able to carry his weight more easily, using the strength in his arms and hands as he climbs. I'm certain Matt has done this before as he begins his descent. He pushes out from the wall with his legs, leaping away from the cliff face as he drops, landing lightly a few metres further down, then bouncing off again, clearly enjoying himself.

"You've done this before, haven't you?" I ask Matt.

"Yeah, a few times. It's been a while though, I forgot how much I enjoy it. Might need to try and find some time to do it when I get home. Are you up next?"

"Looks like it." I sigh.

"You'll be fine. Just take your time."

Once Emily has tied the rope to my harness, I step closer to the wall and look up. I take a deep breath as I study the rockface one last time. I'm ready. "Climbing."

"Climb on," Jackson says behind me.

I feel nervous at first, wedging my fingertips as far as possible into the cracks, unsure of their strength. But it isn't hard to find good handholds and I like the feeling, the rhythm of the climb. Searching, reaching, holding, lifting. I'm completely focused and don't look down, shutting out all distractions, and am surprised when I reach the top. I hadn't expected to reach it so quickly.

"Well done." Skye nods at me. "Good climb, Jess."

I raise my eyebrows at her compliment. "Thanks."

"Enjoy your trip down."

I intend to. After seeing how much fun Matt had, I'm really looking forward to this.

I slowly lean back as my brain declares war on itself, fighting the instinct to hold on to the rock wall. Instinct loses the battle and I force my body backwards until I'm at right angles with the cliff. I look beneath me and see Kai coming up, about mid-way on the other side.

Ugh, shouldn't have looked down. Come on, Jess, you can do it.

I take a few steps backwards, walking slowly at first. When I feel confident that I'm not going to fall, I push out with my legs, testing how it feels, and bounce straight back into the wall. The next bounce I make bigger and let the rope slide through my hand so I can lower at the same time.

A smile spreads across my face. *I can't believe I'm actually doing this!*

As I prepare to jump again, a scream pierces my concentration. I swivel, so I can look below and see Kai hanging flat against the rock, both hands gripping her rope, her face buried into her chest.

"It's okay, Kai, I've got you," Kalen calls out from the ground where he's belaying her. "You can't fall. You're completely safe."

"We won't let you fall, Kai," Emily calls up. "It's safe to let go of the rope. You just need to find a handhold and somewhere for your feet."

"I can't!" Kai cries down to them. "I'm too scared."

I lower myself slowly until I'm at the same level as Kai, then move across the rock until I'm beside her. "Hey, Kai, I'm here too."

She peers sideways at me without moving. "I can't do this, Jess. I'm afraid I'm going to fall again."

"I know it's a long way down, but they won't let you fall. Kalen's got you. I know it doesn't feel like it, but you *are* safe." I reach my hand out toward hers, her knuckles white as they grip tightly to the rope. "I can hold on to you too if you like. Why don't you take my hand? Test it out."

She doesn't move, and I don't want to rush her. She takes a deep shuddery breath and lets go of the rope with one hand and quickly takes mine. Her whole body shakes as she takes another deep breath.

"There's a handhold here, Kai," I say, placing her hand on a ledge in the rock. She digs her fingers into the ledge and clings to it. "And there's another one here." I put my hand on top of Kai's, still gripping the rope, and wait for her to let go. I lift her hand to the other ledge and she grasps it.

I lower myself until I'm just beneath Kai, then push her feet onto small footholds hidden from her view.

"Now all you need to do is put your weight on your feet."

"I'm too scared, Jess."

"The rope has still got you. You can't fall. I'll stay right here with you."

She shakily places her weight on her feet and stands, clinging onto the handholds.

Cheers and "way to go Kai" erupt from the ground.

"What do you want to do, Kai? Do you want to keep climbing or do you want to go down?"

She pauses, pressing her face against the rock. "I want ... I want to go down. But I need to go up. I wouldn't be able to face the others if I give up."

"Don't worry about the others. If you want to go down, we'll go down. But if you want to keep climbing, I'll come with you."

"Will you?"

"Sure. Are you ready?"

She nods, letting out a shaky breath.

"Climbing," I yell down to Jackson below.

"Roger that," he yells back up.

"Climbing," Kai calls down, and everyone lets out a cheer.

Kai gives me a small smile, then looks up in search of her next handhold. I move sideways, making room between us and search for my own, keeping pace with her as she climbs.

"You're doing great, Kai!" Kalen yells.

I look over at her and she's smiling again, Kalen's words urging her to keep going.

"Not much further. We're nearly there," I say, looking up to see Skye watching us.

"Well done, Kai," Skye says as we reach the top of the cliff. "If you don't want to abseil down, you can come up here with me and walk down the side of the hill."

Kai hesitates, then looks down. I cringe, thinking it was the worst thing she could do. There's no way she'll want to rappel back down now she's seen how high we are.

"I want to try abseiling."

"Alright then! Good on you, Kai," Skye says.

"You can lower," Kai calls down, grinning at me.

"Yeah!" Kalen yells. "Lowering!"

"Ready?" I ask.

"As I'll ever be." Kai nods.

We watch each other as we lean backwards and slowly take our first tentative steps down the cliff. We pick up speed as we go, then as we near the bottom, I push off with my legs, landing lightly back on the rockface and spring off with my feet one more time before finally landing on the ground. Kai lands just after me.

Kai is engulfed in a swarm of hugs as everyone gathers around to congratulate her. When I finally glimpse her face, she's beaming, cheeks flushed from the excitement and from laughing. I grin at her over their heads and she waves to me and mouths, "thank you."

I look down, returning to my struggle to remove the rope from my harness.

"Here, let me give you a hand. They can be tricky sometimes." Ethan appears beside me. He reaches for the harness, his hands gently brushing mine as I try to move them out of his way. He bends his head to get a closer look at the problem and his breath is hot on my arms. Goosebumps spring uninvited as a shiver runs up my spine.

"You did really well up there, Jess." He lifts his head to look at me.

"Thanks. I didn't expect to enjoy climbing as much as that."

"No, I mean with Kai." He finishes untying the knot and stands back to look at me. "That was impressive the way you managed to calm Kai and help her."

I let out a small, uncomfortable laugh. "I'm sure anyone would've done the same. I just happened to be in the right place to help."

"Nope. Not everyone." Ethan's eyebrows lift as he shakes his head. "We see this sort of thing all the time. Someone slips when they're climbing and they freak out. But I've never seen another student help like you did. It's always been up to one of the guides to get them down."

I feel heat beginning to build in my cheeks. "Oh …"

"That was real leadership you showed up there. Take the compliment, Jess. You deserve it." He gives me a smile, then turns to help Dean take over belaying for Jackson.

I'm still not sure I deserve his praise, but warmth spreads through me as I absorb his words anyway. I get the feeling he doesn't give compliments lightly and I shouldn't underestimate the significance of this. But whether I believe I deserve the compliment or not, the fact that he said it makes me realise I've misjudged him. *Maybe I'm the arrogant one?*

I turn to see that it's now Kalen and Jackson's turn to climb. I begin watching Jackson, but soon find my attention, along with everyone else, taken by Kalen. He almost leaps up the rockface, barely stopping to look for handholds, his fingers seeming to find purchase in the smallest of cracks.

"Oh my god, it's spiderman!" Oliver says in awe.

And then Kalen reaches the top and calls down that he's lowering. We gasp as we watch Kalen swivel around until he's facing us. He grins and begins to walk forwards down the cliff face. It is the craziest thing I've ever seen.

"Jesus!" Oliver exclaims.

"Thought you said he was spiderman." I laugh.

We start cheering and he's loving it, completely lapping it up. He receives a celebrity welcome as everyone gathers around, wanting to know how he's so good. It turns out that he's been rock climbing since he was four years old and works at his local climbing gym.

We continue to take turns belaying and climbing, and it isn't long before competitiveness rears its head and Kalen challenges Matt to a race.

This is Matt's fourth climb, and he's been getting quicker each time. He doesn't fly up the wall the same way Kalen does, but he's fast, and strong, and feeling brave, taking risks as he pushes himself to move faster and reach for small ledges invisible to us below.

Kalen pauses for a breather when he reaches the top and watches Matt climb for a few seconds before slowly turning, getting ready to rappel facing forwards. But Matt doesn't hesitate when he reaches the top, immediately calling out that he's ready to be lowered, then runs as fast as he can down the slope, his face full of determination. It's almost frightening to watch. Kalen glances over his shoulder when he hears our cheers getting louder. Realising Matt is closing in on him, he picks up speed. He makes it to the ground only seconds before Matt does, both of them panting with the exertion.

I wait until everyone has finished congratulating them and head over to Matt with his water bottle. "Wow, Matt, that was amazing! You may not be spiderman, but that was truly heroic."

He smiles and flops his exhausted arm around my shoulder, using me as a crutch to lean on. "Are you saying I'm your hero?"

"Sure, Matty, you're my hero—just don't go wearing your underpants over top of your trousers though, okay?"

****

We're on such a high as we return to the Lodge. That feeling of invincibility that comes after achieving something you'd thought impossible, adrenaline making us loud and revitalising our tired bodies with renewed energy. All of us roughhousing as we walk across the clearing, chasing, pushing, lifting, carrying—as though we need to connect physically, to make our bonds more tangible, permanent.

Priya darts past me, squirting me with water from her drink bottle. I drop the rope I'm carrying and run after her, chasing her across the meadow until I catch her and spray her with the contents of mine. She falls to the ground giggling, then points behind me. I turn to see Oliver trying to tackle Jackson unsuccessfully to the ground, and then Kai jumping on Jackson's back. Jackson continues to stumble along the grass, dragging both of them with him and it's only when Oliver manages to wrap his legs around both of Jackson's that they topple him to the ground.

We're still laughing when I notice Dean creeping up behind Matt. He looks over at us and holds his finger to his lips and winks. I cringe as Dean lunges toward him, knowing Matt doesn't stand a chance against Dean's huge frame. But my mouth drops open when Matt suddenly crouches and swivels, as though he's expecting Dean's attack, and flings Dean over his shoulder onto the ground in front of him. Dean lies winded, flat on his back, looking up at Matt in complete shock.

"What the? How the hell did you do that?" Dean sputters as Matt helps him to his feet.

"For one thing you walk like a pregnant elephant." Matt laughs. "Plus, I noticed Jess and Priya watching someone behind me, so it wasn't too hard to guess what was about to happen."

"No, I mean, how did you *throw* me like that?"

"Oh, that. *That* would be twelve years of Jiu-Jitsu."

"From now on I'm walking in front of you just to be safe." Dean rubs his lower back. "There's no way I'm risking you ever doing that to me again."

"Well, get a move on then, 'cos I'm starving and it looks like everyone else is already inside," Matt says, turning Dean to face the Lodge and giving him a playful kick on his backside.

CHAPTER 10

We end the day lounging around the fireplace after dinner, talking for hours as we drink hot chocolate and toast marshmallows on the open fire in a kind of sugar fueled celebration.

After two cups of hot chocolate, I head outside to use the toilet, grabbing my jacket from the back of the chair as I leave. My breath billows in the light of my headlamp as I walk and I look up briefly, arcing the beam above me into the darkness. The star speckled sky is clear of cloud and I notice a bright glow coming from somewhere out of view beyond the trees.

I shiver as my body adjusts to the change in temperature and scan the toilet cubicle with my torch to make sure there aren't any creatures lying in wait.

I wonder if everyone feels like this, an innate fear of the dark that stops us from wandering off in the night to fall off a cliff ... or something.

I quickly wash my hands, keen to get back inside to the security of the light and the company of the others. As I round the corner of the Lodge, I see a shadowy figure step away from the building.

"Hello?"

"Hey, it's just me, Ethan. Sorry, I didn't mean to startle you."

"Oh, hi, Ethan. That's okay. I just wasn't expecting to see anyone out here."

"Felt like I needed some fresh air. It was getting a bit stuffy in there."

"You've certainly come to the right place for that." I rub my hands together, trying to warm them. "It's the anti-stuffy out here."

He doesn't say anything and it feels awkward. *Maybe I should just head back inside and leave him alone.*

"Hey, do you want to see something?" he says, shoving his hands in his pockets.

"Sure, what is it?"

"How about we keep it a surprise until we get there?" He smiles. "I think it's something you're going to like. It's not far, just over the bridge toward the hot pools."

Hmm, following a guy you hardly know into the dark on your own probably isn't the smartest move.

"I just realised how dodgy that sounded." Ethan laughs. "I could see if some of the others want to come too if you like. We'd have to be quick though. It'll be gone in a few minutes."

Come on, Jess, don't you think you've misjudged him enough already?

"I'm not worried." I shrug as though the thought hadn't crossed my mind. "Let's go. I don't want to risk missing this surprise of yours. And besides, you'd be taking your life into your hands if you did try anything dodgy. I've got a black belt in yoga, you know."

"Yoga?" Ethan gives a small chuckle. "Good to know. I'll be sure to remember that when I'm fighting the urge to be dodgy then."

I have to jog to keep up with Ethan's long strides as we cross the clearing to the bridge. We follow the path for only a minute, then Ethan pauses, shining his torch off to the side, looking for something. "Here we go. It's this way."

Once we're away from the solar lit track, we only have our headtorches to light the way. There doesn't appear to be a path, but Ethan looks like he knows where he's going. "It's not much further, just up here."

I lift my head, shining my torch in the direction he's pointing and make out a rocky slope rising in front of us. He climbs a couple of steps, then waits for me to climb up behind him. "Take my hand. It's easy to lose your balance in the dark."

I reach up and take his outstretched hand, still holding onto the rock with my other as he helps me step up to join him. We repeat this several more times, but when we reach the top, he doesn't let go.

"Be careful where you step up here. I'd get in a whole lot of trouble if you fell off."

Still holding my hand, we move away from the edge, then Ethan reaches up to my headlamp and turns it off.

"What are you doing?" I ask as he turns off his own.

He doesn't reply, instead taking hold of both my shoulders. I look up at him but can't see his face clearly, my eyes still adjusting to the dark.

What is he doing? Oh my god ... is he going to kiss me?

My heart thumps so loudly I'm sure he can hear it. I hesitate, waiting for him to do something. Then slowly, he turns me away from him, and my confusion is instantly replaced with awe.

We're standing above the tree canopy, our view extending over the tops of the trees to see the mountain range in the distance. And just above the mountains is the most enormous full moon I've ever seen. The moon looks so close it appears to be resting on top of one of the peaks. It is absolutely magnificent.

"Wow!" I exhale.

Ethan's hands drop from my shoulders but he doesn't move away, standing so close I can still feel his arm pressed against mine.

"So, I was right then. You *do* like it."

"*That* would be quite the understatement. I've never seen the moon so big before. Why does it look so big tonight? I mean, I know it hasn't changed size or anything, but why does it *look* so big up here?"

"I looked it up once. When it's close to the horizon, it looks bigger because we compare it to things in front of it that we usually consider large. Like those mountains," he explains. "It's just our imperfect brains trying to make sense of things and getting a bit confused."

"My imperfect brain tends to do that a lot." I chuckle.

"It's setting you know," Ethan says.

"What is? The moon?"

"Yeah, it's going to drop behind those peaks soon. It won't take long if you want to watch?"

He doesn't wait for my answer and sits on the ground, so I drop beside him. I rub my hands together and blow into them to try and warm them, grateful that I have my jacket on, but wishing I had my gloves.

"Are you cold?"

"I'm okay," I lie.

Ethan shuffles closer and takes my hands in his. They feel warm in comparison.

"You *are* cold. Your hands are freezing!"

"They're always cold—it doesn't matter what temperature it is. My feet are the same. Do you want to hold those too?"

He laughs, but doesn't let go of my hands, and I realise I don't want him to.

I keep my gaze focused straight ahead, and watch the moon as it sinks below the distant mountain peaks. I wish it would slow down, to take longer. I don't want this moment to end yet. But all too quickly it's gone, leaving an afterglow of light hovering above the horizon and the surrounding landscape suddenly very dark.

"I've never watched a moon set before. That was amazing."

"Show's not over yet," he says, looking above us.

I follow his gaze and look up. "Oh my god," I whisper.

With the absence of the moon, the blackened sky is now ablaze with the dense band of the Milky Way. I've never seen so many stars before and the longer I look, more and more seem to appear. I let go of Ethan's hands and lie back to take in more of the sky.

"I've only ever seen the Milky Way like this in pictures. This is incredible!" I'm mesmerised. A sense of calm spreads through me as I try to take it all in, lifting a weight I hadn't even been aware of. I breathe deeply, wanting to absorb everything I see, to sear this image on my brain. I never want to forget this.

"My dad says looking at the stars is the closest thing we have to time travel," I say as Ethan lies back beside me.

"What do you mean?"

"Well, because the stars are so far away, by the time their light gets here, we're basically seeing how they appeared hundreds or even thousands of years ago," I explain. "Some of these stars might not even exist anymore."

"I like that." I can hear the smile in his voice. "I hadn't thought of it like that before."

"Thanks for bringing me up here. You were right that I'd like it. Would you've come up here on your own if you hadn't bumped into me?"

There's a long pause before he replies. "I'd, ah … I hadn't planned on coming up here alone. I just hoped you'd want to come with me actually."

"It's lucky we bumped into each other then."

Ethan starts to laugh and I wonder why, and then it dawns on me. "Oh! You were *waiting* for me?"

He doesn't answer, which I take to be an answer in itself.

"So, what did I do to deserve this honour?" I say, sitting up.

"Like I said, I felt like I needed some fresh air, and when I saw you leave I thought maybe it'd be something you'd like to see too."

"Okay," I say, feeling a bit disappointed for some reason.

"Aaand …" he continues, "I thought it might be cool to hang out with you a bit."

And there it was. It hadn't just been random chance. He had *wanted* to spend time with me.

"Can I ask you something weird?" I ask.

"I guess so."

"Can you guys hear much of what people are saying in the Lodge from the bunkroom?"

He lets out a surprised bark of laughter, as though it wasn't what he was expecting me to ask. "Yeah, we can pretty much hear everything."

"So, you could hear Dean when we were making breakfast this morning?" I try to be vague in the hope that maybe he hadn't heard.

"Yeah, we heard."

"That must've been a bit awkward." I laugh uncomfortably.

"Kind of. Skye gave me a bit of shit about it, but Skye's always giving me crap about something. One of the perks of working with your sister."

"Oh, I hadn't realised Skye's your sister. What did she say?"

"Ah, you know," he says vaguely.

"Ah, no. I don't."

"Basically she said that I need to stop encouraging schoolgirl crushes and remember that it's my job to keep you guys safe up here."

Ouch. They think I have a crush on him? That's so embarrassing! "Hang on. So, even after Skye said that, you decided to go ahead and bring me up here?"

"I figured it would be okay, because you obviously *don't* have a crush on me. So, it's only me I have to worry about … I mean … that didn't come out right." He laughs.

"Let me get this straight," I say, turning to face him sitting cross-legged on the ground. "You figured it would be okay for us to hang out because I *don't* have a crush on you. So, you're safe from me throwing myself at you and making everything awkward. Is that about right?"

"Pretty much." He smiles.

I feel so relieved that he doesn't think I have a crush on him that I suddenly feel like having a bit of fun with it. I lean forward and place my hands on his legs, and look intently into his eyes.

"So … If I was to kiss you right now." I smile in what I hope is a seductive way. "That *wouldn't* be a good thing?"

He holds my gaze for a moment, not moving, then takes a deep breath. "Don't mess around, Jess." He takes my hands from his knees and places them back on my own legs. "You don't want to do that." He shakes his head slightly, his smile disappearing.

I'm not sure what reaction I wanted, but this wasn't it.

"Sorry, I was just teasing."

"Yeah, I know." He gives me a reassuring smile. "Don't worry about it. Just don't play games, okay?"

He stands and pulls me to my feet. "Come on, we'd better get back. Someone'll notice we're missing soon."

We turn on our headtorches and begin descending the rocky slope, Ethan holding my hand to help guide me. When we reach the bottom, he leads us through the dark until we get back onto the path. As we approach the bridge, he pauses. "Thanks for your company tonight, Jess. It was nice to get to know you better."

Before I can stop myself, I spring up on my toes and give him a peck on the cheek. "It was nice to get to know you too." I quickly pull away. "I hope that wasn't against the rules."

"I'm pretty sure that's fine." He chuckles.

When we arrive at the Lodge, Ethan hesitates, and I realise he's worried about how it will look if we go back in together.

"I think I might just head to bed," I say. "It's been a long day."

"Good idea. I'm going to do the same. Well, goodnight then."

"Goodnight," I say and head to my tent.

I open the zip and climb inside, and jump as I hear, "And where have *you* been?"

"Jesus, Priya! You gave me a fright. You're in bed early."

"Not really. It's after eleven."

"Is it? I had no idea it was so late."

"Sooo?" she prompts.

"I went to see the moon setting, actually." I say it as casually as I can, but know there's no way that could sound casual.

"By yourself?" she asks suspiciously. "Because I noticed another member of our group was missing tonight as well. A particularly sexy outdoorsy kind of fellow, goes by the name of Ethan. I think you might know of him." She bursts out laughing.

"Shh, keep your voice down. I don't want the whole campsite hearing."

"So, you weren't alone then?" She giggles. "Come on, *tell* me!"

"It wasn't like that."

"It wasn't like what?" She laughs again, clearly enjoying making me squirm. "I didn't say it was like anything. So why don't you tell me what it was *not* like then?"

"Stop it. You know what I mean. There's nothing to tell. I bumped into Ethan outside and he asked me if I'd like to see the moon setting and I said yes. So, he took me to a place where we could see it and then we looked at the stars for a while. Then we came back. Nothing happened."

"Let me get this right. Ethan asked you if you'd like to go to an isolated spot away from everyone else in the middle of the night, just the two of you, so you could gaze in wonder at the heavens together … and nothing happened."

"Yeah, but you're saying it funny to make it sound weird."

"Nope. I pretty much repeated what you said to me. So, if it sounds unbelievable that you went to watch the *moon and stars* together with a complete hottie, all on your own, and *nothing happened*—then it's because it *is* unbelievable."

"Honestly, Priya. Nothing. Happened. We just hung out together." I pause, concerned that she's going to tell the others about this. "You know, Ethan could get in a lot of trouble if anyone thinks something happened between us. Do you think anyone else noticed we were gone?"

"You don't need to worry. I covered for you. When you didn't come back after a while and I noticed Ethan was gone too, I told anyone who asked that you'd gone to bed early because you weren't feeling well."

"Thanks, Priya. I really wouldn't want Ethan to get into trouble … *even though nothing happened!*"

"Oh, Jess," Priya deepens her voice imitating Ethan. "Look at the big bright moon."

"Oh, Ethan," she continues in a high-pitched voice. "Look at the pretty stars." Then she howls with laughter.

"Oh yeah, you're hilarious." I groan as I climb into my sleeping bag. "Go to sleep!"

CHAPTER 11

Straight after breakfast we're loaded up with harnesses and helmets and told that today's activity is an extension of yesterday's, but with a twist. We're going canyoning above a waterfall called Fortune Falls at the head of the river.

It's another beautiful morning, blue cloudless skies promising to burn off the mountain chill, but for now, we're under the cool cover of the dense forest canopy.

Priya and I chat as we walk, lagging behind at the back of the group as we continue up the valley past the swimming hole. She hasn't mentioned anything more about Ethan, and I'm grateful. Not only because I didn't want anyone to overhear, but also because it felt like he was avoiding me today. He had barely acknowledged my presence, other than to reply to my "morning" when I first entered the Lodge.

Either I'd gone too far last night and made things awkward, or I was reading too much into it, which means Priya was also reading too much into it. And either way, I just wanted to forget about it so things could go back to normal.

"Well, well, well, look who we have here," Priya says quietly under her breath.

I look up and see Ethan crouched, doing up his bootlaces further along the track.

"Looks like he probably needs some help, don't you think?" Priya nudges me. "I'll catch you later."

She takes off at a run, leaving me to walk the rest of the way toward Ethan on my own. Hardly subtle.

"What's she in such a hurry for?" Ethan asks as I stop beside him.

"She wanted to catch up with Dean, I think."

He nods as if it is the obvious reason, then stands and we continue to walk along the trail together.

"This week's gone so fast. I can't believe the camp's nearly over." I glance at him. "Are you staying here for the next group after we leave?"

"No, I finish up after this one. I need to get organised to start back at uni."

"Are you looking forward to it?"

"Looking forward to finishing this camp or starting at uni?"

"I meant uni, but both I guess."

"Yeah, I'm really looking forward to seeing my friends and getting back into my study, actually."

"And finishing this camp? You're probably looking forward to getting away from us I suppose?"

"Not at all." He looks surprised. "Why would you say that?"

"I just figured you'd probably prefer to be hanging out with your university friends than having to look after a bunch of high school kids."

"You're not such a bad bunch." He laughs. "If we were all at Ashley together, I reckon we'd get on pretty well, be friends even. I'm not much older than you guys, you know."

"It must be that air of authority that makes you seem wiser than your years. So you're not eighty then?"

"I look that wise, do I?"

"Did I say wise? I meant wizened." I grin at him.

Our conversation cuts short as we catch up with the rest of the group. A few seconds later, the trees open to reveal a cliff with a narrow waterfall cascading down its left side, feeding into a large pool of water at its base. A misty rainbow billows from the waterfall, drenching everything in the surrounding area, including dozens of large boulders along the edge of the pool.

"I'll catch you later," Ethan says as he heads over to join Skye, who's getting ready to climb at the base of the cliff. I look above her and see small metal climbing bolts glinting in the light, drilled into the cliff's yellow and orange face like piercings.

"Above us is the start of Fortune Falls Canyon," Emily calls out over the rumble of the waterfall. "Once we climb to the top of the waterfall, we're going to make our way up the narrow canyon behind it. You're going to love this. The canyon is unlike anything you've seen around here. Skye is going to climb first and get everything roped up, then we'll head up one at a time. So, take a look around. We're going to be here a while."

I watch as Skye begins her climb. She takes her time, not taking any risks, but I can tell that she's done this many times before. A few minutes after she reaches the top, she throws down the rope, now secured to bolts above us.

"Kalen, do you want to go first?" Emily asks.

"Absolutely!" Kalen heads over to Ethan to get set up.

I notice Holly and Priya have climbed from the bank onto the boulders and I make my way over to them. We scramble to the edge of the pool and it isn't as deep as I expected, but there's a watermark on the rocks indicating it gets much higher when it rains.

We climb onto the enormous boulders and begin to jump from one to the next, leaping over smaller rocks and crevices in between. We make our way along the side of the pool toward the cliff. Holly is ahead of me and she jumps to the largest of the boulders, one with a greenish tinge close to the waterfall.

She lands on the smooth surface and slips, and her arms windmill. "Woah!" she yells, as if trying to calm a skittish horse, then looks back at us with a grin. "That was a close one, thought I was going to—" Her words cut off as her feet slip again and she begins to wildly wave her arms trying to stop herself from falling.

I begin to laugh, thinking she's hamming it up, but this time her skittish feet don't settle and I watch in horror as she tips back.

Priya gasps behind me and I pointlessly yell out, "Holly!" warning of the danger she's clearly aware of. In a final attempt to stop herself from falling backwards, Holly swivels, turning sideways, and lets out a panicked scream as she tumbles off the boulder out of sight.

Her scream draws the attention of everyone on the bank, and from the corner of my eye I see Kalen look down from midway up the rockface.

"Holly, are you okay?" he yells.

His question is answered as Holly screams, an agonising cry that makes my stomach churn.

"We're coming, Holly!" I yell.

Priya and I carefully jump to the next boulder and I can now see the one that Holly fell from is slick with spray from the waterfall, covered in a layer of green moss.

I lower myself between the rocks and make my way around the side of the one Holly slipped from, not wanting to risk the same fate. When I reach the other side of the boulder, I'm surprised not to find her there. I follow her cries and continue to squirm my way around the next one, which is where I finally find her, lying on her side, the force of her fall having flung her off the boulder behind as well. She holds her leg, head thrown back in agony.

I clamber onto the slippery boulder next to her, the spray from the waterfall soaking everything, including us. Priya is right behind me.

"My leg. I felt it snap," she whimpers.

"Oh shit, hang on, Holly." I raise my head and yell, "We need help!" and see that Ethan and Emily are already making their way toward us. "Holly's leg's broken."

Emily pauses and looks at Skye, who is standing at the top of the waterfall. "Skye, you need to come down. We need you."

As soon as Ethan and Emily reach us, I move out of the way to give them room while they talk to Holly and assess her injuries.

"Is there anywhere else that hurts, Holly? Did you hit your head?" Emily asks.

"No, it's just my leg," Holly cries through gritted teeth.

"We need to move her to the bank so Skye can treat her. Do you think you can carry her, Ethan?"

"Let's get Dean to help," Priya says. "It might be easier if there's two of you."

"Yeah, that's a good idea." Emily stands. "Dean, can you give us a hand?"

Dean immediately starts hopping over the boulders toward us. As soon as he reaches us, Ethan and Dean begin talking about how they're going to carry Holly. They rule out trying to carry her over the boulders and decide to make their way around them, taking turns to pass her between them in a kind of leapfrog relay.

Ethan moves beside Holly and leans his face close to hers. "You're going to be okay, Holly, but we need to get you to the bank so Skye can fix up your leg. This is going to hurt. I'm really sorry."

Holly nods, her eyes wide from shock and pain. Ethan gently places his hand under her legs and scoops her from the rock. She screams as soon as he moves her, but he doesn't hesitate, knowing it would just prolong the pain. He turns and passes her to Dean, who can only take a step before he can't go any further.

Ethan dashes around to the other side of the next boulder and leans forward with his arms out to take Holly from Dean, propping his leg on the boulder to help support her weight. Holly cries out again as she's transferred into Ethan's arms.

Ethan talks to her, telling her she's going to be fine the whole time as Dean makes his way to the next boulder and leans into the gap so Ethan can pass Holly back to him.

They repeat this until they exit the last of the boulders and Ethan carries Holly the rest of the way across the rubble onto the bank.

Holly clamps her hand to her mouth, attempting to stifle her scream as Ethan lowers her to the ground, and Skye runs over with a first aid kit in her hand.

"I need to take a look at your leg, Holly," she says calmly. "I'm going to cut open your trousers so I don't have to move it."

Skye cuts the side of the pant leg up to the middle of her thigh and separates the cloth to reveal Holly's leg. Holly looks down and sees the bone pushing up underneath the skin and begins to scream again.

"I know it hurts, Holly, and I'm going to give you something to help with that, but it's at the Lodge." Skye looks at Ethan. "I need the large first aid kit and the stretcher. We're going to have to carry her to the lodge. There's no way we can get a chopper in here."

"I need three people to come with me." Ethan turns to face the rest of us gathered behind.

Matt, Kalen, and I offer to go with him. Ethan leads the way as we run back along the track to the Lodge, covering the distance that had taken us almost an hour this morning in only twenty minutes.

Ethan dashes into the storeroom and comes out carrying a first aid kit and a stretcher. He hands the first aid kit to me, then passes the stretcher to the boys.

"You need to get these to Skye. I'm going to call for a rescue helicopter to pick Holly up from here."

I shove the first aid kit into an empty backpack and throw it over my shoulder as I run out the door to catch up with Matt and Kalen.

We run the entire way back, the urgency of the situation spurring us on. I drop to my knees beside Skye as soon as I reach them and hand her the first aid kit from the pack.

"I'm going to give you some morphine to help with the pain, Holly," she says calmly to her. I don't think Holly can really hear what Skye is saying, but Skye keeps talking to her the whole time. Holly doesn't react at all when Skye injects her leg with a syringe. She's already in too much pain to feel anything else.

"Ethan's radioing for a helicopter," I say when I finally catch my breath.

"Good." She nods, then looks up at Matt and Kalen. "I'm going to need your help to get Holly on the stretcher." They move into position on either side of her. "Ready? Lift."

Holly screams as they lift her, then lower her gently onto the stretcher. I take Holly's hand, tears streaming down her face as she grips it tightly. I fight back tears of my own, stroking her hand, unsure how to help.

"Right, we're going to do this in teams, six at a time," Skye commands, tucking an emergency blanket around Holly. "I need two in the front and two in the back and one on each side in the middle. We need to keep the stretcher as level as possible, so I want the strongest people in the front to lift it higher as we head down the gorge. When you get tired, call out and we'll swap to the other team."

Dean and Jackson go to the front of the stretcher, and Marley and Oliver move to the back. I let go of Holly's hand and grip the stretcher on one side as Skye takes the other.

"On three," Skye calls out. "One, two, three." Holly winces as we lift the stretcher, but doesn't scream this time. I reach over and squeeze her hand. She squeezes back, closing her eyes.

We have to walk slowly to make sure we don't lose our footing while trying to keep the stretcher as level as possible. After a few minutes, Holly no longer cries out. The morphine has taken effect and she drifts in and out of consciousness as we continue as fast as we can along the track, changing carriers whenever someone calls for a break. We've just swapped carriers again and I'm following at the back when Ethan appears on the track ahead. Skye asks Priya to take her place, then lets the rest of us past, hanging back with Emily to talk to Ethan.

"What do you mean you couldn't get hold of them? Is there something wrong with the radio?" Skye asks.

"No, I mean, no one was responding. I tried for over half an hour," Ethan replies.

"That doesn't make sense," Emily says. "Even if they were already out on a rescue, Beth would still be there to coordinate. There's always someone monitoring the channel."

"When I couldn't get hold of Search and Rescue, I tried contacting Base to see if they could help get in touch with them, but I couldn't get any response there either."

"And you're sure the radio was working properly?" Skye asks.

"I'm sure."

"Maybe I should run ahead and try again," Emily says. "Just in case."

"Yeah, okay," Ethan replies. "Maybe you should, but I'm positive it's nothing to do with the radio."

"Okay, go," Skye says. "But, Emily, if you can't get hold of them on the radio, activate the emergency locator beacon, okay?" Emily nods and takes off, overtaking the rest of us as she runs ahead down the path.

"If we can't get a helicopter, we're going to have to take her out ourselves," Skye says to Ethan. "I'm worried there might be internal bleeding where the femur has broken. We can't risk waiting. We need to get her to a hospital as soon as possible."

"We'll have to move fast. We don't want to be driving that track in the dark."

"If we can get to the jeep by mid-afternoon, we should have enough light to get us to the main road," Skye replies. "It won't matter if it's dark then."

We continue our slow plod, swapping carriers two more times before we reach the Lodge. Emily runs across the clearing to meet us, shaking her head at Skye and Ethan as she approaches.

"Ethan's right, it's not the radio. No one is responding. I have no idea what's going on. I've activated the emergency beacon."

"Just put the stretcher down here," Skye calls out. "Everyone take a break, get a drink, have something quick to eat and grab your jackets, hats, and torches. We leave in ten minutes."

"What about the helicopter?" Dean asks.

"We've activated an emergency locator beacon so the helicopter should be here soon, but we haven't been able to get in touch with Search and Rescue, so there's the possibility that the helicopter's already in use," Skye answers. "We're going to plan to transport Holly to the hospital ourselves just in case there's a delay though. We'll take the beacon with us and they'll get to us as soon as they can."

I grab my jacket and torch from the tent, then head into the Lodge to see if Emily needs help. I find her in the storeroom filling backpacks with food and spare sleeping bags. She hands me one of the packs and I add my things to it.

Marley is rummaging through papers on the table by the window when I leave the storeroom. "Here it is," he says, lifting a piece of paper, then glances over at me when he realises I'm staring. "Holly's emergency contact details," he explains. He then scans the page. "At least that's some good news. Looks like she's a local, from a town here in Langadorne. We can get her parents to meet us at the hospital. Come on, we better join the others," he says, heading to the door.

I look at Holly lying on the stretcher, covered by the emergency blanket. The morphine is managing her pain, allowing her to sleep, but her face looks unusually pale.

It isn't long before everyone's gathered outside the Lodge, belongings put into shared backpacks. Skye calls to get everyone's attention.

"We've still got a long way to go today and we're going to need everyone's help to get there. We do this just as we did before, taking turns to carry Holly. If you're not carrying the stretcher, you're carrying a backpack. We'll swap every fifteen minutes to keep our pace up. You need to make sure you stay hydrated and eat to maintain your energy as we go. Jess and Emily are carrying food supplies for everyone. Team one, take your places. One, two, three, lift."

Holly stirs as they lift the stretcher, but appears to fall back to sleep when they start walking. We keep up a good pace, only slowing where the track narrows. Swapping carriers regularly to keep us fresh.

We keep this up until we finally reach the clearing near the swing bridge. Holly has begun to stir from her sleep, groaning as the morphine wears off. Skye stops us and checks Holly's vital signs, then gives her another shot of morphine.

I look from Skye to Emily and then to Ethan, wondering what they're thinking. I resist the urge to ask them why the helicopter hasn't arrived yet, knowing they don't know the answer either.

Surely it wouldn't usually take this long though. It's been hours since Emily activated the emergency locator beacon. Even if the helicopter had already been busy on another rescue, it should have been here by now, shouldn't it?

When we reach the narrow swing bridge, Skye stops and asks Dean and Ethan to take over carrying the stretcher on their own. Skye backs onto the bridge ahead of Ethan, steering him by his shoulders as he inches backwards onto it. Dean follows with Emily firmly gripping his shoulders from behind, helping to steady him from its sway. They step cautiously, giving the bridge time to settle as they cross.

I hold my breath, afraid they might lose their balance. There's no risk of Holly falling off the bridge, but there's definitely a risk they could lose their balance while unable to hold on to the railing and tip her from the stretcher.

Several long exhales join with mine when the stretcher safely reaches the other side. We quickly file across the bridge and take over from Ethan and Dean to carry Holly the remaining distance to the jeep, which we find still parked on the side of the road where we left it last week.

Skye and Emily set to work making a bed on the backseat of the jeep using the sleeping bags we'd carried with us. Holly groans as they lift her onto the makeshift bed, panting as she lays back, her face beading with perspiration. Skye straps Holly in place using the seat belts, then packs more sleeping bags around her to try and make her more comfortable. Holly's eyes close again when Skye finishes.

I can't bear to think how horrible the journey on this bumpy road is going to be for Holly when even the slightest movement hurts her. But the morphine seems to be helping for now, so they just need to get through the worst of it while her pain relief is working.

Skye joins the rest of the team leaders at the side of the jeep and Marley hands Skye the sheet of paper with Holly's emergency contact details. After a brief conversation, Ethan climbs into the driver's seat. Skye turns to Emily and wraps her arms around her. As she lets go, Emily takes Skye's face between her hands and tells her she loves her. Skye smiles a rare smile, replying that she loves her too, and then kisses her goodbye.

The engine starts and Skye jumps into the back of the jeep with Holly. And then, without giving anyone the chance to say goodbye, Ethan begins to drive down the road.

I feel empty as I watch them drive away. The adrenaline that has kept me going since the accident drains from my body and I'm left feeling utterly exhausted. I start to shake and I'm not sure if I'm going to cry or be sick.

"Okay, everyone," Emily calls out. "This has been an exhausting day both physically and mentally, and I know you're all feeling tired and probably emotional too. But we aren't finished yet. We still have a long trek back to the Lodge before we can rest, and our biggest risk at this point is that exhaustion can lead us to make mistakes and have an accident … and I think we'd all agree that's the last thing we need right now. I want you all to eat something to replenish your energy, even if you're not feeling hungry."

I open my pack and start handing out protein bars, nuts, and chocolate to everyone, then flop on the ground next to Matt. I nibble at my protein bar, forcing myself to eat, and return Matt's smile when he offers me some of his chocolate. Everyone looks as tired as I feel. We barely talk, the stress and worry of Holly's accident beginning to hit home now that we're no longer distracted by the urgency to keep going. Dean has his arm around Priya as she rests her head against his chest, a tear streaking her face as she blinks blankly at the ground beside them. She looks exactly how I feel. Exhausted, worried, sad. And we still have another four hours' walk ahead of us.

"We need to get going," Emily says. "We want to make as much progress as possible while it's still light. Look out for each other. Once the sun goes down, it'll get cold and we need to be watching for early signs of hypothermia. Remember what to look for—extreme tiredness, stumbling, confusion. If you notice anything, bring it to my attention immediately." She puts on her pack and tightens the waist belt. "I'll take the lead. Marley will bring up the rear. Let's get going."

We walk for nearly two hours, taking a break as the sun goes down to put on warmer clothing and get our headlamps out. We have some more food, resting for only a few minutes before Emily gets us moving again. Our pace slows in the dark, the light from our torches casting so many shadows it's hard to tell whether a shadow is a raised tree root or a dip in the ground. I find myself stepping higher than necessary just to be sure I don't trip, and it often feels foolish to do so. We walk in silence. It uses all our energy. There's nothing left for talking.

We finally arrive at the campsite and pile into the Lodge, collapsing into the seats. Emily lights the fire and boils water to make hot chocolate. I'm amazed that she still has the energy to do it. The rest of us lie everywhere, on the seats, on the floor, desperate to rest our aching legs, backs, shoulders, necks, heads—everything aches.

Emily and Marley start handing out hot drinks and pieces of chocolate, telling us that the sugar will help, and it does. And although I really just want to go to sleep on the floor where I am, I force myself to stand and help Matt when he offers to take over from them, telling them they need to sit down and have a drink too. We finish topping up everyone's cups, then flop wearily onto the bench seat by the table.

"You look knackered." Matt smiles at me.

"Thanks." I manage a small chuckle. "So do you."

"I don't think I've ever been this tired in my life." He sighs.

"Me neither. I feel a bit weird—like my head is disconnected from my body. I don't know how to explain it."

"I get what you mean." He puts his arm around my shoulder and pulls me closer.

My head is so foggy, the tenderness of his gesture barely registers. I close my eyes and lean into him, giving in to exhaustion and letting my body relax. I don't know how long we're like that—I think I may have even fallen asleep.

My eyes struggle to open as the sound of Marley's voice rouses me from somewhere across the room. "I think everyone should head to bed. There's no rush to get up in the morning. We won't be doing anything tomorrow except resting. You did a great job today, everyone. You should feel really proud of yourselves."

Matt's arm slides around my waist and I feel him begin to help me to my feet. I groan, not wanting to stand, and turn toward him, burying my face into his chest. I'm overwhelmed by the sudden need to be held, to be held together, and cling tightly to him. I take long, deep breaths as his arms wrap around me, understanding what I need. He doesn't speak and he doesn't move. I feel his head rest on top of mine and he waits until I'm ready.

I slowly pull away and glance shyly up at him, wondering how he feels about my sudden attachment. If he's unsettled by it, he doesn't let on. His eyes tell me they understand as he smiles and gently ruffles my hair. Then he takes my hand and we follow the others outside to the tents.

CHAPTER 12

I was sure I'd sleep like the dead, but it ended up being a restless night disturbed by dreams of people falling and screaming and trying to run but not being able to move. I wake a few times and hear Priya making unhappy noises in her sleep too, our brains processing the stressful events of the previous day.

After breakfast, we head to the hot pool to relax. We talk quietly, letting the warm water soothe our sore muscles, our mood subdued and reflective in the knowledge that this will be our last time here together. Tomorrow we'll be returning to the real world.

Emily tries to contact the Falls River Base Camp to get an update on Holly throughout the day, but isn't able to get hold of anyone on the radio. At first she tells us Ethan and Skye would have had a late night getting Holly to hospital and are probably catching up on sleep. But as her calls continue to go unanswered, I can see that it's bothering her.

After lunch, we sit on the shaded deck, talking and swapping contact details so we can keep in touch after the camp ends. Dean still can't believe how easily Matt threw him to the ground the other day and asks if he can teach him how to do it. I follow and sit on the soft grass close by and watch Matt teaching Dean different techniques to throw an opponent and sweep them off their feet, explaining how to use their size and momentum to his advantage. Dean tries again and again to get Matt to the ground. Sometimes Matt lets him, but often he doesn't.

"Would you like to have a try?" Dean asks when I begin to laugh at his latest effort.

I raise my eyebrows at Matt. "Can I?"

"Sure, if you want to."

"Actually, I was wondering if you could show me something in particular. I want to know how to fight someone off if I'm grabbed from behind, like they teach in a self-defense class. Can you teach me how to do that?"

"Yeah, there are a few things I can show you."

When Dean agrees to help Matt demonstrate, the other girls come over and join in and soon the rest of the boys gather round as well. Matt ends up giving us all a lesson on basic self-defense. He teaches us how to use our elbows to strike behind us, how to punch properly, and how to use our whole body to add power to our punches and kicks. We take turns pretending to attack each other and practicing the moves Matt has shown us.

"Have you ever had to fight anyone?" I ask after our lesson has finished.

"No, I've stopped a few fights though, but that's the whole point. I didn't take Jiu Jitsu classes to learn how to fight, I did it to learn how to defend myself. My parents thought it would be a good idea for me to learn, so they put me into classes as soon as I started school."

"Why did they want you to learn so young? Don't get me wrong, I think it's a great idea that they did. I'm just wondering why."

"They thought I might get picked on, I suppose."

"Why would they think you'd get picked on?"

"I guess they knew I was a bit different. Not many five-year-olds read books about physics, let alone being able to read a book at all. And I refused to eat any meat. I wouldn't even eat chicken nuggets— what kid doesn't like chicken nuggets? That's reason enough, isn't it?" He laughs. "Some people don't like it when you're different. They're threatened by it. My parents wanted me to feel safe to be myself."

"Have you been picked on a lot?"

"I guess I turned out to be less weird than they thought." He grins. "It probably also helped that I put the biggest guy in school on his arse on my first day at high school, so people knew to leave me alone after that. Occasionally, someone who's had a few too many concussions has another try, but it doesn't happen very often. So no, I haven't been picked on a lot. No more than anyone else."

I feel relieved. I hate the thought that Matt might get bullied or picked on. I like that he's different and has the confidence to be himself. I feel drawn to it—to him. I've felt drawn to him since the first moment we met and I'm not exactly sure why. Well, I do know why. I have a rude man's shove and gravity to thank for that.

But ever since then, I find myself constantly choosing to be near him. I like the way I feel when I'm with him, and it dawns on me what that feeling is. He makes me feel like it's okay to be me.

CHAPTER 13

"Any luck?" Ollie asks Emily when she emerges from the Lodge.

"No, they must've already left to pick us up," she replies. "Which means we need to get going so they don't have to wait for us at the other end."

We make good time on the track, everyone much fitter now than when we arrived a week ago, reaching the pick-up point in only three and a half hours. The jeeps haven't arrived, so we sit down to have some lunch while we wait.

And we wait. And we wait.

After a couple of hours, we're getting pretty restless. There's no point in asking Emily when they're going to get here, but we do. And she replies that she's sure it won't be much longer.

At 4:00 p.m., Emily decides we've waited long enough. "There must've been a problem with one of the vehicles. We'll camp in the clearing so we don't have to walk all the way back to the Lodge. I'll leave a note just in case they show up after we leave so they know where to find us."

She writes a message on a piece of paper torn from a notebook and places it under a rock near the entrance to the walking track, tying a strip of red trail marking string to it.

We're not concerned that the jeeps haven't shown up yet. On the contrary, we're actually happy that it means we get an extra night out here together.

We walk the short distance to the clearing and pitch our tents. Emily sets up a firepit while the rest of us collect wood. Once the fire is lit, we put everyone's food in a pile and Emily rations out portions to each of us, making sure there's still food left over for tomorrow. We sit around the campfire telling stories once it's dark, but it isn't long before we head to bed.

****

Although we aren't expecting the jeeps until midday, we make our way to the meeting point late morning just in case they arrive early. Midday comes and goes. Then 1:00 p.m. Then 2:00 p.m. By this point we're finding it hard to hide our impatience, and there's growing concern about how late they are.

"What if they don't come today too?" Jackson asks. "Are we just going to camp here again and keep waiting?"

"We don't have enough food to wait another day though, do we?" I ask.

Emily nods as we speak. "Look, I don't know what the delay is, and I don't have any way to get in touch with them from here. We'd need to go back to the Lodge to use the radio to make contact. So, if they're not here in the next half hour, I think we should probably do that rather than camp here again."

"Is there anywhere with cell phone reception up here?" Marley asks.

Emily pauses, considering Marley's question carefully, then turns to look back down the road. "We might be able to get a signal if we can climb high enough," Emily says. "I have an idea where we could try it, we'd need to go now though. I don't want us walking back to the Lodge in the dark."

"Can I come too?" I ask. "I'm not very good at waiting, I need to do something."

"Sure," Emily answers. "I'll let the others know what we're planning to do and get them to wait for us at the campsite, then we'll get going."

As soon as she's finished, Emily, Marley, and I jog down the road, wasting no time to cross the shallow river at the bottom of the ravine before scrambling steeply uphill through the trees on the other side. Eventually the forest thins and we exit the tree line and cut across the mountainside.

"Can you see if you've got a signal?" Emily asks.

We stop, puffing hard as Marley checks his phone. "Nothing." He shakes his head.

"Okay, I think our best bet is that point up there." She points at an outcrop ahead of us. "If we don't get any signal there, we'll head back to the others."

As we scramble along the side of the mountain, I realise we've reached the landslide where we stopped for lunch on our way up here last week, and see the narrow road crossing below.

"We'll need to be careful as we cross the slip, the hillside will be less stable without vegetation. We often get rockfalls on the road below here," Emily says.

The hillside is covered in scree and rocks, the surface crumbling as we walk, sending small trickles and sometimes showers of stone below us. I realise we could easily start an avalanche of rock from up here and block the road if we aren't careful.

"Did you hear that?" Marley asks.

"Hear what?" I stop to listen.

"I think I can hear a motor. Maybe it's them?"

He's right, I can hear it now too. The definite sound of a vehicle somewhere out of sight.

"Oh, thank god." Emily exhales loudly. "I was starting to get worried."

"Should we try to get down to the road?" I ask.

"Yeah, we should," Emily replies. "But not here. It's too unstable. Let's go back to the trees and climb back down there."

We turn and start back the way we'd just come, angling down toward the tree line.

"Come on, move faster! They're coming!"

I look around, confused. "Who said that?"

Marley pauses, also scanning for the source of the voice. I follow his gaze toward the road just as four people sprint out of the forest.

"There's nowhere to hide. They're going to find us!" a woman yells. "We should go back and hide in the trees!"

"There's no time. They'll see us. Our only chance is to get to the forest on the other side," a man calls over his shoulder as he continues to run.

"I don't know what's going on, but I think we should get out of sight," Emily whispers. "Keep going. We need to get to the trees."

Just as we reach the safety of the tree line, a small truck appears on the road below. But it isn't one of our jeeps. It looks like a military vehicle.

"Just keep running!" a man screams. "We can make it!"

Without speaking a word, we instinctively crouch, hiding ourselves further amongst the foliage. Every muscle in my body tenses, my body preparing to run even though it hasn't been given the command yet to do so. Their terror is enough to warn us we should be afraid too.

"Stop or you'll be shot," a voice booms from a loudspeaker as the vehicle approaches the people.

The terrified people continue to sprint along the road toward the safety of the trees on the other side until a shot rings out. "That was a warning. The next one won't be."

Their running slows to a stop as they realise they can't outrun the vehicle and reluctantly turn to face their pursuers.

"Put your hands up and stay where you are," a man yells as he climbs out of the truck, followed by three more people climbing out the back doors. I'm surprised when I see they aren't wearing uniforms. They're wearing protective hazmat suits.

"What the hell is going on?" Marley hisses.

"Shh, stay quiet," Emily whispers.

I get the feeling something important is about to happen, so I take out my phone and start to video.

"You are not allowed to leave the quarantine zone," a soldier calls out. "Get into the back of the truck so we can take you to a quarantine centre."

"We don't want to go there," a man replies. "One sick person and everyone gets it. We know what happened at Southport. The quarantine centres are a death sentence."

"This is not a request. Get into the back of the truck," the soldier says, raising his gun at the people.

"We don't have a choice, Martin." The woman looks back at the man, shaking her head. "Just get in the truck."

Slowly she walks toward the truck with the others following. The soldiers back away as they get closer.

"This one's sick!" a soldier yells, waving his gun at the man closest to him. "He's got red eyes."

"It's just allergies." The man shakes his head vigorously. "I have hay fever, that's all."

"If he's infected, they're all infected," a soldier shouts.

"We're not sick!" the woman yells. "We just want to be left alone. We know a place in the mountains where we can stay and keep safe away from everyone else. Please, just let us go!" she pleads, taking a step toward the soldier.

"Stay back," the soldier shouts at her.

Suddenly, a man at the back of the group turns and starts to run away, followed by one of his friends. Without warning, shots fire and the men drop to the ground, unmoving. Emily inhales sharply beside me.

"You've killed them!" the woman shrieks as she runs toward their bodies. Another shot fires and she falls to the ground too.

"What the hell, Jones!" A soldier spins around. "Put your gun down."

"I thought she was going to run for it."

The only member of the group left standing begins to scream and breaks into a run, charging at the soldier called Jones. Jones stumbles as he backs away and falls, scrambling to lift his gun before the man can reach him. A shot rings out, hitting the man mid stride, and he slumps to the ground, groaning.

"Is this the infected one?" a soldier asks as he approaches.

"Yeah, he's the one with red eyes," Jones replies.

The soldier points his gun at the injured man. "I'm sorry, but it's better this way." Then he fires. "You were dead anyway."

How can this be happening? My hands shake uncontrollably, and I struggle to hold my phone still enough to keep videoing. Bile burns my throat and I fight the urge to vomit as my stomach roils. I force myself to take a deep breath and exhale slowly, emptying my lungs before taking my next breath. *Get it under control, Jess. If they hear us, we're dead.*

"This was a complete shit show." The soldier shakes his head.

"We couldn't let them run, Captain. We can't risk them getting out and spreading it."

"I'm well aware of our orders. Doesn't mean we couldn't have handled this better though. Burn the bodies. We can't risk touching them."

"Jesus," Marley says under his breath.

I can't watch, and we can't leave, too afraid to move in case they see us. A soldier dashes behind the truck and lifts his visor, vomiting at the side of the road. I swallow bile again and take another deep breath.

"You okay?" the Captain asks.

"It's the smell. It makes me sick every time." The soldier wipes his mouth with the back of his glove.

"Yep, doesn't get much worse than that." The Captain pats the soldier on the back, then opens the truck door.

"Captain?" the soldier calls. "Something doesn't make sense. Why were they heading into the hills if they'd set off an emergency locator beacon? Wouldn't they be going in the other direction if they were looking for help?"

My body tenses at his words.

"Yeah, that'd occurred to me too. They can't be the ones that set it off. We can't carry on any further now though." The Captain waves his hand at the burning corpses. "We'll report back to headquarters and they can decide what we do next."

After what feels like an eternity, the soldiers climb back into the truck and slowly reverse down the road in the direction they'd come, leaving the smoldering bodies lying on the road.

I stop recording and throw up.

"What the hell?" Marley explodes as soon as the truck is out of sight. "This is insane! What the hell has been going on while we've been up here?"

"We need to get back to the others," Emily says. "I don't know what's going on, but we need to get out of here just in case they come back. Let's keep high and stay off the road for now." She doesn't wait for our response and starts walking, conversation over.

None of us talk. My feet follow numbly as I trail behind Emily and Marley. My brain replaying the horror of what we've just seen over and over until it feels so overwhelming, I'm not sure it was even real.

We drop back down to the road just before the ford, then run the rest of the way to the entrance of the track. Emily picks up the note she'd left under the rock the previous day, then scans the area.

"We don't want to leave anything that might alert someone to us being here," she explains. As she's about to enter the trees, she pauses and turns to look at us. "Let's not tell the others anything until we're back at the Lodge. We need to get back there as fast as we can, and I don't think it'll help if everyone's worried and frightened. We'll tell them later."

I nod. I'm not sure I'm ready to talk about it yet anyway.

We reach the meadow to find everyone sitting around chatting, blissfully ignorant of what we'd just witnessed.

"Okay, everyone, we need to get going so we can get to the Lodge before dark," Emily announces.

"Did you get a signal?" Matt asks.

"No, we couldn't get one," I reply as I pick up my pack.

"Make sure you have everything," Emily calls out. "Don't leave anything behind."

Emily, Marley, and I wait for everyone to leave the clearing, then quickly destroy as much evidence of the fire from the previous night as we can.

"Hopefully it won't be obvious anyone's been here recently," Emily says.

"What about the trail markers?" I ask. "Should we get rid of those too?"

"I guess it couldn't hurt. We could get rid of the cairns on the river bank as well," she replies. "I think it's a good idea."

When we reach the river, we hang back and wait until everyone has re-entered the trees before we go back to knock down the cairns. Just as we're finishing, I look up and see Matt standing at the track entry point, watching. I wave and he walks back toward us.

"I came back to make sure everyone's okay. Why are you knocking the cairns down?"

I look at Emily, unsure how to answer him.

"You can tell him." Emily nods.

"Tell me what?"

Emily and Marley walk on ahead, leaving me to talk to Matt alone, to tell him what we'd seen.

"I don't understand. You're saying there's been some kind of virus outbreak and the army is shooting people if they try to leave?" He shakes his head in disbelief.

"I took a video on my phone. Maybe if you watch, it might help."

I take out my phone and find the video, then hand it to Matt as it begins to play. Matt's brow furrows as he focuses intently on the images on the screen, jumping when the shots fire, his mouth dropping open.

"I don't want to see any more." He hands the phone back when they start to burn the bodies. He stands, shaking his head. "This is crazy! Even after seeing that video, I still find it hard to believe. How can that have happened?"

"I know … I don't know."

"What the hell is going on out there?" He raises his voice. "We've only been here a week. How can this happen in a week? Maybe those guys were just psycho and on a rampage or something?"

"I don't know," I say again. "But we don't want to take any risks in case someone else comes up here. That's why we're removing the trail markers."

"Why would anyone come up here? We're in the middle of nowhere."

"I don't know, but you heard those people tell the soldiers that they knew a place where they could stay, so maybe they were meaning the Lodge. What if other people try to come up here because they think it's safer up here? What if they're sick? We don't want to get infected too. The soldiers seemed really frightened once they thought one of them was sick." I pause. "And what if the military come up here and find *us*? They might not believe that we've been here all this time away from other people … and maybe they'll think we're infected, and—"

"Maybe they'll do that to us," Matt finishes.

"Yeah." I sigh. "Come on, we better get going and catch up with the others."

We reach the Lodge just before dark. Dean and Jackson drop their packs as soon as we arrive and start pulling out their tents.

"Just leave the tents, guys," Emily calls out. "I think we'll all sleep in the Lodge tonight. It's more important that we get some food into us. We've hardly eaten in the last twenty-four hours and I don't want anyone collapsing from malnutrition on me."

"Fine by me." Dean shrugs and picks up his pack again.

Emily allocates jobs to get the fire started and dinner cooking as soon as we enter the Lodge, and it isn't long before we're sitting at the table to eat.

Although I should be starving, I have absolutely no appetite and just pick at my food, moving it absentmindedly around the plate. Matt is sitting beside me and he looks like he's having trouble too. I look across at Marley and he gives me a nod, lifting his fork to his mouth as though showing me what to do. I slowly put a forkful of food in my mouth and raise an eyebrow at him as I do it as if to say, 'see, I did it'.

After we finish dinner, Emily calls everyone over to the seats by the fire and says she needs to discuss something with us. "I know you're all wondering why our rides didn't pick us up, and to be honest, I don't know why they didn't either. I haven't been able to get in touch with any of the guides at Base Camp, and we weren't able to get any cell phone signal this afternoon." She takes a deep breath, looking from Marley to me, then her shoulders slump as she shakes her head. "I don't even know how to begin to talk about this."

Everyone has gone completely silent, wondering why Emily looks upset.

Marley joins Emily in front of the fire and starts to talk—explaining what we'd witnessed, telling them about the people trying to escape and the soldiers shooting them and burning their dead bodies. I look around the group as he talks, watching everyone's reactions. Expressions range from complete disbelief to open-mouthed astonishment, and in some cases I can tell they are skeptical, just waiting for the 'ha ha, got ya, you should see the look on your faces' punchline.

But there's no punchline. This isn't some sick joke. Although it *is* nauseating.

"Oh, come on, this is bullshit, right?" Dean asks.

"Jess has a video," Matt replies, and every face turns to look at me.

"I took a video on my phone. You can watch it if you don't believe us."

I hand my phone to Dean and everyone crowds around him as it starts to play. They're as shocked as the rest of us. Priya's in tears by the end and quite a few say they feel sick. Jackson runs outside, following through on his claim. Then everyone starts talking at once, voices jumbling together as they talk over each other.

"So, there's some kind of plague or something?"

"Do you think it's everywhere? What about our families? Do you think they're okay?"

"Does that mean we can't leave here? If we leave, we'd risk being exposed, wouldn't we?"

"Are we safe here? What if someone turns up here? What would we do?"

"Is this why we couldn't get a rescue helicopter for Holly?"

"Woah! Okay, everyone, let's settle down and talk one at a time," Marley yells above the voices, raising his hands until the room quietens. "Look, I know this is really confusing, and we're *all* worried about what this means. But everyone knows as much as each other. We have no more information or answers than the rest of you. So, we're going to have to work this out together … to come up with a plan together. Who wants to go first?"

Ollie puts his hand up. "I think we need to find out more information about what's going on. How can we make a plan if we don't know what we're planning for?"

There's a murmur of agreement.

"I agree," says Kalen. "What if we've misunderstood what they were talking about? Maybe there isn't a plague and we've got nothing to worry about."

"I can keep trying to contact Base Camp using the radio, and failing that, I can try using other channels on the Citizens Band to see if anyone else can give us some answers."

"Do you think that's why no one answered the other day when you were trying to find out about Holly?" Lily asks. "Are they all dead from the plague or something?"

"Jesus, do you think that's why?" Priya gasps.

"I honestly don't know," Emily answers. "We couldn't get hold of anyone at Search and Rescue the day before either. And that *is* really odd, because someone is always monitoring the channel there."

"You said you called for a helicopter that day and that didn't turn up either," Lily says.

"We activated an emergency locator beacon when we couldn't get hold of Search and Rescue on the radio." Emily shakes her head. "I don't know why it didn't work. Skye took it with them when they left, so it's possible they were met by Search and Rescue once they were on the road. Or maybe they'd turned it off by then, I don't know."

"It doesn't sound like they were met though, otherwise those soldiers wouldn't have been up here," I say.

"They were trying to catch those people, weren't they?" Kalen asks.

"That's what I thought at first too," I reply. "But those people would have been walking for hours—all day even. That road is under the cover of the trees most of the time, so there's no way anyone would see them from above or below. So, how did the soldiers even know they were there? Those people were just in the wrong place at the wrong time."

"I'm not following," Kalen says.

"You heard what they said on the video. They were looking for the people who set off the beacon. Maybe Search and Rescue operations can't function normally at the moment and aren't able to rescue people. Maybe the military is doing the rescues now," I explain.

"So, you think they were coming to rescue us?" Lily asks.

"They didn't look like they were on a rescue mission, they were dressed in hazmat suits," Emily replies. "So, if they *were* coming because of the beacon, I don't think they were expecting to rescue anyone. They looked like they were expecting to deal with infected or dead people."

"So that begs the question, do you think they thought they found the people they were looking for?" Kalen asks. "Because they didn't come any further after they burned those bodies."

"I don't think that's the reason they turned back," I reply. "I think it was because the bodies were blocking the road and they didn't want to drive over them."

"I set the beacon off here at the Lodge." Emily rubs her eyes. "So, this is the location that the satellite would have recorded as the initial activation point. Those people clearly didn't want to be rescued. The soldiers realised that. There's no way they'll think they were the people who set off the beacon."

"So, there's a chance they could come back here?" Jackson asks. We all nod, realising he's right. There's definitely a chance of that. "Back to my earlier question then. Are we safe here? And what should we do if someone turns up?"

"I don't know the answer to that," Emily says. "But I think the best thing is for us to stay put here for now. We have food and shelter here at the Lodge. We're away from other people if there is some sort of plague spreading. In the meantime, we keep trying to get in contact with someone on the radio to get more information and *then* we make a decision. Until then, we just stay here where we know we're safe."

"Should someone keep watch tonight?" Jackson asks.

"That's actually one of the reasons I wanted everyone to sleep in the Lodge," Emily replies. "I don't think it's necessary to have anyone on guard duty, but if it makes you feel better, we can."

"What would we do if someone came here anyway?" Dean replies. "Hit them over the head with a pot? It's not like we have any weapons or anything."

"Rule number one, never open the door to a stranger. They always turn into zombies. Rookie mistake." Ollie's face is completely deadpan.

"You don't think people are turning into zombies, do you?" Priya gasps.

Her question is met with laughter, but she isn't joking.

"I don't think we have to worry about that, Priya," I reply.

"Yet." Ollie nods. "You know we're all thinking it." He looks from face to face and I can't tell if he's joking.

"I think we should probably get some sleep," Emily says. "I'll start trying to make contact on the radio in the morning."

We slowly stand and begin to set up our beds for the night. I choose a spot on the floor near the fire as Jackson drags a bench seat from the table and pushes it up against the door, then lays his sleeping mat in front of it. He turns and sees us watching him.

"Can't hurt to be cautious."

CHAPTER 14

"Good morning, sleepyhead," Ollie says. "I wasn't sure you were going to wake up. I even had to move you to get the fire started this morning."

I sit up, rubbing my eyes, and see that I'm the only one still lying on the ground. "Am I the last one up?"

"No, a few of the others in the bunkroom are still asleep. I'm amazed you managed to sleep through all the noise out here though."

"I had trouble getting to sleep last night."

"Yeah, I think a lot of us had that problem." His eyes are red-rimmed and bloodshot, and I realise it must've been Ollie that I'd heard crying when I woke in the night. He quickly looks away when he sees that I'm staring.

"Has Emily got in touch with anyone?" I ask.

"Not yet. We've only just started generating solar power. It was really cloudy first thing, and we used up all the battery last night."

Matt walks over and hands me a cup of coffee. "This might help."

"Thanks. Any chance of some breakfast in bed too?"

"Not a chance." He chuckles.

"Skye, thank god!" Emily shouts. "I've been so worried about you guys."

I leap out of my sleeping bag and follow Ollie and Matt to join the others crowding behind Emily.

"Em, are you guys okay?" Skye's voice calls clearly over the radio.

"We're all fine," Emily answers. "We waited a couple of days at the meeting point, but no one came to pick us up."

"I know, I'm sorry. We couldn't get back in time to let you know, and by then you'd already left," Skye replies. "Emily, I don't have much time to talk, I need you to just listen to me. What I'm about to say is going to sound crazy, but it's really important that you believe me and you do what I say."

We all look at each other, knowing we're about to have our fears confirmed.

"Okay, go ahead," Emily says.

"After we left you guys and got back onto the main road, we got stopped by soldiers at a roadblock. There's been some kind of virus outbreak in Kavanyah and they've completely cordoned off the city. All routes in and out of Kavanyah are closed and the entire state is under military control to stop people from leaving. It's really bad, Em. Everyone's terrified of catching it. One of the soldiers told us that if you're in Kavanyah, you're either dead or dying."

"Jesus," someone whispers behind me.

"Oh my god, Skye, are you guys safe? What about Holly?" Emily asks.

"The soldiers agreed to take Holly to a field hospital within the cordon and arranged for Holly's parents to meet her there. They wouldn't let us go with her though. They were going to take us to a refugee centre that they've set up to keep people safe from coming into contact with anyone who might've escaped the city, but Ethan and I weren't keen on the idea. We decided to head back to Falls River. We haven't come in contact with anyone yet, so we're okay for now, but we can't stay here, Em. It's not safe. There're reports of looters and groups that have escaped the cordon. We're going to try to get to Morrison. They closed their borders before it spread there, along with some of the other states, like New Ardern. It's safe there, and there's a quarantine centre at Marshall's Pass for people seeking asylum in Morrison. That's where we've decided to go. We just can't get caught trying to leave."

"Why don't you come here?" Emily asks.

"I don't know how long it'll be safe there, Em," Skye replies. "Ethan and I have been talking about it and we think you should try to get to Morrison too. It's not safe to come back this way. We've been looking at maps of the area and we think you should make your way to Three Falls Gorge. It'll take you straight down into Morrison without the risk of coming into contact with any infected."

"Three Falls Gorge? So, you mean we go up Fortune Falls Canyon and across the plateau?" Emily asks.

"Yeah, that's right. I know you've never been up there, but do you remember me talking about the guiding trip Dad took me on up there? There's an old hunting cabin about a day's walk from the top of the canyon. That's about halfway. And then it's another day's hike to the top of the gorge from there."

"Are you absolutely sure about this, Skye? Should I really be taking a bunch of kids onto the plateau?"

"It's the safest option. If you come back this way, you'll get taken to a refugee centre and some of them have had outbreaks. Once there's an outbreak, they lock down the whole facility. That's why people are trying to get out of here. It's just too risky. You can do this, Emily."

"Okay, I'll talk it over with the others."

"You *have* to do this. There's no alternative. And you need to get moving soon. You know this channel isn't secure, anyone could be listening."

"I understand." Emily sighs.

"I better go. We'll see you in a few weeks, okay?"

"Yeah, okay," Emily replies. "I love you."

"I love you too, Em. We'll be together soon. Just stick to the plan."

Emily leans forward, resting her elbows on the desk, and covers her face with her hands.

"Holy shit," Oliver says.

"Yeah, that about sums it up." Jackson shakes his head.

We wait for Emily to say something, but she doesn't move.

"I guess that answers a few questions," Marley says. "From what Skye said, we're safe here for now. So, we don't need to panic and we don't need to rush into doing anything. We have time to think and time to plan."

After listening to Skye, I'd felt panicked, like we needed to run for the mountains right now or risk being overrun by zombies. But Marley's words are calming.

"I know nothing about the plateau and the gorge Skye was talking about," Marley continues. "What do you know about them, Emily?"

"I'll get something that might help me explain." Emily pushes back from the table and walks to the storeroom. We hear rummaging of papers and she returns with a map in her hand and lays it out on the table.

"We're here." Emily circles the spot she's pointing to with a pen on the map. "And this is the plateau that Skye was talking about, here. The only way it can be accessed is through the canyon above Fortune Falls where Holly had her accident. The plateau is really isolated, it's completely surrounded by mountains, but there are a couple of other small canyons or gorges that lead to it. They're not easy to access though. The plateau is owned by the same people who own this Lodge and they have an old hunting cabin up there, about here." She marks the area she's pointing at with another small circle. "That's the cabin Skye was referring to. I've never been to it. The furthest I've been is to the lake at the head of the canyon." She points at a blue spot near the top of the canyon.

"I think the gorge that Skye is talking about is this one over here. I've never guided over there, but from the looks of this map, once you're in that gorge, you're in Morrison."

She sits back and takes a deep breath. "I'd say it'd take us a couple of days to get to the cabin and from what Skye said she thinks it's a day to the top of the gorge, then it could be one, or maybe two days to get through it. I don't know whether we'll be met by border control straight away or if we'll have to walk to a town, which might take another day. So, maybe six days if everything goes ok."

"How much food do we have?" I ask.

"We've probably got enough for about three weeks," Emily replies. "There was supposed to be another leadership camp starting this week, so we have the supplies here for them too. So, we've got more than enough food if we decide to head for Morrison, and we've got enough that we could stay here for a bit longer if we decide to do that instead."

"Skye said we should leave here soon," Jackson says. "I think we should do what they say. They're the ones who are out there and know what it's like. I don't think we should risk staying here much longer, especially after yesterday."

"Yeah, I agree," Matt says. "If those soldiers hadn't stopped those people, they'd have made it here by now. More people could be on their way here right now and we'd have no idea."

"But what if we can't get down the gorge on the other side?" Priya asks. "What would we do then? Could we come back here?"

"We'd have to," Emily replies. "We should make sure we take enough food with us just in case we need to return all the way here. So maybe we take ten days of food as contingency."

"What if we return here and find out that we *can't* come back to the Lodge because there are other people here?" Kalen asks. "That *is* something we're worried might happen, right? If we come back and find other people here, then we can't get access to the food we leave here. So, we'll need extra to get us to our Plan B, wherever we decide that is."

"I understand what you're saying," Emily replies. "But it's going to be hard enough carrying everything already. We're going to have to hoist the packs up the waterfall and at other points in the canyon where it's too hard to climb wearing a pack. I just think it's too much to carry."

"What if we did this as a kind of relay?" Kalen says. "We could take extra food in spare packs and shuttle them to the top of the canyon and onto that cabin. Then we could store the extra food at the cabin and use it as a backup only if we need to come back."

"That could work." Emily nods. "You're right, Kalen. It's a good idea to be prepared for that. We can't rely on any outside help or rescue if we get in trouble at the moment, so we *should* take extra precautions if we can."

"Does that mean we're agreed then?" Jackson asks.

"I think we should put it to a vote," Ollie says.

"What alternative is there?" Jackson sounds frustrated. "We can't go south, and we can't stay here. There's nothing else to vote for."

"I still think we should take a vote and make sure everyone is happy to do this."

Jackson shrugs. "Let's take a vote then. Who thinks we should follow Skye's plan and head over the plateau to Morrison?"

Every one of us raises our hands. Some straight away, including me, and others take a few seconds waiting to see what everyone else does first. But every one of us votes to go to Morrison. Jackson's right, it's the only option we have.

"We're decided then," Jackson says. "So, when do we leave?"

"It'll take a whole day to get to the top of Fortune Falls Canyon, so I think we should plan to leave early tomorrow morning," Emily replies. "We'll get everything packed today and start shuttling the packs up to the waterfall this afternoon to save us time tomorrow. There's going to be a lot to carry. We need to take medical supplies too, and we've got the climbing gear and ropes as well."

"Why don't we have someone on watch further down the trail while we're getting ready, just in case?" Jackson suggests. "That way they can provide a warning if someone's coming and we can leave more quickly. I'm happy to be the lookout."

"I'll come with you," Lily says.

"Make sure you're back before dark, okay?" Emily looks uncertain it's a good idea. "And take some food with you."

"Yes, Mum." Jackson winks at her.

We spend the rest of the morning sorting and packing food and equipment. After lunch, we courier the first lot of packs to the base of Fortune Falls Canyon. Kalen and I help Emily hoist the bags to the top of the waterfall while the others return to the Lodge for the rest of the packs.

While we wait for them to return, we carry the packs a short way up the smooth rock chute of the canyon until we reach a raised area where we can safely stash them away from the mist of the waterfall for the night. We repeat the process after the others return with the remaining backpacks, then finally rappel down to join them.

"That's it for today," Emily says, removing her harness. "Tomorrow we'll work on getting the bags to the top of the canyon."

We arrive back at the Lodge late afternoon and get on with preparing dinner and sorting the last items we need to take with us. Jackson and Lily return in time to help us devour an enormous meal, making the most of the perishable food that we can't take with us, telling us they hadn't seen signs of anyone on the road before they left.

Although it's reassuring to know they hadn't seen anyone, our uneasiness is evident as we prepare to settle down for the night. Our isolated Lodge no longer feels quite remote enough from the outside world anymore and we rush to help Jackson when he drags the bench seat in front of the door. Before adding another … just to be sure.

CHAPTER 15

We leave not knowing if this is the last time we'll be seeing the Lodge or if we'll be returning later that day. I'm not sure what I want it to be. I want to be moving forward toward the promise of getting home to our families, but I also feel nervous about leaving the security of the familiar. I decide as long as we're all together, that's what matters. They would be my familiar, my security blanket against the unknown.

We make our way along the track in the pre-dawn light with the help of our headlamps, but it isn't long before we don't need to use them as the sun's rays scatter across the sky. My nerves fade as we walk, replaced by a rising sense of anticipation, excitement even, at the thought of the expedition we're embarking on. I have the feeling that this is going to be a once in a lifetime adventure.

Despite the breaking dawn, we climb to the top of Fortune Falls in shadow, the cliffs above blocking the sun from reaching us. After everyone is safely at the top, Emily pulls up the ropes and loops them onto the back of the packs. Not only will we need to use them, it will make it impossible for anyone else to follow us up here unless they have their own.

With sixteen packs to transport and only eleven of us to do it, we each carry a backpack and work in pairs to lug an extra bag between us. But it soon becomes too difficult as the canyon narrows and we need to use our hands to climb. In the end, we decide to leave the extra bags and focus on getting ourselves and the backpacks we're carrying to the next resting point, before returning for the ones we'd left behind.

The gorge begins to flatten as we near the top, then finally we exit its narrow walls, emerging above the surrounding tree line. Ahead of us is a large plateau nestled amongst mountain tops. A secret valley, ringed by mountains on all sides, extending until it is blocked by the tall snowcapped peaks in the distance. The plateau doesn't appear to have much vegetation, covered only in rock and tufts of tall yellow tussock, but I can make out green trees in the distance.

An icy wind greets us as soon as we leave the protection of the canyon, blasting our faces and cutting through the thin fabric of our clothing. We stop to put on jackets and hats, and I put my gloves on too, watching the clouds as they whip across the sky above us, an ominous wall of dark cloud visible above the peaks further up the valley.

"I think we made the right decision to leave the Lodge when we did." Marley points at the clouds in the distance. "The wind is coming from that direction. I think we're in for some rain soon."

"I think you're right, and once it starts raining it won't be long before this river is a torrent," Emily says. "The canyon is too dangerous to climb if there's any rain, you can get flash floods. We've been lucky. If we'd waited another day, we might not have been able to get up here."

"We need to get moving and find a place to camp for tonight," Emily continues more loudly. "Looks like rain's coming. Everyone needs to get into pairs and carry an extra pack between you. We don't want to waste time coming back for them."

Priya and I pick up one of the extra packs and begin to walk, swapping sides occasionally to rest the arm that carries the pack between us. My gaze is drawn toward the head of the valley and the approaching cloud, the wind bullish and blustery, often knocking us sideways. Finally, as we approach a large cluster of trees, Emily stops.

"This is where we're going to camp tonight," Emily calls out. "Those trees over there will give us some shelter from the wind without being too close to them, and there aren't any rivers or streams nearby that might flood in the night. I think this is a good spot. I want you to pitch your tents in a circle with your doors facing into the middle. Let's get on to it. We don't have long before it'll start raining."

As if summoned by Emily's words, the first drops of rain begin to fall, warning us of the storm's imminent arrival. I glance up the valley and the wall of cloud has lowered to the valley floor, grey now extending from the sky to the earth in a curtain of heavy rain. It will be upon us in minutes.

"Make sure you've hammered your tent pegs in firmly to secure your fly," Emily yells above the rising wind. "You don't want it blowing off in the middle of the night. And put your packs inside your tent just in case the rain gets in under your fly. I know it'll be cramped, but we want to keep everything dry if we can."

The sky darkens as the storm clouds descend upon us—the rain gusting in sheets as we hurry to finish hammering the final pegs. Then we dive inside, relieved to escape the wind and rain.

I flinch as lightning lights up the tent and jump when it's followed almost immediately by a sharp crack of thunder. I outgrew the fear of thunderstorms years ago, but this is different. We don't have the protection of a house to keep us safe tonight, and I know there's a very real risk we could be struck by lightning camping in the open. But we don't have a choice. We're here now and there's nowhere else to go, nowhere safe to hide.

****

"Morning." I poke my head out of the tent and see Emily emerging from hers.

"Morning," she replies. "I'm glad to see all the tents survived the night intact."

"Me too." I pull the hood of my jacket over my head and climb out. "I thought the tent might blow away with some of those gusts."

"Yeah, last night was really *in-tents*." Ollie grins from the opening of his tent, then winks at me when I chuckle.

"Oh, that's a terrible joke, Ollie," Lily yells from inside her tent.

"At least Jess appreciates my humour."

"Rise and shine, everyone," Emily calls out. "Have something to eat, then get packed up. I don't know how far it is to this cabin, but I'm hoping we'll be able to sleep indoors tonight if we don't waste too much time."

The rain continues its steady bombardment as we pack up the

campsite, the ground a muddy mess from repeated footsteps by the time we leave.

Every creek we come to is now a raging torrent. Emily carefully picks the safest spot she can find and gets us to link arms behind each other's backs to form a human chain. The strongest members stand at the ends—Dean and Marley at one end, and Jackson and Matt at the other—with everyone else linked in the middle. We then enter the river carefully as a single unbroken line, walking in unison as Emily instructs us to take each step.

When the first river rises to the middle of my thighs, the only thing that stops me from panicking is knowing that I'm held on both sides. We're each other's life raft. If anyone loses their footing, they're held securely in place. We're safe as long as we have each other.

After experiencing the full power of a river in flood, we realise how lucky we'd been to make it to the top of the canyon yesterday. It would be impassible today after all this rain, and probably for days to come. Fortune Falls has been true to its name.

We eat lunch under some trees, seeking shelter from the deluge. Not that it makes much difference, we're already so wet. Our jackets have kept our upper bodies dry, and I'm impressed by how well the waterproof covers have worked to keep the packs dry beneath, but our legs, feet, and boots are drenched.

"I think we're nearly there." Emily points at the dense tree line ahead of us as we pause at the top of a small hill. "I remember Skye telling me that the cabin was built from the trees in the surrounding woods. Her dad picked this spot because the forest provided protection from the prevailing winds that come down the valley and there was a river just beyond it where they could go fishing. This has to be it."

"Did Skye's dad build the cabin?" I ask.

"No, he was a guide. He was hired to scout the area and help pick out the site," Emily replies. "The family that owns it used to helicopter clients up here to go hunting and fishing, and Skye and Ethan's dads used to guide them."

The sodden ground becomes slick with mud as we make our way down the slope. Priya and I are halfway down the hill, carrying an extra pack between us, when we start to slip. I put my free hand down to stop from falling, but my feet slide out from under me and I land heavily on my bottom, dragging Priya down with me. We try to stand, but the ground is so muddy we both slip and collapse to the ground again as Jackson and Ollie burst into laughter above us.

"Here, let me give you a hand," Jackson offers as Ollie holds his out to Priya.

We gratefully take their hands and attempt to stand, but our feet slip out from underneath us again and this time it pulls the boys off balance too.

I watch everything in slow motion as Jackson tries to sidestep to avoid landing on me. His foot slides out sideways, his knee bends inward, his other leg dragging behind. He lets go of my hand to try to stop himself, but I realise he's going to fall and there's nothing he can do. I brace, waiting for the impact, but he twists away and then screams out in pain.

His left knee is bent inwards at a strange angle and he's holding his thigh above it, his face contorted in pain.

"Where are you hurt?" I ask, sliding over to him.

"My knee, it's my knee," Jackson gasps, his face grey. He looks like he's going to be sick.

"Emily! Jackson's hurt," I yell to her at the bottom of the slope.

"I'm coming," Emily calls back as I take Jackson's hand and try to comfort him. But it isn't any good. He's oblivious to anything I'm saying, writhing in pain.

Ollie slowly slides down to Jackson's other side, as Emily makes her way up to us.

"It's his knee," I say as Emily reaches us.

"Yep, I can see that. Jackson, I'm going to pull up your trousers and try to have a look at your knee," Emily says.

Jackson nods and leans back on his elbows with his eyes squeezed shut. Emily pulls up his trouser leg and looks for a moment. "I need to move your leg to straighten it. This is going to hurt, but try not to move."

Jackson nods, gritting his teeth.

"Jess, hold Jackson's leg here and make sure it doesn't move. Grip it really firmly, okay?"

I do as she asks and grasp Jackson's thigh with both hands. Emily takes Jackson's calf in one hand and holds just above the knee with the other. Jackson groans as she does it, then she slowly but firmly moves his calf to straighten his leg.

Jackson screams and clutches his leg, his eyes screwed tight in agony. I put my arm around him as he leans forward, tears streaming down his face. Ollie does the same on the other side, and we hold him in a protective huddle.

"The good news is that it isn't broken," Emily says. "But you've dislocated your knee and hyper-extended it. I know that hurt like hell, Jackson, but I've got the kneecap back in place. We just need to make sure it doesn't dislodge though, so I'm going to have to bandage your knee and brace it."

Jackson nods, tears dripping off his chin as he continues to hang his head.

"I'll give you something for the pain as well." Emily pulls the first aid kit from her backpack.

Ollie and I hold the emergency blanket above them to keep the rain off as Emily bandages and splints Jackson's leg.

"Usually, we'd want to get your leg elevated, but we just can't do that right now," Emily says. "I'm really sorry, but we've got to keep moving. We don't have a stretcher, so we're going to have to carry you."

We help Jackson slide to the bottom of the hill while keeping his leg straight. Emily then instructs Dean and Ollie how to carry Jackson between them with Jackson's arms over each of their shoulders and their hands grasped together under him to make a seat. Emily wraps the emergency blanket under his leg as I help to hold it, then ties a rope around the ankle of his boot and up around his shoulders, forming a sling.

"This should help to keep your leg elevated and take the pressure off your knee," Emily says. "I'll support your leg as we walk as well. Ready?"

Jackson grimaces and gives Emily a nod.

Dean and Ollie begin walking with Emily supporting Jackson's leg in front of them. I put on my backpack, then pick up Jackson's pack and hook the arm straps over my shoulders in reverse, so I'm able to carry the pack on my front at the same time.

I turn to the others. "We've got three extra backpacks to carry now. If everyone does this, we won't have to shuttle the packs."

As we get closer to the woods, Emily points further along the tree line. "I think I can see a trail marker up there. Do you see that blaze on the tree? It looks like someone has marked it with an axe."

I can't see what she's talking about until we're nearly at the tree, then I see a scar cut into the bark in a '<' shape and the entrance to a narrow trail beside it.

We follow the path into the forest, occasionally finding arrow markings blazed into trees, confirming that we're on the right track. The trail is sometimes hard to see it's so littered with fallen branches brought down in last night's storm. It isn't long before we emerge into a small clearing, and in the middle of that clearing is a cabin about half the size of the Lodge. But it looks like a palace to me.

I exhale in relief and notice Emily visibly relax too. I realise she's been worrying that we might not find it, and I swallow uncomfortably as it occurs to me what a mess we'd have been in if we hadn't. With the rain now flooding the canyon and Jackson's dislocated knee, going back to the Lodge is no longer an option.

We make our way across the clearing toward the back of the cabin, a large rainwater tank sitting proudly at its back. Firewood is stacked against the wall on the left, covered with a sloping tin roof propped up on posts. As we get closer to the cabin, another small hut becomes visible near the trees at the opposite edge of the clearing. It looks similar to the eco-toilet at the Lodge. We continue around to the front, where a covered verandah extends its length. A door sits in the middle of the wall, flanked by windows on each side.

We dump our packs on the verandah and strip off jackets, boots, and as much other wet and muddy gear as possible before we enter inside. Thankfully the interior of the cabin is dry, and looks like everything is intact. No broken windows or dripping roof. We enter a large square-shaped room with a kitchen bench and sink against the back wall. In front of it sits a wooden table with eight chairs, and on the righthand wall, a wood stove, the cabin's dual-purpose source of warmth for heating and cooking. Surprisingly, there are two worn sofas and two armchairs near the stove. There are mats made from animal skins on the floor and the walls are decorated with deer antlers.

On the left as we enter the room, are two doors. Bunk beds are visible through the closest door. The one opposite the kitchen remains closed.

Dean and Ollie carry Jackson to a sofa. He grunts as they lower him, and Emily helps lift his leg to rest on it, then starts unwrapping the brace from his leg.

"Let's get the stove lit," she calls out to no one in particular.

Marley and Kalen head back outside to get firewood and return with their arms piled high, dropping it beside the stove, and get to work lighting the fire.

I walk to the closed door at the end of the room and slowly open it, apprehensive at what I might find. It reveals a small storeroom, wooden racks of shelves covered in dusty plastic, tools leaning against the wall in the corner. I lift the plastic, taking care not to disturb the dust. The shelves are loaded with canned food and other items such as blankets, a first aid kit, ropes, and tarpaulins. There's a metal toolbox on the floor and lying under the bottom shelf are other tools, saws, shovels, a crowbar. As I turn to leave the room, I see fishing rods propped up behind the door and a tackle box on the floor.

"Wow," Matt says from the doorway. "There's some pretty useful stuff in here."

"There's even extra food. Emily said that the owners use a helicopter to get up here, so I guess that's why it's so well stocked."

"Lucky for us."

I take two blankets and head back into the other room. Kalen is still adding wood to the fire when I come out, but I can feel the warmth from it already. I walk over to Emily, who's checking Jackson's leg as he lies back on the sofa, and hold out the blankets to her. "Do you want to use this to prop Jackson's leg up? We can use the other one as a pillow."

"Thanks." Emily takes the blanket and places it under Jackson's leg. "Where did you get these from?"

"There's a storage room with blankets and tools and even food."

"Great, I'll check it out in a moment."

"There's heaps of stuff in the kitchen cupboards too," Kai calls out. "There're pots and pans, plates, cups, cutlery, there's even dishwashing liquid."

"There's some canned food in this cupboard too," Priya says from the other side of the kitchen. "And the taps work, we've got running water!"

I notice Matt staring at something on the wall. "What've you found?"

"It's a map of the plateau. This is the cabin here." He points at a little hand drawn symbol of a house in a circle. A blue line depicts the river we crossed just before Jackson hurt his knee, the line wiggling its way up the valley. There are blue spots dotted all over the plateau.

"Do you think these are small lakes?" I ask.

"I was wondering that too. There's definitely a lake here not far from the top of the canyon, but these look too small to be lakes. Maybe they're tarns or ponds or something?"

"There's one near the cabin." I point at a blue spot amongst the woods close to the hut symbol. "Maybe we should check it out later."

"Yeah, good idea," Matt says. "It looks like they've marked the map with lots of extra information. They've drawn fish in the river here, so I guess that's a good fishing spot, and they've drawn deer over here."

"What do you think these squiggles mean?" I point at a series of wavy vertical lines. "Some of the blue ponds have them too."

"It looks a bit like steam, maybe it means it's a hot spring, like the one by the Lodge."

"Maybe, but there are the same squiggles in other areas of the map where there doesn't seem to be any water. See?" I point at a few of them.

"Yeah, I have no idea then."

"It could be steam vents or maybe geysers." Emily walks over to join us. "There's geothermal activity all over this region, so maybe they've been mapping it so they know where it's safe to go. Might be something we need to be careful of up here then. We don't want to fall into a boiling pool of water or anything like that."

"There isn't anything else marked near the cabin other than that blue pool and the river." Matt shows Emily where we are on the map. "So, it looks like we're okay in the vicinity of the cabin."

"Until we've checked the area, I think it's safest if we don't go wandering anywhere in the dark." Emily looks out the window. "Which is going to be soon. Look at that rain."

"It's lucky we brought the extra food after all." I lower my voice, nodding at Jackson as he struggles to adjust his position on the sofa. "There's no way he's going to be able to walk anywhere, let alone ford rivers and climb through a canyon. How long does a dislocated knee take to heal?”

“Yeah, I’ve been thinking about that too,” Emily replies quietly. “It’s usually six weeks, sometimes longer.”

My eyes widen. “Six weeks! Our parents will go crazy worrying if they don’t hear from us soon. Do we even have enough food for six weeks?”

“I know … I know. We need to come up with a new plan.”

CHAPTER 16

I wake to the sound of drumming rain and immediately feel grateful again that we found the cabin. We take our time rising from bed and spend the morning lazing around, playing cards and Scrabble that someone found on a shelf in the storeroom.

Not long after lunch the rain begins to ease, the sun forcing its way through thinning cloud, and then it stops altogether. We make the most of the sun to hang wet tents over the verandah railing, and Emily heads off with Dean, Priya, and Lily in search of the fishing spot marked on the map. Although Emily didn't say it, I knew she was thinking about our conversation last night and wanted to see if we could supplement our food stores with fish.

I head off with Matt, Kai, and Ollie in search of squiggly lines. We find a well-defined trail marked by a blaze cut into a tree on the north side of the clearing, and after a short walk, we arrive at a small pool of spring-fed water. Someone has done a lot of work around the pool to make a stone footpath and to build up the edges with rock. The water is beautifully warm, and we relish the opportunity to wash away the mud and sweat from the last few days. Then we return to the cabin to let the others know of our discovery.

Soon after we get back, our fishing crew return, proudly displaying their catch, and we feast on grilled fish and rice for dinner.

"Look, obviously there's an elephant in the room, and that elephant is lying on this sofa," Jackson announces after dinner.

Everyone stops their conversation and turns to look at him. "I know you're all thinking it. I know I have been. What are we going to do? I can't walk, we can't call for a rescue helicopter, we don't have unlimited food supplies. We need a plan."

We all nod, and I'm glad Jackson is the one to say it. I think everyone has been feeling like me. Not wanting to bring it up in case it's misconstrued as being selfish, or possibly suggesting that Jackson is at fault for us being stuck up here. But the reality is, we *are* stuck up here. No one can just hop on a bus and leave if they want to.

"You're right, Jackson, we do need to come up with a plan, and I have some ideas," Emily says. "I just want to talk them through with Marley first though."

"No way! We should talk about this together as a group," Kai challenges. "We're not on a camp anymore. You're not our leaders or teachers anymore. The circumstances have changed and we're all in this together. We should all have a say. No one gets to decide for us!"

"I agree," Kalen says as everyone nods vigorously. "You can't treat us like kids up here when the decisions we make could be the difference between life and death. We need to discuss this as a group, not be told what to do."

"I agree completely," Marley says. "But we also need to remember that Emily has a lot more experience of how to survive up here than we do. So, even if we make decisions as a group, we need to listen to her advice."

"Yeah, of course." Kalen looks sheepishly at Emily. "I wasn't meaning we don't listen to your ideas. I just meant you should tell them to all of us."

Emily gives Kalen a small smile, nodding. "Obviously Jackson can't go anywhere at the moment, and it could take weeks for his knee to recover. Even then, it might not be strong enough to handle the canyon. I've had a look at how much food we have and I would say we have enough to last for six or seven weeks, longer if we ration it, and we can supplement our supplies with fish. So, we could probably stretch the food to last ten weeks—"

"Ten weeks!" Kai blurts. "You can't be serious. We can't stay up here for ten weeks! Our families won't know where we are or what's happened to us. They'll already be panicking because we haven't returned from camp and think we're stuck in the middle of that outbreak somewhere. I only agreed to come up here because I thought we'd be able to get home in a few days. This isn't what we agreed. We can't stay here!"

"We didn't know someone would get hurt," I say defensively. "It isn't Emily's fault that Jackson got hurt."

"I know that!" Kai yells. She takes a deep breath and her hands are shaking. As she begins to speak again, her voice breaks. "I just want to go home."

Priya walks over to sit on the arm of the sofa beside Kai and puts her arm around her shoulder. "Me too." Her voice is barely above a whisper.

I swallow hard as I look around the group. Although no-one else is saying anything, I can tell from their expressions that we all feel the same. We all thought we'd be back home with our families in a couple of days. We certainly hadn't expected it to take weeks. The thought of being away from my parents, my friends, my home for that long makes me feel physically sick, but there's no point in saying it out loud. *What does it achieve? It doesn't help fix this. We didn't plan this. We can't change it. We need to focus on what we need to do next so we can go home.* But I keep these thoughts to myself. I know if I say them, it would just make Kai and Priya feel worse than they already do, and this already feels bad enough.

"Which leads me to my next point." Emily's eyes shift uncomfortably away from Kai and Priya. "I think I should take a small group through Three Falls Gorge to Morrison to get help and get a rescue helicopter to bring the rest of you out."

Jackson lets out a sigh of relief, visibly relaxing.

"Do you think they'll come and get us?" Dean asks. "What makes you so sure they'll send a rescue helicopter when no-one came when Holly needed help?"

"From the map, it looks like we're in a kind of no-man's land, but I think officially the plateau is part of Morrison," Emily replies. "From what Skye said, they've managed to keep the virus out of there, so their Search and Rescue will still be operating. Once we get through the gorge, we'll be able to organise a rescue operation from there, and as this is technically Morrison, it's their territory anyway." She pauses, waiting for someone to object. Encouraged by our silence, she continues, "We could have a rescue helicopter up here to get the rest of you within three or four days, possibly sooner."

We're all nodding again. Kai's tears have stopped, and she's nodding too. Three days sounds bearable.

"So, the rest of us stay here until we're rescued?" Jackson asks.

"Yeah." Emily smiles. "The rest of you stay here at the cabin until we come back with help."

"Who will you take with you?" I ask.

"I need strong climbers, and based on the climbing we've done so far, I think the best climbers are Kalen, Matt, and Jess."

I'm shocked to hear my name. I know I'd taken to the climbing pretty well, but I hadn't thought I was one of the best. I look at Matt, then at Kalen and I can't read their expressions.

"It's completely up to you guys. If you don't want to do it, that's fine. There are other good climbers in the group, but you guys would be my first pick. I could also go with fewer people."

"I'll go," Matt replies immediately.

"I will too," Kalen says.

They both look at me and I find myself nodding before I speak. "Yeah, absolutely, I'm in."

Emily looks around the group. "So, are we agreed? Is this our plan?"

We all look at each other as we nod. We'll be home with our families in less than a week.

"When do we leave?" I clasp my hands tightly to hide their shaking.

"First thing tomorrow."

CHAPTER 17

I'm relieved we're on our way. My nerves have been on edge ever since we agreed on our new plan. I don't like that our group is separating. It feels safer together, but I agree that this is the right thing to do. We need to get to Morrison to arrange a rescue helicopter for Jackson and the others. Jackson can't leave without it, and they can't leave without him.

Now that we're walking, the knot in my stomach begins to release. I always feel better when I'm doing something. It helps relieve the anxiety, which is always at its worst when I have to sit and wait.

The plateau extends ahead of us, rugged and rough with long tussocks of grass nestled between the rocks. Emily finds a narrow path—a track made by animals—and it's much easier to follow as it winds around rocky outcrops and avoids boggy patches still sodden from the rain.

After walking for a couple of hours, we stop to take a brief break. I quickly begin to cool after taking my pack off, exposing my damp back to the wind. I pull my jacket out of my bag and put it on, noticing storm clouds gathering on the mountaintops further up the valley. "I don't think this clear weather is going to last."

"We'll need to be careful when we're in the canyon." Emily follows my gaze. "It's one thing if it's been raining for a while, but there's a whole new danger when the rain starts further up the valley. We need to make sure we don't get into a narrow area that we can't get out of in case the river level rises quickly.”

After another hour, we reach a wide forest that extends all the way to the mountains behind. Trees creak ominously above us as Emily marks our trail with red string. The forest shelters us from the worst of the gusting wind and then the rain, which begins while we’re still under its protection. I’m not aware how hard it’s raining until we arrive at a large meadow with a turbulent, swollen river gushing on the other side. We stop and watch from the cover of the trees.

“I’m trying to decide if we should make camp here for the night,” Emily explains. “I know we’ve got a lot of daylight left, but I’m wondering if we should see what happens with this weather. I’m also not sure how easy it’ll be to find somewhere to camp once we’re in the gorge.”

“Why don’t we carry on a bit further?” Kalen suggests. “We can always decide to come back here to camp for the night if we don’t find anywhere else.”

Emily pulls the map out of her pack and steps back under the trees to shelter from the worst of the rain. “Looking at how close we are to those peaks. I think this is the river that leads into the gorge.” Emily points at a blue line on the map. “I would say we’re less than an hour’s walk from the entrance.”

“Let’s carry on then,” Matt says. “As Kalen said, we can easily come back here to camp. It’s barely one o’clock.”

Emily looks at me and I nod.

“Okay. Let’s go.” Emily puts the map back in her backpack.

We cross the clearing and follow the river back into the trees on the other side, using the river as our guide to the gorge. The mountain peaks that we’d been looking at from a distance a few hours earlier, now loom above us, the river leading us to some hidden crack between them we still can’t see.

I’m so focused on my feet and the ground in front of me that I walk into the back of Emily when she stops suddenly. “This is it. This is Three Falls Gorge,” she says, looking up.

I follow her gaze and see there’s now an opening in the mountain face ahead. The river hugs the cliff on the right as we descend into the ravine, and soon the riverbed funnels into rock, channeling the water downwards. The mountain walls begin to close in on both sides as the torrent gouges deeper, the gorge narrowing with it. As the gorge winds to the left, we round the corner to see a rocky overhang with a large, flat area underneath.

"That could be a good place to camp for the night," Matt says.

As we get closer, we can see that the overhang is deeper than it first appeared, and there's a small opening in the rockface at the back. We take off our packs once we're under the overhang, placing them on the dry ground beneath.

Emily pulls her headtorch out of her bag and shines the light through the low opening, scanning left and right, and then she goes in. Matt and Kalen follow, but I hesitate. I hate small spaces … although it's not actually the size of the place that's the problem, it's whether I think I can get out that's the problem.

I poke my head through the opening and the others are standing in the cave, shining their torches around. "There aren't any bears or lions or anything hiding in here, are there?"

"The ceiling is high enough to stand once you're in," Matt says, coming back toward the opening. "Come on, there's nothing to worry about." He takes my hand and leads me in.

I let go of his hand and hover close to the entrance, scanning the cave with my headtorch. It's a single room, and from what I can see, it doesn't have any other tunnels or openings that lead anywhere. *Come on, Jess, it's no different than a bedroom. It's just a windowless bedroom under a mountain. You'll be fine.*

"I think this is a great place to camp tonight," Emily says. "We can light a fire under the overhang outside. It would be impossible to have a fire anywhere else in this rain."

"There are some dry sticks under the overhang," I say, backing out of the cave. "So, we should be able to get a fire started pretty easily."

"I noticed that too. Let's see what else we can find. Even if the wood's wet, we'll be able to dry it beside the fire once it's going."

We spend the next half hour collecting wood while Emily lights the fire.

"I'm going to take a look further down the gorge so I know what to expect tomorrow," Emily says. "Who wants to come with me?"

"I'll come," I say, standing.

"We won't go far," Emily calls back to Matt and Kalen. "Back in thirty minutes, max."

The ground drops steeply soon after we leave the cave, and it's slow progress trying to find stable footing on the wet ground. The roar of the river seems to get louder and louder the further we walk.

"It's so slippery," I yell above the rumble.

"We won't go much further," Emily calls back. "I just want to see what's around the next bend."

We carry on a few more minutes, then stop as the ground levels out and we see the reason the river has become so loud.

"I guess this is the first of the three waterfalls," Emily says.

The river crashes over the edge of a large horseshoe-shaped cliff to a pool of water far below. The gorge walls close in on both sides of the waterfall, leaving nowhere for us to pass.

"Looks like we'll be climbing tomorrow." Emily studies the rockface beside us.

I scan the wall, wondering how the hell we're going to climb this thing. But Emily seems to see things I don't, pointing at different spots.

"It's doable," she whispers to herself. "Okay, I think I've seen enough. Let's head back to the others."

Climbing back up is almost as hard as it was coming down. I use tree roots as handholds and branches to help pull myself up the slippery slope. We stop briefly at a small waterfall near the cave to wash the mud off our hands before returning to join the others.

"Good timing," Kalen calls out when he sees us. "Dinner's ready."

Matt pushes aside some of the firewood drying by the fire to make room for us. The fire is roaring and its warmth feels wonderful as the rain sheets over the edge of the overhang beside us.

Kalen hands us bowls of steaming stew and Emily fills them in on what we discovered as we eat, telling them we'll be getting on the ropes tomorrow.

"I'm tempted to sleep out here by the fire rather than in the cave tonight," Kalen says.

"That's a great idea! I might too," I reply.

"Would depend on the wind though," Emily says. "The cave will provide better shelter from the wind if it picks up, and it wouldn't be safe to sleep too close to the fire if there is any."

"The cave it is then," Kalen says.

Dammit.

We let the fire burn down to embers before heading into the cave for the night. Emily attaches a tent fly across the entrance in a make-shift door to block the draught as we place our sleeping mats and bags on the ground. I position mine closest to the opening. The fly works well to keep out the wind and I can almost pretend I'm sleeping in the cabin rather than in a cave. Almost.

At some point during the night, I become aware of rumbling. I lie in the dark, trying to work out what the noise is. The ground begins to vibrate and then there's a terrible roaring sound. I bolt upright and switch on my headtorch to see what's causing the noise, even though I know it isn't coming from inside the cave. The others sit up and do the same, then the noise stops.

"Do you think it was an earthquake?" Kalen asks.

"I don't know," Emily replies. "Maybe."

"You don't think it could've been a flash flood, do you?" Matt asks.

"I'm not sure." Emily climbs out of her sleeping bag and walks to the cave opening. She lifts the edge of the fly aside and peers outside with her torch. She steps through the opening, returning a few seconds later.

"I can't see anything. There's no water or anything like that out there. So, we're fine," she says. "I think Kalen is right. It was probably an earthquake. Whatever it was, it's over now. Let's just try to go back to sleep."

CHAPTER 18

"I don't believe it. It's stopped raining!" Kalen says as he exits the cave.

"Finally!" Matt says, joining him. "I thought it would never stop."

We don't bother to light the fire, choosing to eat a cold breakfast so we can get going more quickly to make the most of the dry weather.

"Keep your climbing harnesses and helmets out," Emily says as we pack our backpacks. "We're going to need them straight away this morning."

I put my helmet on my head and start putting on my harness and realise Matt is giving me a weird look.

"Saves having to carry them," I explain.

"Good idea." He shrugs and puts his on too.

"Jess, can you carry this?" Emily hands me one of the coils of rope.

"Yeah, sure." I put my helmet on the ground, then lift the rope over my head to drape it diagonally over my body.

"Kalen, can you take the other?" She holds another rope out to him and he does the same.

"All set?" Emily asks as we put on our backpacks. "Okay, let's go."

We follow the route Emily and I took yesterday. Even though it's no longer raining, it's still incredibly slippery with small rivulets of water running all over the ground. Emily is leading, with Kalen behind her. I watch Emily and Kalen's blue helmeted heads bobbing below me as we descend, and then I realise. "My helmet!"

"What?" Matt says on the track above me.

"I left my helmet behind at the cave." I sigh, turning. "You guys carry on. I'll run back and get it. I'll catch you up."

"I'll come with you," Matt offers.

"No, it's fine. It won't take me long." I step past him and begin to race back up toward the cave.

I climb as quickly as I can, arriving back at the cave as a large raindrop splashes my face, then another, and then the heavens open.

"You can't be serious," I mutter as I pull up the hood of my jacket and run for the cover of the overhang where I find my helmet lying on the ground, exactly where I'd left it.

Look after your gear! I shake my head as I clip the helmet to the outside of my backpack and venture straight back out. I move as fast as I can as the rain continues its downpour, not wanting to keep the others waiting. It isn't long before I make out Matt's shadowy frame and realise he's deliberately hanging back so I don't get left behind.

I lose count of the number of times I fall as I skid my way down the muddy track, hurrying to catch up. As the bank drops steeply in front of me, I hesitate, then grab hold of a branch, using it to slow my descent until my feet wedge safely against a tree root.

I let go of the branch and take another step. Both feet immediately slide in front of me, throwing me off balance. My arms flail and I overcompensate, throwing myself backwards and land heavily on the ground with a thud ... again.

This is ridiculous! I kick at an exposed tree root. *We aren't really going to continue in this weather, are we?*

I look further down the slope and see him waiting for me. His face turned away as he strains to hear the others, who I can just make out through the trees near the top of the waterfall. They're yelling to him, but I can't hear what they're saying. Their voices drowned out by the river echoing off the gorge walls and the rain pounding on the hood of my jacket.

Suddenly they begin to run toward us.

"What's going on?" I yell above the roar of the river, now so loud I can feel it.

He spins around, eyes wide with panic. "Run!" he screams as he scrambles back up the slope toward me. "Jess! RUN!"

His panic spurs me into action. I roll onto my knees so I'm now facing uphill, frantically grabbing at branches and tree roots, anything that will help to pull myself up. Finally, I'm standing, but my feet can't get traction as the earth slides beneath me. The roar continues to increase until it's deafening—terrifying. I *am* terrified, but I have no idea what of. All I know is that I need to get away from whatever it is they're running from.

The ground shakes, making the mud flow faster, the thunder in my ears reaching a crescendo as I make agonisingly slow progress back up the slope.

And then, almost as quickly as it starts, it stops. The ground stops shaking, the noise returning to the low rumble of the river.

I collapse to the ground, panting, and roll over to look back down the slope, expecting to see the others coming up the trail behind me. But the shock of what I see takes my breath away.

They're gone, all of them.

But not *just* them—*everything* is gone. The trees, the trail, the hillside we'd just been walking on. It's all gone.

My hands begin to shake, then my whole body. But this time it isn't the ground that's shaking, it's all me. I try to slow my breathing, to push down the panic. Willing myself to keep it under control.

Come on brain, stay with me. Don't abandon me now.

I shuffle to a nearby tree, clinging to it for protection in the hope that it will stop me from disappearing too. I remove my backpack and take the coil of rope slung across my shoulder and loop it around the tree. My hands fumble as I tie the rope in place and then attach it to my climbing harness. Only then can I breathe.

You're okay. You can't fall now.

I slump against the tree, blinking back tears as I stare at the spot where I'd been standing moments earlier. My entire body shudders as I realise what has happened.

The whole hillside has given way, crashing through the gorge below. The force of its power gouging away rock, so that the river that once flowed over the cliff in a waterfall has now been rerouted around it as well.

This can't be real. This can't be happening.

My lungs draw ragged breaths as I lower myself onto my stomach and begin to crawl down what's left of the slope. I let the rope out slowly, making sure it stays taut in case the ground crumples out from beneath me. I force myself to go as far as I can until I reach the edge.

I scan the chasm, searching for signs of my friends, hoping they've somehow survived and are waiting to be rescued. But I can't see anyone. There's nothing but mud and broken trees and rocks and more mud.

"No, no, no, no, no, no, no …"

I feel the panic begin to rise again. I try to hold it down but I can't, my body shaking uncontrollably.

They're all gone.

I cling to my lifeline and inch away from the edge, slowly turning to make way back up the slope. When I reach the safety of the tree I roll into a sitting position and stare blankly down at the devastation. Thoughts jumble in my head. All of them incomplete and incoherent. I know I need to work out what to do next, but my brain won't function.

You're in shock. This is what shock is.

I tuck my knees into my chest and lean against the trunk, feeling its knobbly bark poke into my back. But I don't pull away, I welcome the pain. It reminds me I'm still alive. I bury my face in my hands and press harder, concentrating on the discomfort. Using it to help me focus.

You don't need to panic. You're safe. The only thing you have to do right now is breathe. Just focus on that. Breathe in, breathe out. The rest can wait.

I listen to my breathing, the sound of the air as it rushes from my lungs, and gradually feel my panicked heart rate slowing. As the blood ceases to pound in my ears, I move my attention to the rain, to the beat of its drumming. *Or is that the rumbling of the river?* I block out everything and concentrate on untangling the sounds, to make sense of them—and then I hear something else. Something so faint I'm not sure I really heard it. *Did I imagine it?* I close my eyes and try to focus my hearing, desperate to hear it again.

"Help!" The muffled cry is so quiet it's almost drowned out by the rush of the river.

Oh my god, someone's alive! But how is that possible? I didn't see anyone!

I hear the weak cry again and realise it isn't coming from the chasm, it's coming from the direction of the river.

Still attached to the rope, I scramble across the hillside until I can see the river. I scan the bank for survivors but can't see anyone and can't move any further. I untie the rope from my harness and carefully slide my way down the bank, holding onto trees as I go. My heart pounds as I cling to the branches, terrified I might lose my grip and fall into the raging torrent beneath me.

And then I see him.

Somehow Matt's been carried out into the river. He's wedged between rocks at the top of the waterfall, the river crashing over him as he struggles to keep his head above water.

"Matt! Matt, I'm coming!"

I race back to the rope and untie it from the tree, picking up my pack and bringing it with me. I scramble down the bank and tie the rope to a tree near the edge, then rummage in my pack for spare carabiners and a belay device. I attach them to my harness and begin to belay myself over the edge of the bank into the water. It's painfully cold and swift, and even at the edge, the current sweeps me off my feet. I try again and again to stand, but I can't and pull myself back onto the bank.

Maybe if I could jump out far enough, I could let the current take me to him.

I climb to the top of the bank and turn back to face the river. Taking a single deep breath, I sprint down the bank as fast as I can and leap off the edge, diving into the water. The current immediately whisks me downstream as I swim as hard as I can toward the middle, trying to line myself up with Matt.

The rope begins to tug, pulling me in the direction of the bank, and I frantically release extra through the belay as I continue to kick toward him.

Shit! I'm not going to make it.

I reach out in desperation and barely manage to catch Matt's foot as I sweep past, then grab hold of him with both hands. I pull myself up his leg until I'm straddling his body, trying to block the water washing over his face.

"Matt!" I shake his head and his eyes flutter open before closing again. *Oh, thank god, he's still alive.*

He's wedged sideways between two rocks, his pack jamming him in place with his arm bent behind him. It probably saved his life. If he hadn't got stuck, he would've been swept over the waterfall.

I attach Matt's climbing harness to mine. "Whatever happens now, we'll be doing it together, Matty."

As I try to pull Matt from between the rocks, his eyes open in shock. "Stop! Stop! My shoulder! Jess, you'll break it!"

I immediately stop pulling and try to think of another way to get him free. But I can't think of anything. There isn't any other way. No matter how I do this, it's going to hurt.

"I've attached you to my harness, Matt, and we're tied to a tree on the bank. I'm going to undo the straps on your backpack and then push the pack away so I can pull you out without hurting your shoulder."

Matt's eyes have closed again, but he gives me a small nod. I undo the straps hoping the pack will just fall away, but nothing moves. It's completely wedged. I clench and unclench my hands. I can't waste any more time. The water is so cold, my hands won't be able to function if we don't get out of this soon.

Come on, Jess, you've got to do this now. He'll die if you don't.

I brace my legs against the rocks on either side of him. "I'm really sorry, Matt, but this is the only way."

I grab Matt's free arm and put my foot on the side of his backpack, then push against the pack as hard as I can while pulling his arm at the same time. I grit my teeth against the sound of his screams as I continue to pull. But then I feel it. Almost imperceptible at first as my body begins to twist, my leg slowly moving away and Matt gradually moving toward me.

All of a sudden, my foot pushes through. I wrap my legs around Matt as I swing forward and grab him with one arm while pushing off the rock with the other, watching as the backpack disappears over the waterfall. But the rope holds and we don't move any further.

"I've got you. You're okay. I've got you." My heart races, adrenaline surging through me, giving me strength I didn't know I had. "I'm going to need you to hold on to me so I can pull us in." He doesn't answer, but his arm wraps around me, his injured arm continuing to hang loosely at his side. "I'm going to have to let go of you now, but you're still attached to my harness. Hold on tight, okay?"

He nods and I let go. I begin to pull us up the rope, removing the slack through the belay as we move away from the rock. I feel a surge of panic as I realise that although we're swinging toward the bank, we're also moving closer to the edge of the waterfall. I start hauling us up the rope as fast as I can, heaving with both arms against the force of the water, until I'm sure we won't go over.

We angle close to the bank and I try to stand while holding onto the rope, but my feet are swept out from under me. As I bang against the rocks at the side, I push my face under the water so I can put all my effort into pulling the rope through the belay. Once the rope is completely taut, I lift my head out of the water and try to stand again. This time I place my feet upstream in front of me and lean back, pulling against the rope, allowing my feet to remain planted.

"Matt, can you get your feet down?" I feel him trying to stand. He nearly pulls my feet out from under me as he gets swept over, but finally we're both standing, facing upstream.

I lunge toward a sapling growing near the edge, grasping it with both hands, and use it to pull myself onto the bank. Matt loses his footing, not expecting me to jerk us forward, but my momentum drags him onto the bank with me. He cries out as he lands on his injured arm and rolls onto his back as I collapse onto the ground beside him.

We don't move, just lying where we landed, exhausted from the exertion and the cold. I shiver uncontrollably and can barely feel my fingers. But Matt isn't *just* shivering. His whole body shakes violently as it tries to warm itself.

"We've got to get you out of your wet clothes, Matt. You'll be hypothermic after being in the water for so long."

I help him stand and put my arm around his waist to steady him and we start to climb the bank, continuing to where the rope is tied to the tree. Matt slumps to the ground and I search through my pack for spare clothing.

"They're a bit small, but it's better than nothing."

I unzip Matt's jacket and help strip off his wet layers of clothes beneath. He can't lift his arm, so I leave it hanging against his body as I put my spare top on him. It's far too small, but I manage to get it on. I put my beanie on his head and try to get my gloves on his hands, but they just won't fit. Getting his wet pants off is almost impossible as they stick to his legs, but I finally pull them off and then struggle to get my spare trousers on him. They won't do up, but it'll do. I then wrap the emergency blanket around him.

I put on my one remaining dry top and the pair of gloves. It only helps a little—I'm still frozen to the bone.

Matt isn't moving, just lying on his side, shivering. I put his boots back on and tie his laces. I leave the rope where it is, deciding to come back for it later, but wrap all our wet clothes in a jacket and attach it to the side of my pack. I put on my backpack and stand in front of Matt, unsure what to do.

"Matt, do you think you can walk? If we can get back to the cave, I can light a fire and we can get warm there."

He doesn't answer. I crouch down and take him by his shoulders and try to sit him up. He cries out in pain as I touch him. "I'm so cold, Jess." He hunches forward, shaking. "So cold it hurts."

"I know you are, Matty. We need to get back to the cave so I can get you warm. But I need you to help me. I can't carry you."

I take his hand and drag him to his feet, then pull him behind me, leading him up the slope. It's slow going and Matt stumbles and falls often. The rain already drenching our dry clothes. Matt falls again in the mud and this time he doesn't get up. I step back down to help him stand, but he's too exhausted.

"Jush leave me here," he slurs. "I'm too tired."

"It isn't much further. Only another five minutes and you'll be able to sleep. Come on, Matt. You can do this."

"I'll just resh here a while. Jush need a lil resh."

I feel tears threatening, panic rising. I don't know what to do. *It's raining, I can't light a fire here, I can't make a shelter here. If I don't get him warm he's going to die—but I can't carry him and he can't walk and there's no one to help me!*

Think, Jess, think! Maybe I should leave him and light the fire and then bring him back something warm to drink? I could just lay the tent over him. Maybe if I wrap him in the tent, it would keep him warm—but his clothes are muddy and wet. I need to get him dry!

I crouch behind Matt's head and hook my hands under his armpits and pull. He moves a little, but I fall back straight away. I don't have the strength in my legs to pull him while crouched. I lay the emergency blanket on the ground and lie him back on it.

"Can I come back to your place?" Matt asks as I wrap the blanket around him. "You're sho bootiful. Even with mud all over your fach, yur bootiful." His eyes start to close.

I take the two edges of the blanket in both my hands, then pull as hard as I can, dragging him half a metre up the hill. I step up with one foot and heave again, using the momentum from my body as I fall uphill to pull him over my leg. I wrench my leg out and stand, then do it again, and again and again. Until I'm finally at the overhang.

"Matt, we're here," I say, shaking him. "Can you hear me?"

He doesn't respond.

I drag Matt on the emergency blanket the last few metres into the cave. The wind has picked up with the rain and is gusting, the area under the overhang too exposed to provide any shelter.

Once we're in the cave, I pull the tent out of my pack and lay it out on the ground to provide an extra layer of insulation under the sleeping mat. I then lie my sleeping bag on top of the mat, unzipping it wide open.

Matt's clothes are sodden, covered in mud. I take off his boots and clothes and roll him onto the sleeping bag. I realise his underwear is also soaked and will make the sleeping bag wet.

Why are you hesitating? This is his life you're trying to save here! I lift the sleeping bag over him and pull his underpants off, then zip the sleeping bag around him. I then wrap the edge of the tent around him too.

My clothes are completely saturated and layered with muddy. I search my backpack for anything else I can use, but there's nothing except a pair of socks. I unzip the bottom of the sleeping bag and put the socks on Matt's feet. They feel like blocks of ice. There's no warmth in them at all. He needs warmth, but I can't light a fire in here, the smoke would suffocate us.

Body heat. Skye said using body heat was a good way to warm someone.

I strip off my clothes and unzip the sleeping bag, pushing Matt onto his side before climbing in behind him. I then zip the sleeping bag up as far as I can with the opening behind me. It's a tight squeeze.

I can't zip it up all the way, so I tuck the tent around us to create a barrier against the cold.

I slip my hand under Matt's injured arm and wrap it around his chest, my body pressed firmly against his back. His skin is icy and he's constantly shaking. I shiver uncontrollably too, my teeth chattering so hard I'm sure they'll break. I clench my jaw to try to control it, adding to the rigidity of my body, every muscle tense from the cold.

After a while, Matt's breathing changes. It had been shallow and laboured, but now I feel him taking deeper, longer breaths. His body isn't shaking in the same way either. It seems to stop for a while, then every now and then he shudders. I've stopped shivering too. He still feels cold, but I'm certain he's warming. He has to be. He can't die too. I squeeze him tighter at the thought.

"Please don't die, Matt," I whisper.

I can't help but feel awkward as I lie here with Matt, even though I know it's silly to be thinking about it. But I'd never imagined my first time naked with a boy would be like this … I thought he would've been conscious, at least.

Eventually I must have fallen asleep. There's no longer any light coming through the cave opening when I wake and it takes me a moment to remember where I am and what has happened.

I let out a sigh of relief when I realise Matt's skin feels warm against me. I'd been so cold I wasn't sure I had enough heat left in my own body to raise his temperature. I'd feared his hypothermia might be irreversible. But I'm surprised at how cozy it feels inside the sleeping bag now. I thought I'd never feel warm again.

I don't want to move in case I wake Matt, but my hip is killing me from lying in one spot for so long. I start to pull my hand from Matt's chest, but he grabs it and pulls it back, drawing me tightly against him. He doesn't say anything, still asleep. I relax and give up on the idea of moving for now and drift back to sleep.

****

"Where am I?" Matt sounds confused, worried, his body tense.

"It's okay, Matt. You're okay. We're in the cave," I whisper.

"Jess?"

"Yeah, it's me. It's okay, you're safe. We're safe here." I feel his body relax, the tension releasing from his muscles as his breathing

133

slows.

"Jess? Am … am I naked?" he asks slowly, then his hand reaches over his side to touch my hip. "Are *you* naked?"

"Well, technically, *you're* not naked, you're wearing socks." I burst out laughing. "They were the only dry clothes we had left. I made the ultimate sacrifice and let you have them."

"So, you *are* naked," he repeats, trying to reach further over my hip toward my butt. I smack his hand away.

"Yes, Matt, I am—there weren't any other socks."

"Right," he says, moving his hand off my hip. "Glad we cleared that up."

"I'm starving," I say. "Don't move."

I lift back the tent I'd tucked around us and climb out into the cold. I feel around for the tent fly and wrap it around me, then search for my pack and find my headtorch and turn it on. I pull out the food bag and look inside. There isn't much. I was only carrying a few snacks because I had the tent. I open a protein bar and take it to Matt.

"You should eat something."

He sits up, holding the sleeping bag around him, grunting as he does, and takes the bar from me.

"How's your shoulder?"

"Sore," he replies, his mouth full of food.

I take a bite of my protein bar and look in my pack for the first aid kit.

"I'll take a look at your shoulder tomorrow when it's light, but take some ibuprofen for now." I hand him the tablets and a bottle of water.

"When I woke up, I couldn't remember where I was," Matt says. "It's so dark in here, I couldn't see anything."

"Do you remember why we're here now? Do you remember what happened yesterday?"

"Yeah, I remember," he says quietly. "I remember the landslide and being swept down the hill. And then I was in the water and I couldn't move … I couldn't move my arm and the water kept splashing over my face, but I couldn't lift myself any higher. That's the last thing I remember, trying to keep my head above the water, and I couldn't move and I … I was so sure I was going to die." His voice breaks.

I don't know what to say, don't know how to comfort him.

"What about …" his voice catches. I can't see his face but I don't need to. His ragged breathing giving away his tears as he tries to calm himself enough to ask his question, even though he already knows the answer. "They're dead, aren't they?"

I swallow hard and take a deep breath. "Yes," I whisper. "I looked for them but you were the only one I found. They must've been swept down river." *Or they're under the landslide somewhere*. But I can't bring myself to say it, the thought of being trapped under mud and rock too terrible to say out loud. My hands begin to shake at the thought. "I heard you calling for help," I tell him, as the shaking gets worse, not just my hands now. "I found you at the top of the waterfall. Your pack had wedged you between some rocks at the top. You were so lucky. It saved your life. You'd never have survived going over the waterfall."

"How did I get here? I don't remember."

"I tied myself to a tree and swam out to you. I had to cut off your pack. It went over the waterfall when I pulled you out. Then I literally dragged you up here."

"And then you took off all our clothes and hopped into bed with me?"

"You mean I saved your hypothermic ass from dying," I reply tartly. My whole body is shaking now. I just want to be warm, but now I feel too embarrassed to get back into the sleeping bag.

"I'm just kidding, Jess. You're cold. I can hear your teeth chattering from here. Get back in the sleeping bag."

"Ha! So, you can tease me about taking advantage of you again?" I say, gritting my teeth to suppress the chattering. "I'd rather freeze, thank you."

"Don't be like that. I was just kidding. You saved my life. Please get back in."

I don't reply and I don't move, still feeling too angry and embarrassed.

"Fine, if you won't get in the sleeping bag with me, you can have it." He starts to climb out.

"Stop," I say, realising how ridiculous I'm being. "Don't get out. You need to keep warm. I'll get back in."

"Good," he says as he slides back down into the sleeping bag. "'Cos it's freezing out there."

I turn off my headlamp and drop the fly on the ground and begin to climb into the sleeping bag. "You need to lie on your side, otherwise we can't both fit."

He starts to roll toward me.

"I think it might be better if you face the other way."

"Right, gotcha." Matt rolls the other way. "Don't think I could lie on that arm anyway. Do you think it's broken?"

"I don't know." I squeeze up against him, trying to pull the sleeping bag zip up behind me. "I don't know what to look for, but I'll check it out in the morning when it's light."

"Thanks, Jess."

"I haven't done anything yet. You can thank me tomorrow."

"No, I mean, thanks for everything, for saving me. I'd be dead if it wasn't for you."

"How about you warm up my feet then?" I say, pressing my ice blocks against his leg and my frozen hands against his back.

"Ah! They're freezing!" Matt tries to squirm away.

"Your whole body felt that cold when I got you here." I move my hands and feet away. "I was really worried about you, you know. I thought you were going to die. I'm really glad you didn't."

"So am I," Matt says, moving his legs back to intertwine with my feet, warming them. I slide my hand under his injured arm and around his chest and he takes hold of it in both of his.

CHAPTER 19

I creep into the cave to check on Matt for the umpteenth time, worrying that he might stop breathing while he sleeps. Even though I know it's unlikely to happen now that his temperature is back to normal, I can't stop myself from checking. Popping in to listen to his breathing each time I return from washing clothes at the nearby waterfall, before heading back outside to hang them by the fire to dry.

"Morning," he says as I'm turning to leave.

"I thought you were still asleep. Don't move. I'll be back in a second." I dart back outside and return with my arms loaded. "Fresh laundered clothes, m'lord," I say, placing the pile of clothes beside him.

"I was just trying to decide if I should wrap the sleeping bag around me or leave it behind and cover myself with a sock."

"Dammit, that would have been worth seeing. Now I wish I hadn't brought you the dry clothes." I laugh. "I've just cooked some noodles for breakfast. I'll wait for you outside."

"Thanks, I'll be out in a minute."

He comes out a few minutes later, his injured arm still inside his top, and sits down on the tent fly by the fire.

"Thanks," he says as I hand him the cup of noodles. He takes a tentative first mouthful and smiles. "Who would've thought noodles could taste so amazing?"

Despite the fire and the sunshine, he shivers. I take his jacket over to him and drape it over his shoulders. "Do you want me to look at your shoulder?"

"Yeah, I guess we probably should. I can't move my arm at all."

"Okay, let's take a look." I kneel in front of him and move the jacket off his shoulder, lifting his top. "I think it might be dislocated. There's something bulging out beneath the shoulder here." I touch the bulge gently. "I don't know, though. What do you think?"

"It's got to be better than a break. At least we can fix a dislocated shoulder, right?"

"I don't know *how* to fix a dislocated shoulder."

"I saw a guy on my basketball team get his shoulder put back in. It looked pretty simple. I'll tell you what to do."

"I'm worried I'll do it wrong and I'll hurt you, though."

"It's going to hurt no matter what. I know you've never done this before. We'll just have to work it out together, but I think we need to get it in sooner rather than later. I remember the coach saying the longer you wait, the harder it is to get it in and there's more risk of damage."

"Okay." I let out a shaky sigh. "Tell me what to do."

"You need to lift my arm out in front of me so that it's straight, like this." He lifts his other arm up as an example. "You'll need to pull it a bit to help the bone go back in the shoulder socket."

I take his hand and put my other hand on his chest. "Are you ready?"

"Yeah, do it." He nods, then clenches his teeth.

I start to lift his arm and he grimaces straight away. The bulge swivels and I pause. "Are you okay?"

"I think you need to pull the arm out as you lift, to help get the bone away from the socket. I can feel it jamming on it," he says, panting.

I put both hands around his wrist and begin to pull down and then out as I slowly lift his arm straight in front of him. He cries out, but I keep the pressure, then see the bulge disappear. As I release his wrist, Matt drops to his knees, cradling his injured arm with this other hand.

"I'm sorry, Matt." I crouch beside him. "Are you okay? Have I made it worse?"

He doesn't look at me, hugging himself, gently rocking back and forth. After a minute, he wipes his face and lifts his head. "It's okay, I'm okay. I think it feels better."

"Can you move your arm?"

He lifts his arm slowly, grimacing as he does. "I think it's back in."

"I'll get you some ibuprofen and then I'll make a sling for your arm."

I grab the first aid kit out of my pack and hand him the pills, then unravel a length of bandage. I stretch Matt's top away from his body to help him slip his arm into the sleeve, then take the bandage and wrap it diagonally across him to make a sling.

"There, that should hold it. You need to keep warm." I reach forward and zip his jacket up over top of his arm.

"Thanks, doc," Matt says, putting his good arm around me to give me a hug. "I honestly don't know what I'd do without you. You're a life saver, literally."

"Yeah, and don't you forget it." I hug him back. "I need to get the rope and harnesses I left behind yesterday. It won't take me long. I'll be back in fifteen minutes."

"I'll come with you." Matt reaches for his boots.

"No, I really think you need to stay here and rest as much as you can."

"I should come with you," he insists, trying to hide a grimace as he stands.

"You nearly died yesterday. You should really be in a hospital, definitely not walking around in the mountains." I take the boots out of his hands. "We don't have enough food to last us more than a couple of days, so we're going to have to start making our way back to the cabin soon, probably tomorrow. You need to get as much rest as you can in the meantime."

"How much food do we have? I thought we had enough with us for a week?"

"We did, but I wasn't carrying much food because I had the tent, and—"

"My pack went over the waterfall with everything I was carrying," Matt finishes.

"Exactly."

"So, what do we have left?"

I pull the bag of food out of my pack and lay it out on the ground. There are only a few packets of noodles, some protein bars, a block of chocolate, and some dried fruit and nuts.

"Okay, we can work with this. We're only a day's hike from the cabin, so if we leave tomorrow, we've got enough food to get us there. And even if it takes us a bit longer, people can survive for three weeks without food, right?"

"Yeah, I'm not worried, but I do think we should leave tomorrow. So, you *really* need to rest as much as you can today. I'm not dragging your heavy ass up this gorge. You're going to need to be able to do it yourself."

"Yeah, okay, I get it." He sits down.

"Good." I smile. "Glad we're on the same page. I'll be back soon."

I pick up the empty pack and throw it over my shoulder, leaving before Matt can change his mind. It doesn't take me long to get back down to the spot where I'd left the rope tied to the tree and pack it into the backpack with the harnesses. I then decide to head to the river again. I'm not exactly sure why, maybe in the back of my mind I'm hoping that Emily and Kalen have somehow survived and I'll find them sitting on the bank together. But of course, no one's there.

I walk further along the bank toward the waterfall. When I get to the end, I stare at the rocks that had stopped Matt from being swept over the edge and shake my head at how close he'd been to going over. I force myself to look at the river beneath the waterfall, my stomach churning, afraid I will see them lying there, but I have to check. I let out a long, shaky breath. There's nothing except rocks and water and mud.

I peer across the gaping scar that the landslide has cut from the earth to the rockface that we'd been planning to climb yesterday. A chasm now between us. I then scan the other side of the waterfall. There isn't a bank there either. The river flows right against the cliff face and has done almost the whole way since the top of the gorge. I take my phone out of my bag and take a photo of the waterfall and the cliffs on either side. It's impossible to get through here now.

I don't want Matt to come looking for me if I take too long, so I head back to the cave as quickly as I can.

He looks relieved to see me when I arrive back, but doesn't let on that he's been worrying. "Did you find it okay?"

"Yeah, no problem." I sit next to him on the tent fly. "I don't think we can get through that way anymore. We can't get down the gorge on the other side of the river, and the landslide took out the route to the rockface on this side. I just can't see how we can get through that way now. I took some photos while I was there if you want to see. But I understand if you don't."

"No, I'd like to see them."

I take out my phone and bring up the photos. He swipes through them slowly. When he sees the photo of the rocks at the top of the waterfall, he pauses.

"Yeah, that was where I found you," I say.

He doesn't say anything, just nods and swipes to the next photo. He studies the photo of the landslide for a long time, his brow furrowed as though he's trying to remember, or he *is* remembering. When he's finished, he hands me back the phone and lets out a deep breath. "I can't see how we can get through there either. So much for reaching the safe haven of Morrison and getting a rescue helicopter."

"Yeah, I know. We're going to have to go with Plan B."

"What was Plan B again?"

"Exactly."

****

After resting at the cave all day, Matt is adamant he'll be alright to walk tomorrow, insisting that we start our way back to the cabin in the morning. I'm concerned about him and know he really needs more time to recover, but I agree. Because the reality is, with so little food, we can't risk staying here any longer.

After sharing a single packet of noodles for dinner, we let the fire burn down, then head into the cave when it gets dark.

"You get in first," Matt says. "I'll lie against the sleeping bag opening tonight." I'm about to protest, but Matt doesn't give me the chance. "I'd feel bad if you slept with the draught all night."

"It isn't draughty. I tuck the tent in under me and it acts as a barrier."

"I won't be cold then either. And besides, I want to be the spooner. And as we're clothed tonight, there's no chance of inappropriate spoonage." He chuckles.

"Fine." I laugh, climbing into the sleeping bag.

Once we're in the bag, Matt can't reach around to pull up the zip with his injured arm. I roll over to face him and reach behind him, pulling the zip as far as I can, then tuck the tent beneath him. I try to turn back over and realise I can't—there isn't enough room to turn without pulling the zip undone again. So instead, I shuffle down as far as I can until my face is resting against his chest. Matt places his injured arm over my waist and I slide my arm under his, wrapping it around him. My cheek presses against his chest and I can hear his heart beating. It seems fast.

"This is cosy." I laugh nervously.

"Sure is." He chuckles.

"Are you okay? I'm not squashing you, am I?" My hands shake, but I'm not cold.

We were naked in this sleeping bag together last night and I wasn't nervous then. Why am I feeling nervous now?

"I'm good. You're shaking, are you okay?"

Oh my god, this is so embarrassing. Get yourself together, Jess! "I'm just a bit cold, I'll warm up soon."

He hugs me tighter, trying to warm me. "I'm sure it won't take long."

Gradually the adrenaline subsides and I stop shaking as Matt's slow, rhythmic breathing relaxes me. I like the feeling of Matt's arms around me. He feels strong and warm, and even though I don't need protecting, it *feels* protective and safe. I listen to the soothing sound of his heart, its regular beat lulling me toward sleep. And just as I'm about to drift off, I'm vaguely aware of the sound of my name murmured so quietly I'm not sure if I'm dreaming. Followed by the gentle brush of lips on my forehead.

CHAPTER 20

After sharing a measly breakfast of a single packet of noodles, I help Matt into his jacket and tie his bootlaces for him. Matt watches as I hoist the backpack over my shoulder and clip the waist belt in place. I give him a smile when I'm ready and he nods in reply. It's time to go.

I lead the way, intentionally keeping my pace slow, not wanting to push Matt too hard. We've eaten so little food over the last couple of days, we don't have any reserves to call on, and I'm worried how Matt will cope walking the long distance we plan to cover today.

We finally escape the gorge and its shadowy cliffs after nearly two hours of continuous plodding. The land flattens and widens and I find myself repeatedly glancing at Matt as we walk side by side, concern pricking at the back of my mind. He walks with shoulders hunched, intently focused on his feet. His eyes, usually sparkling with wit, are flat, almost sunken into the dark patches beneath. His breathing is laboured, even though our pace is barely more than a shuffle. By the time we reach the meadow, I know we can't continue any further. Matt desperately needs to rest.

"Let's take a break." I put my pack on the ground by a fallen log and sit down.

I open a protein bar and hand it to Matt when he sits next to me. He takes the bar and stares at it for a few seconds, too tired even to eat, then reluctantly takes a small bite.

"I think we should make camp here for the night."

"We're not even half way," Matt mumbles.

"I know, but there isn't really anywhere else to camp between here and the cabin, and I don't think it would be a good idea to keep going today … I can see how tired you are. You're still recovering from hypothermia, remember?"

He takes a deep breath and nods without looking up from the ground.

I open my pack and take out the tent. Matt helps to lift the poles into place, then sits down again, exhausting the last of his energy. I lay the sleeping bag inside and help Matt out of his jacket and boots. He sighs as he collapses onto the sleeping bag and closes his eyes. The corners of his mouth hint at a smile as I scruff his hair and zip the sleeping bag up around him, but he doesn't move. I swallow the lump in my throat as I study his face. He's so weak, and we still have so far to go.

I head into the forest to collect fallen branches and get to work lighting a fire. Once the fire's blazing, I check on Matt and he's sound asleep. I contemplate having a protein bar, my stomach growling at me for not feeding it, but I decide against it. Matt's going to need all the energy he can get if we're going to make it to the cabin tomorrow.

When I've got enough firewood to last us until night, I plonk on the ground by the fire. I blink slowly as I stare into the flames, its flickering hypnotic as an overwhelming sense of tiredness washes over me. The non-stop stress and fear and worry of the last few days has masked my grief, but now with nothing to distract me, I can't avoid it any more. Tightness builds in my chest as I try not to think about what has happened. There's too much to grieve for. The thoughts all jumble inside my head as my brain jumps from one thing to another until I don't know what these tears are for. But I need to cry for all of it and it all comes crashing down on me at once.

Although I hadn't known Emily and Kalen long, they were my friends and they were good people that I truly cared about. I hug myself as I remember Kalen on our last morning. Reliving the memory of him holding his book to his chest like some tangible link to his father, before placing it into his pack. That's the memory of Kalen that I cling to. His smile as he held his book. I could see the comfort it gave him, and it made me wish I had something that could link me to mine.

Then I think of Emily, her kindness, her compassion, the way she made us feel like everything was going to be fine. She was more than just one of our group. She was our protector, our saviour, the person who was going to keep us safe until we could get home. Our surrogate parent until we could get back to our real ones. And now she's gone, and there's no one else to look after us.

I don't want to be here on my own, to be the one who's responsible for keeping us alive. I want to feel safe, to be home with my parents, who'll make sure nothing bad happens to me. I want Matt to be in a hospital where doctors will make sure he's okay. Not here with me in the middle of nowhere. *How can I look after him when I'm not sure I can even look after myself?*

This wasn't supposed to happen! We weren't supposed to be here! We're supposed to be in Morrison by now and our friends being rescued. I'm supposed to be running into my mum's arms and these tears are supposed to be ones of relief. Not grief from losing my friends. Not fear of not knowing how we're going to get out of this mess and whether we could die up here. And what if something happens to Matt?

The thought of Matt dying is more than I can bear, and a sob escapes me as I hug my knees to my chest. *How do I look after him? How do I keep him safe?*

I hear Matt stirring in the tent and quickly wipe the tears from my face, taking deep breaths to try and calm my breathing. I don't want him to see me upset. I can't let him know I don't have it all together, not when he needs me to keep us alive. The last thing Matt needs, on top of everything else, is to have to worry about me too.

"I'm going to make some noodles," I say as Matt emerges from the tent. "You'll feel better after you have some more food."

I open the packet, trying to keep Matt from seeing my face in case he can tell I've been crying.

"That's our last packet, isn't it?"

"Yeah, it is." I take a deep breath, then when I'm certain the tears have gone, I look up at him. "I've been thinking … if I leave early tomorrow morning, I could get to the cabin and be back here with extra food and bring a few of the others with me before it's even dark. It would give you the chance to rest a bit longer and then we can take our time to go back when you've regained your strength."

"What, and I stay here?" he asks angrily. "No way. You're not going on your own! I'll have some food and get some rest and I'll be good to go by morning."

"It's just that I'm really worried about you. If you push yourself too hard, you could end up having a heart attack or something. Remember, Skye said there was a risk of that if you get hypothermia?"

"I'm not going to have a heart attack," Matt scoffs. "You're overreacting."

I hold his gaze, neither of us wanting to back down. And then I realise that even if I force the issue and leave against his wishes, he'd probably just follow. I let out a frustrated sigh and break eye contact. *Fine, you win.*

We sit in uncomfortable silence, waiting for the noodles to cook and then cool enough to eat. Matt grunts 'thanks' when I hand him the cup. He eats half, then holds the cup back out to me.

"No, thank you." I shake my head. "They're for you."

"This is the last packet, right?" He frowns.

"If you're going to be in any state to walk tomorrow, you're going to need all the energy you can get."

"No way!" He shakes his head. "I'm not going to eat it all and you have nothing."

"Either you eat all of it or I go back on my own tomorrow and bring back help." I fold my arms in front of me. "I'll have one of the protein bars tomorrow and there's chocolate. I will be *fine*." I narrow my eyes at him.

"*Fine*," he huffs back, but continues to eat the noodles.

When he finishes, I take the mug to the stream to wash it out. I stand and stretch my back as I look further up the valley toward the hills still basking in the last rays of the sinking sun. Just as I begin to turn away, something catches my eye. I look back, wondering what it was that seemed out of place.

There it is. Something shining—catching the sun in the distance, like a mirror reflecting sunlight. *Could someone be up there?* I squint, trying to make my eyes zoom in, but I can't make out any more detail. Just a bright spot of light.

I shiver, my nerves prickling in warning. *What if there are other people up here?* I look over to the fire and wonder if I should put it out just in case. The smoke would be a beacon, making us visible to anyone looking.

Don't be ridiculous, there's no one else up here other than us and our friends ... and if they find us, that would be a good thing!

I shake the thought out of my head and decide it isn't even worth mentioning to Matt as I walk over to rejoin him. We sit by the fire, watching it burn down to embers as the sun sets, and I find myself looking forward to the dark. Glad for the excuse of having to sleep together in our only sleeping bag. Butterflies replace the growling in my stomach. I want to feel him close to me, his arms around me. I'm sure I hadn't been dreaming that he kissed me last night. I wonder, hope, maybe he will kiss me again.

Matt and I squeeze into the sleeping bag and I zip it up as far as I can, then tuck our jackets around the side to cover the gap where it doesn't zip all the way to the top. We face together, arms wrapped around each other as we had the night before. I'm shaking, this time a mixture of anticipation and cold, hoping he won't realise why.

"You're shivering again," he says, wrapping me tightly in his arms. "It does feel colder tonight. Maybe we shouldn't have sat out there for so long."

I snuggle into him, enjoying his warmth and the closeness. I can't think of anywhere I'd rather be than with him right now.

"You know, as awful as the last couple of days have been," I say. "This—being here with you—I've liked being with you." I hold my breath, wondering if I've said too much. Maybe he'll think I'm a terrible person for saying this when two of our friends have just died. I wait.

"I've liked being with you too."

I peek up at him, trying to make out his expression in the dim light. He looks at me, smiling, and slowly tips his head forward until his lips touch my forehead. I pause, my face and lips still tilted expectantly toward his ... waiting. I swallow, my heart thumping uncontrollably as he pulls his head back and smiles at me again. His arms briefly squeeze tighter, then he closes his eyes, the smile still on his face.

I feel confused, but mainly disappointed. His response felt loving, but I'd expected—hoped for something more. We've become so close over the last few days. It doesn't feel like *just* friendship to me anymore, it feels more than that—he means more than that, to me. And I'd been certain he felt the same way. But now I'm not so sure.

****

The ground is white with frost when we climb out of the tent, our breath billowing in front of us in the crisp morning air. I help Matt put on an extra top and his jacket, then put my beanie on his head.

"There you go, pal." I give him a slap on the back. "That should keep you nice and toasty."

"Thanks … *pal*," Matt replies, giving me a strange look.

"You ready?" I ask.

"Yep, let's go."

The ground crunches beneath our feet as we walk across the clearing and into the trees on the other side. Each time we come across one of the pieces of red string that Emily had used to mark our trail, my stomach clenches, reminding me of who and what we've lost. We'd been so full of hope at the prospect of making our way to Morrison and getting help for our friends when we came through here. We would've been on our way back to our homes and our families by now if the landslide hadn't happened. But now only two of us return, our companions and our only route to safety, gone.

We walk at a good pace at first, quickly making our way through the forest and onto the plateau on the other side, but soon it begins to slow. We manage to keep going until we reach the stream, the midway point to the cabin, where we decide to have a break and some chocolate.

Matt's renewed energy doesn't last long though, our pace reducing further, and we need to stop more frequently to rest. Matt eats our final protein bar and we share the last of our nuts and dried fruit, hoping it'll be enough, but he's weakening so quickly and we still have an hour or two to go. I keep thinking about Skye's comment that the biggest mistake people make in the mountains is to continue trying to get to shelter instead of stopping and making one where you are. *But Matt isn't hypothermic anymore—he's just tired. This is different, isn't it?* I'm worried I'm making a mistake pushing on.

"How are you doing, Matt? Honestly."

"I'll be okay," he replies, but he looks shattered. "It isn't much further now."

"Why don't we put up the tent? It wouldn't take me long to get to the cabin from here, I would be back—"

"No, we go together." Matt starts to walk. "Come on."

148

We don't talk as we walk, conserving our energy as Matt's feet plod heavily, step after step after step. I have no idea how he manages to keep going, but he doesn't give up, and after what feels like an eternity, we crest a small hill and see green.

"We're nearly there. It's just through those trees."

He gives me a small smile, but it makes me feel uneasy. It's painfully clear how much he's struggling. I take his hand and we follow the markers through the trees. And then finally … finally we reach the clearing in front of the cabin.

"We made it." I hug him.

He wobbles, as though I might knock him over, and slumps into me, taking a deep shuddery breath. I look up and see a tear run down his cheek.

"It's okay," I say. "We're going to be okay."

He rests his head on mine, holding me tightly, then he goes limp and I feel all his weight on me. I try to hold him up, but he's too heavy and I fall to the ground with him landing on top of me.

"Matt? Matt?" I'm pinned to the ground. I use the last of my energy to roll his unresponsive body off me and put my fingers on his neck, feeling for a pulse. *Please don't be dead!*

"Help! Someone help us!" I scream at the top of my lungs.

I keep fumbling around his neck for a pulse, but can't find one. "Help! Help! Someone help us!"

I put my cheek against Matt's mouth and am relieved to feel his breath on my face. I don't know what to do. I lift my head to scream again, but see figures running toward me. They heard me—they're coming!

"Jess!" Marley calls as he runs to us.

"It's Matt. He needs help," I say to Marley and Ollie as they reach us first. The others close behind.

"What happened to him?" Ollie asks as Marley starts checking for vital signs.

"He was just so exhausted. We've hardly eaten. He's had hypothermia," I blurt.

"What about this bandage?" Marley opens Matt's jacket and sees the sling underneath. "Why's he got this sling?"

"He dislocated his shoulder too. Sorry, I forgot about that."

"Matt." Marley leans closer to Matt's face. "Matt, it's Marley. Can you hear me?" He gently shakes him.

Matt's eyes flicker open briefly and then close again.

"Come on, Matt," I say, taking his hand, tears streaming down my face. "Please, Matt, wake up." Someone takes off my pack and I feel arms hugging me. I look up and it's Priya. I squeeze Matt's hand. "We made it. We're at the cabin. Please, Matt, wake up."

I feel his hand squeeze back, just a small squeeze, but it's enough. His eyes open again and this time they stay open. He looks up at all the concerned faces standing over him and frowns, then closes his eyes again. "Can't a guy sleep in peace?" he mumbles.

"Come on, guys, let's get him inside," Marley says. "Then you can sleep for as long as you like."

Marley, Ollie, and Dean lift Matt from the ground and begin to carry him. Lily picks up my pack, and Priya and Kai put their arms around me and help me walk. Jackson is standing on the verandah with a wooden crutch made from a Y shaped stick under his arm.

"Welcome home," he says as I climb the stairs.

"Thanks, Jacks," I say as we walk through the doorway into the cabin.

They lie Matt on one of the sofas by the wood stove. He tries to sit and Kai grabs blankets from a chair and puts them under him to help prop him up.

Dean hands us both a bowl of some kind of stew from a pot on the table. It's warm and it tastes good, but most importantly, it's food. We both eat slowly, being careful not to eat too much too fast. I can only eat a small amount of what they give me. Matt is the same, only eating a few mouthfuls before putting the bowl on the ground.

"I'll finish it later," he says, closing his eyes and laying his head back down. No one has said anything since we sat down, just quietly watching us eat.

Finally, Priya breaks the silence. "Where are Emily and Kalen? Are they still coming?"

I don't know how to tell them. I try to speak, but a weird choking noise comes out instead, taking me by surprise. I try to wipe the tears off my cheeks, but they just keep coming. Priya kneels in front of me and wraps her arms around me. I don't need to tell them; the answer's now clear.

After a couple of minutes, and a lot of deep breaths, I get the tears under control. Everyone is waiting patiently for me to give them more information. Dealing with their own shock at the realisation that Emily and Kalen are dead.

"There was a landslide when we were in the gorge," I say, shaking my head, the memory of it suddenly very fresh. "Emily, Kalen, and Matt got caught in it, but Matt was the only one I found. The others got swept away."

"Saved my life," Matt murmurs.

"I found Matt stuck between some rocks in the river. It took me a while to get him out. His shoulder was dislocated, and he was hypothermic. He nearly died."

"When did it happen?" Dean asks.

I have to count back the days and work it out. "Four days ago, I think. It was only our second day after leaving here. We lost most of our food in the landslide. That's part of the reason Matt's so weak."

"You've been without food for four days?" Dean asks.

"We had a few packets of noodles and some snacks, but that was it. We rationed it, but it wasn't enough. Matt wasn't in any state to be walking really, but we couldn't wait any longer. We didn't have enough food to wait." I take a deep breath, tears threatening again. "I should've left you, Matt, and come back here and got help. You should never have walked all this way." I begin to cry.

Matt opens his eyes and reaches out his hand to me.

"I'm sorry, Matt, you nearly died all over again." I take his hand.

"Don't be stupid. I wouldn't let you, remember? This was my decision as much as yours. Anyway, we made it, didn't we? I'm still alive—well, partially." He smiles.

I give him a small smile and nod. *But it was the wrong decision. I knew what needed to be done. I just hadn't been strong enough to do it. I was too afraid of upsetting Matt, too afraid of over-reacting. But it *had* been up to me. I had the power to act, to follow my instincts, and I had chosen not to. I shudder at the thought of how differently this could have ended.*

If Matt had died, it would have been my *fault. Not the landslide's, not the river's, not Matt's. Mine.*

CHAPTER 21

The hot pool washes away thoughts of 'what if' along with dirt and dried sweat, leaving me warm and cleansed. I return to the cabin dressed in clean clothes lent to me by Priya and find Matt has woken from his nap. Although he says he feels fine, his eyes tell a different story, still weighed down by heavy bags and lacking their spark. But he looks relaxed and happy, smiling and chatting as he rests on an armchair by the wood stove.

Dean and Ollie serve us fish and rice for dinner, and Matt raises a few eyebrows when he eats some of the fish. I'm relieved no-one makes comment or teases. This choice would be difficult enough for him as it is, and he needs to take advantage of every calorie.

"So, the fishing's been going well then, Dean?" I say as we eat.

"Lily caught tonight's fish, actually." Dean nods at her.

"There are a couple of really good spots along the river on the other side of the trees," Dean explains. "We've been able to catch fish every day since you left. We've hardly touched the canned food since we got here."

"That's good to hear." Matt nods. "Especially now we're going to need to stretch the food out for longer."

"What do you mean?" Jackson asks.

Matt looks over at me as if not sure he should've said anything. "Well, because of the landslide in the gorge. We can't get to Morrison that way anymore.”

“I hadn’t realised that the landslide meant we couldn’t get through the gorge,” Jackson replies quietly.

“I hadn’t either,” says Lily.

Everyone else is nodding too.

“The landslide carved a big hole in the bank beside the waterfall,” I explain. “It was the only way to get to the cliff we needed to climb to get around it. I took some photos in case someone else has any ideas … but without Emily, I don’t see how we could climb any of it, even if we could get to it.”

Dean’s body suddenly stiffens. I look up at him hesitantly, expecting an outburst, but his eyes are fixed on the window behind me, every muscle tensed.

“What’s the matter?” Priya follows his gaze. “Did you see something?”

“I thought I saw a light or something.” Dean keeps his eyes focused on the window as he gets up from the table.

My heart leaps into my throat at the memory of the light flashing up the valley. I bolt past Dean to the storeroom as he grabs an empty pot off the bench and return with the axe and a shovel.

“Take this.” I push the axe into Marley’s hands as I run behind Dean toward the door.

Dean stands on one side of the door and Marley and I on the other. Dean makes eye contact and lifts his finger to his lips, then raises the pot above his head, poised to strike. I force myself to breathe, every muscle on high alert.

As the handle slowly begins to turn, I thrust my foot in front of the door to stop it being thrown open. The door rebounds off my foot and I hear a thud as the attacker’s face hits it, not expecting it to stop so suddenly.

“Ow!” someone yells, followed by the sound of a woman laughing.

“You’re a muppet, Ethan.”

Dean’s face reflects my shock, both of us recognising Skye’s voice. I remove my foot, pulling the door open. Ethan is standing on the other side, holding his hand over his nose.

“Boy, am I glad to see you!” Dean grabs Ethan in a hug.

"I think that's about the best welcome I've ever had." Ethan laughs.

Dean stands aside and lets Ethan into the room, then hugs Skye as she steps through the doorway. Ethan startles when he notices Marley and me hiding behind the door holding our shovel and axe, then looks at the pot in Dean's hand.

"Let me see if I've got this right. You thought we were intruders, and you were going to have to defend yourselves?"

"Pretty much," I reply.

"Seriously, Ethan." Dean shakes his head. "Knocking. Have you heard of it? We could've cut your arm off!"

"And you would've cooked it up by the looks of things." Skye points at the pot in Dean's hand.

"It was the closest thing I could find."

"Come on in, guys," Marley says. "You must be tired and hungry. Let's get you something to eat."

They dump their packs and the rifle Ethan is carrying by the door and head over to the table, where they're greeted with more hugs and offered seats.

"Where's Emily?" Skye says, scanning the cabin.

The room falls silent.

"Guys, you're making me nervous. Where's Em?"

More silence.

"Just bloody tell me." Skye's eyes flash from person to person, then swing onto Matt as he takes a deep breath, preparing to answer her.

"Emily and Kalen were caught in a landslide when we were trying to get to Morrison." The words rush out of his mouth, wanting it over with. "I'm so sorry, Skye."

"What do you mean, a landslide? Are they hurt? Where are they?" Skye shakes her head.

Marley puts his hand on Matt's shoulder, letting him know he'll take it from there. "When we were making our way here, Jackson dislocated his knee and we couldn't go any further," Marley explains. "So, Emily took Kalen, Matt, and Jess with her to try to get to Morrison. The plan was for them to arrange a rescue helicopter to come back for the rest of us. But Emily and Kalen didn't make it.

Matt and Jess only got back a few hours ago."

Skye looks at Matt, then at me. "You were with her?"

"I was—we were."

"She's dead?"

I nod. I can't even bring myself to say it.

"So, how is it that you two survived when Emily and Kalen didn't?"

"Matt nearly didn't," I reply. "He got caught in the landslide too, but he was the only one I found. I looked for Emily and Kalen, but I couldn't find them. I'm really sorry, Skye."

"How hard did you look?" Skye demands. "If you found Matt alive, then maybe they're alive too!"

"There wasn't any sign of them. After the landslide, I looked for all of them, but I only found Matt. I even went back the next day to look again, but I ..." I shake my head.

"So, you stopped looking for them when you found Matt, did you?"

"I don't get what you mean?" I frown at her. "I'd already looked and there was no sign of them. Not a boot, not a glove, nothing. They were gone. Either swept down the river or so far under the landslide ... I don't know, but they weren't there anymore. Matt *was* though, and I could save Matt. But he was the only one I could. I'm sorry, I really am." My voice breaks. "I wish I could have done more, but I couldn't. I really am sorry, Skye." I can barely say the last words as tears run down my cheeks.

Marley cuts Skye off as she bristles, preparing to respond. "That's enough, Skye. I know you're in shock and hurting, but you're out of line. Jess did everything she could."

"You don't know that." She glowers at him.

"*I* do," Matt says. "There was nothing else she could've done. This isn't Jess's fault. It's no one's fault. It was just a terrible, *terrible* accident."

Skye shoves her chair back from the table and storms out of the cabin. Ethan slowly gets up and follows her.

They don't return for a long time, and when they do, they huddle together at one end of the table. Skye sits with her head in her hands, not wanting to talk to anyone, refusing food, only accepting a cup of hot tea. Ethan doesn't leave her side, comforting her, obviously concerned about her and also dealing with his own loss.

We do what we can for them, but in the end, it feels better to give them time on their own, so we all head to bed.

****

Skye keeps to herself, but avoids me in particular, and I'm okay with that. I know she's hurting and I don't want to make it worse, and for some reason my presence does.

After breakfast, I sit outside on the verandah with Priya, Kai, and Lily, making the most of the warmth from the sunshine in the morning chill.

"So." Priya gives me a sly look. "You lost Matt's pack over the waterfall?"

"Yeah, that's right." I nod.

"And you only had one sleeping bag left?"

I look at Kai and Lily and they're both grinning at me too. I shift uncomfortably, knowing where this is going.

"Yep." I study my mug of tea.

"So?" Priya asks.

I give her a confused look and shrug. I'm not going to make this easy for her.

"Oh, come on, Jess," Lily says. "Did anything happen between you and Matt?"

I laugh out loud, shaking my head. "No, Lily. Nothing happened."

"Seriously?" Kai blurts. "How is that possible? We saw how friendly you two were getting before you left. How could you have spent days alone together sharing a sleeping bag … and nothing happened?"

"I guess, amongst other things," I say in as off-handed a manner as possible. "Matt nearly died and had a dislocated shoulder and we'd just lost two of our friends and were trying to stay alive. But also it's probably because we're just friends."

"No way." Kai shakes her head. "There's much more to you guys than just friends."

"I thought so too. But I don't know what's going on, to be honest." I sigh, shaking my head. "After everything we went through together, it connected us, made us closer. But I'm not sure he feels the same way. I think maybe I'm confusing our friendship for something more. I'm telling you the truth though, nothing happened."

We hear voices approaching and the boys appear around the corner of the cabin, returning from the hot pool. Matt with his arm in a sling, and Jackson using Dean and Ollie as human crutches.

"If it isn't the walking wounded and their aides," Lily says, giving them a big smile.

Dean and Ollie help lower Jackson onto the step to sit down, then take a seat beside him.

"Hey," Matt says as he sits next to me. "Did you sleep okay?"

"Yeah, good," I say. "You?"

"It was alright." He shrugs, then leans closer and whispers. "Felt strange having all that room to myself and no-one snoring in my ear." He ruffles my hair and then places his hand on the deck of the verandah behind me, leaning up against me.

I blush, knowing the girls are watching. *What is going on here? Is he flirting or just being friendly? I can't tell with him!*

The cabin door swings open and Skye walks out, followed by Ethan and Marley.

"Morning," Lily greets them.

"Morning," Skye replies, giving her a small smile.

Her smile disappears as she glances down at Matt's arm around me and stomps off toward the toilet. Matt immediately sits forward, removing his arm and our connection, and I'm left feeling more confused than ever.

"Ethan and Skye have just been telling me what happened to them after we spoke on the radio and why they changed their plans and came here," Marley says. "Ethan, I think you should fill them in."

Ethan swallows uncomfortably as we all turn to look at him. "As you know, we were planning to head to the quarantine centre at Marshall's Pass and try to enter Morrison from there. We were keeping off the roads, it was too risky to travel by vehicle. If you got caught trying to leave the quarantine zone you'd be detained, but we'd read reports that people were actually being shot on sight if they thought they were infected."

"I told them about what we saw when we were waiting to be picked up," Marley says.

"While we were on our way there, we read there'd been a riot at the quarantine centre, and Morrison announced it was closing its border to all refugees. It was a bloodbath. Dozens of people were killed in the riot at Marshall's Pass, and then people started attacking military blockades all over the state, saying it was illegal and they couldn't stop them leaving. It's completely out of control out there. No one's safe. It's just everyone for themselves."

I'm shaking my head as he talks. *How could everything have fallen apart so quickly?*

"There was a mass exodus from the Kavanyah quarantine zone. Everyone wanted out," Ethan says. "We knew that meant it wouldn't be long before infected people were all over the state. We decided the safest option was to stay off the roads and get up here and follow the route Skye had told you guys to take to Morrison. We got stuck at the Lodge because of all the rain, though. We had to wait for the water level to drop in the canyon before we could climb it. We were sure you'd be long gone by now."

"But here you are," Skye finishes.

"Can I just ask one thing?" Ollie asks. "There are still no zombies, right?"

Ethan and Skye look taken aback by his question.

"He's kidding," Kai says and then looks uncertainly at Ollie. "You are, aren't you, Ollie?"

"Yes, I'm kidding—unless there are zombies. In which case, no, I'm not, and it's a completely serious question."

"No, it's not a zombie apocalypse, just a regular apocalypse." Skye almost manages a smile as she answers.

"So, what are we going to do now?" Jackson asks.

"That's what we were just talking about inside," Marley answers. "If the gorge isn't passable, and it isn't safe to go back into Langadorne, what's our next plan of action?"

We wait, looking from Marley to Skye and Ethan, wondering what plan they've come up with.

"That wasn't a rhetorical question, guys." Marley laughs. "Come on, we agreed we would decide as a group. That there aren't any leaders anymore. So, let's see what everyone thinks."

"Are there any other routes down to Morrison from here?" Dean looks at Skye and Ethan.

"We're not sure, to be honest," Ethan replies. "We haven't been up here since we were kids. Our dads used to guide for the Jacobs family who owns this land, but they stopped bringing people up here about ten years ago."

"We've looked at maps of the area, and it's hard to tell where there are traversable routes," Skye adds. "We know of one route that goes back down into Falls National Park further up the valley to the East, but that's going in the wrong direction back into Langadorne. I knew of Three Falls Gorge because I've climbed the bottom section from the Morrison side years ago, but we didn't climb all the way to the plateau. There looks to be another mountain pass further North that would take you down into New Ardern, but it's a pretty serious alpine pass. You'd only want to attempt that if you're experienced mountaineers, and we don't have the right equipment anyway." She pauses. "And the other thing is that the weather is really unsettled at this time of the year. It's risky enough to try anything in these mountains without the right equipment and experience, let alone with the potential for storms being thrown in. We can't take the risk, especially when there's no chance of a rescue if we get in trouble."

"So, do we stay here until this all blows over, then?" Jackson asks. "If we can wait it out long enough, they'll either come up with a vaccine or get the outbreak under control, then we can return to Langadorne when it's safe, can't we?"

"How long would we have to wait, though?" Priya asks.

"Once the snows come, it won't be easy to leave, maybe not at all even until next Spring," Ethan says. "We could be stuck up here for four or five months. We'd need to be prepared to stay that long, just in case we can't get out."

I hear someone muttering under their breath and scan for the source. Kai is sitting with her hands clenched, head shaking slightly from side to side.

"What about going back down to the Lodge?" Matt asks. "It's still isolated and there's more room at the Lodge. It'll be easier to get out from there when things settle down. We wouldn't be stuck there for the whole winter if we stayed there, would we?"

"Yeah, but what about the risk of people coming back up that road? Remember, we thought those people were probably heading there and maybe the soldiers were too," Jackson says.

"Fortune Falls Canyon is probably our biggest barrier to stop people," Skye replies. "Only climbers with equipment can get up there, and they would need to know there's something worth climbing to in the first place."

"What about food?" Jackson asks. "Whether we're at the Lodge or up here, we still don't have enough food to last the winter, do we?"

"Emily estimated we probably have about six weeks' worth of food here," Priya says. "But we haven't used that much of it. We've managed to catch fish every day so far, so we could stretch it out to last longer."

"Even if we ration it, we couldn't stretch it out to last sixteen weeks though," Marley says.

"Stop! Just stop!" Kai slams her hands onto the wooden railing. "We can't stay here for sixteen weeks! I can't stay here for one more day!" She lifts her hands to her head. "We were supposed to be back with our families by now and they have *no idea where we are!* How can you even talk about staying here? I have responsibilities. I have a family I need to look after. I need to go home." Her voice trails off as she covers her face with her hands.

Priya steps toward Kai and puts her arm around her shaking shoulders. "I know. I want to go home too."

Kai looks up from her hands, her head still shaking. "You don't understand, it's not *just* that I want to go home, I *need* to go home. I live with my elderly grandparents and they rely on me for almost everything. I managed to get them into a rest home for a couple of weeks so I could come on this camp. But they're expecting me back. I was supposed to pick them up two days ago. I need to go back."

I look from face to face as I rack my brain, trying to think of a solution that doesn't involve us losing our lives on a mountain pass or dying from a virus. We can't stay. But how do we go?

"We've all got families we want to get back to, Kai," Marley says. I feel on edge at his words—they sound dismissive. "My wife is four months pregnant and I want more than anything to be back with her."

"Your wife can take care of herself." Kai scowls. "My grandparents need me to look after them."

"That's even more reason you can't take the risk, Kai," Marley says. "What use are you to them if you're dead?"

"Shouldn't it be up to each of us to decide if we're prepared to take that risk?" Matt asks. "If some of us want to leave, that should be our choice."

"Do you want to leave?" Kai asks quietly.

Matt pauses, considering his answer. "Yeah, I do, but I'm not sure it's the wise thing to do. I think my family would prefer me to return safely to them in a few weeks or months rather than die trying to get back to them now. But I might feel differently if they depended on me. So, I think if you want to leave, no one should try to stop you."

"I'm really sorry, Kai," Jackson says. "This is all my fault. If I hadn't got hurt, we wouldn't be stuck here. I wouldn't blame you if you wanted to leave. I wouldn't blame any of you. If you want to leave, you should go."

Kai's mouth drops open. "Oh my god, Jacks, I wasn't thinking. I'm such an idiot! I was just so worried about my grandparents I completely forgot about your leg. Of course, we won't leave you."

"Is there any way we could use the radio at the Lodge to get a message to our families?" I ask.

"We might be able to get hold of someone and ask them to contact the Leadership Institute and pass on a message to your families," Ethan nods. "The Institute would have everyone's emergency contact details, wouldn't it, Marley?"

"Yeah it does." Marley nods. "If the Institute's able to get a message to your grandparents, do you think they could extend their stay at the rest home until it's safe for us to leave?"

"Yeah, they might be able to," Kai replies.

"Could the Institute organise a rescue operation from Morrison to come and get us?" I ask.

"If we can get a message to them and let them know where we are, I'm sure they could," Marley replies.

"But what if they can't?" Kai asks.

"We'd have to prepare for that, just in case," Marley says. "Which brings us back to what we were talking about before. Can we make our food last the winter if we have to stay here?"

"There's still food at the Lodge, isn't there?" I ask. "We need to go back there to use the radio. What if we brought all the remaining food up here?"

"What if it still isn't enough? We'd risk starving if we stay up here, wouldn't we?" Kai asks.

"Yeah, that is the risk we'd be taking if we decide to stay up here." Ethan nods.

"We don't need to decide right now, though, do we?" I ask. "We could bring the food back from the Lodge, then decide in a couple of weeks if we haven't been rescued by then."

Everyone nods, murmuring in agreement. "So, is everyone agreed?" Ollie asks. "I think we need a show of hands to make sure."

I watch as everyone raises their hands, Kai included. Because the reality is, she doesn't have a choice. None of us do.

CHAPTER 22

Lily and Dean leave with Ethan to go hunting for something other than fish, and I decide to head to the river to wash some clothes. As I'm about to leave, I realise Matt could probably do with some clean clothes too and can't exactly wash them one-handed. I try to be discreet asking him if he wants me to wash his clothes for him, but he hands them to me in front of Jackson.

"Hey, Jess, I'm injured too, you know," Jackson says loudly. "Can you do my washing?"

I blush as the others turn to see what he's talking about. "Sure, Jacks. What do you need washed?"

He hops to his pack and holds a pile of clothes out to me.

"I'll give you a hand." Priya intercepts Jackson's clothes. "I've got a few things I need to wash too."

She returns from the bunkroom a few seconds later and we head to the river together.

"God, I miss washing machines." I groan as we scrub our clothes in the river. "Seriously, how did our ancestors get anything else done? Washing clothes by hand takes forever, and even then, they still don't seem clean."

"And don't get me started on trying to wring them dry," Priya says. "No matter how much I squeeze them, the water just keeps dripping out."

We finish our washing and head back to the cabin with our sopping clothes. As we cross the clearing and approach the back of the cabin, I make out voices talking loudly ahead.

"You're being unreasonable, Skye," Matt says. "There was nothing else Jess could do."

Priya puts her hand on my arm to stop me.

"If it wasn't for Jess, I'd be dead," Matt continues. "She didn't go back to look for them again that day because she was trying to keep me alive. I had hypothermia. I'd have died if Jess hadn't stayed with me."

"No. She didn't go back to look for them because she was too busy cosying up with you playing mummies and daddies," Skye says bitterly. "I've seen how you two are together. You're all over each other. She's doing your washing like a good wifey, for god's sake."

"I don't know what you think is going on between us, but you've got the wrong end of the stick," Matt snaps. "Jess and I are nothing more than friends—we're bloody good friends—don't get me wrong. After what we've just been through, she's probably the best friend I've ever had! But there isn't anything more than that. She's like a sister to me."

Even though I'd been telling the girls that nothing had happened between us and we're just friends, hearing it come from Matt stings. His words dashing my hope that there is something more between us, or at least something that might grow beyond friendship. He couldn't have been clearer. The closeness I'd been feeling is only good friendship and gratitude for saving his life. Nothing more.

It's better to know, I try to tell myself. *At least now there's no doubt about how he feels. It's better to find out this way than suffer the humiliation of him rejecting me to my face.*

Priya seems to know how I'm feeling and puts her arm around my shoulder, giving me a sympathetic squeeze.

"See, I told you." I shrug my shoulders. "Now you've heard it from both of us."

She doesn't look convinced.

"Come on." I start to walk, and raise my voice to alert Matt and Skye that we're coming. "We better get these clothes hung out or they'll never be dry before tonight."

Skye and Matt stand awkwardly on the verandah, their

conversation over as soon as they heard us coming.

"Hi," I say brightly, immediately setting to work draping the clothes over the verandah railing.

"Thanks, Jess. I really appreciate it," Matt says.

"No problem, you can return the favour once your arm's better," I reply. "Actually, Matt, maybe you should get Skye to check your shoulder. You'd be able to tell if the arm is properly back in the socket, wouldn't you, Skye?"

Skye looks at me blankly and then at Matt. "Yeah, of course I can. Do you want me to take a look?"

"Yeah, that'd be good if you could, actually." He glances at me before following Skye into the cabin.

****

Ethan and the others return later in the day, excited to show everyone the rabbit and fish they've caught.

"We've set snares to catch more," Ethan says as we eat dinner. "Lily knows how to check and reset them while we're gone."

"Aren't you coming with us, Lily?" Kai asks.

"I'm going to stay to help look after Jackson and Matt while you go back to the Lodge," Lily explains. "Someone needs to stay behind to look out for them, and I'll keep hunting and fishing in the meantime too."

"Oh, of course," Kai replies. "I forgot they'd need someone to stay with them."

"It's a tough job, but someone's got to do it." Lily sighs loudly, then winks at Jackson and Matt sitting across the table from her.

"So, you guys used to come up here as kids?" Ollie asks Ethan and Skye.

"Yeah," Ethan replies. "Our fathers used to guide a lot of hunting trips for the Jacobs family up here over the years, but they only brought us here a couple of times though."

"It wasn't long after that last trip that the Jacobs stopped bringing anyone up here," Skye says. "I remember Dad talking about old Jack Jacobs, saying he was going batty. That he kept talking about the end of the world and needing to prepare for a nuclear war or something and that this was the best place in the world to bug out to."

"Yeah, I remember that," Ethan adds. "Dad said that Jack had

165

them scouting the plateau for a location to build a bug out shelter. And then he just stopped bringing anyone up here. When Jack died a few years later, he left everything to his sons. I think they stopped coming up here then too."

"Do you think there's any chance they could've built something else up here?" I ask. "The reason I ask is that when Matt and I were camping at the clearing near the gorge, I thought I saw something further up the valley. Something was shining in the sunlight."

"You didn't tell me about that?" Matt's head whips around to look at me.

"I wasn't sure if it was a trick of the light or something," I explain. "It was nearly night, and the fire had burned right down. I figured there wasn't anything to worry about, so I didn't say anything."

"What do you mean, something was shining?" Marley asks. "Do you mean like a mirror or something?"

"I'm not sure, maybe," I reply. "Or maybe something metallic. The sun was setting and most of the valley was in shadow by then, but its rays were still on some of the hills higher up the valley and I saw something shining."

"Was it shining all the time or did it come and go?" Marley asks.

"It wasn't flashing, it was shining all the time. It didn't seem to move or anything like that either."

"So, there's got to be something artificial up there, right?" Marley says. "It's unlikely to be something natural that's reflecting light like that, isn't it?" He looks at Skye and Ethan.

"Yeah, I'd say it's pretty unlikely to be something natural." Ethan answers. "What do you think, Skye? Do you think it's possible that they built another cabin up here?"

"I guess anything's possible," Skye replies.

"We should check it out then." Marley's eyes are wide with excitement. "It might have food or other stuff we could use."

"If someone built a bug out shelter up here to use in an apocalypse," Jackson says, "isn't it possible there might already be people using it given everything that's going on?"

"So, we're not alone up here after all?" Priya asks. "Should we be worried about that? They might see us as a threat."

"Yeah, and as we know, it's not the zombies that are the real threat," Ollie says. "It's other people."

"Exactly!" Jackson replies.

"We need to find out if there are people up there," Marley says. "And the sooner, the better."

"Do we delay going back to the Lodge then?" Jackson asks.

"No," Skye replies. "We need to get that message to the Institute and get the food from the Lodge as soon as possible too. If we wait too long, someone else might find the Lodge and then we've lost all that food. We can't take that risk."

"What if we split up?" Ethan says. "I can scout out the valley and see if there's anything up there. And the rest of you go to the Lodge and get the food."

"I think that's probably the best idea, but you can't go on your own, Ethan," Skye says. "You need to take someone with you."

"Fine. Jess should come." Ethan looks at me. "You saw where the light came from. You'll be able to help narrow down where to look."

"Don't we need to have as many people go back to the Lodge as possible to carry the food, though?" Matt says. "Why don't I come with you, Ethan, so Jess can go to the Lodge with the others? I may not be able to carry a pack with my shoulder like this, but I can walk fine."

"I don't think you should be going anywhere yet, Matt," I say. "Have you forgotten that you collapsed only yesterday after a few hours' walk?"

Matt starts to object, but Skye cuts him off. "Jess is right, Matt." It looks like it physically pains her to say it. "I know you think you're feeling better, but it's only because you've been resting all day. You've been through a lot in the last few days. You need to recover properly or you'll end up having an accident or collapsing again. And we don't need any more injuries."

"Fine," Matt says, clearly unhappy.

"Jess." Ethan walks over to the map on the wall. "Can you show me where you were when you saw the light?"

I join him and point to a spot on the map near a blue line leading to the gorge. "We were camping in a clearing about here."

"Where do you think the reflection might've been coming from?"

"I'm not sure. It was further up the valley on a hillside without any trees. It was at sunset, so maybe over here somewhere."

Ethan studies the map for a few seconds and then draws a line with his finger from where we are to where I'd pointed on the map. He goes to his bag and comes back with his phone and takes a photo of this section of the map.

"So we can refer to it if we need to," he explains. "Let's get packed. We'll leave as soon as it's light."

As I pack my backpack, I notice Matt walk over to Ethan. Ethan stops packing to listen and lifts his hands as if to say 'it's out of my control'. Matt shakes his head in reply, frowning back at Ethan. Marley then gets involved in the conversation too, so I carry my bag to the kitchen table to pack some cooking utensils, trying to get close enough to hear.

"Look, I get what you're saying, Matt," Marley says. "There is a risk that there might be people up there, and that's exactly why we need to find out. We need to know what we're dealing with as soon as possible. If there is someone up there, we don't want to wait for them to find us."

"We'll just check things out," Ethan says. "I'll make sure no one sees us unless we want them to, and if we decide to make contact, I'll make sure we think it's safe first. I'll take this just in case." He picks up the hunting rifle beside him.

"Do you think that's wise?" Matt says. "We don't want to start a fight with anyone."

"I'm not planning on *starting* anything, trust me. It's just in case. Besides, one minute you're saying it's too dangerous and now you're worried about me taking a gun to defend ourselves. I'm not sure what you really … oh, okay." Ethan's expression softens. "Look Matt, I think I understand. I'll look after her. I promise I'll bring her back in one piece."

"I'm not worried about Jess," Matt scoffs. "She can take care of herself. If anything, she'll be the one looking after you."

CHAPTER 23

We're rugged up in jackets and hats, ready to head out into the frosty air. Jackson, Matt, and Lily watch us put on our packs and take turns to hug us all goodbye.

"Don't take any risks, okay?" Matt hugs me tightly.

"I promise to keep my head screwed on at all times." I try to lighten the mood, then pat him on the back, letting him know it's time for me to leave.

After crossing the river, Ethan and I say goodbye to the others heading on to the Lodge, before we turn north up the valley.

"I think we should head up there." Ethan points at the hill directly ahead of us and makes a beeline toward it.

I inhale deeply as we climb, enjoying the cold in my lungs, certain I've never breathed anything purer. As we gain height, more of the valley comes into view and I'm amazed to see fountains of mist rising from hidden cracks all over the valley floor, venting steam from invisible hot springs. By the time we stop for a break, the sun's rays have erased the fountains from view but instead have revealed a landscape unlike anything I've ever seen. I'm mesmerised by its otherworldliness. The earth is a mixture of reds, greys, and yellows, the land dotted with small tarns varying in colour from milky blue to deep azure.

"I've never seen anywhere like this," I gush. "It looks like we're on a completely different planet."

"It does, doesn't it? There are a few places like this around here, especially in the National Park." Ethan hands me a bag of nuts and dried fruit from his pack. "Do you think we're close to where you saw the light?"

I look in the direction of the gorge. "I can almost see the clearing that I was standing in when I saw it. I think we need to climb higher though until I can see the clearing better."

"We should probably keep a watch out for people from here on too," Ethan says as we put on our packs.

After walking for another hour, I'm starting to wonder if we're in the right area. Or worse, that there's nothing to find at all. I scan the rockface above us and look for signs of a building or people below, but there's nothing.

As we continue to round the bend in the hillside, a forest spreads beneath us and then a small clearing appears in the trees below. I feel my spirits begin to lift. This would be the ideal place for a cabin. We eagerly make our way around the hilltop until we have a direct line of sight into the clearing, but it's completely empty. I let out a sigh, louder than I'd intended.

"I was sure there was going to be something there." Ethan echoes my thoughts, then shakes his head and carries on.

We continue along the hill until we pass beyond the northern edge of the forest and Ethan stops. "That looks odd, don't you think?" He squints at the rocky ground below.

"What do you mean?"

"The ground looks like it has markings on it. It doesn't look natural. Almost looks like a symbol or something."

I tilt my head to one side, studying the area where he's pointing, and make out marks on the ground, like a trail etched into the surface.

"Have you seen pictures of the Nazca lines?" I ask.

"Yeah, sure."

"You know how you can see the picture that the lines form from a plane but you can't see it at ground level? Maybe those lines are like that. Something that's meant to be seen from the air."

"Like a helicopter?"

"Exactly like a helicopter. Maybe it's letting a helicopter pilot know where to land."

"So, if that's where you want a helicopter to land," Ethan says. "Then …"

"The shelter should be nearby!"

"Let's take a closer look." Ethan grins at me.

We keep watch for signs of people as we scramble our way down to the valley floor and scan the area for anything that resembles a cabin.

"There isn't anything." I kick a stone in frustration. "No trail, no cabin, nothing."

"Why don't we head toward the river? Maybe they built a cabin close to a water supply." Ethan turns toward the trees.

We find an animal trail soon after entering the forest and follow it.

"This doesn't make sense," I say.

"What doesn't?"

"Why would you land a helicopter so far from where you'd want to drop your supplies? If there's a cabin by the river, they would just land there, wouldn't they?"

"So, it wasn't a helicopter landing site then," Ethan replies. "Maybe it's a sign to give the pilot directions where to land."

"Maybe." I'm not convinced.

"Woah, Jess!"

I stop behind him, looking around to see what he's reacted to, and then the smell of rotten eggs wafts up my nose.

"Oh my god. What is that smell?"

"I thought that was you."

"Oh, shut up! You did not."

"Honestly, I didn't think you'd have it in you." Ethan laughs. "But who am I to judge what you're capable of?"

I roll my eyes at him. "Seriously, what *is* making that smell? Is it a dead animal or something?"

"It's sulphur. There must be a geothermal spring or something nearby."

"The other hot pools don't smell like this."

"No, not all of them do. It depends on the sulphur content of the soil. There must be more sulphur around here."

"So, you knew it wasn't me." I whack his arm with the back of my hand.1

"I think I would be pretty foolish to underestimate *anything* about you, Jess." He darts out of reach. "Let's see if we can find the source of this smell then."

He starts sniffing the air with a wink. As I begin to follow him he darts off behind a tree and then jumps out behind me. "A-ha, found it!" he proclaims loudly, throwing his head back, laughing.

"You're not funny." I push him away.

"Come on, I'm hilarious."

I shake my head in resignation and continue walking down the animal track. I haven't gone far before our trail appears to intersect with a wider path, one that has been deliberately dug into the ground and cleared of saplings and other undergrowth.

"This isn't an animal track, is it?" I look along the new path.

"Only of the human kind."

I turn to Ethan, excitement bubbling inside me at the realisation of what we've found. My face breaks into a grin and I start jumping up and down. "So, this means we're right."

"Might be a bit soon to count our chickens, but yeah, it's a good sign." He grins back at me.

"So which way? Left or right?"

Ethan heads to the right. "Right it is." I follow him.

"It doesn't look like anyone has been through here recently." Ethan lifts a fallen branch and throws it to the side. "Not since it rained last week anyway, or there'd be footprints." He points at the impressions our boots have left on the soft ground behind us.

It isn't long before we reach the path's destination, arriving at a pool of water. Like the hot pool at the Lodge, a small stream flows into it at one end and exits at the other where it has been artificially dammed to create a swimming hole. I kneel and touch the water and it's blissfully warm.

"This isn't where the smell is coming from," I say, inhaling the steam wafting off the water. "It must be coming from somewhere else. I guess the cabin is in the other direction."

"Guess so." Ethan takes one last look around the pool and begins walking back along the path we'd just followed.

We retrace our footprints back to the crossroads where the tracks intersect and continue to follow the man-made path in the opposite direction. Ethan leads the way, occasionally clearing a fallen branch from the trail. Even though there's no sign of anyone having been through here recently, we walk in silence, listening carefully for sounds of people as the path leads us back in the direction of the hillside and its rocky cliffs.

Surely there can't be a cabin on this side. We would've seen it from the hill.

Ethan stops at the edge of the clearing that we'd looked down on earlier, blocking the view beyond him. "Oh my god."

I nudge him aside and my mouth drops open. Set into the cliff directly in front of us is a huge steel door recessed into the rock, as though barring an entrance to a cave. The doors are grey, camouflaging it to match the surrounding rockface.

"They didn't build a cabin," Ethan says. "They built a bunker."

CHAPTER 24

"Do you think we should be going closer?" I grab Ethan's arm as he steps forward. "Don't we have to be careful in case someone's in there?"

"There's no sign of anyone being here for weeks, probably longer. I really don't think we need to worry about it. Come on." He takes my hand and tugs me forward.

As we walk side by side across the small clearing toward the door, I see it isn't just a single door. There is one large steel door the size of an oversized triple garage, and on the left is a smaller, regular sized door, also made of steel. There aren't any windows, and the entire front is sealed. There's no way of looking in or getting in unless the door is opened.

The smaller door has a five-spoke handle and there's a combination lock above it. Ethan reaches up to pull the door handle.

"Hey, I was just thinking about what Dean said the other night," I say. Ethan jumps, not expecting me to speak. "Maybe we should knock first?"

Ethan lets out a deep breath, obviously feeling more tense than I'd realised. "Yeah, okay."

He knocks on the door, but it makes no noise at all, the thickness of the steel completely absorbing the sound. Ethan gives me a sideways look as if to say, 'Okay. Now what, genius?'

I shrug my shoulders and pull my water bottle out of my pack and hand it to him. "Try this."

He bangs the water bottle against the door and it makes a dull thud, but not much more.

"Fine, we tried. See if it opens then," I say.

Ethan takes hold of the handle and pulls. The door doesn't budge. He then tries to turn the five-spoke wheel, but it doesn't move either.

"Of course, it's locked," Ethan says. "Why would you leave your bunker unlocked?"

"You don't think they'd have chosen a passcode like 123456?"

"Doubtful," he replies, but punches in the numbers anyway and presses the OK button.

Nothing happens. He presses 000000 and OK. Nothing.

"Do I keep trying?"

"I don't know. Will it lock us out?"

"Probably, but they usually reset after a while."

He punches in another set of numbers and another. Each time, nothing happens.

"It's locked us out," Ethan says. "This is an electronic lock, you know."

"Okay." I shrug my shoulders, unsure why it's important.

"An electronic lock needs a power source," he clarifies. "So, the bunker must have a power generator or something. Maybe solar, but we haven't seen any panels or anything. But maybe that was what you saw reflecting the sun the other day."

"So now what? Do we keep plugging in different combinations in the hope that we pick the correct one?"

"I guess we set up camp for tonight. And tomorrow we can see if there's another entrance somewhere. Maybe there's an escape hatch or something further up the rockface."

"You think there's still a chance we can find a way in?"

"There's no way this is what you saw reflecting the sun the other day. It's too well camouflaged, and it's surrounded by trees. The only way you can see this is if you're right here in front of it. We couldn't see it from the hilltop, it's recessed. You'd probably have a hard time even seeing it from a helicopter. There has to be something else further up there that made that reflection."

"Yeah, you're right." I look up the rockface directly above us. "There must be something up there. There's no way I saw light reflecting off this. Do you think this clearing is big enough for a helicopter to land?"

"Yeah, I'd say this will be where they land. Right on the front lawn."

"Should we camp here?"

"I think we should camp closer to the river so we've got access to water," Ethan replies. "Let's check it out at least. We can always come back here if it isn't suitable."

We head back across the clearing to the path, following it until it crosses the animal track we were on earlier. The animal track seems to widen from this point, as though human feet have helped solidify it. Eventually the track leads us to the river we'd watched winding through the valley from the hillside. The smell of rotten eggs is stronger here and there are lines of yellow in the soil at the edge of the water.

"Hey, check that out." Ethan points downstream.

In the middle of the river is a small rocky island with steam billowing out and water is gushing from an opening on the top.

"Is that a hot spring?"

"Yep," Ethan says. "I've only heard about hot springs coming up in the middle of a river. Never seen it though. Pretty cool, huh?"

"Very cool! Will it make the river warm below it?"

"I don't know by how much. There's a lot of water flowing through here. Let's get the tent up and then we can check it out."

After pitching the tent, I'm keen to check out the stream, but Ethan wants us to get a fire going first. While he sets up the fire pit, I head along the riverbank collecting wood. I return with a few armloads, then head further down the bank to take a closer look at the hot spring island.

Steam wafts from a hole in the rocky outcrop where the water gushes out, making bubbling sounds as it surges and then quietens for a few seconds before surging again. The river becomes cloudy where the spring splashes into it, eventually clearing as it dissipates further downstream.

The bank drops half a metre down to a muddy looking flat that stretches the rest of the way to the river's edge. I'm curious to know how warm the water is and decide to quickly check it out before returning to Ethan with the wood I've collected.

After placing the sticks in a pile on the ground, I take off my boots and socks, roll my trousers above my knees, and step off the bank to the mud flat beneath. I expect it to feel cold, but instead it's lukewarm as my foot sinks into the mud. I take a step toward the river and my back foot sinks down to my knee. When I try to lift it out to take another step, it won't move. I pull again as hard as I can and it gives a little, and then releases all of a sudden and I lose my balance, falling forward. I throw my hands out in front of me to break my fall, but my arms sink in past my elbows and my face plants fully in the mud.

I roll onto my side, unable to open my eyes, and shake my hands to try to remove their coating of the stinky sludge. I hear laughing and hurriedly wipe away the mud until I can finally see again. Ethan's head is thrown back as he howls in laughter, standing above me on the bank.

"Do you need a hand?"

I don't reply. Ignoring him, I try to regain some sense of decorum as I heave myself upright, but it's impossible. Every time I try to take a step, the mud sucks onto me, making a loud farting sound as the suction releases my foot. I lose my balance and fall into the sludge all over again. Finally accepting defeat, I lie back and try to catch my breath, listening to Ethan's laughing.

"Don't go anywhere, Jess. I'm just going to get my phone. I've got to take a photo of this."

"Don't you dare!"

"Relax, I'm kidding. Do you think you can make your way back to the bank, or do I need to get a rope?"

"I'll get there eventually," I grunt as I try to stand up and fall, yet again.

"Looks like we found the source of that smell." Ethan can barely speak, he's laughing so hard. "You can't deny it isn't you anymore. You're literally covered in it now."

I give him a withering look but realise it was a wasted effort. He's doubled over, too busy laughing to notice.

"I'm just going to take a little rest for a moment," I say, exhausted from my effort.

Ethan takes off his boots and socks and carefully takes a step with one foot down onto the edge of the mud flat. He keeps his other foot on the firm side of the bank and reaches out toward me. I stretch up and take his hand and try to stand, but decide better of it when he starts laughing at me again.

"You should see yourself! I don't think I've ever seen anything so funny before." He clasps my hand tightly, getting ready to pull me up.

I reach up with my other hand and grip his wrist so I'm now holding onto him with both hands. A grin creeps across my face as I pretend to stand, but instead I pull back as hard as I can. He's already off balance, leaning well over his grounded foot, and it takes him by surprise.

"Ah!" He tries to jerk his hand free, but I hold tighter and keep pulling, refusing to let go, and he lands heavily in the mud beside me.

Ethan rolls over to face me and I place both my hands on his cheeks, smooshing mud all over them. "Thanks for coming to rescue me."

"You, Jessica Maddox, are going to pay for this!" he says, throwing a handful of sludge at me.

I scramble away from him as quickly as I can toward the river and hear Ethan trying to crawl after me. I collapse, laughing as Ethan grabs one of my feet and pulls me squealing back toward him until our faces are next to each other. Anticipating my next move, he grabs my hands to stop me from getting any more mud.

"You'll keep." He laughs.

"I really want to know how warm that spring is," I say when I finally catch my breath.

"We need to wash this muck off anyway. Let's check it out."

We discover a commando crawl is the most efficient way to keep our bodies from getting sucked back into the mire. Finally, we reach the edge of the river and drag ourselves into the flow of water.

The water is painfully cold, much colder than I was expecting. A trail of muddy water instantly forms downstream of us as it washes the sludge from our clothes. I face upstream into the current and push my head beneath the water, trying to wash the mud from my face and hair, scrubbing my scalp with my fingernails. Ethan does the same and by the time we finish, we look more human than bog beast.

"Hope it's warmer over there," I say through chattering teeth.

"Don't get too close to the water coming straight from the spring," Ethan warns. "Some springs can be a hundred degrees. Best to approach it from further downstream."

I feel the temperature begin to rise as soon as we reach the cloudy patch. It isn't exactly warm, but it's definitely not as cold as the rest of the river. I move further toward the island and the temperature continues to increase.

"I think I prefer the hot pools," I say after a couple of minutes.

"Me too. We've got most of the mud off now. Why don't we go to that hot pool and warm up?"

"Yeah, I think I need to get out before I get too cold."

"Okay, let's go downstream a bit. We need to avoid that mud."

We let the current carry us downstream until we see the mudflat disappear, replaced by rocks at the river's edge. We climb onto the stony bank and race back up to our boots, dripping wet in our now mud-free clothes.

We shove bare feet into boots and grab our backpacks, not bothering to waste time looking for dry clothes, then head down the track to the hot pool. I'm so cold by the time we reach it I just kick off my boots and step straight into the water fully clothed, desperate to feel warmth as soon as possible.

"Whose bright idea was it to go for a swim in that river?" I say as my body lets out an involuntary shudder, my muscles trying to relieve the tension from the cold.

Ethan immediately follows me into the pool, groaning as he slides into the water up to his chin.

"It doesn't look like we're going to get anything useful from that bunker, does it?" I say after a few minutes. "I feel like I've sent us on a wild goose chase up here and wasted our time. It would've been better if we'd just gone with the others to help bring the food back from the Lodge."

"I don't agree." Ethan shakes his head. "We had no idea what we'd find when we decided to come up here. We could've found a cabin stocked full of food, or another group of people. Just because we didn't, it doesn't mean it was a waste of time. We needed to know."

I give him a small smile, grateful that he doesn't blame me for a wasted trip. I'm always surprised when people show kindness. I'm not sure why that is. It's not as if people are unkind to me very often, but for some reason I seem to expect it.

Although I've known for some time that I unfairly judged Ethan when we first met, he continues to show me how wrong I was. His actions have shown him to be nothing like the shallow, arrogant jerk I thought he'd be. He's self-assured and confident, but he isn't arrogant. He shows an interest in others and compassion toward his friends. He's smart and capable and isn't afraid to work hard. And the more I get to know him, the more I find myself liking him.

"How long have you been working as a guide?" I ask.

"I've been involved in guiding one way or another since I was a little kid. My dad started up Falls River Guides with Skye's dad before we were born. Skye and I hung around all the time growing up, even getting to go on some of the trips with them. After they died, Skye's mum, Monica, took over the company. I think I was about sixteen when Skye and I officially started working as part of the crew. So, that would make this my fourth summer."

"You're only nineteen?" I'm surprised, he seems older to me.

"Yeah."

"But Skye's older, though, isn't she?"

"She's twenty-two."

"You guys are pretty close, aren't you?"

"Yeah, for sure. When our dads died, Monica took me in. She'd been like a surrogate mother to me ever since my mum died anyway, so the adoption just made it official. So, technically, Skye's my big sister. She definitely treats me like an annoying little brother, anyway."

"And what about Emily? How long had you known her for?"

"Emily joined the crew about four years ago. It was love at first sight for Skye, and they've been inseparable ever since. So, Emily basically became part of the family then too."

"I'm really sorry about Emily. I liked her a lot."

"Yeah. Me too," he says, nodding. "So, what about you? You've been asking all the questions. What's your story?"

"Ha! I don't have a story."

"Come on, you have to have something interesting you can tell me."

"I'm so normal it's embarrassing. My mum's a lawyer and my dad's an accountant. I'm an only child. I go to school, I study, I hang out with friends. I'm allergic to sports, but I like to run, and it turns out I'm not so bad at climbing. See? Very normal. Very boring."

"And boyfriend?" he asks casually.

"No, there's no boyfriend. You?"

"No, I don't have a boyfriend either." He grins at me. "So, what about Matt?"

"What about Matt?"

"You guys seem close," Ethan says slowly, as though he's picking his words carefully. "Is there something going on between you guys?"

"No." A small laugh escapes as I shake my head, remembering Matt's conversation with Skye. "No, not at all. We're just good friends. There's nothing going on."

"Okay." Ethan nods.

"Well, I'm feeling much warmer. Probably time to get out."

"Yeah, I guess so," Ethan replies, but instead of moving to get out, he strips his top off over his head and wrings the water out, then throws it onto the stones at the edge. "It's easier to take wet clothes off in the water," he explains, seeing my confusion. "Warmer too."

"Good idea," I reply.

I take my trousers off under the water, then wring them out as much as possible, squeezing them into a ball before throwing them onto the rocks. I start to pull my top off, but it clings and gets stuck, covering my face. I struggle to lift it over my head, grunting as I try to pull out my arms. Finally, it comes free, and I see Ethan has helped lift it off my head.

"Oh, thanks." I give an embarrassed laugh, imagining how silly I must've looked.

He hands me my top and I wring the water out and throw it onto the rock with the other clothes. I turn back and see Ethan is still watching me. I smile at him. He has a smear of mud down the side of his neck from where he'd taken off his top.

"You've got some mud on you." I reach out and gently wipe the smudge from his skin. I feel his body tense as I touch him and immediately worry I've done something wrong. "Sorry, I probably should've asked first."

He catches my hand as I pull it away, holding it until it drops back under the water. A shiver runs up my spine as he releases my hand and his fingers brush slowly up my arm.

"There's some on you too," he says as he gently strokes the skin on my shoulder, electrifying every nerve ending.

I watch his face as he touches me. I don't smile. My whole body on edge, wondering what he's going to do. Excited … nervous, very nervous. *Surely, I can't be reading this wrong? Can I?*

I swallow hard, trying to calm the thumping in my chest. "Now who's playing games?" My voice is barely audible.

He looks up at me, eyebrows pulling together. "I'm not *playing* anything." He shakes his head.

His hands slide down to my waist and he pulls me very gently, very slowly closer, giving me the chance to pull back or stop him if I want to. But I don't want to. This is exactly what I want him to do. He doesn't take his eyes off mine as he draws me closer and I don't take mine from his.

Just before our bodies touch, he leans forward. His lips brush gently against mine, testing, checking, and then, as I respond to his kiss, his arms wrap firmly around me, my body tight against his. His kiss becomes harder, more intense, his hand sliding up my back and into my hair. I wrap my legs around his waist, wanting to be closer, to touch more of him with more of me.

My heart feels like it's going to explode as our bodies intertwine, hands running over each other's skin. Our kissing becomes urgent, breathless. I begin to feel lightheaded and break my lips away from his, tilting my head back to catch my breath. Ethan's lips skim my neck, small kisses up to my jaw. I didn't know anything could feel this amazing! I want more, more of him, and lower my mouth back to his, his hands on my body, caressing me.

My skin feels electric, my heart pounds out of control … I *feel* out of control, overwhelmed … I need to breathe. I put my hand on his chest and slowly, firmly push him back, making space between us, breaking our kiss.

"Are you okay?"

"I need to stop." I take a deep breath. "If I don't stop now, I don't think I'm going to be able to … and I'm not sure that would be a very good idea."

He lets out a small laugh and pulls me in close again, his breathing as heavy as mine as he holds me. His fingers run up and down my back, setting off lightning bolts, and I let out a sigh, using all my willpower to stop myself from kissing him again.

"Probably for the best," he says quietly in my ear.

Neither of us moves. I don't want to let go of him and he isn't in a rush to let go of me either. After a few seconds, we finally pull apart. Ethan climbs out of the pool first and takes his towel out of his pack and holds it out to me.

"Thanks." I smile shyly as I climb out of the pool, wrapping it around me. I find my towel in my bag and hand it to Ethan to use.

"Thank *you*." He reaches for the towel, but instead grabs me around the waist and pulls me in for another kiss. It takes me off guard, and when he moves away, I'm left breathless, speechless. He grins, pleased at the effect it has on me.

We quickly dress in dry clothes and head back to our tent. Ethan lights the fire and I collect some more wood, adding it to the pile. The temperature drops quickly as the sun sinks behind the hills in the distance, leaving the valley floor now in shadow. I look up at the cliff, still bathed in sunlight above the trees to see if there's anything reflecting the late afternoon light. But I can't see anything, at least not from this angle.

After we finish eating dinner, Ethan puts his arm around me, pulling me close beside him as we watch the fire. I find it hard to shake the feeling that this is some crazy dream. I still can't believe it's happening. It seems impossible to think that someone like him could like someone like me, and I have no idea why he does. Maybe it's because I'm the only girl here, the metaphorical last girl in the world. Well, not exactly, but close enough. But right now, I don't really care. Because tonight he does want me, and I want him. And I'm certainly not going to mess this up by having some insecurity fueled conversation seeking reassurance that he does.

"No beautiful moon setting tonight," I say.

He doesn't reply. Instead, he leans forward and kisses the tip of my nose. I turn to look at him and smile and he places his lips on mine. He grasps my waist in both his hands and pulls me around to straddle him as our kisses become more urgent, more desperate. Suddenly, he stops and moves me off his lap, and stands. He holds out his hand and pulls me to my feet and begins to lead me to the tent.

I hesitate and pull back. I'm afraid of going into the tent with him, afraid of us going so far that it can't be undone. But mostly, I'm afraid that tomorrow he'll come to his senses and I'll feel the humiliation of his rejection.

He turns to face me, the light from the fire flickering on his face. "We don't have to *do* anything, you know."

"I know." I nod, but I still don't move.

"I mean it, we can just kiss, nothing else. I *am* capable of restraint, you know." He gives me a wink and then puts his hands around my waist, pulling me closer.

"It's not *you* I'm worried about," I say under my breath.

He steps back, holding me at arm's length, his hands on my shoulders as though assessing me. "I promise you, no matter how much you want to, we will *not* have sex tonight," he says seriously. "Scout's honour."

I laugh, despite my nerves or maybe because of them, and wrap my arms around his neck. I look up into his smiling face and kiss him, and then, letting go of my fear, I take his hand and lead him into the tent.

CHAPTER 25

It's already light when I wake. I stay perfectly still at first, lying with my eyes shut, listening to the sound of Ethan's steady breathing. His arms are wrapped around me, blanketing me in the warmth of his body as much as the sleeping bag that covers us.

I pull the bag up under my chin and smile, remembering the night before. We'd spent hours kissing and getting to know each other, finally falling asleep in each other's arms. Ethan had been true to his word, and we hadn't had sex. I think he quite enjoyed denying me as my inhibitions disappeared, but he'd said teasingly, "I have many flaws, but if nothing else, I'm a man of my word. I always keep my promises."

I couldn't think of any flaws.

Although it's light, the sun hasn't reached this part of the valley yet and it's cold outside the sleeping bag. I scan the tent, looking for my clothes, and see my top at the end of the tent. I carefully lift Ethan's arm off me and lean out of the bag, trying not to pull the cover off him. I've just reached the top with my fingertips when Ethan grabs me from behind and pulls me back into his arms.

"Where do you think you're going?" He nuzzles into my neck.

"Nowhere, I was just looking for my clothes," I say, enjoying that he doesn't want me to go.

"And why on Earth would you need clothes?" He chuckles

quietly, then kisses down my neck to my shoulder, turning me to face him.

"No idea. Absolutely no idea at all." I smile at him.

"So, do you *still* think this was a wasted trip?"

I laugh, not bothering to answer, knowing he isn't expecting one.

"I'm not sure I want to go back." Ethan sighs as he stretches his arms above his head. "How about we just forget about the others, forget about going back? We could build a little cabin and live out the apocalypse here, just the two of us. What do you reckon?" He wraps his arms around me again. "Or … maybe we could just stay up here for one more night? I don't think I'm ready to give you up just yet."

"Don't give me up then." I kiss him, wanting to make the idea too difficult to contemplate.

"I'm not planning on it." He lifts me so I'm lying on top of him. "I just don't think there'll be much opportunity for this when we go back."

I look down at him, my hair falling around his face. "Oh, really? You don't think *this* would be acceptable bunk-rooming behaviour?"

"We might need to get creative, otherwise things could get a bit awkward."

"Why would it be awkward?"

"It just might be a bit uncomfortable with the others if we're suddenly behaving like a couple or something," he explains. "Especially around Skye at the moment, you know, because of Emily. I think it would be hard for her to see us together when she's just lost her partner, you know what I mean?"

"I hadn't thought of that. I guess it would be pretty insensitive. Maybe your 'build a cabin' idea isn't such a bad one after all." I laugh, trying to hide my disappointment.

"I think, maybe we should keep this just between us for a while …"

I get a sinking feeling as I realise I'm about to become an embarrassing little secret.

"You know, just until Skye's had some more time to get over losing Emily."

Yeah, because everyone knows it doesn't take long to get over losing the love of your life, no big deal. Great. What do I say to that?

I look into Ethan's eyes and realise I don't need to say anything. *When I left the cabin yesterday, I had no idea this would happen or was even a possibility. He's not my boyfriend. No promises were made ... well, apart from that one promise, and he kept that one.*

"Jess?"

I look into his concerned eyes and smile.

"Thought I'd lost you for a second." He returns my smile as I lower my lips to his jaw and slowly kiss down to his neck. He laughs, pulling me back up until my face is level with his, and kisses me gently. "*You* are going to be trouble, I can tell."

****

It's nearly midday when we finally manage to drag ourselves out of the tent. The valley is now in full sunlight and the frost has thawed from the ground. We don't pack up the campsite, having already decided we'd stay one more night. Not yet ready for our time together to be over. Ethan packs water bottles and some snacks into his backpack, along with rope and climbing harnesses, in case we need them. Then we head back to the bunker.

Ethan studies the rockface for a few minutes and then walks along the bottom of the wall, looking for a place to climb. He chooses a spot further down from the bunker doors where the rockface slopes back and isn't as steep, allowing us to climb without needing to use ropes. Ethan leads and I stay close behind, watching carefully where he places his hands and feet so I can copy his movements.

About fifteen metres up, it levels out onto a ledge a couple of metres wide before climbing again. The ledge continues along the cliff as far as we can see until it curves out of sight, providing a safe path for us to traverse. As we walk, I look up and down the rockface for anything metallic that might reflect the sunlight, but I don't see anything. When we're directly above the clearing in front of the bunker doors, we take a break and sit with our legs hanging over the edge to peer down at the ground beneath us. Even though we're right above it, the bunker doors are completely hidden from view, recessed into the wall beneath.

I lie back on the ledge, staring up at the cloudless sky, enjoying the warmth on my face. Strange this sense of contentment is in the middle of an apocalypse ... uncertain of whether we'll be rescued or have enough food to survive the winter, and with no idea if our loved ones are safe. But I guess I have the indisputable power of hormones to thank for that.

I turn my head to look further along the ledge and notice what looks like a metal line barely visible a few metres away. I tilt my head, trying to make sense of what I'm seeing, but it doesn't make it any clearer. I move back from the edge and stand up, intending to walk over to it, but once I'm standing, I can't see it anymore. I take a couple of steps and get down on my knees, placing my cheek on the ground to look along the ledge again, and there it is, right in front of me. I reach out and touch it.

"What *are* you doing?"

"I think I've found something. It's a metal edge on something," I reply as I try to brush the stone and dirt away from the top, hoping to reveal the metal underneath, but it doesn't shift.

Ethan crouches beside me and I point to it. He tries to brush the stone off too, and then stands and scuffs at it with his boot, but it still doesn't move.

I trace the metal with my finger and it forms a large rectangle. I'm certain it's a door of some kind, with stone from the rockface attached to the top to camouflage it.

"It's got to be an escape hatch for the bunker," I say. "It's right above the bunker doors. It would make sense for the bunker to have an escape route, wouldn't it? In case something blocks the other entrance."

"Yeah, makes sense. They've done a good job hiding it. There's no way you'd see it from a distance. I didn't even see it and I was standing right beside it."

He tries to get his fingers under the edge and lift, but it doesn't budge. "We need a lever."

"I saw a crowbar at the cabin. Maybe we could bring it back up here and try to lift it?"

"Yeah, that might do it."

Ethan takes a red trail marker out of his pack and ties it to a loose rock lying nearby, before placing it on top of the hatch.

"This still doesn't solve the mystery of what was reflecting the sunlight," I say. "We came from that direction, so we already know there isn't anything that way. Why don't we follow this ledge back round the other way and see if there's anything else we can find?"

I take the lead this time, being careful to stay away from the edge. The ledge narrows after a few minutes, and I can see that it becomes little more than a crack further ahead. We haven't seen anything out of the ordinary … but then again, we nearly didn't see the escape hatch either. I scan the slope above us. The top of the face is only another fifteen metres above, then it rounds off before connecting with another hillside where it continues to climb again.

"We need to go up," I say as Ethan follows my gaze.

Ethan picks a route up the rock, climbing cautiously, both of us conscious of how far we'd fall if we're to lose our footing. He helps pull me over the edge when we reach the top, and I step onto level ground.

"I think we've found your mystery reflector."

Steam wafts from crevices all over the rocky ground in front of us. And poking out of one vent, partially hidden at the base of the steam, is a metal chimney.

I look across the valley and can see the small clearing in the distance where Matt and I had camped. "I think you're right," I reply. "What is it?"

"I'm not sure, but I think it might be part of a power generator. Maybe the bunker is powered by geothermal energy. There are steam vents and hot springs everywhere around here. It would make sense to use it as a power source. You'd have power twenty-four-hours a day, and you aren't reliant on sun or wind or fuel. It's kind of genius actually, if that's what they've done, chosen a location where they've got an unlimited energy source."

"It's not going to be much use to us though, if we can't find a way in."

"The others might have an idea." Ethan puts his arm around my shoulder. "If we can't get in through that hatch, I'm sure we'll find another way."

CHAPTER 26

The sun is already high in the sky by the time we start our hike back to the cabin. We decide to use the path of the river as our guide and it proves to be a much faster route than the one we took on our way up here, shaving an hour off our time.

As we enter the forest surrounding the cabin, I take Ethan's hand, forcing him to stop. He looks down at me and smiles as I lift onto my toes and take his face between my hands. I memorise every detail, the feeling of his lips, the rush of electricity that it sparks in my body, not knowing when we'll have another opportunity.

The sound of voices and laughter greets us as soon as we exit the trees. We quickly make our way around to the front of the cabin, eager to see if the others have returned from the Lodge. My question is answered as soon as I see Priya and Dean sitting with Jackson and Lily on the verandah.

"Hi!" I call out.

Priya jumps up and runs over to us, grabbing us both. "I was getting worried."

Lily hugs us as we climb the stairs and then Dean lifts me off the ground, squeezing me tightly. "We were going to send out a search party if you guys didn't come back tonight."

The door bursts open and Skye comes running through, ignoring me and grabbing Ethan. "You took your time, didn't you? Goddam it, little brother, I was starting to get worried."

"You know nothing would happen to me. I'm too annoying to die, remember?" He laughs as he wraps his arms around her.

"Ugh, don't say that. I can't believe you even remember me saying that. You would've been, what, nine?"

"Thirteen."

"Were you? Oh god. No wonder you remember. I wish I'd never said that. You know I didn't mean it."

I turn to walk into the cabin and Matt is standing at the door, his arm still in a sling.

"Hey." I grin at him.

"Hey." He smiles back.

"Don't I get a hug?" I drop my pack to the ground and hold out my arms.

He takes the couple of strides toward me and wraps me with his good arm as I hug him back. "Welcome home."

It's funny that he uses that word, because as soon as he says it, I realise that's how it feels seeing him. Like coming home.

"Thanks. I missed you."

"Missed you too." He squeezes me tightly.

"Hey, hey, hey," Oliver yells as he comes around the corner with Kai and Marley. "They're back!"

He walks over and pats Ethan on the back. "We thought you might have run off and left us or something."

"I tried, but Jess wouldn't let me," Ethan says.

Ollie gives me a strange look and I realise I'm laughing a little too loudly. I clear my throat. "How did you go at the Lodge?"

"It's good we're all back," Marley replies. "Let's head inside. We've got some catching up to do."

I look from face to face, searching for information, but no one reveals anything as we file into the cabin.

"Come on, can someone tell me what's going on? The suspense is killing me," I say as I sit at the table. "What happened at the Lodge? Did you get the food okay?"

"Yes, we got all the food," Marley replies. "No one had been at the Lodge since Skye and Ethan had been there. So, we packed it all up and even brought some extra gear back—sleeping bags, ropes, first aid."

"Soooo?" I say impatiently. "What's the problem that we need to catch up on?"

"I was getting to that," Marley says. "We were shuttling the bags up the waterfall and Ollie and Kai went back to get a couple of the solar lights from the bridge."

"We thought we could use the lights to make trips to the toilet a little less creepy at night," Ollie explains. "Kai and I had just finished getting the solar lights and were about to head back to join everyone when we saw two men come around the side of the Lodge. They had guns raised and were walking toward the toilets. I guess they were checking for people. We ran into the trees so they wouldn't see us and we watched them from there. When they went back to the Lodge, we could hear them talking to someone else, but we couldn't see them."

"Couldn't hear what they were saying either," Kai adds.

"As soon as they got back and told us what they'd seen, we got out of there as fast as we could. We didn't want to risk being found," Marley says. "We already had everything we needed, so there was no need to risk going back." He gives Dean a pointed look. "The important thing was that we knew there were people there and it wasn't safe to go back anymore."

"We should've tried to find out how many there were," Dean retorts. "We should know what we're up against."

"We're not *up against anything* if they don't know we're up here," Marley replies. "And Skye took care of that."

"Did you get rid of the bolts?" Ethan asks.

"Yeah, they're gone except the top ones. I took the crowbar with me just in case we found people at the Lodge when we went back," Skye replies. "We brought all the remaining climbing gear back with us, so unless they've got their own ropes, there's nothing left for them to use."

"Why would anyone climb up that waterfall, anyway?" Jackson asks. "They'd need to know there's something at the top of the canyon worth climbing to, right? You guys only knew this cabin was here because your dads worked up here. Most people wouldn't know about it, would they?"

"That's right," Skye answers. "Most people wouldn't know about it."

Jackson visibly relaxes at her response.

"But that doesn't mean no-one else knows though. A lot of locals do know about it." Ethan looks at Jackson. "I know what you're worried about, and it is something we need to be thinking about. We should be prepared just in case."

"So, is there anything we can do to stop people coming up that canyon?" Jackson asks.

Skye shakes her head. "I honestly don't think it's something we need to worry about. Once we get some more rain, it'll be too dangerous to climb it anyway. And then it'll be winter and it'd be crazy to come up here in winter if you don't know exactly where you're going."

"Unless you're desperate," Jackson says. "When it's your life on the line, people do some pretty desperate things to survive. I know I'm not the only one thinking it." He looks from face to face. "We need to be ready to protect ourselves and each other. I know we've been focused on getting rescued, but now that's looking unlikely, we need to protect what we have if we're going to survive up here. It's worthless if we can't defend it."

"Why is it looking unlikely we'll be rescued?" I ask.

"We couldn't get hold of anyone on the radio to get a message out," Skye answers.

"Did you try all the channels?" Ethan asks.

"All of them. I tried for hours and no-one responded."

"So, that's it then? Are we just giving up on the idea of getting out of here?" I ask.

"We're not giving up, Jess. We just need to buy some time until Jackson can walk out of here. We can't leave him," Kai replies.

My eyes widen. I can't believe Kai is the one saying this after she was so upset the other day. "Of course we can't leave Jackson. That wasn't what I meant. I would never suggest that." I shake my head. "What I meant was, if we don't think we'll be rescued, does that mean we still plan to stay here?"

"What alternative do we have?" Marley replies. "Obviously, we can't use the Lodge as a fallback plan anymore. So unless anyone can think of somewhere better, staying here until Jackson has recovered, and it's safe to leave, is our only option." He looks at Ethan and me. "Unless you guys have some news for us. Did you find anything?"

"We did actually." Excitement ripples through the group at Ethan's words. "But I'm not sure it's going to be useful. We found what we think is a fallout bunker built into the hillside about four hours' walk up the valley. But it's locked and we couldn't find a way in."

"How do you know it's a bunker then?" Kai asks.

"We don't know for sure," I reply. "But it does look like it. It has steel doors and we think we've found an escape hatch further up the hillside, and Ethan thinks it has power."

"The keypad on the door is electronic, so there has to be a power source for it," he explains. "We found what looks to be a chimney from a steam vent, so I think it uses a geothermal generator."

"You guys have been busy … and here we were thinking you were slacking off in a hot pool somewhere." Ollie laughs.

"It's all really well camouflaged." Ethan ignores him. "There's no way anyone would see the bunker doors unless you know where to find it, and it was just luck that we found the hatch."

"If we can get in there, it would be a pretty secure location," I add. "Even if people did come up here, they'd never find it."

"You found it," Jackson says.

"Yeah, but that was only because Jess saw the chimney reflecting the sun from that clearing," Ethan says. "If we can hide that, no one would be able to see anything, and they wouldn't have any reason to look for the bunker. And remember, the only reason we knew there might be anything worth looking for was because we remembered Skye's dad saying old Jacobs kept talking about needing to prepare for a nuclear war. If we hadn't heard about that, we wouldn't have gone looking in the first place."

"So, how soon can we start breaking into this bunker then?" Ollie grins.

CHAPTER 27

"Holy shit!" Ollie exclaims as we reach the clearing and he sees the steel doors of the bunker. "That's massive! Now I see why you said we wouldn't be able to force the doors open."

"How would you even get these up here?" Kai asks.

"I figure by helicopter," I reply. "Maybe they were flown up in smaller sections and then welded together?"

"It's got to be a bunker by the looks of it," Marley says. "Why else would this be here?"

"Yeah, it's got to be. It couldn't be anything else." Matt nods.

The six of us had left the cabin early this morning, leaving everyone else behind to focus on foraging and hunting for food.

"Let's see if we can get this baby open," Ethan says as he hands the crowbar to Ollie. "I'll take Ollie and Marley up to the hatch and see if we can get it open. You guys take another look at the lock."

Ollie and Marley follow Ethan out of the clearing, and Kai, Matt, and I walk up to the bunker door.

"It's definitely electronic," Kai confirms as soon as she sees it.

"You said it's a six-digit combination?" Matt asks.

"Yeah, I think so," I reply. "The screen let us put in six digits, so I assumed that means it needs six. Don't you think?"

"It would certainly make it harder to crack the code if you need six," Matt replies. "We've got a one in a million chance of guessing the right combination in that case."

"What if we could short circuit it?" Kai asks. "Do you think it would disable it?"

"I think it would have some sort of failsafe if the power supply is interrupted," Matt says. "It would probably just stay locked or open, whatever state it's already in. Otherwise, it'd be too easy for people to break into places using electronic locks."

"Why couldn't it have just been a good old-fashioned lock that uses a key?" I say. "*That*, I could've worked with."

"What do you mean?" Matt frowns at me. "Are you saying you know how to pick a lock?"

"Not all locks, but there's one I've been able to pick quite a few times."

Matt raises his eyebrows at me.

"Don't give me that look. It's not as bad as it sounds." I laugh. "My best friend's parents used to go away a lot, and they'd lock their liquor cabinet before they'd go. So, we watched a few YouTube videos and worked out how to pick it. Once you get the hang of it, it's pretty simple. Her parents have never suspected a thing."

"So, can you pick other locks?" Kai asks.

"I've never tried, but I don't see why not. If it's just a basic key lock and I have the right tools, I could probably work it out."

"Who'd have thought lock picking would be such a useful skill?" Matt says, laughing. "Think I need to add it to my list of life goals."

"You have a life goals list?" Kai screws up her face.

Matt hesitates.

"Don't answer her, Matt. You'll just incriminate yourself."

"Yeah, think you're probably right. I have nothing more to say."

"Definitely guilty." Kai laughs. "So, what else is on your list, Matt?"

"Well … *if* I had a list … and I'm not saying I do. Learning when to keep my mouth shut would definitely be on there."

"So, does anyone have any bright ideas on how we can crack this lock?" I ask.

"I guess we could just start trying different combinations," Matt replies. "I assume it locks you out after a certain number of wrong attempts?"

"Yeah, it locks you out after four incorrect codes. I don't know how long for exactly, but at least a few minutes."

Matt starts punching in different combinations, each one wrong. After his fourth attempt, it locks him out and we time it. It locks us out for five minutes.

"We're not going to get anywhere just guessing," Kai says. "It would take hundreds of years to try all the possible combinations. This is just a waste of time."

"Yeah, I agree," I say. "Unless we can find a number written somewhere, or can get in through that hatch, we don't stand a chance."

"Maybe that's it!" Matt's eyes widen. "Maybe the code is somewhere at the cabin. The same people who built this bunker built the cabin, right? So, maybe they wrote it down somewhere there just in case."

"I didn't see any six-digit numbers written anywhere." Kai shakes her head.

"Neither did I, but we weren't looking for them. They could be anywhere," I say.

"It could be on that map on the wall," Matt almost shouts. "There are numbers all over that map. It could be coordinates or anything."

"Hellooo down there," Ethan's voice booms out from above us. We look up and Ethan, Ollie, and Marley standing on the ledge high above us.

"Hey," I yell as we wave up at them. "Any luck?"

"We've only just got here," Ethan calls back down. "Haven't tried yet. I'll let you know."

They move back from the edge and along toward the location of the hatch. We wait and listen. After a while, their legs appear as they sit down again, and then their faces as they lean over to look at us.

"Sorry, guys, it won't budge," Ethan calls out.

Matt lets out a disappointed grunt as Kai says, "Dammit."

"Okay," I call back up to them. "Be careful climbing down, guys."

"Yeah, we'll be down soon," Ethan shouts back.

They look as dejected as us when they return to the clearing. "It wouldn't budge at all," Marley says.

"Even with all three of us pushing on the crowbar," Ollie adds. "It's impossible. No one could lift that."

"I take it you've had no luck down here either?" Marley asks.

"Actually, we were thinking maybe the map at the cabin might hold the key," Kai says.

"Well, we've done what we came here to do," Ethan replies. "Let's get going."

Although we'd cut across the plateau on our hike up here, we decide to follow the river on our way back.

"Wow, look at that!" Matt says as the steaming island comes into view. "Is that a hot spring coming out of the middle of the river?"

"Yeah, it is." I smile at him, remembering how excited I'd felt when I first saw it too. "It's cool, isn't it?"

"Looks like animals have been rolling around in there." Ollie points at the mudflat.

"That's a very good observation, Ollie," Ethan says, trying not to laugh.

"Do you think it might have been pigs or boars or something?" Ollie asks.

"Certainly looks like one's been rolling in it." Ethan grins as I snort with laughter and then try to cover it up with a sneeze.

By the time we reach the cabin, we're all tired and glad to be home. As soon as Matt has his boots off, he walks to the sofa and lies down. He looks exhausted. I lift his feet and sit down, placing his legs on my lap.

"That was a huge day today, and it was your first time out since we got back here. You must be feeling it. How are you doing?"

"I'm alright. Just need to rest for a bit." He reaches out to take my hand. I give it a squeeze and he closes his eyes.

We take turns telling the others about the bunker, the hatch, and the combination lock. I watch everyone's faces as they listen. Their reactions fluctuate from excitement at the prospect of there being a bunker we could live in, to disappointment that we can't get in, to excitement again at the possibility that there might be a code hidden somewhere in the cabin.

As everyone crowds around the map on the wall searching for six-digit numbers, I look at Matt and see he's fallen asleep. I slide out from under his legs and cover him with a blanket, shaking my head in disbelief that he can sleep through all the noise. "Well, that's one skill you can tick off your list of life goals, Matty," I whisper, and without thinking, I bend down and kiss his forehead.

There isn't any space left around the map to even attempt to have a look, so I join Dean and Priya in the kitchen, preparing dinner.

"How did your hunting go?" I ask.

"Not bad actually," Dean replies. "We got three rabbits and two fish. Enough for tonight and tomorrow."

"We found mushrooms too," Priya adds. "There aren't many yet, but Skye says there'll be lots more soon."

"So, how much food do we have?" I ask. "With all the supplies you brought back from the Lodge, plus what we already have here, how long do you think it'll last us?"

"We spent a few hours going through it all today, actually," Priya replies. "It's hard to be sure, but we think we have enough food for at least eight weeks, and that's allowing for generous portion sizes and three meals a day. So, if we reduce the portion sizes and ration the food, it could probably last another week or two."

"And we should be able to continue to supplement with fish and rabbits and mushrooms, so that'll help stretch it for another couple of weeks," Dean adds.

"Is that going to be enough if we need to stay here over the winter?" I ask.

"It'd be pretty touch and go," Ethan says, coming up behind me. "Once it snows up here, we'll be stuck for the next few months. The snow will last at least mid-way into spring. We'd need about twelve weeks from when the snow starts and that's still weeks away." He sits beside me.

"So, we just hunt more," Dean says matter-of-factly.

"Yeah, we can try," Ethan replies. "We could set more snares and if we could get a few deer, we could dry the meat and we'd be able to store it."

"What about pigs?" Ollie says as he joins us. "We saw wild pig tracks earlier," he explains to Dean and Priya.

I see a grin spread across Ethan's face. "They're pretty rare up here, but we can try." He gives my knee a squeeze under the table.

"So, how long do we have before we need to make a decision?" I ask.

"Is there even a decision to make anymore?" Ollie replies. "What other option is there? We can't go down that gorge to Morrison and we can't go back to the Lodge. Where else is there? It's here or the bunker, and we can't get into the bunker."

"Yeah, I guess you're right." I suddenly feel uncomfortable at the realisation that we no longer have any other options.

"We're just going to have to make this work," Ethan says. "There is no other choice."

CHAPTER 28

I jolt awake in the dark bunkroom, the dawn light barely visible through a crack in the curtains.

"What the hell was that?" Matt calls out.

"It sounded like a plane," Jackson answers.

"Yeah, but it was flying so low," Matt replies. "I haven't seen any planes flying over here the entire time we've been up here."

"Maybe that means things are getting back to normal if planes are flying again," I say hopefully.

"That wasn't a regular plane," Jackson says. "It sounded like—"

The sound of a jet suddenly roars overhead, drowning out Jackson's voice. We all jump out of our beds, running outside as fast as we can, and in the dim light we see two fighter jets heading over the top of the mountain peaks further up the valley.

Ethan, Skye, and Dean come sprinting out of the trees in front of us, looking up at the sky as they run across the clearing.

"Did you see that?" Dean pants as he reaches us.

"That's rhetorical, right?" Ollie replies.

"Shhh," Priya says. "Can you hear that?"

We fall silent, listening. And then I hear it. Quiet but distinct, the sound of a helicopter somewhere in the distance.

"I can hear it, but I can't see it," Lily says, peering further up the valley. "Do you think we should get inside in case they come back this way?"

We look from one to the other, none of us having thought about the need to keep undetected.

"Yeah, that's probably a good idea," Marley replies.

"Wait!" Priya calls out, her arm pointing up the valley. "There!"

I narrow my eyes and then I see it. A small dot steadily growing as a helicopter crests the top of the mountains at the head of the valley. The two jets suddenly appear out of nowhere, sweeping past the helicopter and then immediately turn back toward it.

A split second before we hear it, we see it. We watch in stunned silence as the helicopter explodes in midair … and then the deafening boom slams into us. I flinch as the sound hits me and stagger backwards, covering my ears while the roar of the explosion continues to echo in the valley, and look on in horror as the helicopter disintegrates in slow motion until it falls out of sight.

"Get inside!" Lily yells as the jets complete their arc and turn back toward us. "Everyone get inside! They're coming back!"

We race inside the cabin and stand at the window, listening as the planes fly overhead and then fade into the distance.

I glance at the stove and am relieved to see that it's still cold and empty. "They will have seen the cabin," I think out loud. "But at least they wouldn't have seen smoke or signs of anyone being here."

"Shit, what about the solar lights?" Ollie says behind me, trying to look through the window.

"It's okay," I reply. "They're not on anymore."

Everyone begins talking at once, shocked, frightened, unsure of what we've just witnessed and what it means. But one thing is for certain though, the world is definitely not back to normal.

Skye picks up a backpack and starts grabbing first aid kits and ropes and other equipment. "We need to see if there are any survivors."

"No one could've survived that," Marley says. "It exploded in midair."

"Maybe. But we need to check," Skye replies. "Someone might need our help."

"It's not that simple, Skye." Marley shakes his head. "What if those people are infected? That's probably why it was shot down. If you go up there and one of them is sick, you're not only risking your own life, but the lives of every one of us here."

"What if it was you or someone you love who was in that helicopter? You'd want someone to help if they could."

"This isn't the time to be a hero, Skye. We need to put ourselves first, to protect each other, not people you don't know. Are you really prepared to risk our lives so you can help a stranger?"

"I'll go alone then. I won't approach anyone if I think they could be infected."

"Oh, come on, Skye, be realistic," Marley huffs. "How would you be able to tell if someone who is injured and covered in blood is infected or not? You can't know. Don't do this!"

"Look, I understand what you're saying. But this is something I *have* to do. I can't just ignore what we saw. If I find survivors, I'll wait a couple of days to make sure they aren't showing symptoms first. I won't bring them back until I'm sure they aren't infected. I promise not to put any of you at risk."

"I'll come with you," I say. "I won't go near any survivors, but I'll come with you to make sure you get there okay." I look at Marley. "I'll quarantine as well if I think I've been exposed. I won't put anyone else at risk."

"I'll go too," I hear Dean say as I head into the bunkroom. "Same deal as Jess. I'll just be part of the escort party."

"Yeah, I'm coming too," says Ethan.

"Pack food and tents and bring the stretcher in case we need it. We leave as soon as we're ready," Skye instructs.

Marley approaches me as I'm putting the final items into my backpack and hands me a small can of lighter fluid. "Take this, just in case."

He doesn't need to tell me what it's for. The memory of those burning bodies is seared on my brain. I nod and place the can in my pack.

Ethan and I lead the way up the valley, familiar with the route we need to take at least as far as the bunker. We walk quickly, much faster than we have on previous days, a sense of urgency that lives may depend on us driving us to get there.

Skye takes the lead after we pass the forest near the bunker, using the pillar of smoke from the crash as her guide. She picks up the pace and charges ahead, going so fast I have to jog occasionally to keep up.

As we begin to find debris from the helicopter, Skye suddenly dashes away from us and stops a couple of metres from something lying on the ground. When we reach her, I see it isn't part of the helicopter. It's the body of a woman. We don't get close to her; there's no point, she's clearly dead. Even if she'd survived the explosion, there's no way she could've survived that fall.

We see the wreckage well before we reach it, smoke billowing from the helicopter's shell.

"Skye!" Ethan yells as she breaks into a run. "Not too close, okay? We need to check things out first."

Skye slows as she arrives at the crash site, then stops and scans the area in front of her. The site is a mess of mangled metal, barely recognisable as a helicopter. Only the ragged remains of the passenger compartment are left; the front has been blown off and the tail completely severed from the body by the impact. It lies motionless on its side with its one remaining skid facing us.

"Over here." Dean runs toward a body partially covered by debris. I stay back as Ethan and Skye help him carefully lift the metal away from the body and watch as they shake their heads at each other and immediately move on.

Skye walks toward the helicopter and pulls herself up onto the landing skid, using it to stand on. I take a deep breath and haul myself up beside her. She glances at me when I join her, then we lean over the top of the compartment and look inside. The smoke we'd seen from a distance is coming from inside the passenger compartment and the smell is overwhelming. And then I see the charred remains of bodies. I don't know how many—four or five, maybe more. I gag as I realise what the smell is and jump down from the helicopter skid. I take a few steps before I drop to my knees, taking deep breaths, trying to suppress the urge to vomit.

"Is that the first time you've seen a dead body?" Skye asks behind me.

"You mean apart from the other two we saw earlier?" I reply snarkily. I don't have the energy to deal with Skye being nasty right now.

"The first time is definitely the hardest," she says quietly. "I'd like to say it gets easier, but it doesn't really. You just get better at finding ways to deal with it."

I look up at her, surprised she isn't mocking me. "What about this time?"

"This is about as bad as it gets." She holds out her hand to help me stand. "I didn't really think they would be alive, but I had to make sure. Thank you for coming with me."

"I just didn't want you to come up here alone."

"I'm going to check the rest of the crash site." She nods in acknowledgement and walks away.

"Are you okay?" Ethan asks as he and Dean walk over.

"Yeah. I wouldn't recommend looking inside the helicopter though. Skye's checking out the area on the other side of it."

"We should probably keep looking around too," Ethan says. "The sooner we can get out of here, the better."

"Why don't we stick together, Jess?" Dean puts his arm around my shoulder and gives me a squeeze as he notices my hands still shaking.

"Thanks." I nod, grateful for his company.

Dean and I begin lifting debris to check underneath, slowly moving away from the main crash site toward the tail of the helicopter. Near the tail is a large piece of metal, torn from the side with letters saying 'ACOBS INDUS'.

"Oh my god," I say. "Ethan! Skye!"

"What's the matter?" Dean asks. "Why are you yelling?"

Ethan and Skye both come running. They look confused when they reach us and don't see a body. "What's going on? Are you okay?" Ethan looks us both up and down.

"What was the name of the man who owns this land, the one who built the bunker?" I ask breathlessly.

"Jack Jacobs," Ethan answers. "Why?"

I point at the letters. "I think this used to say Jacobs Industries … This helicopter must have been taking people to the bunker."

"I thought you said he died years ago?" Dean says.

"He did, but he had two sons," Skye answers. "They used to come up here with him too. They've been running the family business since Jack died."

"I think you're right, Jess," Ethan says. "This can't be a coincidence. They must've decided it was time to get to the bunker."

"Thomas had kids." Skye looks at Ethan. "I can't be sure, but some of the bodies in the helicopter looked small. They could have been children." She folds her arms across her stomach as though she's in pain. "Does that mean this was Tom and his family in that helicopter? Oh my god, why would anyone shoot down a helicopter carrying kids?"

"They must've thought they were trying to cross into Morrison." Ethan puts his arm around her. "They couldn't have known they were only planning to come this far."

"There's a bigger picture here, guys," Dean says. "We've had no news of what it's like out there for over a week. The fact that people are trying to escape to bunkers and the air force is shooting down anyone trying to fly across the border has got to tell us it's a complete mess out there."

"I think we need to head back to the cabin and let the others know what we've found out. They'll be worried about us," I say. "If we leave now, we'll be able to get back before dark."

"What about their bodies?" Skye asks. "We can't just leave them like this. We need to bury them."

"I know you knew these people, Skye, but we shouldn't be touching their bodies," Dean says. "We can't risk it in case they were exposed to the virus."

"We can't just leave them lying out here. Scavengers will eat them. We just can't …" her voice breaks.

"There's another reason we shouldn't leave the bodies to scavengers," I say, pulling the lighter fluid out of my pack. "If they're infected, maybe it will infect the animals too. The soldiers burned the bodies of those people for a reason. I think we probably should as well."

"You brought lighter fluid?" Ethan asks.

"Marley gave it to me before we left."

"Good old Marley," Dean says. "Always two steps ahead."

"I'll take care of it," I say to Ethan and Skye. "You knew these people. You shouldn't have to do this."

"Thank you." Ethan nods and puts his arm around Skye, guiding her out of the crash site.

"I'll help." Dean follows me as I walk toward the body that he and Ethan had uncovered earlier.

I squirt lighter fluid along its length, trying not to look too closely at it as I do. Dean lights a match and throws it on the body. It ignites immediately and we move on to the helicopter.

"Don't look inside," I say as we climb onto the landing skid. "You don't want this image in your head."

"Okay, thanks, I won't." Dean nods, then puts his hand on my arm as I'm about to open the can of lighter fluid. "As soon as I throw the match in, we should get away as quickly as we can. Just in case it explodes or something."

"Right, I hadn't thought of that. Good thinking."

Dean stays back from the edge as I lean forward and pour lighter fluid into the compartment. He waits for me to move away, then lights a match and throws it through the opening. We hear a whoosh as the lighter fluid ignites and leap from the helicopter, sprinting as fast as we can to get as much distance between us and the helicopter.

A large popping sound bursts from the helicopter and Dean slams into me, throwing me to the ground, covering me protectively with his body while we wait for it to explode. The popping turns into crackling and then stops altogether.

Dean rolls off me and helps me to stand. As he dusts himself off, I impulsively grab him in a hug. "Who'd have thought you'd be such a hero? Literally putting your body on the line to protect me!"

Dean starts to chuckle quietly. I stand back and look up at him in surprise as it turns into a full-blown belly laugh. *Maybe he's suffering from post-traumatic shock?*

Tears run down Dean's face as he looks down at me, gulping deep breaths. "I tripped."

"You what?"

"I wish I could take credit for it. I really do. But the truth is, I tripped and fell on you," he says wryly.

I raise my eyebrows at him. "As far as I'm concerned, an accidental hero is still a hero."

"I'm not sure I want the accolade, to be honest." Dean shakes his head, taking a deep breath. "Playing the hero is a sure-fire way to get yourself killed." He picks up my backpack and hands it to me. "Come on, we've still got work to do." He puts on his own pack and begins walking away from the crash site.

I throw my bag over my shoulder and hurry to catch up with him. A few minutes later, we see Ethan and Skye waiting for us near the body of the woman we'd found when we first arrived.

"You carry on, we'll catch up." I wave Skye and Ethan on. They nod and silently turn away, continuing toward the riverbank.

I try not to look directly at the twisted body of the woman, focusing on the ground instead. I don't want to see this. I don't want the details of her face imprinted on my brain.

My hands tremble as I pour the last of the lighter fluid and wait for Dean to set it alight. My chest tightens as we turn away from her. I need to cry, but the tears don't come. As though reading my thoughts, Dean takes my hand and squeezes it tightly. I cling to it and the comfort it provides, and glance quickly up at his face. He swallows hard, fighting to hold back tears, and I realise he needs this as much as I do. After a minute, he releases my hand and puts his arm around my shoulder, giving me a quick hug, then we continue on in silence until we catch up with Ethan and Skye.

"If they'd got here, they would've unlocked the bunker," Skye says to Ethan. "They would've helped us. I know they would have."

"Yeah, they would've," Ethan replies. "And we would've helped them too."

"And now that bunker is just going to sit there, unable to help anyone. Everything they did to prepare for something like this and it was for nothing and now they're dead. They were good people. They didn't deserve this … and Emily's gone too." She bursts into tears and stops walking. Ethan puts his arms around her and holds her as her body shakes with each sob.

"Do you remember the time we went on that hunting trip with them when I was about nine?" Ethan says as they walk again. "Tom and Joe would've been, what, sixteen and seventeen? And Jack found out that Joe had taken credit for that deer you shot and Tom said nothing. I remember he was so angry at them, going on and on about the importance of being men of honour. He said the Jacobs family name carried a lot of responsibility. It was a name that people trusted and he would disown them if they brought shame to it."

"Sounds like he was pretty big on the whole family honor thing," Dean whispers to me as we walk behind.

"Yeah, well, their company *was* called Jacobs Industries," I whisper back. "I guess their name was their brand. It was the key to everything."

Jacobs is the key!

"Six letters," I blurt out. "It's got six letters!"

"What are you talking about?" Dean gives me a confused look.

"Jacobs is six letters. Numbers on the keypad can represent letters." The words tumble out of my mouth. Ethan and Skye stop and turn to stare at me. "Instead of it being a numerical code we're looking for, it could be a password!" I jump up and down as I put it all together. "Jacobs could be the passcode to get into the bunker!"

CHAPTER 29

I break into a run as we cross the clearing, too excited to walk the last few metres. But as soon as I reach the door, I hesitate. *What if I'm wrong? I will have built up everyone's hopes for nothing.*

"Come on!" Ethan says impatiently beside me. "What are you waiting for?"

"Here goes nothing," I mutter. I reach up to the keypad, looking for the small letters underneath each number, and punch in the code for JACOBS. My hand shakes as my finger hovers above the OK button. I take a deep breath and press.

There's a click and then the sound of something moving within the door. My heart thumps as I turn the five-spoke wheel as fast as I can until it won't move any further, then pull the handle. The door is heavy, but it begins to move. Ethan grabs the handle to help, and the door opens.

I stand in astonishment, overwhelmed with relief, but only for a second. I burst out laughing as whoops of joy erupt behind me and I'm lifted off the ground and swung around. We all grab each other, jumping up and down, bubbling with excitement.

"Come on," Dean says. "Let's take a look inside our new home!"

The steel door is enormous, probably thirty centimetres thick. It opens into a rectangular chamber big enough for ten people to stand comfortably, and there's another steel door at the end of the wall on the right-hand side. White hazmat suits hang on hooks along the wall with a bench seat underneath, and on the other side are two adjustable shower heads. There are also outlets in the middle of the ceiling and a drain covered by a grill on the concrete floor.

"I guess this is a decontamination room. You're supposed to wash off radioactive dust in here before you go in the bunker," Ethan says as he opens the door at the end of the room.

The second door also has a five-spoke wheel, but no lock this time. Ethan grunts as he pulls it, not expecting it to be so heavy, but it moves more easily than the outer door. Lights automatically turn on as it opens, and we follow him into a small L-shaped passageway surrounding the decontamination chamber. There are shelves on the wall just inside the doorway stacked with towels and what looks like jumpsuits. More shelves line the wall at the end of the room with racks just above ground level. I assume for placing boots or other equipment that you don't want to bring into the interior. An ordinary wooden door marks the exit at the foot of the L around the corner.

"It's like a maze to get in this place," I say.

"It'll be to reduce exposure to gamma rays from a nuclear explosion," Ethan explains. "Gamma rays travel in straight lines, so if you build access with right angles, it prevents it getting inside. That's why the doors are so thick. They're probably lead-lined too."

Sensor lights instantly turn on when Skye opens the door, revealing an interior that feels more like we've walked into an apartment than a bunker. We enter a large living room with polished concrete floors and decorative rugs. Sofas and armchairs surround a large square coffee table in the area closest to the outer wall.

"It's so warm in here." Dean follows us into the room.

I bend and touch the floor. Instead of cold concrete, it feels warm. "It feels like there's some kind of underfloor heating."

"It's probably geothermal," Ethan says. "Remember the chimney we found and all the steam? I said I thought there was probably a hot spring down here. The whole area will be warmer because of it."

I continue to gaze around the room. There's an enormous bookshelf against one wall, packed full of books, and a cabinet beside it. In the middle of the room is a large rectangular wooden table with twelve seats. The back of the room is taken up by a kitchen with an electric stove top and extractor overhead.

"Oh my god, there's even a fridge!" Skye calls out from the

kitchen. We open cupboard doors and find the kitchen is fully stocked with pots and pans and plates. Everything you would expect in a normal kitchen at home.

"Come and check this out," Dean calls from the other side of the kitchen wall.

We follow Dean's voice through a doorway opposite the one we'd just entered, into a wide passageway. Immediately through the door on the left is a staircase heading up to a second floor. A bannister runs the length of the passageway in front of us to where another staircase descends to the floor below. The staircases fitting into the same area, one directly above the other.

"There's a shower!" Dean calls out from a room on the right.

We excitedly squeeze into the doorway to confirm what he said is really true, and as promised, it contains a shower cubicle … with a shower … and it works!

I rush to the next door along the hallway, already suspecting what it contains. "Yes!" I exclaim. "An indoor toilet! No more trips to the loo in the dark!"

Dean opens large cupboard doors and discovers a storeroom stacked with shelves of towels, sheets, blankets, and clothes. There are jackets and hats, trousers, tops, socks. Everything you can think of and each pile neatly labelled to tell you what is stored there and whether it is 'Adult' or 'Child'. Further confirmation that they'd been planning to bring an entire family here.

"Up or down?" Ethan calls out.

"Up," Dean replies, and they walk back to the staircase and begin to climb the stairs. Skye and I run to catch up, not wanting to be left behind.

There's a door at the top of the staircase and this time Dean has to feel along the wall on the other side until he finds a light switch. We enter a long passageway that runs the length of the bunker. The hallway is lined with doors, all of them open to reveal bedrooms, another shower room and a toilet. There are four bedrooms—two have queen-sized beds and the other bedrooms contain two sets of bunk beds in each. There's a ladder attached to the wall at the end of the passageway on the left, leading to a trapdoor in the ceiling.

I point to the ladder. "I'd be willing to bet you a week of dishes that leads to the escape hatch on the ledge we found."

"I'd say you're probably right," Ethan replies.

"There are enough beds for twelve people here and there are twelve seats at the table downstairs," Dean says. "But there weren't twelve people on that helicopter."

"So, you think more people might be coming?" I ask.

"I don't know," Dean replies. "But it's something to consider."

"We should probably mention it to the others once we're all back together," Skye says.

"Let's see what's downstairs," Ethan calls from the stairwell.

We follow him back down the stairs, then around to the top of the other staircase, descending to the door at the bottom. Ethan opens the door and feels for a light switch, turning it on, and we follow him into a huge room that runs the entire length and width of the bunker.

"Holy crap!" Dean says as he looks around.

I'm speechless. The amount of thought and effort that has gone into building this place. The back of the room is lined with rows of shelving, all packed with what looks to be food and other items. The other half of the room is full of wooden planter beds, and hanging directly above them are rows of lights. There are barrels lining the wall and then there's another set of shelves containing plastic containers and books, with a fridge beside it. I walk over to the fridge and open the door and immediately feel a rush of cold air. It's full of plastic containers labelled 'Carrots', 'Tomatoes', 'Lettuce', 'Beans' and on and on.

"It's a seed bank," I whisper under my breath.

There are books stacked on the shelves and I scan through some of the titles: *How to Grow Food Indoors*, *Indoor Kitchen Gardening*, *Survival Gardening*. The barrel is labelled 'liquid fertiliser'.

"Washing machine!!" Dean yells out from further down the room near the food shelves. "And a dryer! And a freezer! And another fridge!"

"I can't believe all this," Skye says as I walk down to join them. "There's everything we could possibly need here. There's enough food to last us for months, probably longer."

"And it's set up so we can grow fresh food too," I say. "There are containers of different seeds in a fridge down there."

I feel almost light-headed at the relief of knowing we're going to be okay. We now have enough food to last us the winter.

I walk over to a small room built under the staircase and try to open the door, but it's locked. "I wonder what's in here?" I say to myself. No keypad on this one. I look around with the vague hope of finding a key hanging nearby, but I can't see anything.

"Is it locked?" Ethan comes up behind me.

"Yeah, there must be a key somewhere. I'll have a look around for it later."

"Hey, there's another door back here. It's got a combination lock," Dean calls out.

We follow his voice to the back of the room behind the shelves of food, and sure enough, there is another solid steel door with a combination lock.

"I've already tried *Jacobs* and it didn't work," Dean says.

"A mystery for later then." Ethan shrugs. "There's another door over there. Surely this has to be the last one." Ethan points at the door at the other end of the room past the rows of planter beds.

We walk to the door, and Ethan opens it. A wave of warm, humid air floods into the room, but we can't see anything apart from some lights flashing in the darkness. There's a lever beside the door with the word 'Lights' on it. "I guess they couldn't have made that much more obvious." He laughs as he pulls it.

"Woah," Dean says, echoing all our thoughts.

"This is amazing," Skye says.

I'm speechless for the second time in less than five minutes. In front of us is an enormous cavern. The roof of the cave is so high I can't see it in the lights that illuminate the area in front of us. There's machinery at the far end, and as we walk across the rocky soil, I see pipes entering the ground beneath it and a chimney disappearing up into the darkness. The hum of machinery fills the air.

"I knew it!" Ethan says excitedly. "It's a mini-geothermal power plant! This is awesome!" He looks at us when we don't react. "Okay, obviously you have no idea how awesome this is. Let me explain. This generator uses the heat from the Earth to create steam to generate power twenty-four hours a day, 365 days a year. It won't run out. It doesn't create any pollution. And once it's built, the energy is free."

"Wow, that *is* awesome," Skye says.

"I already knew all that, you know," I whisper into Dean's ear.

"Me too," he whispers back. "I just wanted to see if he did."

"So," Dean says more loudly. "Are we staying in our new five-star accommodation tonight or are we going back to the cabin to tell the others?"

"If it's alright with you guys, I'd like to stay here tonight," Skye says. "I'm completely knackered. It's been a big day for a lot of reasons and I'd rather we told them tomorrow."

She looks exhausted and I realise I am too. The excitement of getting into the bunker has kept us going, and I'd forgotten that Skye and Ethan were also dealing with the death of their friends on that helicopter. I don't think I'd have much energy left to walk any further today either.

"That's okay with me," I say. "If we leave early in the morning, we'd still have time to bring everyone back here for tomorrow night."

"Yeah, I'm okay with that." Dean nods.

"Race you for the shower," Ethan says, pushing Dean aside and darting back through the door as Dean races after him up the stairs.

"There *are* two showers." I smile at Skye.

"Let's just hope there's unlimited hot water." She smiles back.

****

"I will *never* take for granted having a shower again." I flop into an armchair by the coffee table. The others finished their showers before me and we're all dressed in clean clothes from the cupboard in the hallway.

"Here." Dean hands me a steaming cup.

The smell of coffee wafts from the mug. "Oh my god, there's coffee! Thank you."

"There's pretty much everything." Dean replies. "It's like a supermarket down there. A supermarket *and* a pharmacy *and* a hardware store. It's not just food, there's medicine too. I looked in the fridge downstairs and it has antibiotics and other medicines in it. There are tools and everything you could think of that you might need, from duct tape to nails and shovels, electrical wiring ... everything."

"What are you reading?" I say to Ethan, who's flicking through pages in a ring binder.

"It's an instruction manual for this entire place." Ethan looks up at me. "There are engineering and maintenance plans for everything. The ventilation system, the pump, the power generator, the air-

215

cooling system, security system. Come and have a look." He pats the sofa next to him. "You know that room under the stairs in the basement? It's an armoury. That's why it's locked."

"Why would you lock your ammunition separately? You already have to get through that beast of a door to get in here," Dean says.

"They probably want to keep it locked because of the kids," Skye answers.

"Right, of course," Dean says. "What about the door with the combination lock? Is that marked on the plans?"

"Yeah, it says 'Laboratory'. It looks like it extends underground quite a long way," Ethan replies. "It seems weird that it uses a different access code though. Don't you think?"

"It's probably for the same reason the armoury has a separate lock," I say. "I guess they don't want the kids getting in there."

"Yeah, probably." Ethan nods.

"There's an inventory of all the supplies." Skye shows me the folder she's holding. "It's broken down into categories. God, they've been thorough."

I scan along the books on the shelf. There are first aid books, survivalist medical books, engineering, farming, history, encyclopedias, beginner's guides to everything from plumbing and electronics to making radios and then a wide range of fiction. It would take years to read everything here. At least half is for reference or educational purposes, and half for pleasure.

"Has anyone looked in here?" I point to the cupboard doors beside the bookshelf.

"Yeah," Ethan says, flicking through pages in his folder and holding it out to show me. "It's a home theatre system. According to this, there's a projector up in the ceiling and it projects onto the wall behind us here." He points at the blank exterior wall behind the sofa.

"So, all we need is popcorn," I say.

"There's popcorn downstairs in aisle two, middle shelf." Skye reads from her inventory list. "Condoms are on the bottom shelf of aisle three by the way, Dean."

"Why would I need to know that?" Dean replies innocently, trying to look offended.

"I was thinking maybe you and Priya should take one of those double rooms," Skye says. "Would save the rest of us from having to keep knocking every time we enter the bunkroom."

Dean raises his eyebrows, trying to work out if she's joking. "I'll talk to Priya about it, but I'm sure she wouldn't say no to a bit of privacy if everyone's okay with us having it."

I glance at Ethan. Skye doesn't seem to be bothered by Dean and Priya being together. *Maybe it would be okay if she knew about us?*

"Fine by me," Ethan says without looking up from his manual.

"Me too." I smile at Dean.

"Let's bring it up with the others tomorrow, but I can't imagine anyone objecting," Skye says. "It's not as if anyone else needs their own room, do they?"

"Unless of course, you and Matt finally stop pretending you're not keen on each other." Dean grins at me.

I swallow uncomfortably, feeling my cheeks blush and very aware that Ethan's head has shot up to look at me. I avoid looking at him and focus on Dean. Skye is staring at me too.

"Why would you …" My voice sounds constricted, unnatural as I speak. "I don't know what you're talking about," I finally manage to say.

"Oh, come on, Jess," he teases. "Everyone can see what's going on between you two. You've been almost inseparable, and on the few occasions when you are apart, Matt doesn't stop talking about you when you're not around."

"I think you're mistaking good friendship for something else." I laugh. "He's like a brother to me."

"Well, I don't know about you guys, but I certainly don't look at my sister the way he looks at you," Dean replies, laughing. "Where I come from, that sort of relationship with your sibling is kinda frowned upon."

I look at Skye and then Ethan, shaking my head. "Seriously, it's not like that. We're just really good friends."

"Sure, whatever you say." Skye raises her eyebrows at me.

"Whatever you guys get up to is your business." Ethan shrugs and looks back down at the folder on his lap. "You don't owe us an explanation. You can do what you want."

Even though I'm sure he doesn't mean it, I'm taken aback by his words. I study his face, wondering if that's how he really feels. But whether he means it or not, one thing is very clear, what's going on between us is still a secret and he wants it kept that way.

"Who's up for some beef stew and mashed potatoes for dinner?" Skye says, putting down the inventory book.

"Sounds good to me," Ethan replies. "I'll help."

Fifteen minutes later, we're sitting at the table eating reconstituted mashed potato from dried potato flakes and canned stew. It tastes amazing.

"I have to say it feels different here," I say. "I hadn't realised until now, but I guess I've been feeling on edge ever since you guys saw those people at the Lodge. It's always in the back of my mind that someone else could be up here. But now that we're in here, knowing that no one can get through that door without the passcode, I feel like I don't have to worry about it anymore."

"Yeah, I get it," Dean says. "I feel the difference here too. It'll be good to have Priya and the others here tomorrow. I know they've been feeling worried about it as well."

After dinner, we take sheets from the hall cupboard and head upstairs to the bedrooms. Dean and Skye take the two double rooms and Ethan and I each take a separate bunkroom. Everyone is keen to make the most of the opportunity to have some space to ourselves after sharing tents and bunkrooms for the last few weeks.

Climbing into the fresh, clean sheets feels like luxury. Despite the temperature falling below zero outside, the bedrooms, like the rest of the bunker, are warm and there isn't any need for heavy covers. My head is so unused to sleeping with a pillow, it takes me a few minutes to get used to the feeling of the softness under my head. But I'm so tired after all the walking and the emotional rollercoaster of today that I quickly fall asleep.

I don't know what time it is when I wake. The room is pitch black, so dark I can't even make out my hand in front of my face. I hear a noise, a click of the bedroom door shutting.

"Ow, dammit!" Ethan mutters. "Jess, where are you? I can't see a bloody thing."

I reach up and flick the switch above me, turning on the light above my bed. We both wince and cover our eyes at its harshness.

"Okay," Ethan says. "You can turn it off now."

I turn the light off and feel Ethan's hands pat the bed, then he climbs in beside me.

"Hope you don't mind me dropping by. I figured we might not get this opportunity again for a while."

"Yeah, probably a good idea … because once Matt gets here, he'll want us to take one of those double rooms together." He doesn't reply, and I feel annoyed he didn't rise to the bait. "'Cos, you know, what *I* do, and *who* I do it with, is *my* business, right?"

"You know I couldn't let them think it mattered to me about you and Matt … or anyone else."

"But it wouldn't *really* bother you though, would it? If I did this with someone else?" I begin to kiss his neck.

"Yes," he says quietly.

"Yes, what*?*" I murmur innocently. I want him to have to say it out loud, to say that this means something to him.

"Yes, it *would* bother me."

CHAPTER 30

At some point during the night, we'd fallen asleep, and when we woke, Ethan had kissed me goodbye and silently crept back out of my room. It wasn't long after that Dean was knocking on our doors to wake us, keen to get back to Priya and the others.

We dress in the dirty clothes we'd been wearing yesterday and quickly eat breakfast before heading out the door with near-empty packs, only carrying a few snacks replenished from the bunker's supermarket. The only other thing we take with us is the stretcher that we'd brought with us yesterday. We would need it to help carry Jackson to the bunker.

It's barely light when we leave and we're bubbling with energy, excited at the thought of telling everyone the news of the bunker. We reach the forest surrounding the cabin in just over three hours, not just quicker because we're walking faster, but also because we decide to take a more direct route rather than following the river this time.

We don't arrive unannounced. Ollie appears to be on guard duty, wandering around the outside of the cabin with the rifle slung over his shoulder. He sees us coming and calls out to someone in the cabin before walking over to greet us. Priya darts out seconds later and runs to join us, leaping into Dean's arms when she gets to him. The two of them kiss, oblivious to everyone around them.

Then the rest of our friends appear around the corner of the cabin. Everyone's talking, wanting to know about the helicopter. Did we find it? What did we see?

A whistle pierces through the voices, startling us into silence, and I'm surprised it came from Kai. "Let's give them a chance to get inside and then they can fill us all in at the same time."

Once we're seated in the cabin with hot drinks in hand, Dean begins to speak. He tells them about the helicopter and the bodies, reassuring everyone that we hadn't touched any of them and had burned their corpses before leaving in case they were infected. And then he tells them about our theory that the helicopter was carrying Tom Jacobs and his family with the intention of reaching the bunker.

Everyone listens intently, hanging on every word, shocked at the possibility that the helicopter contained the owners of the bunker. Their faces turning to horror when they realised that the air force had shot down a helicopter transporting children.

"And then Jess worked out the passcode to the bunker." Dean says it nonchalantly, as though it's an unimportant afterthought, but his face breaks into an enormous grin.

For a moment, no one says anything, unsure they've correctly understood because he'd said it so casually. Finally, Matt turns to me. "Are you saying you unlocked the bunker?"

I'm grinning from ear to ear, looking forward to their reaction. "That's *exactly* what we're saying."

The room erupts in screams of excitement, everyone jumping up and down, hugging each other. Matt drags me to my feet, hugging me, and then plants a big kiss on my lips before letting go. He grabs Dean and the two of them link arms and start jumping around doing some weird jig.

I throw my head back and laugh as I'm grabbed by person after person, everyone wanting to hug and celebrate, euphoric at this wonderful news. All of us united in our shared joy that our new family of friends will now have the best possible chance of survival.

It takes a while, but eventually the excitement calms, and we start to make plans. Everyone wants to get to the bunker as soon as possible to see our new home. We discuss what we want to take with us, agreeing to take all the perishable food and leaving the canned food behind. We take some tents and sleeping bags, but not all of them, deciding to come back for the rest later. Today our priority is to get everyone to our new home, and we'll need to carry Jackson, who still isn't able to walk.

****

Priya, Lily, and Jackson are completely stunned when they see the steel doors for the first time, but soon join in the excitement as we cross the clearing. Everyone falls silent while I enter the passcode, watching eagerly behind me. I hold my breath, suddenly feeling anxious as I enter the pin. *What if it doesn't open this time?* There's a click as soon as I press 'OK', and I quickly begin spinning the spoke wheel to unlock the door. Dean leans forward to help pull it open, revealing the decontamination chamber inside.

The four of us stand back, letting the others in first, knowing how keen they are to see inside. Once everyone has entered, we take them on a tour of the bunker, showing them the bedrooms upstairs and the supermarket and seed bank below, then out into the cavern behind. It feels a bit like an over-excited birthday party, except one where the guests open every drawer and cupboard to find out what treasures are stored inside.

Before long, Priya creates a booking system for the showers after a queue forms in the passageway. Bedrooms are allocated, and Dean and Priya take the double room that Dean slept in last night. Marley gets the other double room after the boys draw straws (in this case, twigs). One bunkroom is assigned to the remaining four boys and the other to the girls.

"It feels like Christmas," Kai says, taking a book off the shelf and flicking through the pages. "Dean said there's even a home entertainment system, so we'll be able to watch movies!"

"Yeah, it does feel like that," I reply. "If we forget everything that's happened and why we're here, we could almost pretend that we're just a bunch of friends on holiday together."

"Yeah, I like that. Let's just pretend that for a while." Kai gives me a hug. "Happy holiday, Jess!"

The celebratory atmosphere continues through dinner, all of us sitting at the table to enjoy what feels like a feast after the last couple of weeks of rations. We even have music playing after Jackson works out how to use the entertainment system. We eat and talk and laugh and enjoy being together again, safe in the comfort of our new home.

We agree that there's a lot of planning to do, but for tonight, we're going to have fun. Tomorrow the work will begin.

After dinner, the music is turned up and Ollie and Lily began pulling everyone up to dance, even Jackson with his crutch. Although the songs aren't recent, they're ones we all know and as each one starts, we cheer as we recognise it and our mish mash of dance moves resume all over again.

An arm goes around my shoulder and I turn expecting to see Ethan. Instead, I look into Matt's smiling face. I'm already smiling and wrap my arm around his waist and then take his hand and try to twirl him under our arms. He complies and ducks down, spinning under our joined hands, laughing.

"Hang on," he says, tugging his sling off over his head.

"How does your shoulder feel?" I yell over the music.

"Yeah, it's much better. I don't need to wear this all the time anymore, but Skye said I should try to wear it for another week if I can."

He takes my hand in his and puts his other one on my waist and we begin to dance together.

"Don't tell me you know how to waltz?" I look up at him.

"No, but I know how to step side to side a bit without standing on your feet. I wouldn't call it dancing exactly, but it's got to be better than nothing."

I laugh as he pulls me closer and I rest my head on his shoulder. "Learning to dance isn't on your list then?"

"I'm thinking of adding it." He gently pushes me away and then spins me around.

"I think you can probably tick it off already."

He puts his arm back around my waist and leans closer so he can speak without yelling. "I was worried about you when you left. I wanted to come with you, but I felt like I would probably be more of a hindrance than a help at the moment."

"That's sweet that you were worried. But you know you didn't need to. Skye, Ethan, and Dean are probably the most capable people in our group. I couldn't have been in safer hands."

"Yeah, I know," he replies. "But I—"

"You two are looking pretty cosy," Ethan says, slapping his hands on our shoulders.

Matt flinches, immediately pulling away, and I realise Ethan's hand is on his injured shoulder.

"Are you okay?" I say to Matt.

"Yeah, I'm fine," he says, looking pale. "Just think I'll sit down for a bit."

"Oh, shit, I didn't think! I'm such an idiot. I'm really sorry!" Ethan follows Matt to the seat, leaving me standing by myself.

I study Ethan's face as he sits next to Matt, helping him to put his sling back on. *He didn't do that on purpose, did he?*

I reluctantly turn away and head over to Jackson, who's now dancing while sitting in a seat in the middle of the room. I take his hand and dance with him, while occasionally glancing over at Matt and Ethan, who are still talking to each other.

After a while, I notice Dean and Priya are missing. Soon after that, Skye says she's going to go to bed. Marley comes over and says he's going to head up to bed and asks Jackson if he wants some help to get up the stairs.

Marley helps Jackson stand and we both support him as we make our way slowly up to the bedrooms. I've just returned to the bottom of the stairs when Ethan walks through the doorway from the living room, shutting it behind him.

"Are you off to bed too?" I ask.

"I was looking for you actually." He smiles, joining me at the bottom of the stairs. He puts his hands on the wall on either side of my head and then leans forward until our lips meet. I put my arms around him and pull him toward me.

"Were you trying to make me jealous?" he asks cheekily.

"No." I inhale sharply. "You didn't hurt Matt on purpose, did you?"

"Of course not." He pulls back. "You don't seriously think I would do something like that, do you?"

His eyes lock with mine. He looks genuinely shocked, but there's something more and it takes a second for it to register. It's hurt. My accusation hurt him.

"No, I don't think you'd do that. I don't know why I even said it."

"I feel pretty shitty about it to be honest. I thought it was his good shoulder because there wasn't a sling on it. I hadn't realised he'd taken it off."

"I'm sure Matt's not angry."

"No, he's not angry at all. He even told me it was *his* fault for taking the sling off." He leans forward until our faces are almost touching. "He's a nice guy, Jess, don't lead him on, okay?"

"What *are* you talking about?" I snap at him, trying to move away, but I can't. I'm stuck between him and the wall.

Before he can reply, the door to the shower room opens, the light shining into the passage. Ethan's head spins around and we see Skye silhouetted in the doorway as she reaches back in to turn off the light.

Ethan moves away from me onto the staircase and starts up the steps, calling back, "Night, Jess, see you in the morning."

I step away from the wall, intending to go back into the living room as Skye walks toward the stairs.

"Jess?" Skye says as I open the door.

"Yeah?"

"I … um…" She hesitates. "Oh, don't worry, it's nothing. Good night." She turns away and walks up the stairs, leaving me frowning at her back in confusion. *What was that about?*

I enter the living room just as everyone seems to be heading toward the door, the music no longer playing.

"We're calling it a night," Lily says. "We're all beat."

She gives me a hug and I stand back to let her through the door, waiting for Matt.

"How's your shoulder? Are you okay?"

"Yeah, it's fine. That'll teach me to take my sling off against doctor's orders." He chuckles. I narrow my eyes at him, unconvinced he's telling me the truth. "Seriously, Ma." He puts his good arm around my shoulder as we climb the stairs. "Now who's worrying too much?"

CHAPTER 31

After breakfast, we gather around the table for our first bunker meeting. Marley called the meeting, suggesting that we meet regularly to discuss jobs that need to be done and any issues that come up. He said we need to make sure that we operate like a proper community, dividing the workload and making sure everyone contributes equally. Otherwise, animosity and divisions will grow.

"So, are you the group leader then?" Lily asks Marley.

"No. I'm not sure we need a leader, but if we decide we need one, then we can vote on it. But I'm happy to lead this meeting for now though, if that's okay with you all."

We all nod, not sure how it should be run anyway.

"I think the first thing we should do is work out what we need to ensure our survival up here, then make sure that we're doing everything that needs to be done. We should identify jobs, allocate them and make sure we're all contributing. It's important that we all have a role in our community and feel a sense of purpose.

"So, the key things for survival are shelter, water, food. We've got the shelter and water sorted. Which leaves food," Marley continues. "Even though we've got a lot of food stored downstairs and we're fine for now, it won't last us forever and we don't know how long we're going to have to stay up here. We need to make that store of food last as long as possible. I think we should try to become self-sufficient."

"I completely agree," Skye says. "We've got the ability to grow our own vegetables all year-round downstairs. It'll take a while before it produces anything and it'll take a lot of work. But once we get it producing, we won't need to rely on canned food anymore. We can keep fishing and hunting just like we did at the cabin."

"Does anyone know much about growing vegetables?" Marley asks.

"My nan had a vegetable garden. I used to help her plant it every year. I have a pretty good idea of what to do," Kai says.

"I can help," Jackson offers. "I used to spend a lot of time helping my aunt and uncle on their farm when I was younger."

"I'd like to help with the garden too," Matt says. "I figure it's going to be pretty important, especially if I don't want to have to keep on eating meat."

"It'll take a while before there's anything ready to eat though," Kai says. "I think lettuce takes about a month. Other vegetables will be two months, even three."

"I saw a book downstairs about the fastest crops to grow," Jackson says. "We should probably sit down and make a plan before we plant. We don't want to get this wrong."

"I can gather mushrooms and roots and other plants that grow wild around here in the meantime," Skye adds. "I found a good survival guide that includes wild edible plants that'll help give me some other ideas too."

"How about I help you with that?" Marley says. "The more of us who know what to look for, the better."

"Yeah, sure."

"Okay, great," Marley says. "And I assume Ethan, Dean, Priya, and Lily will continue with fishing and hunting duties?"

"Absolutely," Lily replies as the others nod in agreement.

"So, that's shelter, water, and food taken care of. What else?" Marley asks.

"I was actually thinking the shelter part is only partially taken care of," Ethan says. "There are a lot of systems in this place that will need to be kept maintained. There's the generator and the pump, the air filtration system, the water filtration system. There's a huge list of things. I think we need to have someone who understands how they all work in case something breaks down. I've already had a look through the manual and I understand the basics of most of it. I think I should probably be that person."

"I'd be interested in helping with that too," Ollie says. "I'm pretty good with electronics and mechanical stuff. We should have more than one person who knows how it works."

"Yeah, I agree," Ethan says. "I'll still help with the hunting though."

"I know you all think I'm obsessed about this." Jackson holds up his hand, preemptively silencing our reactions. "The other thing we need to think about is security. We need to be prepared in case those people at the Lodge come up here … or anyone else, for that matter. We need to be able to protect ourselves."

"I agree," I say. "There have been a few of times that I've thought someone else might be up here. It made me nervous, not knowing if we're in danger. We need to be prepared. We should know how to protect ourselves, and we should have a plan so we know what to do. I'd be keen to help with that."

"I would too," Ollie says as a murmur of agreement spreads through the group.

Jackson looks relieved to have our support.

"On the floor plan it shows an armoury under the stairs in the basement," I say. "We need to find out what's in there and make sure everyone knows how to use it. We just need to find that key."

"It doesn't use the same passcode?" Jackson asks.

"No, it's not a combination lock. It's just a regular old key lock. We think it's locked because they were expecting to have kids here. The key has to be here somewhere. We just need to find it."

"If we can't find it, you can always try picking the lock," Kai says with a laugh.

"Let's see if we can find the key first." I feel myself blushing as everyone looks at me. "I was also thinking medical skills is something else we need to have. Maybe Skye could teach some of us so we have more people who can help in an emergency or if we get separated or something."

"I think that sounds sensible," Marley replies. "We need to make sure we have back up people for every core skill, just in case."

"Yeah, sure," Skye says. "Fine by me."

"Okay, I think we all know what our jobs are for now," Marley says. "We can have another meeting in a couple of days and see how we're all going."

Everyone heads off toward their job, so I decide to look for the missing key.

"Do you want a hand?" Ollie asks as he pulls the folder containing the operation manuals out of the bookshelf.

"That'd be great if you want to."

We search the entire living room and kitchen area first, looking in every cupboard, under the table, on top of door frames. We leave nothing unturned. We then head down to the basement where Matt, Jackson, and Kai are examining the contents of the seed bank and working out how long they take to grow. Kai is writing growing times in a notebook as they read out the details on the packets.

After half an hour of searching, I'm resigned to the fact that we might not find the key. "I think I might start trying to pick that lock," I say to Ollie.

"What do you need?"

I walk to the shelves full of tools and find a small flathead screwdriver and some wire, cutting off a piece. "This should do it."

I kneel in front of the door under the stairs and bend a kink into the end of the piece of wire. Inserting the screwdriver into the lock, I push the wire in and start to move it, feeling for the indentations of the pins inside. Ollie stands behind me, watching.

"This might take a while." I look up at him.

"I might head back upstairs and start studying that manual then. I'll check on you later."

"Okay, I'll let you know how I go."

I close my eyes to help focus, feeling for the pins inside the lock. Soon my shoulders and neck begin to ache as I constantly hold tension in my arms, not wanting to relax just in case I'm nearly there. After what feels like an eternity, the last pin finally lifts and I twist the screwdriver. Click. I turn the handle and the door swings open.

I collapse back on the floor in relief, a huge grin on my face. *I can't believe I actually did it!*

"Hey Jess, you won't believe what I've found," Matt calls excitedly from the end of the room.

I roll my head sideways on the floor to look over at him. He's holding up a key. I burst out laughing and kick the door wide open so he can see it's unlocked. "Your timing is impeccable, Matt."

"Oh my god, you actually picked the lock!" Kai exclaims.

They come rushing over to look. I open the door fully and reach inside, feeling for a light switch, and turn it on. The room floods with light and we all stare in amazement at the racks of guns lined along the wall—hunting rifles, shotguns, handguns. There are shelves stacked with boxes of ammunition and even bows and arrows, machetes, and some other nasty looking knives.

And then, the icing on the cake …

"Woohoo," Ollie yells as he and Skye join us in the room. "There's booze!"

On a shelf in the corner of the room are dozens of bottles of spirits and even more bottles of wine.

"Tonight, we celebrate!" Ollie picks up a bottle of vodka.

"Not with that you aren't." Skye takes it out of his hand. "We can use this as antiseptic if we need to."

"Fine," Ollie says, picking up a bottle of wine instead. "Tonight, we celebrate!"

****

It turns out we have more than one reason to celebrate when our hunters return with their first deer. They spend the next hour working outside on a plastic sheet to harvest the meat, filling the fridge with venison to feed us for the rest of the week and storing the rest in the freezer in the basement.

"That deer should provide us with all the protein we need for the next three or four weeks," Dean tells us when he returns from the basement. "There's more than enough room in the freezer for another if we can catch one."

"What about fish?" I ask, thinking of Matt. He's eating fish now, but I doubt he would eat the deer. "Do you think there are any good fishing spots up here?"

"There's a couple that look promising," Dean replies. "We'll take a closer look at them tomorrow."

"I think a bottle or two of red should complement the venison nicely, wouldn't you agree?" Ollie says, producing one of the bottles of wine he'd picked up earlier.

"Wow, where'd you find that?" Ethan asks.

"It was in the armoury," Ollie explains. "Jess picked the lock."

"You're kidding?" Priya says from the kitchen. "I can't believe you managed to do that!"

"You should come and take a look."

They follow me downstairs. I open the armoury door and turn on the light.

"Wow, look at all of this." Ethan picks up a rifle.

"We should all know how to use these. Do you think you could teach us?" I ask.

"Yeah, definitely," Ethan replies. "We can start tomorrow."

"Great, the sooner the better."

CHAPTER 32

Not long after lunch the following day, Ethan and I head out for my first shooting lesson. Even though I'm eager to learn, I'm surprisingly nervous at first, almost fearful. The gun feels dangerous, as though it might kill me for even touching it. But I swallow my nerves and take the rifle from Ethan and then adrenaline does the rest as I fire my first shot. The bullet misses the target entirely, but my aim improves quickly as Ethan teaches me how to time my breathing and adjust my stance to hold the gun steady. Before long, I'm hitting the target every time.

"Not bad," Ethan says as I hit the target exactly in the middle.

I'm just about to grab him in a celebratory hug when I hear Skye call out from behind us.

"Don't let him fool you, Jess. That's high praise coming from him."

I turn to face Skye, my smile as much from relief that she hadn't caught me hugging Ethan as it was to see her. "Hey, I thought there were rules about sneaking up on people with guns?"

"There are!" Ethan growls. "You should know better, Skye."

"I just wanted to see how you guys were going. I was curious to know whether I was going to lose my trainee medic to the hunting crew."

"You must've read my mind." Ethan smiles at her. "I was just about to suggest to Jess that she joins us on our hunt tomorrow."

"Oh, that's a shame. Because I was going to suggest we start first aid training tomorrow," Skye retorts.

"Maybe you could do that when we're finished," Ethan replies.

"Ollie and I thought we'd probably spend the whole day on it." Skye's eyes narrow. "That's what I came to tell Jess."

I have no idea what is happening here. Neither of them is looking at me. It almost feels like they're fighting over me, but something tells me it's more than that.

I look from one to the other. "If one of you tries to pee on me, I'm out of here."

Their heads jerk toward me, mouths gaping. I'm not sure if their surprise is from my comment or because they'd forgotten I'm even here.

"Actually, Jackson and I are going to start work on our security plan tomorrow." I ignore their stunned faces. "But I would love to join the hunting crew when you go out in the morning, Ethan, and maybe we could start the first aid training in the afternoon instead, Skye?"

"Fine by me." Ethan looks back at Skye.

"I'll tell Ollie we'll start in the afternoon then," Skye replies.

"We'll see you back at the bunker when we're finished here," Ethan says when Skye doesn't leave. "There's still a couple of things I want to go over before we finish today." Finally, he looks at me.

"Okay." I shrug. *What the hell is going on?*

"Fine, I'll see you later." Skye reluctantly turns and walks away.

Ethan watches her leave and as soon as she's out of sight, he packs the guns into the bag. "Come on, let's go for a walk."

"I thought you said you had something else you wanted to teach me?" I say as we start following the river upstream.

"It was more that I just wanted some extra time alone with you."

As he takes my hand and gives me a smile, butterflies take flight in my stomach. I can't believe that I still get nervous at the thought of being with him. I thought it would have started to feel more normal by now. I give his hand a squeeze, returning his smile.

****

It's nearly dark when we make our way back to the bunker. We walk hand in hand, not yet ready to let go of each other, knowing we won't be able to do this once we're back with the others.

"What was going on with Skye? You two were a bit weird with each other earlier."

"Yeah, looks like Skye's warmed up to you a bit. She certainly wants you to be her medical protégé." Ethan smiles at me.

"It's definitely been easier with her lately. At least it doesn't feel like she's blaming me for Emily anymore."

"Try not to hold that against her. Grief can have a strange effect on people. They want to blame someone for their pain, to make it someone's fault. Being angry seems to make it more bearable … for a while, anyway."

"I guess so," I reply. But I wouldn't know. I've never had to deal with that kind of grief before. "I got the feeling that Skye was checking up on us."

"I wondered that too. I think she may have picked up on something between us."

"If she has, she doesn't seem too upset about it."

"Maybe, but I don't think she's exactly thrilled about the idea."

"Do you think it's because she doesn't like me?"

"No, I don't think that's it. Skye never seems to approve of who I'm with. I used to think it was some kind of overprotective sister thing, but I'm not so sure that's it this time."

"So, do you think it would be a big deal if she found out about us anymore?" I feel awkward saying it, because I don't know what 'us' is. I know he likes me and I like him, but what are we to each other anyway?

"I don't know, but it isn't just Skye we need to think about here. What about the others? How do you think they'll react if we're suddenly together?"

"Does it really matter what they think?"

"Let me put it this way. How would you feel if Matt knew about us? Would you be comfortable with him seeing us together?"

I'm about to say that it wouldn't matter, but as the image of Matt's face flashes into my mind, I realise suddenly that it would. I know Matt isn't attracted to me. I heard him tell Skye as much. But deep down, something inside me says it's not that simple.

"I don't know. Maybe. I hadn't really thought about it."

"I know you keep saying nothing was going on between you guys and that you're just friends, but everyone else thinks there's more to it than that, and I see it too." He stops walking and turns to look at me. "I think it's one of the things I find most attractive about you. You're completely unaware of the effect you have on everyone around you … including me. But *also* on Matt. And as much as I'd like to ignore what the others think, I don't think flaunting our relationship in front of them, *especially Matt*, is going to make us all a happy family. We're all stuck with each other up here. So, I think we should try to keep things as amicable as we can, don't you?"

My brain whirrs as I try to process everything he said. *What effect do I have on people?* I've always been aware of my power to annoy and piss people off without much effort, but certainly not of any effect that would make someone attracted to me!

"What about Lily? You must've noticed how keen she was on you when we were at the Lodge … You're a good catch, remember?"

"How could I forget?" Ethan laughs. "She seems to have lost interest since we got up here though."

"I guess other things have taken priority. That, or your novelty wore off." I smile cheekily.

He pauses, studying my face as I grin up at him, and then puts down the gun bag.

"You really have no idea, do you?" He shakes his head, bending his face down to mine. "You smile your sexy little smile and you have no idea—" He cuts off his words as he kisses me, the intensity of his kiss moving us back until I'm pressed against a tree. His hands reach down, fingers intertwining with mine, making sure he has complete control over me. As though trying to retake the power he believes I have over him.

I take his face in my hands when he releases me, and peer into his eyes. *Does he really feel this way about me? No-one has ever used sexy in a sentence with me in it before. How could I possibly be having this effect on him?*

"I've just realised something." I laugh. "You're completely delusional. Either that or it's those mushrooms Skye found."

"See, that's exactly what I'm talking about." He shakes his head at me and picks up the gun bag. "Come on, we better get back."

I take Ethan's hand as we begin to walk and look up at him. He smiles and squeezes it affectionately. A few seconds later he lets go, using it to adjust his cap, then shoves his hand in his pocket.

The back of my neck prickles as I realise he doesn't want to risk anyone seeing us. My subconscious crying out for my attention. I try to ignore it, but I know what it's trying to tell me. Why are we doing this if we think it might cause problems? Because Ethan *is* right, we *are* stuck up here with each other. Is it really worth the risk?

But maybe it won't cause any trouble with the others?

Sure, maybe it won't, but you know this isn't going to last forever. You may be new to this, but you're not completely naïve.

Can't I just enjoy this while it lasts? If no-one else knows, no-one will get hurt?

But what about you? Because the reality is when this inevitably ends, it will end badly, as break ups tend to do, and then *you* will be stuck up here together.

Maybe it won't end badly? Can't we have just a little longer? I won't let myself get hurt. I promise.

But what about Ethan? Can you promise he won't get hurt?

I look up at Ethan as we walk, so confident, so strong, so sure. I can't imagine anything hurting him, especially me.

CHAPTER 33

Warm air, laced with the scent of venison stew, greets us as we enter the living room. We say hi to Priya, Dean, and Skye, working their culinary magic in the kitchen, then head down to the basement to return the guns to the armoury.

"Hey." Matt smiles as soon as we walk through the door. "How did your lesson go?"

"Great," Ethan replies. "She's a natural. As soon as your shoulder is out of that sling, I'll take you out for a lesson too. Maybe you'd be keen to have a turn in the next few days as well, Kai?"

"Sounds good," she replies. "I should have some time later tomorrow."

Ethan takes the guns to the armoury and I walk over to check out the row of new seedling trays covering the shelves. "Looks like you've been making good progress."

"Yeah, we've got the planting all planned." Kai holds out a notebook showing a diagram of the planter boxes with names of plants allocated to each area. "We've planted all the seeds in these trays and now we're getting the soil in the boxes ready."

She reaches behind my head and pulls a twig out of my hair, giving me a quizzical look.

"I got caught in a low-hanging branch," I reply.

"Right." She nods skeptically, reaching back up to my hair. "And there was grass on that branch too, was there?" She smiles cheekily, holding out the evidence for me to see as a tool clatters to the floor behind us.

I turn toward the source of the noise and Matt is staring at me, open mouthed. He looks from me to Ethan, who's avoiding eye contact with all of us, then back to me again. His jaw clenches as his lips pull together, eyes narrowing as they lock with mine, silently asking me if it's true. I look down, breaking eye contact for only a second before getting the courage to meet his gaze again, but it's all the confirmation he needs. He exhales a sharp huff of disbelief and bends down to pick up the dropped trowel.

"We'll transplant the seeds into the planter boxes once they've begun to sprout." Kai looks warily from Matt to me, wondering why Matt looks upset as he returns to his work, stabbing at the soil with his trowel. "That way we can be sure we're not wasting space on seeds that aren't going to grow."

"Sounds sensible to me." I nod, barely listening as I look from Matt to Ethan, who shakes his head at me. He lets out a small sigh, as if to say 'I told you so'.

"We've decided to plant potatoes in the cave too," Kai continues. "There are some spare grow lights and we thought we'd set some up in the cave so we can use that space as well. It's pretty rocky in there, but we figured if we brought in some soil, it would be a good way to extend our garden over the winter."

"That's a good idea." Ethan nods. "Looks like you guys have thought of everything. It'll be great to have some fresh food."

"Yeah, I guess we reap what we sow," Matt mutters to himself.

****

The room hums with conversation as we eat, everyone sharing their progress of the day and any discoveries they've made. Although Matt takes part in the conversation, he seems quieter than usual and has avoided talking to me or even looking at me since we left the basement.

Until Ethan had brought it up, I hadn't considered how Matt might react if he found out about us. It hadn't occurred to me that it would bother him because I thought Matt only saw me as a friend. But the hurt and disappointment I saw on his face told me that either his feelings have changed or he disapproves of me being with Ethan. And either way, it wasn't what I'd expected.

Although I'd had to push my feelings for Matt aside when I found out he didn't feel the same way as me, it hadn't stopped me caring for him. If anything, the opposite is true. His friendship means everything to me. I hate that I've hurt him, no matter how unintentionally, and I need to fix this, to talk to him. But now is definitely not the right time.

My attention returns to the conversation as everyone bursts into laughter at something Marley has said, and Matt's face breaks into a grin. He glances across the table at me and I smile as soon as our eyes connect. His grin falters briefly, and for a second I think he's going to ignore me, but then he nods and the smile returns to his eyes before he looks back at Marley. It isn't much, but it's all I need. This small gesture is his way of telling me we're going to be alright.

"And we even found a patch of wild asparagus!" Marley says. "It looks just like the ones you buy at the supermarket!"

"So, why aren't we having asparagus tonight then?" Lily asks.

"They were dying off. It's too late in the season," Marley explains. "But now we know where to look next spring!"

"I take it you like asparagus?" Jackson laughs.

Marley looks a little embarrassed when he realises we're all grinning at him. "It's more that I find this kind of fascinating, really. As you've probably guessed, I'm a rather theoretical kind of person. I read a lot. And for me, this is like theory brought to life. I've read about doing this but never imagined I'd actually be living it … you know … in the wild, living off the land to survive, that sort of thing."

"Yeah, I get it. It's like a real-life zombie movie," Ollie says. "Except without the zombies and the fighting for our lives part. But, hey, maybe there's still hope for that!" He grins. "I wonder if there are any zombie movies on the entertainment system? We should probably check—important survival research."

"I'm up for it if you can find one," I offer.

"Wouldn't have picked you for a zombie movie kind of girl," Jackson says.

"You're kidding! I love a good zombie movie. Science fiction, fantasy, post-apocalyptic … love it all."

"Star Wars?" Ollie asks.

"LOVE Star Wars!"

"No way! Are you real? Can I pinch you?" Ollie reaches out to pinch my arm.

"I think the whole pinching thing only works on yourself ... Ow, okay, okay, okay." I laugh as he pinches me. "You have your proof! No more pinching!"

"She's real!" he yells. "*You* are officially the perfect woman!"

"Because she's real?" Lily guffaws. "Why am I not surprised that would be your most important criteria to be considered perfect?"

After cleaning up the dishes, we move the sofas and chairs to face the back wall as Jackson selects a movie to play. Skye leaves as soon as she hears it's a zombie movie, saying it isn't really her thing, taking a book and heading to the bunkroom. Someone turns off the lights, and the room becomes completely dark, making the projection as clear as if we're at a cinema.

We would have been thrown out if we'd been watching in a real cinema though, all of us calling out as we watch. We chastise the characters for making predictable mistakes. "Why would you go in there? You know there's going to be zombies!"; "Don't let him go! He'll just come back and kill you later!"; "Don't split up, never split up!"; "Yeah, 'cos of course you wear skimpy shorts and a crop top in an apocalypse ... and she's wearing makeup!!!"

I smile at the normality of it all. Just a group of friends, hanging out and watching a movie together, not a care in the world. It's hard to believe we're actually living in a fallout bunker, built into a cave in the mountains, with no idea what is going on in the rest of the world. All we know is that it isn't safe to leave. We don't even know if our families are okay or if they're safe from the virus. As my eyes fill with tears, I force the thought of my parents from my mind. I don't want this moment to be sad. I need this sense of normality, even if it's only for a few hours.

This is exactly what movies are for, to escape your life, to take you to another place, another time, another reality. Maybe a post-apocalyptic movie wasn't the best choice then. But at least we don't have zombies.

I glimpse Ethan's head slumping forward from the corner of my eye. I have no idea how he can nod off with all the noise of the movie, but somehow, he has. He startles and drags himself from his seat toward the door, giving up the fight to stay awake. I watch him and wonder if I should follow and talk to him about what happened in the basement earlier.

After a few minutes, I get a drink of water from the kitchen, then head into the hallway. As soon as I close the door, I hear Skye's voice coming from above, drifting through the door left ajar at the top of the stairs. I turn to leave, realising there's no longer any chance of speaking to Ethan alone.

"What Jess and I choose to do is none of your business, Skye."

I freeze.

"It *is* if you're going to mess her around, Ethan. We're stuck up here together. She can't exactly go home when you get bored of her."

"I'm well aware of that," he says. "Thanks for pointing out the obvious. I'm not planning on messing her around, as you so nicely put it. Why do you always have to make me out to be the bad guy?"

"Ah … history! Maia, Katie, Sarah, Katie … Katie … Katie … Need I say more?"

"Come on, Skye, that's hardly fair. That's just how it is with Katie, you know that. It's as much her as it is me. We've always been like that."

"I thought you guys were back on again."

"We were, but it was just for the summer. It was going to be over once I started back at university anyway."

"When were you planning on telling Katie that? And what about Jess? When were you going to tell her? Or did you just figure you'd never have to see her again after the camp was finished?"

"Nothing happened between us until after we got up here, until after the camp. It wasn't like that."

"But I bet she doesn't know about Katie though, does she?"

"No, but why does it matter? It's not as if I'm seeing Katie anymore. Like I said, it was going to be over soon anyway."

"And Jess?"

The door slams into my back as it swings open behind me.

"Oh, sorry, Jess. I didn't know you were there. Are you okay?" Priya bursts through the door with Dean.

"I'm fine. I was just coming back in." I push past them and head straight to my seat. Grateful for the dark.

I know I shouldn't have eavesdropped, but as soon as I heard my name, I wanted to know what they were saying about me. I certainly wasn't expecting to find out that Ethan had … has a girlfriend. And even though everything with Ethan is so new and I could hardly consider him to be my boyfriend, I still feel betrayed. Disappointed. Foolish.

When the movie finishes, the lights turn on and we all make a move to head to bed. I turn toward the door and Ethan is standing beside the light switch. I glance away, avoiding eye contact. I'm not sure if he knows I overheard his conversation with Skye or not, but I'm not ready to talk about it. I need time to think.

"Night." I give him a small smile as I walk past.

"Can you stick around? I was hoping we could have a chat." He catches my hand, stopping me.

"Yeah, okay." I stand aside and let the others pass.

I follow stiffly behind Ethan as he walks to a sofa and sit next to him. My hands ball into fists. I'm not sure I'm ready for this.

"I was talking to Skye." Ethan's eyes probe mine, looking for a reaction. I realise he isn't sure if I overheard their conversation or not. "About us."

I nod, keeping my face blank.

"I think maybe … you might have overheard us?"

I nod again.

He swallows. "I know it sounded bad, but I want to explain."

"Okay." I shrug.

"I was already seeing someone when I met you—"

"Katie."

"Yeah, Katie."

"You told me you didn't have a girlfriend," I say flatly.

"Technically, I told you I didn't have a boyfriend." He grins.

"Don't be a jerk. You know exactly what I was asking you." I shake my head. "You lied to me."

"I know it might seem that way, but I don't think of Katie as my girlfriend. Katie and I have always been on and off. We've been like this since high school. We go out for a few months and then we stop and see other people. Sometimes she breaks it off and sometimes I do. It's so normal for us now we just expect it."

"Sounds romantic."

He takes a deep breath, eyes locked with mine. "I know you must think badly of me, but I swear, neither of us saw it as anything more than that. I wouldn't call that a relationship, would you?"

I shake my head.

"I didn't tell you about her because I didn't think it was important. I wasn't cheating on her because we had an understanding. I wasn't cheating on you because I was with you. I *am* with you. At least, I hope I still am?"

Now it's my turn to take a deep breath as I study his face, wishing I could read his mind and know for sure if he's telling me the truth, or just saying what he thinks I want to hear. I want to believe him, to let him make his excuses for deceiving me. Because he had. Whether he believes it or not, he had kept this information from me.

His eyes search mine, trying to guess what I'm thinking. I can see he's worried. I want to believe him, to trust him, to erase this … but I can't. And it isn't just this. I can't forget the look on Matt's face when he found out something was going on between us, confirming Ethan's warning to be true, that our relationship would cause problems if anyone found out.

"I don't know." My words take him by surprise—he hadn't expected this. "I don't know what to think. I like you Ethan, you know I do. But what are we doing? Like you said earlier, we're all stuck up here together. We don't have any choice but to live with each other. And this … us, you said it could cause problems and I think you're right. It's just going to end up hurting someone, and then what do we do?"

"Is this about Matt?"

I let out a sigh, trying to find the words to explain how I feel, when I'm not sure I understand it myself.

"No … well, yes. But not in the way you think. The way Matt reacted made me realise we shouldn't be doing this. You've got to admit that there's something wrong with what we're doing if we feel we need to hide it from everyone. It's not normal, Ethan. And I do understand why you felt we needed to hide it. You were right, it is going to create problems. But I don't think that's the only reason you wanted to keep this a secret. I don't think you wanted Skye to find out because of Katie."

"I wasn't trying to deceive you." He shakes his head. "I can see how it might look like that, but honestly, I wasn't. I just thought it would be better for everyone, especially Matt, if they didn't know about us.”

I look down at my hands. I don’t want to hurt him and I can see that I am. But I realise now that this is for the best, for both of us. This was only ever going to end badly and I’d been kidding myself that it wouldn’t. It’ll be a lot less painful if we end this now, before too much damage is done.

“I believe you. I do.” I take his hand. “But I think maybe we should slow things down a bit. Hit pause and just be friends while we see how this whole situation is going to work up here. We’re only going to be stuck up here for a few more months. Then when this is all over and we’ve managed to get out of here, we can try again, when we don’t have to worry about all of this complicating everything. Do you think we could do that, just be friends?”

“So that’s it? Just like that, you want to end this?”

I recognise the look in his eyes. Disappointment, hurt, the sting of rejection, trying to work out what he can say to fix this.

Be strong.

“I do. I think we should stop this now, before someone gets hurt.”

He shakes his head in frustration and goes to speak, then stops. Fighting an internal battle to stop himself from saying something that he might later regret. Finally, his shoulders slump in defeat and he sighs. “I really am sorry. I wish you hadn’t found out this way. I should have told you myself. I didn’t mean to hurt you.”

Be strong.

“You haven’t hurt me.” I swallow the lump in my throat. “But I think it’s probably for the best.”

He pauses and sighs again, then nods slowly as he realises he isn’t going to be able to change my mind. “Fine. If that’s what you really want. I’d rather have you as a friend than nothing at all.” He gives me a small smile that fails to mask the hurt in his eyes. “I just hope I can prove myself to be a better friend than I was a boyfriend. Then maybe one day I’ll get the chance to show you I can do that better too.”

CHAPTER 34

It's still dark when we head outside the next morning, only a faint glimmer of light visible in the sky above the mountains to the east. I pull my hat down over my ears and zip my jacket up to my chin, shoving my gloved hands into my pockets for further warmth. The ground crunches underfoot as Ethan leads the way, carrying a rifle over his shoulder. Lily also carries a gun, and Priya and Dean have fishing rods. We all have our hunting knives and I carry a backpack.

"We're going to head to those woods near Three Falls Gorge," Priya explains as we reach the stream. "Ethan told us there's a meadow with a river there and thought we might have more luck hunting further away from the bunker."

After crossing the stream, we head across the plateau toward the mountains on its western border. When we arrive at another river, narrower and deeper than the one by the bunker, we follow it the rest of the way to the forest at the top of the gorge. Making it there in just under an hour.

We walk in silence once we reach the woods, taking care not to alert any animals. Ethan indicates for us to stop when we arrive at the meadow, wanting us to remain concealed within the trees as he scans the clearing for signs of movement.

I'm not sure what Ethan sees, but he raises his gun and takes aim. He waits, exhales, then pulls the trigger. As the shot rings out, I see rabbits scatter and he fires again. We follow Ethan into the clearing and he picks up a dead rabbit, turning to show it to us. He then walks a few more steps and picks up another, lifting them both high in the air in triumph, his face grinning.

"You got two, very impressive!" Lily congratulates him.

"Did you see how many rabbits there were?" Ethan says. "There must've been at least twenty. It's a great spot to set some traps."

"It'll be good to have an extra hunting ground, and it's not too far from the bunker," Dean adds. "I'm going to head downstream a bit. There's a fallen tree over the river. Should be a good place to catch some fish." He points to where the river disappears into the trees.

"I'll come with you," Priya offers, and they head off together, holding hands.

"Let's set some traps." Ethan walks to the edge of the meadow near some scrubby looking bushes and crouches down, gesturing for Lily and me to join him.

"Can you see the small track here through the underbrush?" He points at a small trail barely visible. "This is what we need to look for. It's where small animals like rabbits or stoats travel to get to a burrow hidden somewhere in the bushes. This is the perfect spot for a trap."

Ethan pulls some string out of his backpack and cuts off a length, then shows us how to tie it into a loop. "You tie the other end up here with the loop hanging over the opening in the scrub above the trail. Then when the rabbit jumps through, bam! It gets caught." He ties the string to a sturdy branch above the small trail. He says it to both of us, but I know this explanation is really for my benefit because Lily had already been helping set traps back at the cabin when we were there.

"Right, your turn. Have a look around and see if you can find any other good trapping spots."

Lily and I head off together. After a few minutes, we find another small track further upstream. Ethan hands her a piece of string. "See if you can remember how to knot the loop."

He cuts another piece and holds it out to me. While Lily ties hers to a branch, I practice tying the knot, repeating it over and over, trying to memorise how to do it.

"Let's head to Dean and Priya. I think we've set enough around here."

"Any luck?" Lily asks as we reach them.

"It's got potential," Dean replies. "Priya's spotted a trout, just got to be patient."

While the others watch for the elusive fish, I head to the edge of the clearing and look for signs of animal trails until I find one leading under some bushes. I tie the loop and attach the rope to a branch above the trail, making sure the loop hangs into the path.

"Nice work," Ethan says behind me.

I tug at the rope, thinking of how it works. "Will they suffer?"

"It's not the most humane way to kill an animal. Shooting them can be quicker as long as you get a clean shot."

"*Humane* … I've always found that term ironic." I shake my head, looking up at him. "We use it to mean killing something painlessly or quickly, but in reality humans are the most violent, cruel species on the planet. We're the only animals that kill for fun or sport, no other species does. They only kill for food or to protect themselves."

He raises his eyebrows at me and nods. "I think you're oversimplifying it though. Have you ever seen a predator killing its prey? It's seldom quick or painless. Animals don't care if their prey is suffering, all they care about is feeding themselves and their young. I think that's where the term 'humane' comes from. It's referring to the fact that humans are one of the few creatures that have the *ability* to feel empathy and compassion."

"I hadn't thought of that."

"We aren't the only species capable of empathy though," he continues. "Elephants, whales, great apes—they all display compassion and grieve at the loss of loved ones. Whales will swim with a calf for weeks mourning their death before letting go. I do get your point though, the irony of the term given how cruel humans can be. Maybe we should replace 'humane' with 'whalene' and 'whalenity'." He laughs at his own joke.

"Oh, the *whalenity*." I laugh. "I like it."

"The Hindenburg sort of looked like a flying whale. It's kind of fitting."

"Is that what the quote is from? I had no idea! You constantly surprise me. You are most definitely not just a pretty face."

"Careful." Ethan wags his finger at me. "That sounds suspiciously like a compliment. We're just friends now, remember?"

"The last time I checked, compliments *are* considered friendly." I smile at him, grateful that he's able to make a joke and not make things awkward. *Maybe the adjustment to friends isn't going to be so hard after all.*

"Just can't get too friendly though, right?" He grins.

"Yeah, something like that." I feel my face beginning to blush.

"There's one more lesson we need to cover today."

"You mean like yesterday's lesson?" I raise an eyebrow at him suspiciously. "Because I think that *would* be considered a bit too friendly."

"Ha! Not exactly." He picks up the rabbits. "You need to learn how to field dress your catch."

I grimace.

"I know it's not pleasant, but it's an important skill to learn if we're going to be living up here for a while. You need to learn how to do this to make sure the meat doesn't get contaminated and is safe to eat. It would be an *inwhalene* waste of a beautiful creature if we weren't able to eat something we kill, don't you think?"

How can I argue with that?

"Come on." He starts walking downstream.

I watch as Ethan field dresses the first rabbit. He then washes his knife in the river and holds it out to me. "Your turn."

I don't object, determined to learn how to do this, to be able to do my bit. I take the knife and repeat the steps Ethan had shown me, finally placing it in the container with the other rabbit.

"I'm impressed!" he says as we wash our hands. "Where is the girl who vomited after she caught a fish a couple of weeks ago?"

I shake my head at the memory, barely able to believe the change myself. "I know. So much has happened in the last few weeks. I'm not sure I'm even the same person anymore. It hasn't been like that for you though. You don't seem any different."

"I wouldn't be so sure about that," he says, moving some hair from my face as he smiles down at me. "I may have been able to do this sort of stuff before, but a lot *has* changed for me."

Damn butterflies, why are you still here? Maybe this *is* going to be harder than I thought.

****

We return to the bunker mid-morning, and my plan to find Matt and talk to him are dashed as soon as I enter the living room to find Jackson and Ollie waiting for me, eager to begin our security meeting.

"We've been talking through some ideas, and we think there are two main scenarios we need to plan for," Jackson says. "The first is that we come across people in the valley, away from the bunker. The second is that someone actually finds the bunker. We're thinking that it doesn't matter whether we know for sure if they're aggressive or not, we need protocols in place to deal with both circumstances."

"Makes sense," I reply. "What were you thinking?"

"We think our priority should be to keep the bunker a secret," Ollie says. "So, if we come across anyone away from the bunker, we can't tell them about it."

"But wouldn't they want to know where we've been living?"

"Yes. We think the protocol should be that we take them to the cabin, not to the bunker, and we'll stock the cabin with food just in case we need to use it."

"And it also gives us a backup in case something goes wrong here," Jackson says. "Then we don't have all our eggs in one basket."

"Good idea." I nod, impressed. "I think that's a really good suggestion."

"We can't tell anyone about the bunker until we're absolutely certain that they aren't a threat to us," Ollie continues. "Which might mean living with them for a while at the cabin until we get to know them better and are sure we can trust them, even if we don't really want to. The priority always has to be to protect the rest of the group."

"If any of us don't return to the bunker by midnight," Jackson says, "we need to assume that they've gone to the cabin and the protocol will be to change the passcode on the bunker lock. The only way into this bunker is through that front door, and the only way through that door is if you have the code. So, we can't risk one of us being out there with other people and knowing the code. That way, if someone gets taken hostage, they can't be forced to open the bunker."

"Okay." I nod. "I can see a problem though. What if the reason someone doesn't come back by midnight is because they've hurt themselves? How would we know if we don't go looking for them?"

"It doesn't matter at that point," Jackson says. "We change the passcode at midnight, and send out a search party once it's light. But we don't go near the cabin. We can't risk being seen and the outsiders finding out there are more of us. If we can't find them anywhere else, we assume they're at the cabin."

"And if you're at the cabin, then what? What if you're in danger?"

Ollie and Jackson look at each other, neither of them wanting to answer.

"If you're at the cabin, you're on your own," Jackson says. "You won't be rescued. There won't be any help coming. It has to be the rule. We can't risk anyone else. The safety of the group has to take priority."

I raise my eyebrows, taken aback. He's effectively saying that a few may be sacrificed to save the many. "We wouldn't even try to rescue them?"

"I know it sounds harsh, but it's the only way," Ollie says. "What if the rescue fails? Then more of us might be captured, or even killed. It's too risky."

"I guess." I nod. "I can't say I like it very much, but I agree."

"We're all going to have to," Jackson says. "Every one of us. Because if someone decides to go against the protocols and play hero, they could put us all at risk. And we can't have that."

"What else?" I ask. "What if other people find the bunker? What then?"

"Everyone needs to be trained to use the guns," Ollie says. "We all need to be ready to fight if it comes to it. We'll get Ethan to give everyone lessons, and it needs to start soon."

"But if we're in here, we won't need to fight," I say. "We could just hide in here and no-one could get in. Those doors are blast proof. We've got everything we need in here. We wouldn't need to go out. Why would we need to fight?"

"What if they take us by surprise?" Jackson says. "We should all know how to defend ourselves, just in case. But, yeah, if it comes to it, we want to avoid a fight, and hunkering down in the bunker is the safest place to be."

"Okay, what else?" I ask again.

"That's it," Jackson replies. "Unless you can think of anything?"

"What about the escape hatch?" I ask. "We should make sure we know how it works in case we need to use it in an emergency. It could also be useful for getting in and out of here without anyone seeing us if people discover the bunker and set up camp outside."

"Yeah, definitely. Good thinking," Jackson says.

"So, when do we tell the others what you've come up with? As you said, we all need to agree on the protocols."

"We'll tell them at lunch," Ollie replies.

"Okay. Well, this meeting was quicker than I thought it would be. You've already thought of everything." I smile and begin to stand.

"Hey, there's something I want to show you," Jackson says. "I found this when I was scrolling through the entertainment drive contents the other day. Consider it security training."

He starts up the projector and turns off the light in the lounge section of the room so we can see the image on the wall.

"It's a survival series," he explains. "There's an episode on how to escape if you've been tied up using zip ties and duct tape."

We watch in disbelief as they show how to use shoelaces to saw through zip ties. They also demonstrate how to break your hands free from duct tape just by pressing your fingertips together and pushing out with your wrists while swinging your arms down from above your head.

We decide we absolutely *have* to see if it really works for ourselves. We find duct tape and zip ties in the basement and head back up to the lounge as everyone gathers for lunch. I go first, everyone laughing and asking what's going on as Jackson binds my wrists with duct tape. But the look on their shocked faces is priceless when I swing my hands down from above my head, and break them free using the method shown in the video.

I'm as shocked as they are. I can't believe it worked either. It's definitely harder than it looked in the video, and it hurts a bit, but it really worked. And then everyone wants to try it for themselves.

Ollie and Jackson fill everyone in on our meeting over lunch, describing the different scenarios and explaining the protocols they want us to agree to.

An uncomfortable silence follows their proposal that anyone who encounters strangers will be left to fend for themselves to protect the safety of the rest of the group. But in the end, everyone agrees. There will be no contact, no rescue, no heroics. We all understand what it means. We just hope it never comes to that.

"Matt, can I talk to you about something?" I lower my voice, trying to avoid anyone overhearing as we clean up after lunch.

"Sure." He shrugs, turning to face me. "Fire away."

"It's a bit personal." I smile uncomfortably. "Can we go somewhere less crowded? Maybe we could go for a walk?"

He raises his eyebrows at me. "Funny. That's the second time someone's asked me to do that today."

"Well, aren't you popular? Who else was so eager for your undivided attention?"

"Wouldn't you like to know?" He gives me a sly smile.

I shake my head, ignoring his attempt to bait me. "Come on then, Mr. Mysterious. Let's get out of here."

Neither of us speak for the first few minutes as we walk side by side across the clearing. We don't discuss where we're going, the destination irrelevant as I try to get the courage to say what I need to.

"So, what did you want to talk to me about?" Matt finally gives up waiting for me to speak.

"I feel a bit awkward even bringing this up." I take a deep breath, trying to calm my nerves, focusing on the ground. "But yesterday I got the impression that you were upset with me after Ethan and I got back from our shooting lesson."

"Shooting lesson?" Matt scoffs. "Is that what you guys call it?"

I swallow uncomfortably, unable to bring myself to look at him. I'm surprised at the spitefulness of his words. I've never heard him speak like this to anyone, especially not me.

I shake my head and stop walking. Finally, I get the courage to look at him. "I'm not sure why you're so angry. It's not like you're my boyfriend."

"I'm well aware of that," he huffs.

"Then why are you so angry?"

"I'm not angry." He looks taken aback. "Why do you think I'm angry?"

"You sound … bitter." I hesitate, trying to find the right word. "It almost seems like you're jealous."

Matt lets out a derisive snort. "I'm not jealous. I just think you could do better, that's all. And besides, I'm seeing someone, so why would I be jealous?"

My stomach lurches at his revelation. I'd been so worried *my* relationship with Ethan would cause problems with Matt that I'd ended it. And now I find out that he's in a relationship himself and couldn't care less!

I clamp my lips together, realising my mouth has dropped open, and break my gaze from his. I scuff at a rock with my boot. I feel embarrassed, stupid. I swallow hard, trying to push down the lump in my throat.

As my initial feeling of shock slowly subsides, anger rises to take its place. I wrestle with my thoughts, realising it's ridiculous to feel angry at him for being with someone, especially when I've just been seeing Ethan, and the emotion takes me by surprise. I try to shake the anger from my head, confused by it, trying to rationalise it.

Oh my god, you've got to be kidding me. I let out a loud sigh as the truth sinks in. *Am I jealous?*

"I didn't realise," I say, looking up at him. "Who are you seeing? How long?"

"Lily. Not long, it only happened recently."

"Oh." I take a deep breath and force myself to smile as I battle my feelings of jealousy. "I'm happy for you, Matt. Lily's great," I say sincerely.

"Yeah, she is." His face softens. "Look, I'm really sorry I snapped at you before. I was out of line. It's none of my business that you're with Ethan. I guess it just took me by surprise. I suppose I was feeling … I dunno … protective of you." He gives me one of his trademark smiles, the warmth returning to his eyes. "It's just that I think you're awesome, and I wouldn't want to see you get hurt. And it's not that I don't like Ethan—I think he's a good guy. He just seems like he's got a bit of history and you should probably be careful with him."

He takes my hands and pulls me in for a hug. I wrap my arms tightly around him, relieved that he's not angry anymore. Relieved that he still cares.

"Just don't sell yourself short, okay?"

I sigh into his shoulder. "Thanks, Matty. But you don't have to worry about that anymore though. It's over between me and Ethan. We decided it would be better just to be friends."

Matt immediately pulls back, holding me by the shoulders as he studies my face. "I don't understand. When did that happen?"

"Last night, after the movie."

"Oh!" His eyebrows shoot up in surprise. "So, how're you doing? Are you okay?"

"Yeah, I'll be okay. It was my decision to end it, actually. Ethan isn't exactly thrilled about it, but he understands why."

"I bet he isn't. I'm glad you're okay though." He gives me a reassuring smile. "Thanks for clearing the air with me. Your friendship means a lot to me. *You* mean a lot to me. You know that, don't you?"

"Yeah, I do. You too, Matty." I put my arm around his waist as we turn back toward the bunker. "I don't know what I'd do without you," I say, suddenly feeling the urge to cry. "I don't want anything to ever come between us."

Matt stops, turning me to look at him. He gives me a small smile and pulls me into his arms again, hugging me tightly. "That's one thing you *don't* have to worry about. There's no chance of that."

CHAPTER 35

The next few weeks pass quickly, each of us working with a sense of purpose, driven by our need to prepare as much as possible before winter sets in. Everyone has their specific jobs and roles, and we work hard. We know there'll be time to rest once winter comes.

After agreeing on our new security protocols, we make it a rule that no-one is to leave the bunker alone, and we have to complete a register before leaving. Recording who is going, the time they're leaving, and where they're planning to go. We need to make sure we know where to look if anyone goes missing.

I become a permanent member of the hunting crew and we manage to supplement the group's diet with rabbit or fish on almost a daily basis, even adding to our supply in the freezer.

Ollie, Marley, Lily, and Skye make a day trip to the cabin to restock it with extra canned food as well as medical supplies, sleeping bags, and spare clothing. Our back up shelter in case of an emergency or if we come across other people in the valley.

We all help carry hundreds of bucket-loads of soil from outside to replenish the planter beds and to create a new garden in the cave. And Ethan and Ollie set up the extra grow lights above it, effectively doubling our indoor gardening capacity. Our gardeners finish planting the indoor garden, transferring the seedlings into the planter beds and the cave garden soon after, and everyone excitedly watches their progress as they steadily grow under the dedicated care of Kai,

Matt, and Jackson.

Ollie and I spend a few hours with Skye each week to continue our medical tuition. Matt and Jackson often join us, Skye insisting that they both have regular checkups while they're still recovering from their injuries. Matt has made a full recovery from his hypothermia and no longer wears his sling, and Jackson's now able to walk without a crutch, preferring to use a knee brace we found stored with the medical supplies in the basement.

Every afternoon, Ethan takes a few of us out for a shooting lesson, making sure we all understand the basics of gun safety and how to fire a gun. He insists we need to practice until it becomes instinctive, until our bodies can react without thinking, to reduce the chance that we might freeze or panic when the time comes … if it comes. *Prepare for the worst and hope for the best* soon becomes our new mantra.

Ethan and I have managed the transition to friends *pretty* well, although I seem to need more shooting lessons than anyone else and often on my own. He's an incorrigible flirt and enjoys making me blush, often testing the boundaries of friendship when no-one is around. It hasn't been easy to stay within those limits. We often find ourselves standing unnecessarily close, making excuses to touch each other, looking longer than we should. But we haven't crossed any lines, although sometimes it's a little hard to tell where they are as the distinction between friendly affection and desire seems to blur.

My friendship with Matt has recovered from our small bump in the road. If anything, we're actually closer than ever. Most of the time I'm able to suppress my feelings of jealousy, but occasionally I find I have to look the other way when Lily and Matt share a moment. But they don't happen often, and I think maybe it's because Matt deliberately tries to avoid any displays of affection when I'm around.

With each passing week, the days have noticeably shortened, and the temperature has continued to drop. Most mornings, a frosty landscape welcomes us as we head out early to hunt, and we spend our evenings in the warmth and safety of the bunker reading, playing cards or a board game, or watching something from the entertainment system.

We've found comfort in our routine and acceptance of our reality as we prepare for the coming snow. The paradoxical winter, which will both imprison us and inevitably set us free. We have to endure being trapped here to allow enough time to pass so we can safely return home.

Without windows in the bunker, we exit its confines each morning oblivious to the weather outside. Some days we encounter gales and rain, but more often than not it's frozen, clear skies. Today, however, it isn't frost *or* rain that greets us.

It's snow.

CHAPTER 36

We can't contain our excitement as we venture out into the snow. All of us whooping when we see it and running out into the clearing, kicking white clouds with our feet and throwing handfuls in the air.

I don't know what it is about fresh snow that makes me feel this way, but it never fails to fill me with a childish wonder, making me almost gleeful when I see it. Maybe it's a reminder of the way it felt when I was little, when everything was wondrous. When I believed in magic and everything my parents said. When anything was possible and Mum's cuddles fixed anything that wasn't.

We set out hopeful of bringing home a good haul, using the animal tracks that crisscross the snow to lead the way. But we return to the bunker hours later, cold and empty-handed for the first time in weeks.

We arrive just as everyone's finishing lunch, about to return to their work. I decide not to join Ethan and the others when they sit down to eat, instead making a beeline for the shower. I'm chilled to the bone and the thought of a long hot shower with no one waiting impatiently outside is too good an opportunity to miss.

Eventually I emerge, warm and relaxed, and am surprised to find the living room completely empty. It's such a rare occurrence, I'm not sure I've ever been in here alone before, and I relish the idea of a few more minutes of solitude. I pull the bunker manual from the bookshelf and flick through its pages, studying the floor plan.

"Hi." Matt walks through the door from the hallway.

"Hey." I return his smile. "Where is everyone?"

"Kai and Jackson are downstairs, and Ethan and Ollie are in the cave. I think some of the others headed outside to check out the snow." He fills a glass from the tap before turning to look at me. "So, what's on your agenda for this afternoon, Miss Maddox?"

I turn the floor plan around so Matt can see what I'm looking at. "I told Ollie and Jackson I would check out the escape hatch. We want to make sure it works okay in case we need to use it in an emergency." I cringe.

"I take it you're not exactly happy about the idea?"

"Not particularly. I hate small spaces."

"Why did you offer to check it out then?"

"Well, Jackson obviously can't, and Ollie already has so much on his plate with learning how all the bunker systems operate. So, I felt like I should be the one to do it. I keep putting it off. I said I'd do it weeks ago." I take a deep breath, steadying my nerves at the thought. "I'll be fine … it'll be fine."

Matt raises his eyebrows in amusement. "Would you like me to come with you?"

"Would you? That would be awesome!" I blurt. "Are you sure your shoulder's up to it though?"

"Yeah, it's fine. It's feeling really good actually. It's pretty much back to normal now."

"Great! Are you free now? I'd kinda like to get it over with."

"Sure." He chuckles. "Come on, we'll have this done before you know it."

We grab torches and head upstairs to the end of the passageway, where the ladder leads to the trapdoor in the ceiling. Matt climbs first and unlatches the door, then pushes it up until it rests vertically against the wall behind it. I peer up into the darkness and swallow. It's pitch black, no glint of light anywhere in the shaft above. Matt arcs his headlamp above him and I see wide metal rungs climbing in a vertical tunnel until they eventually disappear out of sight.

"It can't go too high. We know the escape hatch leads to that ledge," he calls back down.

"Is there a light switch?"

Matt feels around and looks down at me. "I can't find anything. We'll just need to use our headlamps. The light coming through the trapdoor helps too." He steps off the ladder onto a ledge beside the opening. "Come and check it out and see what you think."

I climb the rungs until my head breaches the opening and see that Matt is standing on a small platform at the side of the trapdoor. I take a deep breath, forcing my lungs to empty in an attempt to slow my heart rate. *Come on, you can do this.*

Although I told Matt I don't like small spaces, the irony of my claustrophobia is that it actually stems from an incident that happened *outdoors* at a soccer game with my dad when I was ten years old.

We were standing in the milling crowd, waiting to leave the stadium, when the faint smell of smoke wafted over us and then someone yelled, 'FIRE!' My dad tried desperately to hold on to me as the people at the back pushed toward the exit and the crowd surged in panic. Bodies fused so tightly around me I was lifted off my feet, pinning me helplessly between them.

I screamed for my dad, clinging frantically to his fingertips as his hand was ripped from mine, then my face became pressed against the chests of the adults crushing me. As they continued to scream in terror, I no longer could. I remember tilting my head back, the only part of my body I could still move, and looking up at the cloudless sky. All that beautiful air, all around me … but I couldn't breathe any of it.

That's the last thing I remember until I woke lying on the ground with a woman leaning over me. Later, I found out that the man beside me had realised my upturned face wasn't breathing and had got the people around us to help lift me above them. I'd then been passed above the heads of the crowd, handed from person to person until I reached safety, where the woman was able to revive me.

I was one of the lucky ones. Twelve people died that day, either crushed by the surrounding crowd or beneath their feet. Seven years later, and it's still something I struggle with. Only my family and closest friends know this is even an issue for me. I keep it so well hidden. I have techniques I use to help control my panic, to focus my breathing, to think rationally about the true risk of a situation. But I always know where the nearest exit is—I do it subconsciously—it's ingrained in my psyche. 'Confront your fears', people say, but I've found avoidance to be an equally effective strategy. If I don't think I can get out, I don't go in.

It'll be fine ... and even if it gets too much, you can just come back out. Matt will understand if you have to. He'll be fine with it. You'll be fine.

I take another deep breath to steady myself and then continue to climb the ladder until I'm standing at the same level as Matt.

"Can you go first?" I ask.

"Sure, come over here and we'll swap places." Matt reaches out to take my hand and I move onto the small platform beside him, allowing him to step past and take my place on the ladder.

I wait until Matt's feet have cleared the bar above me, then step back on. I've only managed to climb a couple of steps when I clip my headlamp on the rung in front of me, pushing the torch painfully into the bridge of my nose and smashing the lamp in the process. My foot slips as I jerk my head back, and suddenly I'm dangling by my hands.

"Ah!" My feet kick out and my left foot hits something. I hear a creaking noise as I scramble to get my feet back on the ladder, and then it's followed by a deafening boom. The noise explodes off the enclosed tunnel walls, leaving my ears ringing long after.

"Are you okay?"

I look down into the darkness, the trapdoor now closed and my broken headlamp no longer working.

Breathe, Jess, breathe.

"I knocked the trapdoor closed and I've broken my headlamp. My nose is a bit sore, but other than that, I'm fine," I say through gritted teeth.

"Do you want me to come down?"

"No, keep going. I can feel my way behind you."

I watch as Matt's shadowy form begins to ascend and exhale deeply, preparing myself to follow.

I focus on the rungs, counting as I climb, trying to distract myself from the suffocating darkness. I close my eyes. *Just pretend you're climbing a ladder outside. You're not in a narrow tunnel ... beneath a mountain ... without light ... without air. Breathe, breathe, there's air, you can breathe.*

"I'm at the hatch," Matt calls down.

I hug the bars of the ladder, eyes screwed shut to the darkness, and feel momentary relief at knowing we'll soon be out. I listen as

Matt works to open the hatch, scraping, grunting.

I'm not sure I can do this much longer. "What's taking so long?" *I need to see light, to feel air, to get out.*

"I don't know what I'm doing wrong. I can't get it to open." Matt's words suck more air from the tunnel.

I begin to feel panicked realising I'm going to have a full-blown anxiety attack, squeezing my chest further. *Don't do this. Not here with Matt. Breathe, breathe. You can't let Matt see you like this.*

"Do you want to come and have a look?" Matt asks. "Maybe you can work it out."

"No, let's just go back down." My voice sounds constricted, as though my lungs don't have enough air. I begin to feel lightheaded. I've got to get out of here *now*.

I make my way down the rungs as fast as I can, afraid that I might pass out and fall. As soon as I reach the trapdoor, I move onto the platform beside it and try to lift it, but it won't budge. I try again, nothing.

My heart races out of control, my breathing coming in rapid, shallow huffs. I don't have long. I'm going to suffocate in here. *There's no air, THERE'S NO AIR!* I huddle into a ball at the back corner of the platform and put my head between my knees. *Don't pass out, don't pass out.*

"Jess? Are you okay?" Matt steps onto the platform beside me.

"Can't open it," I wheeze.

I hear him grunt as he tries to lift it. "Shit, it must have latched on the other side when it shut."

I let out a low groan and begin to gently rock.

"Jess?"

"Can't breathe," I choke.

Matt sits down next to me and puts his arm around my shoulder. "There's lots of air in here, Jess. You just need to breathe. We'll do it together. Come on, take a slow breath in …"

I can't bear it any longer—I can't calm myself enough to breathe. I push Matt's arm away, his closeness suffocating me. I open my eyes, but I can't see his face, blinded by the light from his headlamp. I rip the torch off his head and use it to frantically scan the tunnel as if the light will somehow help me find my self-control.

I lunge onto my knees and bang my fists on the trapdoor. "Help! Can anyone hear me? Help!"

The noise echoes off the walls, the sound smothering me further. I bang on the door again and again until finally I hunch over in a ball and begin to cry. "We're going to die in here. We're going to run out of air and die in here."

"We're going to be fine. We just need to wait until someone comes up to the bedrooms and then they'll hear us."

"We'll run out of air before then," my voice shrills. My chest pulsates with short sharp breaths, my body under attack from my panicked brain.

"Jess, listen to me." Matt's hands take my shoulders and he pulls me back next to him. "There's lots of air in here. We are *not* going to suffocate."

"There might be air in here." I hyperventilate. "But I can't get any. I can't breathe." Tears run down my cheeks as I look up at Matt in desperation.

"You need to think of something to help distract you. Why don't you tell me about your family? Tell me about your friends and your school." He pulls me closer and begins to gently stroke my hair and back.

"I …" I can't think to talk. The only thing my brain can think about is air and my lack of it.

"Come on, you can do this. I'm not going to let anything happen to you, I promise. We're going to get out of here. You're going to be fine."

I nod as I try to take a deep breath and then let out an involuntary whimper.

"Jess, look at me." I feel Matt's hands on my face, turning me to look at him. "Jess, open your eyes."

I look up through tear-blurred eyes into his calm face, continuing to gasp shallow breaths. Slowly he leans toward me until we're sharing the same air, still holding my face between his hands. And then he places his lips on mine.

I pull back, inhaling sharply, my eyes locking with his in confusion, and then, very slowly, I exhale. He smiles as I take another deep breath, then leans forward and kisses me again. This time I don't move away.

His kiss is soft and gentle, giving me time as he waits for me to push through my fog of confusion. Finally, I understand that this is really happening and my body wakens. My lips open as I respond to his kiss and I reach up to his neck and into his hair. Matt's hands slide down from my face to my hips and he pulls me onto his lap to straddle him. A small moan escapes me as his hands reach under the back of my top to stroke my skin beneath, and I feel his lips smile. His mouth presses harder, our kiss becoming more urgent, until finally I have to break away, gulping air in deep breaths.

"Looks like you've remembered how to breathe." He chuckles.

Oh my god, is this really happening? I stare at him in complete astonishment as I try to work out if I'm in the midst of some crazy oxygen deprived hallucination.

"Not quite." I shake my head, my heavy breathing slowing. "Still need more distracting."

I silence his laugh with my lips and pull myself tightly against him. This time he's the one taken by surprise as I kiss him with the full force of the feelings that I've been hiding, ignoring, neglecting. Finally setting them free.

Matt's breathing is as heavy as mine when we break from our kiss. As I study his shadowy face, I become aware of the darkness surrounding us, and I'm suddenly reminded of how this all started. "Seems you've worked out how to cure a panic attack." I give him an embarrassed smile.

"Glad I could be of service." His hands continue to stroke my skin, his eyes on mine.

I don't move, meeting his gaze, my breathing continuing to calm. *Was he just trying to distract me, or was this real? It felt real ... but I can never tell with Matt.*

"Do you kiss all your friends like this, or just the ones you think of like a sister?" I swallow shyly.

"Huh?" His hands stop moving. "What do you mean?"

"I heard you tell Skye that you thought of me like a sister."

A look of realisation crosses his face. "I didn't know you heard that. Well, that explains a lot." He shakes his head as though everything now makes sense. "I just said that to get Skye to stop giving you such a hard time about us after the landslide. I thought if she knew how I really felt about you, it would just make things worse.”

“How you really felt about me?” My heart begins to race.

“Well, yeah, I thought you felt the same, but then everything changed after we got back from Three Falls.” His smile is tinged with regret. “It still felt like we were close, but it was different. It didn’t feel the way it had when we were in the gorge together. I figured I must have got it wrong, got my wires crossed and just been imagining you felt the same way.”

“You didn’t.” I shake my head, my eyes still locked with his. “I did feel the same way, but after I heard you talking to Skye, I thought *I’d* misread things.” I swallow and take a deep breath. “I need to know, Matt. Was this just you trying to distract me? Or does this mean something more?”

“I can’t believe you have to even ask. Can’t you tell?”

“No, I honestly can’t. I can’t tell with you! And I don’t want to keep guessing and get it wrong again. I need to know.” I begin to move away to make some space between us, but he takes my hands and holds them in his.

“Ever since we found out about the outbreak, I’ve felt like I’m in some crazy never-ending nightmare, and I keep wondering if this is really happening, if it’s all real. Everything, that is, *except* for you. The way I feel about you is the *only* thing that feels real, the only thing that doesn’t feel like a nightmare.” He inhales deeply. “Maybe it did help to distract you from being stuck in here, but that wasn’t the reason I kissed you. You have to know that. This … us now, this is real.”

Warmth spreads through my chest, a smile sneaking across my face as I try to suppress the urge to laugh. I lean back and allow the laughter to burst out of me, releasing coils of tension from the fear, the anxiety, the shock of his kiss, the worry that I was misreading this.

If he didn’t think you were crazy before, he definitely does now.

I inhale deeply, trying to get my laughter under control, and then cup his confused face in my hands. Just as I lean in to kiss him, I pause. “What about Lily?”

“Lily and I aren’t together anymore.” He shakes his head. “We ended it a couple of weeks ago. Not long after you and Ethan split up actually.” He gives me an awkward look.

"Really, why?"

"Isn't it obvious?"

I begin to shake my head. "Oh!" My eyes widen as I understand what he means.

He laughs, shaking his head at my shocked reaction, then stops as we suddenly hear voices coming from the hallway.

"Did you hear that?" I ask.

As I turn toward the trapdoor, Matt grabs hold of my shoulders and stops me. "Jess, wait."

He pulls me closer, wrapping his arms firmly around me and kisses me. Making sure I understand how he feels.

Making sure there can be no doubt.

CHAPTER 37

Marley and Skye's bemused faces peer up at us as we lift the trapdoor.

"Thank god you heard us," I say, climbing down the ladder. "I thought we were going to die in there."

"She's not exaggerating," Matt calls down as Skye and Marley both laugh.

"What were you doing up there?" Skye asks.

"We needed to make sure the hatch works in case there's an emergency," I explain. "Lucky we did, because it wouldn't open."

"Really?" Marley asks. "Are you sure?"

"Yeah, it wouldn't budge," Matt replies. "We'll need to take in some lights and have another look. It probably just needs to be oiled or something."

"I might skip going back in for another look if that's okay." I give Matt a sideways look.

"I think that would probably be a good idea." Matt chuckles. "Maybe Marley or Skye could come and check it out with me instead."

"Yeah, sure," Marley replies. "We can check it out after dinner. It's just about ready. I'll see you down there in a few minutes."

"Great, I'm starving," Matt says as he begins to walk down the stairs.

I follow Matt to the kitchen where Priya and Dean have already started serving up bowls of stew. Matt heads straight to the table and takes a seat across from Kai and Jackson, and I take the one next to him. As soon as I sit down, Matt's hand slides onto my leg under the table, giving my thigh a gentle squeeze. Heat rushes to my cheeks as my heart begins to race. I swallow nervously as I peek up at him and give him a shy smile, then glance across the table at Kai and Jackson, wondering if they noticed anything.

I feel dazed, still trying to get my head around this and what it means. I still can't believe it happened, that Matt kissed me … that *we* kissed. I feel stunned, my hands shaking.

The room suddenly fills with voices as everyone arrives for dinner.

"Hey." Ethan takes the seat next to me, moving his chair closer so his leg presses up against mine. He places his hand on his leg, his fingers brushing against me. My eyes dart to his face and I see he's grinning, then his hand slides onto my thigh.

Oh my god. This can't seriously be happening.

I'm sure my expression is more a grimace than a grin as I try to return his smile. I feel completely flustered, my breathing bordering on hyperventilating again, terrified one of them will look down and see the other's hand on my leg. I slide further under the table, making sure my legs and their hands are completely out of sight. Just when I think I can't take it any longer, both hands simultaneously lift from my legs as bowls are placed on the table in front of them. It takes every bit of self-control I have left not to audibly sigh in relief.

I can barely eat, completely distracted by thoughts of what just happened with Matt and the fact that Ethan is sitting right next to me, his leg still lightly touching mine as though nothing has changed. But it has changed, everything has.

I'd had to push aside my feelings for Matt when I thought he didn't feel the same way, and it hadn't been an easy thing for me to do. Even though I denied it, it always felt like something was simmering beneath the surface with him, something that I constantly had to suppress. But now, sitting here next to Ethan, the excitement I'd initially felt at finding out Matt shares my feelings has been replaced by confusion and guilt and shame.

Although I hadn't wanted to admit it, I'd been hurt by Ethan's deceit. But other than not telling me about the girl he'd been seeing before we met, he'd done nothing wrong. He certainly hadn't cheated on me. And even though we're no longer together and trying just to be friends, I'd be kidding myself if I thought that's all we are to each other. We may have hit pause on the physical intimacy, but the attraction and emotional connection are still there.

I know I haven't done anything wrong, and that Ethan and I aren't together, but I feel like I've betrayed him, cheated on him. Even though I could justify why it's okay, it doesn't really matter. What matters is that I know Ethan would be hurt if he found out about Matt, and I can't bear the thought of hurting him.

I glance from Matt to Ethan.

How is this possible? How am I sitting between these two amazing guys, both of whom I utterly adore and who seem to feel the same way about me?

CHAPTER 38

Not wanting to risk coming home empty-handed two days in a row, we make our way to the meadow by Three Falls Gorge to check the traps we'd set there a couple of days earlier. We left later than usual, giving the sun a chance to reach the valley floor, the ground now clear other than the patches of snow that remain beneath the trees.

"It feels like another cold snap's coming," Ethan says as we check the traps in the meadow. "The wind has changed. Think we might be in for more snow."

"I'll check the traps by the river if you guys want to head back to the bunker with this lot," I say as I reset the snare from which I'd just taken a rabbit. It's a good haul today. A few rabbits, and Priya even managed to track a deer through the trees when we first arrived, a clean kill with a single shot. "It'll feel like a long walk carrying the deer."

"You're not wrong," Ethan says. "Give me a hand, will you? I'll take the first turn."

Dean and Lily pick up the deer and lift it over Ethan's shoulders.

"I'll come with you, Jess," Priya calls out. "I noticed some tracks in the snow earlier. Might be a wolf. And we're not supposed to be out here alone, remember? You guys go ahead, we'll catch up."

"You sure?" Dean asks. "Maybe I should stay with you if you've seen tracks?"

"Yeah, I think that might be a good idea, Dean." I nod.

I lead the way and Dean and Priya follow behind, chatting happily to each other.

"I'll check the traps over here. Can you check that one?" I say, pointing further downstream.

I glance over my shoulder and see Ethan and Lily leaving the clearing behind us, disappearing into the trees. My muscles relax as soon as they're gone and I realise I've been tense around Ethan all morning. He's been just the same with me as always, friendly and teasing as he flirts with me, but I've felt guilty with every smile and every touch. I'm dreading going back to the bunker and being in another situation like yesterday, trapped between the two of them, worrying they'll find out about each other. I need to tell them before they find out another way. I owe it to them to tell them myself. I need to tell Ethan about Matt … and I need Matt to understand that things aren't completely finished with Ethan. But I have absolutely no idea what I'm going to say.

I shiver and pull my jacket collar tighter around my neck. We need to be quick; I can feel the weather changing. It won't be long before it packs in.

When I reach the trap, I can see it's been triggered, but is empty. As I reset the snare, I hear a click behind me.

"No luck this time," I call over my shoulder.

I swivel while still crouched, pivoting on my toes, then jolt backwards in fright as I look up into the face of a man pointing a gun at me.

I freeze, too afraid to move in case he reacts and shoots me. I swallow hard, staring up at the man, a soldier, with a rifle slung across his shoulder and pointing a 9mm directly at my face.

"Put your hands above your head and stand up."

I move slowly, taking care not to do anything that might startle him, and lift my hands in the air.

"Turn around and put your hands on the tree behind you. I'm going to check for weapons." His voice is steady. I do as he asks, keeping my hands high and placing them on the trunk of the tree above my head. He pats me down, removing the hunting knife attached to my belt and taking my backpack.

"Go to your friends. Move."

My heart is pounding, a million thoughts racing through my head as I walk toward Priya and Dean, who are kneeling with their hands raised in front of two more soldiers. When I get closer, I see that one of the soldiers is a woman. She tells me to kneel beside the others. Dean looks up at me and subtly shakes his head, warning me to keep quiet. I kneel beside him, keeping my hands in the air the whole time.

"Are there any more of you?" the male soldier guarding Dean and Priya asks.

I say nothing. I don't think I could even if I wanted to.

"No, it's just us," Dean replies.

"We *will* find out if you're lying. It's better for you if you tell us the truth now." The soldier watches each of us carefully and then points his gun at Priya's head. "Is he telling the truth?"

Priya lets out a small noise and closes her eyes. "There's no-one else. It's only us."

"Did you check her for weapons?" the man asks the soldier who found me. He nods in reply and adds my hunting knife to the rifle and knives they'd already taken from Dean and Priya.

The female soldier walks behind us and zip ties our hands behind our backs.

"Johnny, find out where KJ and Rhys are. See if they've found signs of anyone else," the man says without taking his eyes off us. He takes a step back so he can cover all three of us with his gun. Johnny, the soldier who found me, heads off across the clearing.

Shit, shit, shit! There'll be footprints in the snow where Lily and Ethan have headed back to the bunker. Maybe he'll think they're our footprints, maybe it'll be okay ... but he'll see them going off in a different direction, he'll know! I close my eyes, willing myself not to react and let my panic betray me. *What will they do when they find out we're lying?*

We'd talked about this, the possibility that we might come across other people, but we didn't think it would happen until next spring. No one would be stupid enough to come up here this close to winter. It would be too dangerous to risk getting stuck up here without shelter and food. We'd been so sure we were safe from outsiders for now. *What the hell are these people doing up here?*

I stare at the soldiers in front of us as we kneel in silence. The man is tall, maybe six foot three, and big, really solid, muscle, not fat. He looks tired and worn down, as if he's been out here a while. The woman is about my height, and she looks like she has short hair, although it's hard to tell, covered by a cap. Her demeanour is calm, unruffled, unconcerned by us. But her eyes don't leave us for a second, weighing us up, analysing the risk we pose to them. After a few minutes, two soldiers emerge from the trees across the clearing, a man and a woman.

"Find anything?" the big soldier guarding us asks them as they approach, still keeping his eyes on us.

"No. Some traps, but nothing else," the female soldier they referred to as KJ replies.

Then I see Johnny returning from the other direction. I feel like I'm going to be sick. *He must've seen the tracks. There's no way he could've missed them.*

"Did you find anything?"

Johnny shakes his head. "There were some tracks in the trees on the other side, but I didn't see signs of anyone else."

"We were tracking a deer in the trees earlier. It got away," Priya says quietly.

"Not such a hot shot after all." The big soldier looks at Priya.

"Yeah, I saw deer tracks, Sarge," Johnny says to the big soldier in front of us.

Sarge takes a deep breath, and then slowly exhales, looking directly at me. "How long have you been up here?"

I've already decided the best approach is to stick to the truth as much as possible. Less opportunity for us to contradict each other and get caught out in a lie.

"About six weeks. We were camping at the Lodge at Fortune Falls when the outbreak happened and then we decided to head further into the mountains until things settle down."

"I don't see a tent." Sarge waves his arm around the clearing. "Where's your camp?"

Priya gives me a small nod. We know what we need to do.

"We've been living in a hunting cabin further down the valley," I reply.

"How far?" Sarge asks.

"About ten kilometres that way." I point in the direction of the cabin.

"Let's get moving then. We're going to need to get there before this storm sets in. You lead." He looks at me.

I stand and begin to walk across the clearing with Johnny and the other two soldiers, KJ and Rhys, right behind me. Priya and Dean follow with Sarge and the other female soldier behind them. We walk in silence initially, but after about an hour, Johnny comes up to walk alongside me.

"How much further?"

"Not far. Maybe another hour," I lie. It's at least two.

"Long way to go to set traps." He looks at me sideways under his cap.

"We have a few different hunting grounds. That's one of the best ones, so we head up there every few days."

He nods, satisfied with my explanation, and continues to walk beside me. "I'm Johnny."

"Yeah, I gathered that. I'm Jess." I give him a small smile, hoping this is a sign he's going to be a friend, not a foe. "You guys look like you've been out here a while. Where are you based?"

He looks over his shoulder, checking how close the others are following.

"Our unit was posted at a refugee centre outside the Kavanyah quarantine zone."

"I heard about the refugee camps at the border, but why are there refugee centres near the quarantine zone?"

"They were for the people we brought in from the countryside where we couldn't provide protection from looters and people who'd escaped the quarantine zone. Patrols kept finding people dead in their homes, so they decided we needed to bring them into the centres to keep them safe."

"So, what happened? 'Cos obviously something must've happened, otherwise you wouldn't be here."

He checks over his shoulder again.

"Fighting broke out in Kavanyah after a rumour started spreading that the virus was a hoax. People were saying that the government had fabricated it to take away their rights. They started attacking the military blockades, and it wasn't long before they overran the troops holding the perimeter. When the refugees in the centre heard about it, some of them wanted to leave, but we were ordered not to let them out for their own safety. One night they took us by surprise and we couldn't stop them. We couldn't risk using our weapons because of the kids, and once they overran us, it was complete mayhem. I found Sarge and Rhys pretty soon after, then we found KJ and Maria a couple of days later. I have no idea what happened to the rest of our unit. I don't even know if they're still alive."

"So, how did you end up *here*? Why didn't you just go back to your base?"

"Once the infected got out of Kavanyah, the government cordoned off the state to stop it spreading any further. They're not letting anyone in or out of the entire state. We only found out when we radioed for backup at the refugee centre that we were on our own. They said there'd be no backup and no evac until there's a vaccine."

"So, they're just abandoning everyone?"

"They said they can't risk it getting out. It's just too deadly. No-one survives once they're infected. They reckon it could wipe out the entire human race before they can roll out a vaccine. They're hoping if they can contain it in Langadorne, it might buy them enough time."

"So, they're just leaving us here to die!" I spit the words.

"I figure it doesn't make much difference anyway. Without a vaccine, everyone is going to die." Johnny shrugs. "So, I guess a few million lives has to be better than billions."

"Yeah, I get it … sacrificing the few to save the many." I shake my head. "I understand why they'd do it, but it sure sucks when you're one of the few."

"Exactly." Johnny nods. "That's why we headed up here. Our only chance to survive this is if we can avoid the infected and live long enough for them to produce the vaccine."

"How long ago did this happen? When the refugee centre got overrun?"

"About a month ago. We stayed in a farmhouse for a while, and then made our way up to a cabin in the mountains south of here that KJ knew about. We were there for a few weeks until we decided we needed to move on. What about you guys? How have you survived up here?"

"Luck mainly. We found this hunting cabin stocked with food, and we've been trying to stretch it out to last as long as we can by hunting and fishing. We were planning to head through a gorge to Morrison, but we couldn't get through."

"And it's just been the three of you this whole time?"

I hesitate. *Will it be obvious there were more of us when we get to the cabin? I don't know how we left it. Keep to the truth as much as possible.*

"There *were* more of us. When we tried to get through the gorge there was a landslide, and some of our friends got swept away. The rest of us were in a bad way. We were lucky to survive."

I glance over my shoulder to see how close the others are, and trip as I'm looking back. I begin to stumble, but with my hands tied behind my back, I can't steady myself and start to go down. Johnny reaches out to try to stop me falling, and although he saves me from completely face planting, I land hard on one knee. Pain shoots up my leg as I fall to the ground.

"Get her on her feet," Sarge calls out.

"I think she's hurt. Give us a second," Johnny calls back. "Can you get up?"

"I think I can if you untie me?" I look up at Sarge as he approaches. "Can we have our hands untied? I can barely feel my fingers in this cold. We aren't going to run off. We all need to get to the cabin before this storm hits."

Sarge shakes his head.

"Please," I plead. "We aren't a threat to you. We need to trust each other, and from the looks of this weather, we're going to be stuck together for a while."

"Alright." Sarge nods. "Untie them."

After Johnny cuts my hands free, I roll up my pant leg to assess the damage. The skin on my knee has split open, but other than that, it's okay. Johnny kneels down to take a look and then helps me stand. I take a few tentative steps and although it's sore, I'm okay to walk. "I'll be fine. Not much further now."

"Let's keep moving," Sarge grunts.

Johnny and I don't resume our conversation. He seems reluctant to talk now that the others are following closely behind. As we walk, I try to work out how long it will be before Lily and Ethan realise something's happened to us. When we still haven't returned by the time they've finished dressing the deer, they'd head back to the meadow to look for us. They'd look for tracks when they don't find us, and see them heading toward the cabin. It won't take long for them to work out we must've come into contact with other people. They'd know that would be the only reason we'd go there instead of back to the bunker.

They won't follow us to the cabin, they'd return to tell the others. We all agreed on the security protocols. We're on our own. At least until we can decide whether we can trust these soldiers anyway. Until then, the cabin is our new home, and we have five new companions, whether we like it or not.

We're nearing the edge of the trees by the cabin clearing when Sarge calls out, "This is the longest ten kilometres I've ever heard of. Either you're a really shitty judge of distances or you're lying to us."

"We're nearly there," I call back. And a few minutes later we come into view of the cabin.

The sky is now heavy with cloud and it won't be long before it starts to rain, or possibly even snow again. We're all relieved to arrive at the cabin; at least we now have shelter. Safe from the coming storm, if not from anything else.

"Wait here." Sarge instructs us to wait in the trees. "Johnny, Maria, you're with me."

"Keep quiet," Rhys says, pointing his gun at us.

Sarge, Johnny, and Maria head to the cabin with their guns raised and check the outside. Sarge points at the toilet hut and indicates for Maria to check it. Once she returns, they quietly step onto the verandah and Sarge cautiously looks through the windows. Johnny opens the door and they enter, guns raised. A minute later, they come back out and call that it's clear. Rhys waves us forward.

The cabin feels cold and uninviting. We'd been in such a hurry to get to the bunker the day we left we hadn't really tidied up much, which I'm now grateful for, because it doesn't feel as empty as I thought it would as a result.

"We need to get a fire started," I say. "The firewood is stacked at the side of the cabin. Can I get some?"

"Take Rhys with you," Sarge replies.

"We should have something to eat too." I look at Dean. "I bet everyone's hungry. I know I am. Once we get the fire going, let's cook up some of those rabbits."

As Rhys and I start to head outside, Johnny clears his throat. "Sarge, maybe I should help too."

"They'll be fine," Sarge replies. "Take it easy, Johnny. You stay here."

I glance at Johnny as I walk to the door. His face is blank, but the muscles in his jaw look tense. Rhys follows me around the side of the cabin to the woodpile.

"How's your leg?" Rhys asks.

"It's okay."

"You're limping. Why don't you let me take a look? I'm a medic. I might be able to help."

"Thanks, but I'm sure it's just a bit of bruising. I'll be fine."

He puts his hand on my shoulder and points at the chopping block. "It wasn't a request. Doctor's orders."

"I guess if it's doctor's orders, then." I shrug and sit on the large tree stump.

He rolls up my trouser leg and presses around my knee at the sides and back, asking if it's tender. He then lifts my foot up and down, slowly straightening and bending my knee. He seems to know what he's doing and is careful not to hurt me. He takes my calf in his hand and squeezes it. "You'll be fine, good strong legs." He winks at me.

I let out a bark of laughter and remove his hand from my calf. "The compliment every girl wants to hear. How *strong* their legs are!"

I begin to stand, but Rhys doesn't move back to give me room as I expected him to, and it feels uncomfortably close. I look down so I'm not face to face with him and awkwardly turn to the side, bending to pick up a piece of firewood. "Put your arms out and I'll load you up."

He steps back this time, making room for me to place the wood into his outstretched arms. I continue to pile on the firewood, *lots of it*, and then get some kindling and follow him back inside. Dean and Priya are in the kitchen preparing food; they turn to look at us as we enter and Priya raises her eyebrows in silent question. I nod and give her a smile. I realise Johnny is looking at me too. His expression is still blank, but his jaw looks more relaxed. *Has he been worried?*

We get the fire going in the stove and soon the stew is cooking while Sarge and the other soldiers take a look around the bunkroom and the storeroom.

After we've eaten and the cabin has warmed, it feels much easier to believe this is our home. The soldiers begin to relax, hands no longer on their guns.

It's only 3:00 p.m. but it's almost dark outside already, with snow gently falling. I watch out the window and wonder how long this storm is likely to last, hoping that Ethan and Lily have stopped looking for us and made it safely back to the bunker.

Johnny offers to go outside to get more firewood and makes a few trips in and out, suggesting we stock up wood inside before it gets dark.

Sarge, Johnny, and Maria take turns to keep watch at the window, while Priya, Dean, and I play cards at the table. We're doing our best to pretend that this is no different than any other afternoon for us. That this is our home and how we'd be spending our time. We just happen to have uninvited guests.

KJ is the only one who takes our invitation to join in, and Rhys sits in a nearby armchair and watches. When Johnny isn't standing at the window, he stays away from everyone, keeping to himself. He doesn't speak unless spoken to, quite different to how he was when we'd been walking together, when he'd seemed so eager to talk.

Rhys suddenly stands and casually walks over to Johnny, whispering something in his ear as he looks over at us and laughs. Johnny says nothing. He doesn't smile at Rhys's joke, but I see his jaw tightening.

Johnny moves away from Rhys to the kitchen. He picks up a pot, grunting something about wanting a hot drink, and asks if we have any coffee. Priya replies that we don't, but have some leaves that we use to make a tea with if he wants to try it.

"Sure, why not?" He shrugs.

Priya goes to the storeroom to get the tea and Johnny turns on the tap. "There's no water," he says.

Priya returns with the dried leaves and tries the tap too. "It was working before. Must be something wrong with the water tank. It can't be empty. We've had plenty of rain."

"I'll check it out," Dean stands.

"Go with him," Sarge says to Johnny.

As soon as they're gone, Rhys comes over to the table. "Room for one more?"

"Sure," says Priya. "You want to play?"

"Absolutely." He smiles at her and then me.

My muscles tense. *Is he flirting with us?* Beneath the layers of beard and dirt, his eyes look kind and he had been nice to me outside earlier. But the thought of one of our captors showing an interest in us suddenly makes me feel very nervous.

"The tank's got water in it, but there's something wrong with the feeder pipe to the cabin," Dean says when he and Johnny enter the room. "I think it might be blocked, but it's getting too dark to see. We'll need to check it out tomorrow. The tap on the side is stuck too. We couldn't budge it either." He shakes his head, confused.

"We're going to need water," Johnny says. "Where's the closest source?"

"There's a river on the other side of the trees beyond the clearing," Priya replies.

"I'll go and get some water before it gets too dark," Johnny says.

"Alright." Sarge nods. "Go now."

"I need a guide," Johnny says, looking at the three of us.

"You afraid you'll get lost in the dark again, buddy?" Rhys chuckles.

Sarge doesn't smile, but nods at Johnny. "Fine."

"Jess, can you come with me?"

"I'll show you." Dean immediately stands.

Rhys shakes his head. "Sit down, buddy. He's made his choice."

I pat Dean on the shoulder as I pass him to let him know it's alright. And it is. I'm not worried. I have a feeling Johnny's okay. I grab an empty pot, put on my jacket, and follow Johnny out the door.

The wind has dropped, the air now completely still apart from the large snowflakes falling heavily from the dark sky. The magical silence of snow, absorbing all sound as the flakes land noiselessly on the ground, already beginning to turn white as it settles.

"I love it when it snows," I say as we walk to the other side of the clearing. "I think it's my favourite weather."

"It's alright I guess, as long as I have somewhere warm to sleep."

"You'll be glad to have found us and the cabin then," I say. "Where were you camping?"

"Further up the valley a bit."

"I guess you'll have to wait until this storm passes before you can get your things from your campsite."

"I guess so."

"It's not much further," I say as I lead him through the trees to the other side of the woods. "There's a hot pool in the trees over that way too." I wave my hand in its general direction.

"There seem to be a lot of hot springs around here," Johnny replies. "There was one near the cabin we stayed at before we came up here."

He has to be talking about the Lodge.

"There it is." I point at the river ahead. I lead him to a spot where there are some large rocks near the edge and step out onto one and dip the pot into the flow of the river. I hand it back to Johnny and he passes me the pot he has carried so I can fill it too. I hand it back before stepping up onto the bank.

As I reach down to pick up my pot, Johnny puts his hand on my arm to stop me. "I know you're lying to us," he blurts. "I know you haven't been living in the cabin, and I know there are more of you. I saw the tracks in the snow where the deer was shot."

"You're mistaken." I straighten, so I'm face to face with him. "They were *our* footprints from when we went looking for the deer, but it was already gone."

"That deer didn't walk off on its own. Someone carried it." He pauses, waiting for me to react. "I haven't told the others, but you need to tell me the truth."

"I don't know what you *think* you saw, but there isn't anyone else. It's just the three of us. The rest of our friends died in that landslide. I already told you that."

I bend to pick up the pot, indicating I'm finished with the conversation. But Johnny isn't. He grabs my arm again, forcing me back up to look at him.

"Let me go," I say angrily, trying to pull away.

"If you don't tell me the truth, I can't protect you." His grip tightens.

I jerk my arm away from him, slipping on the snowy bank as he lets go, and I fall to the ground. He does nothing, just stares down at me. I get to my feet and begin to stomp away, and when I'm a few metres from him, I break into a run, trying to get back to the safety of the cabin.

I hear footsteps closing behind me, and then his body slams into mine as he tackles me. I hit the ground hard, all his weight on top of me preventing me from getting up. As he moves off me, I try to roll over, but he pushes me back onto the ground face first, holding me down with his knee on my back. Adrenaline surges through me as he grabs my arms and I use all my strength to try to pull them from his grip, kicking as hard as I can with my heels into his back.

"Calm down, Jess! You need to calm down!"

I thrash, trying to roll him off me, but he holds me firmly in place.

"Stop fighting me! I'm not going to hurt you. I'm trying to help you, for god's sake!"

I try to roll one last time and finally give up when I find I can't move at all. He's too heavy and too strong for me, and I realise there's no point in trying to fight him. All it's doing is weakening me further.

"I'll let you up, but you need to listen to me."

I don't reply, but he takes my lack of struggling to mean agreement and removes his knee from my back, allowing me to roll over and sit up. He helps me to stand but continues to hold my arms, preventing me from running again.

"*How* are you trying to help me?" I growl. My hands shake as I realise how vulnerable I am out here alone with him. "Why do you think I *need* help?"

"You're shaking." He looks concerned, moving his hands down to mine.

"It's cold," I say through gritted teeth.

"You're scared. I'm sorry, I don't want you to be scared of me," he says sincerely. "But you should be scared, Jess. Just not of me."

"So, who should I be scared of then?" I'm surprised at how angry my voice sounds, angry that he's making me feel afraid. "Your friends?"

"They aren't my friends. I told you earlier, we were all that was left of my unit. KJ's alright, and I thought Sarge was okay until recently, but Rhys is a psycho. He was a jerk before everything kicked off, but since then I've seen a side of him that's really scary. He does what he wants, to whoever he wants, whether it's necessary or not."

"But he's a doctor, isn't he?"

"He's a medic." Johnny laughs. "As far as I'm aware, there's no requirement for medics to take a Hippocratic oath."

"Right." I let out a deep breath, trying to make myself look calm. *I need to get away from him, to get back to the cabin.* "Well, thanks for the heads up about Rhys. I'll warn the others."

"I don't think you understand what I'm saying," Johnny persists, gripping my hands tighter as I try to leave again. "If you go back there, you're going to end up dead. And if I try to protect you, I'll end up dead too."

"Awesome! So, what do you suggest I do then?" I raise my eyebrows at him.

"You need to go back to your other friends ... Wherever it is you've been staying." He looks at me expectantly. "We should go now."

"There. Isn't. Anywhere. Else!" I yell in frustration. "There. Aren't. Any. Others!"

"Stop lying!" He shakes me.

My heart hammers as I stare at him, eyes wide with shock. Suddenly terrified of what he might do.

"That farmhouse we were staying at," he speaks more calmly, trying to regain control of his temper. "There were people living there, a couple and their teenage daughter. They were good people. They'd taken us in and helped us. They fed us and told us we could stay as long as we needed to." He takes a deep breath. "Sarge, KJ, and I were out helping the old guy on the farm fixing a fence that had come down. When we came back, we found Rhys and Maria sitting on the verandah by themselves. Maria looked upset and went straight over to Sarge to talk to him as soon as she saw us. But Rhys just sat there, drinking coffee and whistling to himself. It felt off. He didn't say anything to anyone. The old man asked where his wife was and Rhys told him she was inside, so he went in looking for her. A few seconds later we heard him screaming and when he appeared at the door, Sarge just shot him, dead. There was no warning, no discussion, no threat from the old guy. He just shot him. KJ and I freaked out, yelling at Sarge, wanting to know why he'd done it. Sarge just looked at Rhys and said 'ask him' and then walked away."

Johnny loosens his grip on my arms, knowing he's got my attention.

"Why did he shoot him?"

"Rhys wouldn't answer us. He just kept whistling. It makes me sick thinking about it. We went inside to see what had happened and found the wife and daughter dead in one of the bedrooms." He pauses, letting it sink in. "Rhys had taken a liking to the daughter as soon as we arrived. We'd all noticed it, but hadn't thought anything of it. When we went to help fix the fence, Rhys stayed to help out with some jobs around the house … or so he said. The wife walked in on him with her daughter and when she tried to fight him off, he shot her … then he shot the daughter too. Maria said she ran in and found them after hearing the shots. When she confronted Rhys, he just walked to the kitchen and made himself a coffee."

"Oh my god! But why did Sarge shoot the dad?"

"He said he didn't have a choice after what Rhys had done. He said he couldn't just leave the old guy there after that, otherwise he would've tried to kill us. I argued with him, saying he didn't know that. But he said he did know, because that's what he would do if it was him."

"So, why is Rhys still with you guys if he's such a psycho?"

"If it was up to me, he wouldn't be. But Rhys is Sarge's brother. There's no way he'd leave him."

"Why didn't *you* leave then? *You* didn't have to stay with them."

"It's not that simple." Johnny shakes his head. "There's no way anyone could survive out there on their own right now. If I left them, I'd be lucky to last a week. There's safety in numbers. Look at you guys, there's three of you, but you're outnumbered, you don't stand a chance against us … unless there are more of you."

"But if you and KJ would help us, we would outnumber them."

"And then what? We kill them? Are you really prepared to do that? 'Cos I don't know that I am. Maria isn't a bad person, but she's sleeping with Sarge and she'll stick by him. And Sarge will protect his brother with his life. The only option is to leave here, but we need somewhere to go."

Is he trying to trick me into telling him about the others?

"So, you're the good cop then, are you?" I sneer at him. "You're the guy who can help me if I help you, but if I don't, then you'll have to leave me to take my chances with the bad guys. Is that it?"

"Are you serious?" He shakes his head in frustration. "Fine, go back in there. I've tried my best to warn you … to help you. I've seen the way Rhys has been looking at you. I'll do my best to keep him away from you, but I can't promise you anything." He begins to move away. "But do yourself a favour and stop lying that you've been living in this cabin. You may have been staying here at one point, but we know you haven't been here for at least the last four days … because we've been staying here since then."

My stomach sinks. They knew we were lying this whole time.

"Now do you understand?" he says.

"We were camping …" My voice trails off as I realise how hollow my lie sounds. Johnny shakes his head, disappointed that I won't let it go.

"I can't leave them," I say. "I can't just leave Dean and Priya there with them if Rhys is as dangerous as you say. I can't just save myself and leave them behind. And what about KJ? You wouldn't just leave her with them, would you?"

"No, I wouldn't, but we could bring back help. If we had the numbers, we could negotiate with them, get them to agree to let your friends go, and Sarge and the others could stay at the cabin."

"You really think they'd agree to let them go?" I ask hopefully.

"I don't know, but it'd be worth a try." Johnny sighs. "Better that than you all end up dead, isn't it?"

I don't know if I can trust him. He seems sincere. Either that, or he's a very good liar. I want to believe him. But I also know that if I put my trust in the wrong person right now, it could put the lives of all my friends at risk. Not just Dean and Priya and my own, but everyone else's too. We agreed we'd be on our own until we're certain any strangers could be trusted.

I can't take that risk. Not yet.

"I want to go back to the cabin now please." I look up at him.

He looks disappointed, the anger from earlier now gone. "I'll do what I can to help you and your friends." He nods. "But you need to trust me, okay?"

CHAPTER 39

"The prodigal twins return," Rhys calls out as we enter the cabin. "I was starting to wonder if you two had run off together."

Dean and Priya don't even try to hide the relief on their faces when they see me.

"Snowing pretty hard out there now." I smile, trying to reassure them. "I think it's settled in for the night."

We carry the pots to the kitchen and Johnny places one on the stove before walking over to Sarge, who's still keeping watch by the window. He speaks quietly to him as Sarge looks at me and then replies, nodding. Johnny walks to the storeroom and returns with a shovel.

"Last call for the toilet before we lock up for the night," Sarge says.

One by one we take turns to visit the toilet with a soldier accompanying us, not prepared to risk us choosing a snowstorm in the dark over the warmth of the cabin. Once we're back inside, Johnny wedges the shovel under the door handle to prevent the door from being opened, then they move a heavy armchair behind it as an extra barricade. I catch Johnny's eye when he finishes and he looks guilty.

Son of a bitch, he was playing me.

Eventually Sarge tells us we should head to bed in the bunkroom and that he and Maria will stay on guard duty in the lounge.

We file into the bunkroom and I notice that some of the beds already have sleeping bags and other gear laid out on them. Definitely not how we'd left it.

A look of panic crosses Priya's face as she realises the soldiers have been sleeping here. It takes a moment longer for Dean to register and then I can tell he's trying not to react.

"So, where are *your* sleeping bags then?" Rhys asks smugly.

"There are some blankets in the storeroom." KJ shakes her head at him. "I'll get them for you."

KJ returns with the blankets, holding them out.

"Priya and I will share." Dean takes one, leaving the other blanket for me.

The three of us climb to the top bunks, and after a few minutes, the light turns off. We lie in silence; the only sound is of bodies shuffling in sleeping bags below. I lie under my blanket fully dressed. I'm going to need every layer of clothing to keep me warm under a single blanket tonight.

****

I have a terrible night. It takes me ages to fall asleep, and once I finally do, I wake up cold and can't get back to sleep again. I'm tempted to climb in with Dean and Priya at one point, but am worried I'd give them a fright. And besides, there just isn't enough room for three of us on a single bunk bed anyway.

I pretend I'm asleep as I listen to the soldiers get up. Priya and Dean seem to be asleep too, so I wait, hoping the soldiers will leave so I can talk to them in private. Finally, KJ leaves the room, and as soon as she closes the door behind her, Dean and Priya look up and I scoot over to join them.

"They knew we hadn't been staying here. They knew we were lying," Priya hisses. "*They've* been staying here!"

"I know. I found out from Johnny when we were getting the water last night."

"You knew!" Dean says. "Thanks for the heads up."

"I didn't exactly get the chance to talk to you after we got back," I say defensively. "But there's more I need to tell you."

They listen attentively as I recount everything that Johnny told me last night and how he'd tried to convince me to take him to the others. "But I don't know if he was telling the truth. When we got back, he told Sarge something and then they barricaded the door. He looked guilty, like he'd betrayed my trust somehow."

"Okay, so they know we weren't staying here, so they've assumed we have somewhere else and that there's more of us. But they don't know for sure, and if we don't tell them, then they can't find the bunker," Dean says.

"We could tell them we were staying in that cave in the gorge where Matt and I camped after the landslide," I say. "It wasn't far from the meadow. We could say we camped there for a few days because it was closer to the meadow than here."

"It doesn't explain the other footprints and the disappearing deer though," Priya reminds us.

"So, what do we do then? Wait until they trust us and then run for it?" I ask.

"In the absence of a better plan, yeah." Dean shrugs.

Priya lies back and covers her face with her hands. I raise my eyebrows at Dean as if to ask, 'is she okay?' He shrugs his shoulders again and touches her arm.

She takes her hands away from her eyes. "I'm fine. I'm just wondering how the hell the world turned so completely upside down so quickly. Do you know, for a while there I actually wondered if this was all part of the leadership camp. That they were pretending this was happening to test us or help us develop leadership skills or resilience or something. Obviously, I don't think that now, but it just doesn't seem real sometimes. Like I imagined this all up, and it's all in my head."

"If this is all in your head, that would make me the man of your dreams then, wouldn't it?" Dean says, grinning at Priya.

"I guess then you would be." She smiles back.

"I think I'll join the others." I roll my eyes and jump down from the bed, closing the door behind me.

"Morning," I say as I enter the living room and walk over to the soldiers at the table.

"Morning. Do you want a drink?" Rhys asks, filling a mug from a steaming pot.

"Sounds great, thanks."

I take the mug and walk over to the window to look outside. Everything is covered in a deep blanket of fresh white snow, and although it's no longer snowing, the sky is still cloaked in thick grey cloud, threatening the possibility of more.

"Johnny said you know of a hot pool near here, Jess?" KJ calls across the room. "Maria and I are keen for a bath. Could you take us?"

"Yeah, sure," I reply as Dean and Priya emerge from the bunkroom and make their way to the table.

Rhys hands them both mugs of tea and serves up bowls of porridge. We eat in uncomfortable silence, other than KJ asking Priya if she'd like to come with us for a swim after breakfast. Dean doesn't look happy about the idea, but Sarge tells him he'll need to stay behind and will get the chance to go with Johnny and the others when we return.

As we get ready to go, I remember there used to be towels in the storeroom and dart in to find them. I pick up the towels from the shelf and notice the hunting knives that the soldiers removed from us in a pile in the corner. I quickly pick up one of the knives and tuck the sheath under the waistband of my trousers, making sure my top is pulled down to cover it. I have the towels in my arms and am just about to leave when I'm met by Maria at the doorway.

"What are you doing in here?"

"I remembered there were towels in here and thought we'd need them. Do you want one?" I hold out the towels for her to see.

Her eyes narrow as she tries to work out if I'm lying, and scans the room. Her eyes rest on the weapons still lying on the floor, then steps aside to let me pass. I hand her a towel and walk to my jacket and put it on, wanting to make sure the knife is properly concealed beneath.

"Keep an eye out, okay?" Sarge says to Maria and KJ as we prepare to leave. They nod in reply, and I notice they're both carrying guns.

"We'll take good care of your boyfriend while you're gone." Rhys masks his warning with a smile.

Priya and Dean hug before we leave, and I hear Dean whisper he'll be fine when she seems reluctant to go.

"I need to use the toilet," I say once we're out the door.

"Fine, we'll wait here," Maria replies.

I hand the towels to Priya before running across the clearing to the toilet and quickly close the cubicle door behind me. I'm breathing hard, my heart pounding, terrified they would find the knife on me. *I've got to find somewhere to hide this.*

I frantically look around the hut and see a beam at the top of the wall where the roof slopes down to meet it. It's too high to reach, so I put the toilet lid down and stand on top of it to get the extra height I need. I place the knife on the beam and push it back from the edge out of sight, checking from a few different positions to make sure I can't see it. Once I'm completely satisfied it isn't visible, I leave the toilet and return to the others. My heart is still beating fast, but I'm relieved that I'm no longer at risk of being caught with the knife on me.

As we cross the snow-covered clearing, Maria comes up alongside me. "Don't think for a second I believe this act of yours." She grabs my arm roughly, stopping me. "I'm going to give you one chance to tell me if this is some kind of trap, because I'm warning you, if it is, they won't hesitate to kill Dean."

I'm confused by her sudden aggression. Maybe she suspects I took the knife?

"What do you mean, a trap? I don't know what you mean?"

Her eyes lock with mine as she grips me. I'm not sure whether she's trying to read my mind or intimidate me, but I refuse to back down, holding her stare. After a few seconds, she lets go of my arm and instructs me to keep walking.

Even though I know Ethan and the others won't come to check on us, I scan the meadow for tracks as I jog to catch up with Priya and KJ. But there's nothing. The perfect white carpet is completely untouched by footprints other than our own.

****

"Oh, this is bliss." KJ sighs as she sinks into the water, placing her gun on the rocks at the side of the pool. Maria does the same, but keeps her hand resting on hers.

"I'm surprised you hadn't found this already," I say. "We found it on our first day here."

"We had other priorities," Maria says.

"Such as?" I ask.

"Hunting," she replies. "We were out of food when we found this place, and we didn't want to burn through the supplies we found at the cabin too quickly."

"You came up here without any supplies?" Priya asks incredulously. "What if you hadn't found any shelter or food when you got up here?"

KJ looks at Maria as if seeking permission to speak. Maria nods.

"I grew up around here," KJ replies. "Most of the locals know about the Jacobs having a hunting cabin up here. So, I was pretty sure we'd find it once we got onto the plateau."

"Is that how you knew about the Lodge at Fortune Falls too?" I ask.

"Yeah, I thought there might be some food stored there. We headed there after it got too dangerous in the valley."

She didn't mention staying in the farmhouse. I wonder if it's because she doesn't think she should tell us about it, or the other possibility. It never happened, and Johnny made it all up just to scare me.

"Johnny said your unit was posted at a refugee centre after the outbreak started?"

"Yeah, that's right." KJ nods.

"Did the virus get into the centre?" I probe, wanting to double check Johnny's story. "We heard that some of the refugee centres ended up having outbreaks spread through them."

"Yeah, that happened in some of the centres at the border, but not the one we were at," KJ says. "Ours was different. We were there to protect the refugees. It wasn't safe for them in their homes anymore and they couldn't cross the border, so they were taken to the refugee centre for their protection."

"Why weren't they safe in their homes?" I ask.

"There are a lot of desperate people out there," KJ replies. "People were terrified. If they stayed in the quarantine zone, it meant death. But if they left, it meant everyone else would die if they took the virus with them. So, the government brought in the military to make sure that didn't happen."

"But why weren't people safe in their homes *outside* the quarantine zone though?" Priya asks.

"Because some people did get out of Kavanyah," Maria answers before KJ has a chance to. "And those people had nothing and nowhere to go. Like KJ said, they were desperate people, and desperate people do desperate things." She shakes her head as though annoyed that she has to explain something so obvious to us. "When there's limited resources, like food and shelter, and there isn't enough for everyone, people will do what they need to do to survive. And sometimes that means taking what they need from someone else. They'll take it by force, even kill if they have to. That's why people weren't safe in their homes. That's why we needed to take them into refugee camps. It was to protect them."

"So, what happened at the refugee camp if there wasn't an outbreak?" I ask.

"People happened," Maria spits the words. "The virus isn't the most dangerous thing out there. You know how to deal with a virus, you can isolate and avoid the infected. But it's the people who are dangerous. They're unpredictable, they're selfish, they're afraid, and a lot of the time they're just plain stupid. They won't listen to what they're being told to do to protect them. They would rather believe that the government is out to get them than is trying to help them. They turned on *us*, the people who were trying to protect them. We were their *only* line of defence, and they turned on *us*!"

"So, they wanted to leave?" Priya asks.

"Some did, but a lot of them didn't. That's what made it so hard," Maria replies. "There were so many families in there, kids and the elderly who needed our protection. But there were enough other people who didn't want it."

"Why didn't you just let the people who wanted to leave, go? And let the people who wanted protection stay?" I ask.

"I know," KJ says. "That's what I said too. But we were given orders not to let anyone leave. We needed to stop the virus spreading, and the only way to do that was to stop people moving around. But in the end, they took us by surprise and got into the armoury. We weren't expecting them to *force* their way out. They overran the place, taking hostages, shooting anyone in a uniform. It was a complete mess. We were lucky to get out of there alive."

"Johnny said you were the only ones from your unit who survived?"

"We weren't the only ones." Maria shakes her head. "There were others. I saw them get out, but we got separated. I found KJ pretty soon after, but we didn't find Troy and the others for about a week."

"Who's Troy?" Priya asks.

"Troy is Sarge's name." Maria laughs. "You didn't think Sarge was actually his name, did you?"

"You didn't find them for a week?" I ask. "Johnny said you found each other a couple of days later and then you stayed in a farmhouse with a couple and their daughter."

"No." Maria shakes her head, narrowing her eyes at me. "KJ and I went back to the refugee centre after everyone left and barricaded ourselves in. We were hoping some of our unit would come back and we'd regroup, but after about a week, we had to run for it when a group of looters smashed their way in."

"Troy and the others found us when we were making our way to the Lodge at Fortune Falls," KJ continues. "Johnny may have stayed at a farmhouse, but we weren't with them."

Despite the warmth of the pool, I shiver as the hair on my head prickles. Johnny said Maria and KJ had been with them at the farmhouse, but they weren't, and there's no reason for KJ and Maria to lie about it. *I can't believe that whole story was a lie! He'd been trying to trick me into telling him where our friends are!*

"It sounds really scary," Priya says. "I can't imagine what you've been through."

"You must've been through some scary stuff, too," KJ replies. "Johnny told us about the landslide."

"I told Johnny about how we were trying to get through the gorge to Morrison and that we got caught in the landslide," I say to Priya before she has a chance to say anything.

"He said some others in your group were killed?" KJ asks.

"Yeah, two of our friends died," I say. "Emily and Kalen."

KJ's eyebrows shoot up, a brief look of surprise registering on her face, and then it's gone. *Did I imagine it? But why would she react to what I just said? It's what I told Johnny, and it's all true.*

"I'm sorry to hear that," KJ says.

We stay at the pools a while longer and then Maria tells us it's time to go back to the cabin. We quickly dress and follow our footprints back through the snow—the clouds parting occasionally to let fingers of sunlight break through, turning our meadow into a glistening wonderland.

Maria opens the door and stands back to let us enter the cabin. Priya walks through the doorway and stops so suddenly that I walk into the back of her.

"Sorry, Priya, I wasn't expecting you to stop," I say as I step to the side to move around her. Then I see why she froze.

Dean is sitting in a chair, his head slumped forward with his hands bound behind his back. He lifts his head to look at us, his mouth covered in duct tape and blood streaking his face from a cut in his eyebrow.

CHAPTER 40

"What the hell!" The words rush from my mouth as Priya runs toward Dean.

Rhys intercepts her, grabbing her arms and then forcing her into a chair as she struggles to break free.

"What have you done to him? Let me go!" she screams, throwing her head back as she thrashes, and it connects with Rhys's face while he's bending to bind her hands.

"Ah, you bitch!" He slaps the side of Priya's head. "A little help here," he calls out. Johnny walks over to hold Priya's arms while Rhys finishes strapping her wrists together with duct tape.

My initial shock is replaced by the urge to run. I turn, intending to go back out the door, but Maria's blocking my way. She just shakes her head and points at the table. I glance at KJ—she looks as stunned as I am. She hadn't known this was going to happen either.

Rhys places a chair in front of me as I walk toward the table and I sit down. I don't resist as he takes my hands and places them around the back of the chair where he binds my wrists with duct tape.

"That's more like it," Rhys says behind me. "Now if you two had behaved a bit more like this, we wouldn't have had to be so rough!"

"Why are you doing this?" I direct my question to Sarge.

"Why do *you* think we're doing this?"

I ignore him and look at Dean. "You okay?"

He nods. I then look at Priya. "What about you? Are you alright?"

She doesn't reply, just continues to glare at Rhys who's now standing beside Sarge, holding a towel to his bleeding nose. I'm surprised by the look on her face, jaw clenched and chin lifted, defiant.

"I'm fine too," Rhys retorts. "Thanks for asking."

I decide to say nothing more, waiting for them to make the next move. I'm don't know what triggered this, but I'm pretty sure I know what they want to find out. I watch Johnny closely as he joins KJ and they whisper to each other, too quiet for me to make out what they're saying. But from the look on KJ's face, she's not happy with what he's telling her.

"So," Sarge barks into the silence. "We've been having a little chat with Dean here, haven't we, Dean?" He walks over to Dean and slaps him on his back. Dean makes a herculean effort not to flinch. "But I'm done talking to Dean and I think he's had enough of talking to me, haven't you, mate? So, now it's time for me to have a chat with each of *you*."

Sarge smiles at me. "Jess, I think I'll start with you." He walks over to me and lifts me so my hands clear the back of the chair and plants me on my feet. He then takes me by my elbow and guides me to the bunkroom.

"Sit." He puts his hand on my head as he pushes down, making sure I don't hit the frame of the top bunk as I sit on the bed beneath.

He shuts the bunkroom door and then sits on the bunk opposite me, clasps his hands on his knees and leans forward. I resist the urge to shuffle back and return his stare.

"So, as I was saying, we've had a very interesting chat with Dean while you were out. And now I'd like to give you a chance to corroborate some of the things he's been telling us." He pauses waiting for me to say something. "Jess, it's important you understand that if you tell me something that's different from what Dean has told me, I will punish him for lying to us. So, if you lie to me, I'm still going to hurt your friend, because I've decided I'm going to believe that you're telling me the truth. Okay?"

I swallow and nod.

"And, just so you know. After we've finished our talk, I'm going to have the same chat with the lovely Priya, and I'm going to believe everything *she* tells me."

He lets it sink in. I'm screwed no matter what I do. I don't know what Dean has told them, and I don't know what Priya might tell them. But my gut tells me that Dean wouldn't have betrayed our friends. He wouldn't have told them about the bunker. And I need to do the same.

"Right, let's get on with it then," Sarge says in a relaxed manner, placing his hands on the bed on either side of him. "How about I just mention a couple of things that Dean told us so you know what we've covered already, and then we can move on to the important stuff. We know about the bunker, and we know there are more of you." He sits forward, studying me. I try not to react, but the realisation that Dean has told them the truth knocks the wind out of me.

"We *know* that's where you've been living. What we *don't* know for sure is *where* this bunker is located and how many others are in your group. And that, Jess, is where you come in. Dean has told us some information, but I want to make sure he's telling us the truth, which is why your answers *really* need to be the same."

"Fine. What do you want to know?" I sigh, defeated.

"How many people are at the bunker?"

I picture the faces of each of my friends as I count in my head. "Eight." I feel sick as soon as I've said it, my stomach churning with betrayal.

Sarge nods. "Good, we're off to a good start. Well done, Jess. Now describe where this bunker is."

I take a deep breath, deciding to tell the truth, but avoid as much detail as possible. "It's a few hours' walk further up the valley, hidden by some trees."

"Come on, you can do better than that."

"It's really well hidden. You'll never find it without someone showing you."

"You managed to." He shrugs.

"We got really lucky."

"What side of the valley is it on?"

"The eastern side."

"Yes, it is." He smiles at me. "So far you're doing very well. Now tell me about security. How do you access the bunker?"

I hesitate. *What should I say? What would Dean have told them?* I close my eyes, trying to calm the feeling of panic crushing my chest. I take a deep breath, then exhale slowly, and then another, slowing my heart rate. "It's got a steel door with a combination lock."

"What's the code, Jess?" His voice sounds deeper, more intimidating.

"It doesn't matter what the code is." I smile at him. "Because they would've changed it as soon as we didn't return to the bunker yesterday."

"Then it doesn't matter if you tell me the code, does it?" He smiles back, knowing he's winning.

"Shit," I mutter under my breath, feeling completely trapped. Even though our security protocol is to change the passcode as soon as anyone goes missing, what if they haven't? What if I give them the correct code to the bunker?

"I'm waiting." He leans forward impatiently.

"It's …" I start to cry. I feel like a traitor. "I'm not going to tell you."

"I understand. But you said it yourself. If they've changed the code, it doesn't matter if you tell us." He walks toward the door. "I don't want to have to hurt your friends, so I'll give you one more chance." He pauses with his hand on the door handle.

"Jacob," I whisper. Close enough to corroborate Dean if he's told them the correct passcode, but missing a vital digit if he hasn't and for some reason the others haven't changed the code.

He takes his hand off the door handle and returns to his seat on the bunk. *Does this mean Dean didn't tell them the code?*

"One last question. What sort of weapons do they have?" He leans back, trying to look relaxed, but his eyes are intently focused, eager. And I realise that *this* is what he wants to know. Everything else has just been a test, confirming information he already knows. But he doesn't know this. Dean didn't give him this.

"There are some knives and tools, like axes and shovels, things like that. But we don't have any weapons." I sigh, as though disappointed with myself.

"Any guns?" His eyes narrow, suspicious that we don't have guns.

"We only have one, and you've got it. We were hunting with it yesterday.”

“Remember, I’m going to be speaking to Priya next. If she tells me something different, I’m going to believe her over you.”

“I’m telling you the truth.” I shake my head.

He stands and tears a piece of duct tape off the roll he’s brought in with him.

“Sorry to do this, but I can’t have you saying anything to Priya, can I?” He places the duct tape over my mouth, then pulls me to my feet and leads me back to my seat in the living room.

“Are you okay?” Priya’s concern is clear in her voice. I nod, unable to say anything.

Sarge moves in front of Priya, then squats down until they’re at eye level.

“She’s fine, and you will be too. We’re just going to have a friendly chat.” He stands her up, helping to lift her arms over the back of the chair and then leads her into the bunkroom. She doesn’t resist, doesn’t argue. She knows there’s no point.

I watch them until the door closes and then look over at Dean. He raises his eyebrows in question. I shake my head in dejection and shrug my shoulders as if to say ‘what other option did we have?’ His eyebrows pull down in a frown as he closes his eyes. A look of frustration? Annoyance? I can’t tell. But he isn’t happy with my response, and I’m not sure why.

I watch Rhys with Maria, KJ with Johnny, as they talk in pairs, and I wonder if this was their plan all along when they asked me to take Maria and KJ to the hot pool this morning. They wanted to separate us so they could question Dean on his own. By removing Priya and me it reduced the risk of any complications if we resisted or fought back. Dean wouldn’t have stood a chance against the three men on his own. They would’ve overpowered him easily, and he wouldn’t have seen it coming.

Here I was thinking we would be the ones to outsmart them, planning to build a rapport with them and get them to let their guard down around us. Instead, the opposite happened, and we’d been completely clueless. I’m furious at myself for being so stupid. I glare at Johnny talking to KJ. Although I have no reason to feel betrayed by them, I do. I’d wanted to believe that Johnny was telling me the truth. But now I know it was all a lie. His way of getting *me* to let *my* guard down around him. And it had worked.

When Priya emerges from the bunkroom, her mouth is covered by duct tape and her face is streaked with tears. Sarge returns her to her chair and I try to make eye contact with her, but she doesn't look at either of us, her eyes focused on her knees. Dean is staring at Priya, willing her to look at him, his forehead creased with concern.

Sarge walks to Rhys and speaks quietly to him. Rhys's eyes flick over to us as he listens, his face expressionless. Then Sarge tells the other soldiers to come outside with him. I turn my head, trying to see them through the window. Johnny and Rhys are leaning against the verandah handrail facing toward me, and Rhys is still watching us as he listens to Sarge. KJ begins to talk, becoming animated, lifting her hands as though unhappy about what she's hearing. Maria places a hand on KJ's shoulder, attempting to calm her as KJ continues to shake her head. Johnny nods as Sarge says something, but I can't read his expression, his face a stony mask.

Sarge has complete control over these soldiers. Whatever he's telling them is a command, not a request; he is their leader. He finishes, then leads them back inside the cabin. Rhys pulls a chair away from the table and straddles it as the rest of the soldiers begin packing items into backpacks. He rests his arms on the back of the seat and stares at the three of us as we watch all the activity, wondering what they're planning to do.

Sarge finishes packing and comes over to stand in front of us. "I want you to listen to me very carefully." He looks at each of us in turn. "We're going to go and find this bunker of yours and meet your friends. Priya has kindly agreed to come with us to make sure we don't get lost and make the introductions."

Priya shakes her head dejectedly. She hasn't willingly agreed to anything.

"And just to make sure Priya doesn't change her mind about helping us, you two are going to stay here with Rhys." He smiles at us. "And as a thank you, I've promised Priya that Rhys will take good care of you both … but!" He lets it hang there. "Sadly, there's always a but, isn't there? If one of my guys doesn't return to tell Rhys that we've become friends with your bunker mates within twenty-four hours, Rhys has orders to kill you both." Sarge looks at his watch. "So, midday tomorrow. How does that sound to all of you?"

CHAPTER 41

Priya's in tears as they untie her. She doesn't want to go. They won't let her hug us, all she can do is call out "I love you" to Dean as they push her out the door. Dean can't do anything. Unable to speak, he tries to stand, but Rhys firmly keeps him in place. I see tears in his eyes, powerless to stop them taking her, powerless to do anything.

"I don't think we really need these anymore, do we?" Rhys says after a few minutes, tearing the duct tape off my mouth. I flinch as he pulls it off, tasting blood where the tape tore at my cracked lips. He then walks to Dean and removes his.

"Can I have a drink? I'm thirsty." I say.

He walks to the table and returns with a cup, holding it to my mouth so I can drink. He then goes to Dean and holds it for him.

"What did you tell them?" Dean's voice is hoarse; he coughs to clear his throat.

"Just the same as you. The general location of the bunker, how many people there are and—"

"I didn't tell them anything." Dean shakes his head.

"It's okay, we *all* told them."

"I'm telling you. I didn't say anything! They took me by surprise, held me down and tied me up, put duct tape over my mouth and then we sat here until you guys came back. They didn't ask me anything, and I didn't tell them anything."

"How is that possible?" I shake my head. "They knew about the bunker. I don't understand. If you didn't tell them, how did they know about it? He said you'd already told them about the bunker, Dean! He told me that if I didn't give him the same answers you gave him, he'd hurt you, so I told them the truth." Panic rising. "Oh my god, what have I done?" I burst into tears at the realisation that they'd completely fooled me. "He said *bunker*." I try to justify why I thought he'd told them. "How would they have known about it? He didn't say cabin, he specifically said *bunker*," I ramble through my tears.

"Jesus," Dean mutters, shaking his head. "I don't know, but it wasn't me. Maybe they heard you talking to Priya?"

"Ahem." Rhys clears his throat loudly. "Maybe you should just ask me?"

"Fine. How did you find out about the bunker?" I glare at him.

A smile creeps across his face. "Well, to start, Dean's right. He didn't tell us. We already knew about the bunker before we even came up here."

"How could you have known?" Dean asks incredulously.

"It's an interesting story, actually." He's thoroughly enjoying that he has our full attention. That he has information we want. He takes his time, pouring himself a mug of tea and sitting back in an armchair.

"About a month ago, a family was found hiding in a farmhouse and brought into the refugee centre where we were based. They started telling some of the soldiers that they had a bunker in the mountains and offered them a place in it if they'd help them get there. We didn't think anything of it until the shit hit the fan at the refugee centre and we were overrun. That same man started pleading with the guards to help him and his family get to his bunker. He said it would provide a safe place to stay for anyone who went with them until this all blows over. At that point, when we realised that the centre was going to fall, some of us agreed to take him."

"*You* agreed to help them get to the bunker?" I ask.

"No." Rhys laughs. "Not me, but Johnny the good Samaritan did."

"What happened to the family?" I feel a sense of dread, suspecting the worst.

"Dunno. Johnny said he got separated from them during the riot. And lucky for us, we found Johnny. Fortune favours the bold, so they say!"

"Yeah, they also say dumb luck," Dean replies.

"Oh, Dean, do I detect a note of sarcasm in your voice?" Rhys smirks.

"I think the word you're looking for is condescension." Dean lifts an eyebrow.

The smile disappears from Rhys's face. He mentally checks himself, then smiles a small smile that doesn't spread to his eyes. I'm not sure it's anger I see. No, it's malice, and I suddenly feel scared. I'm afraid for Dean and what Rhys might do to him.

He calmly gets up from his seat, eyes focused on Dean, and walks slowly to him. He bends down so that he's at eye level, only inches from his face.

"You think you're smarter than me?" Spit flies from his mouth, hitting Dean in the face. "You think you're—" Dean whips his head forward, smashing his forehead into Rhys's face.

Rhys roars in pain as he covers his face with his hands, blood trickling through his fingers. He kicks out with his leg, hitting Dean squarely in the chest, knocking him and the chair backwards. Dean's head smacks onto the wooden floor with a loud thud, no longer moving.

I try to get out of my seat, but I can't lift my hands over the back. "Dean? Dean?" I repeat more loudly. "Let me check him. I think you've killed him!"

Rhys ignores me, holding the same bloody towel he used earlier against his nose, trying to stem the bleeding. I shuffle my chair toward Dean to see if he's breathing. I try to lean closer to him and knock the chair over sideways. Rhys continues to ignore me as I wiggle my way up the back of the chair until my arms are free and then crawl over to Dean. I place my face next to his mouth and feel warm breath on my skin. He's not dead, just unconscious. Tears stream down my cheeks, dripping onto his face, and I hear him whisper, "I'm okay."

"Get away from him." Rhys shoves me away with his foot, and I fall back against the base of the sofa behind me.

"You could've killed him," I yell.

"Shame I didn't."

"Do you really think our friends will let you stay in our bunker if you've killed one of us?" I shake my head in disbelief at his stupidity.

"Do you really think we care whether your friends want us there or not?" He glowers down at me.

"They won't let you in if they think you've done something to us. They'll want to know we're okay first. And you don't know the code to get in. I didn't tell Sarge the right code."

"Priya told us the code."

"It doesn't matter anyway." I sneer at him. "They'll have changed the code as soon as we didn't return yesterday. And there's no way you can get into that bunker without the code. I know, because we tried."

"Oh, Jess." He lets out a deep breath as though speaking to a silly child. "We don't *need* the code. We have Priya, remember? And Priya is going to ask your friends to let us in."

"Priya wouldn't do that," Dean mumbles from the ground as he tries to roll away from the chair.

"Oh, yes, she will. You forget, if she doesn't get us into that bunker and help us meet your friends, I'll kill you both, and she knows that."

"But just because they let you into the bunker, it doesn't mean they'll let you stay." I glare at him.

"You're right." Rhys throws his hands up. "You're absolutely right. Your friends might decide *not* to share, and that isn't a risk we're prepared to take."

"What do you mean?" Dean has untangled himself from his chair and is now sitting with his back against the sofa next to me.

"I mean, if anything looks like it isn't going to work in our favour, we'll make sure it goes our way. Fortune favours the bold, remember?"

"So, if they don't let you stay?" I already know the answer.

"Let me put it this way. You need to stop thinking of it as *your* bunker. From now on, that bunker belongs to *us*." He points at himself. "And it's *you* and *your friends* that'll be begging *us* to stay."

I can't look at his gloating face anymore, the sick realisation that he's right. They've thought of everything. Priya will help them get into the bunker because she's afraid they'll hurt Dean and me if she doesn't. Sarge will tell her it's just so they can talk and negotiate the possibility of them joining our group. She won't know that they'll kill anyone who stands in their way. Once that bunker door is open, they'll easily overwhelm our friends inside. They're soldiers, this is what they're trained to do. Our friends won't stand a chance. The only hope they have is to keep the door closed. They can't let Priya in.

I close my eyes. *We have to get there before they do. We have to stop them before they open the door.*

"I need to take a piss," Dean grunts.

"Fine," Rhys says. "Stand up. You can go off the verandah."

Dean rolls onto his knees and stands. "Unless you're planning on holding it for me, I'm gonna need my hands."

"I'm not untying you. You'll just have to make do."

"Come on, man. I'll end up pissing all over my pants and *you'll* have to sit here smelling it."

Rhys hesitates, then moves over to the table. He starts pulling out duct tape from the roll and then picks up his gun and a knife. "I'm going to cut your hands free and rebind them at the front. If you try anything, and I mean *anything*, I'm going to shoot her in the head. We clear?"

"Yeah, we're clear," Dean replies.

Rhys slices the duct tape from Dean's wrists. "Put your wrists on the tape."

Dean does as he says, and with the gun still pointed at me, Rhys wraps the tape around Dean's hands. He then points the gun at Dean. "Okay, outside."

Dean walks to the door and waits for Rhys to open it for him, then goes outside.

We've got to get to the bunker before they do. But how the hell are we going to get away from Rhys when we're tied up?

I frantically look around the room for anything that I can use to cut my hands free, but before I have a chance to do anything, Rhys and Dean re-enter the room. As I watch Dean walk in with his hands bound in front of him, I realise what I have to do. I just have to find the courage to do it.

"I need to go too," I say.

"Seriously?" Rhys looks at me in disbelief. "What is this, synchronised bladders or something?"

"Something like that." I stand up and turn my back to Rhys. "I can't go with my hands tied either. And no, you're not helping me."

"Over here." Rhys points to a chair by the table. I begin to walk to the chair. "Not you, him." He points at Dean. "Put your feet around the table leg, ankles together."

Dean does as he says, and Rhys binds his ankles with duct tape, trapping his feet around the leg of the table so he can't move away. "Don't think I need to tell you not to go anywhere now, do I?" He slaps the back of Dean's head as he turns toward me.

He picks up the 9mm and the knife and smiles at me, lifting the gun so I can see it clearly. "Just don't be stupid, okay?" He then reaches behind me and cuts my hands free. I grab my jacket as I walk to the door and put it on as we cross the clearing to the toilet with Rhys following behind. I climb the steps to the hut and look back at Rhys as I close the door.

"Don't worry, I'll be right here," he calls out.

I lock the door and sit on the toilet, looking up at the beam above me. *Am I doing the right thing? This could backfire. He's much stronger than either of us, and as much as I hate to admit it, he's smarter, too.* But I can't think of an alternative. This is our only chance.

I put the toilet lid down and stand on it, reaching with my fingertips to the beam where the knife is hidden. I manage to crab pinch it between two fingers and pull it to the edge. I'm about to lift it off when Rhys bangs on the door and I jump, knocking the knife from the beam, and frantically fumble with both hands to catch it as it falls. My heart pounds as I call out, "Nearly done," and tuck the knife into the belt at the back of my pants, hidden beneath my jacket.

I open the door and smile at Rhys. "Sorry, I'd been holding it a while. Big bladder."

I push past him and walk down the stairs and head across the clearing to the cabin. As I reach for the door handle, I stop and turn to look at Rhys. "I've been thinking about what you were saying. That it will be *us* that'll be asking *you* to let us stay in the bunker once you're in there, and I realise you're right. I'm not stupid. I know you and Sarge and the others are trained for stuff like this. There's no way my friends will be able to stop you."

"Yeah, so?" Rhys looks at me warily.

"So … I want to be in that bunker, and I was thinking you probably have the power to make that happen." I swallow nervously as I say the last words, trying to get the courage to say the rest. "I thought maybe you might want me to be there with you if I was, like your girlfriend or something."

"Huh." He grunts at me, unconvinced, and then narrows his eyes. "*If* ... and that's a big if ... I wanted a girlfriend, why do you think I'd be interested in *you*?" He flicks my hair dismissively and I realise I've misjudged him.

My smile falters and I begin to blush. "Oh, I ... I just thought maybe ... Oh, forget I said anything," I mumble, shaking my head. Even though I wasn't really wanting to seduce him, I'm mortified that he rebuffed me so harshly. I feel stupid and embarrassed that he wasn't even slightly interested.

So much for that idea. Now what, genius? What's your big plan to get him away from Dean now?

I realise he's staring at me and I look shyly up at him and see that he's studying me. *Oh my god, I think he's actually considering it!* I can almost hear his brain whir as he tries to work out how he can make this to his advantage without the risk of it going wrong.

"Alright." He shrugs. "How about I give you a chance to show me whether you're up for the role? Consider it an audition of sorts."

I let out a shaky breath and nod, forcing myself to smile.

Rhys reaches for the door handle and I quickly put my hand on his arm to stop him. "Not here." I shake my head. "I'd be too self-conscious with Dean in the other room." I pull him gently toward me until we're in front of the window, making sure Dean can see us, hoping he can hear what I'm saying. "I was thinking, how about the hot pool? It's private there, no one around. I'll feel more relaxed."

Rhys glances through the window at Dean, who quickly looks away.

"You don't have to worry about him, he can't go anywhere. You've tied him to the table!" I laugh and then say more loudly, "Hot pool. Come on! I promise you won't be sorry." I take his hand and begin to lead him away from the door. I feel him resist for just a moment, and then he follows.

"Why the hell not?" he mutters under his breath.

I walk at a leisurely pace across the clearing, wanting to give Dean as much time as possible to get himself free before we get there. I just hope Dean remembers the method we watched in the video. It wouldn't have been possible if his hands had been bound behind his back, but now that they're in front of him, he should be able to get his hands free within seconds. I just need to hold Rhys off until Dean gets here, and then we can overpower him together, tie him up, and get to the bunker before Priya and the others do.

Neither of us speak as we walk. I'm too nervous to talk, going through different scenarios of how this will play out when we get to the pool. I just need to make sure Rhys doesn't see the knife, and I need to make sure he doesn't see Dean when he arrives.

I stop as we reach the small clearing around the pool, the steam so thick it obscures visibility of the other side. "Here it is," I announce with more confidence than I feel.

Rhys stops beside me and takes my hand, gently turning me toward him. He places his finger under my chin and tilts my head to look up at him. I swallow nervously as our eyes meet, and then he takes my face in his hands and leans down to kiss me. He's much gentler than I'm expecting him to be and I immediately feel relieved. I force myself to kiss him back, trying not to cringe as I do. I need to make sure he thinks I'm interested, that this isn't just a ploy to distract him.

His hands slide down from my face to my waist and then begin to move to my back and I quickly pull away, worried he'll find the knife. "How about we get in the pool? It's kinda cold out here, don't you think?"

"Ladies first," he says, holding his hand out toward the pool.

I smile and walk to the edge of the pool where I take off my clothes, keeping the knife concealed within them as I place them in a pile on the ground. Rhys watches as I undress to my underwear. I then step into the steaming water and sink down to my shoulders, turning to face him.

"Your turn." I smile.

He quickly discards his clothes in a pile next to mine, placing the gun on top. He sighs as he steps into the water, enjoying its warmth, sinking down to his chin.

"This was a very good idea." He says, tilting backward to let the water warm the back of his head. He lifts his head and makes his way toward me, steam swirling around him as he moves.

His hands reach for me under the water and he pulls me toward him, kissing me softly, his hands running over my body. His eyes close as he kisses me, and I sneak a look behind him at the path, hoping to see some sign of Dean coming. But I don't.

I feel his hands move to my back and begin to tug at my bra strap. Before he has the chance to undo it, I put my hand on his chest and gently push him back. "What's the hurry?"

He doesn't seem annoyed by my resistance, in fact the opposite, as he grins at me. He moves so quickly it takes me by surprise. One hand grasps my arm and pulls me toward him; with the other he reaches around to the back of my neck and grabs a handful of hair at the base of my head. He pulls the hair sharply, snapping my head back so I can't move, his face still smiling. But something has changed in his eyes. He pulls my head toward him and he kisses me, but the gentleness of his previous kiss is now gone, roughly grinding his lips into mine, stubble tearing at my skin.

I try to push him away, but he pulls my hair harder, trapping me so I can't move, unable to even turn my face from his. He follows as I back away from him, until I'm pressed against the rocks at the edge of the pool, trapping me. He stops kissing me, still holding my hair in his hands. "You know what I really like?"

I stare at him in terror, unable to think of anything that is going to help me, realising I'm completely out of my depth.

"I like a girl with a bit of fight in her." He pulls my hair back so far my head can't go any further, and I have to grit my teeth to stop from crying out.

"You don't need to do this," I plead. "I want to be here with you."

Still pulling my head back with one hand, his other reaches up to my exposed throat, gently running his fingers down from my jaw. Then, without warning, he grasps my throat tightly in his hand. "I don't think you get it, Jess. I don't *care* what you want."

He squeezes my throat so hard it feels like it might break. I grab his hand with both of mine and try to pry his fingers away, but the more I try, the harder he squeezes. I hear a strangled choking sound and realise it's coming from me. I can't scream. I can't do anything. *He's going to kill me!*

He lets go of my hair, holding me in place, pinned against the rocks by my throat. I can't breathe. I give up trying to remove his hands and hit at his face instead. Darkness begins to crowd the edges of my vision, a roaring noise fills my ears, and just as I feel I can't carry on, he lets go.

I drag in a deep breath, filling my burning lungs with air and cough as it irritates my throat. I suck in another breath and cough over and over. Tears run down my cheeks, as I choke and cough, terrified he might do it again.

"You're just lucky that I don't have a thing for dead girls."

He reaches out to me, and I reflexively push his hand away, afraid of him touching me and what he might do. Slowly, I edge toward the entry point of the pool. My only means of escape.

Dean, where the hell are you?

"Oh, come on, Jess, we're just messing around, aren't we? Got to see whether you're right for the role. Wouldn't want to vouch for you getting a spot in the bunker if you're not up for it."

"I told you I'm here willingly," I croak, my voice barely above a whisper. "You didn't need to hurt me."

He reaches out and grabs my hair again, stopping me from continuing any further. "Are you, though? Are you *really* here willingly?"

I let out a sob, unable to control my fear. "I … I thought …"

"You thought what? That you could seduce me and be my girlfriend and get to play house with me? Is that what you thought? Or maybe you thought you could get me to let my guard down so Dean could rescue you?" He yanks my hair back and I let out a strangled gasp. He grips my forehead in his other hand and pushes my head under the water.

I try to push him away, kicking out with my legs, scratching at his skin with my nails, frantic to make him let me up so I can breathe. Nothing I do is having any effect. If anything, it makes him hold me down harder. And then I realise he's just going to keep doing this to me over and over until I break, and there's nothing I can do to stop him. So, I give up. I stop fighting. I go limp and wait. He *wants* me to fight, so if I don't, it removes the pleasure for him. That, at least, I can take from him.

I resist the urge to gulp for air as he raises my head above the surface and lie limp in his arms, trying to breathe inconspicuously through my nose. But I can't control the spasm in my lungs, desperate for more air than I'm giving them, and I begin to cough, gasping for air.

"Woah-ho-ho! Thought I'd lost you there for a second. Have to say, Jess, I'm thoroughly enjoying myself. This was a great idea!" he says enthusiastically as I continue to cough, trying to calm my breathing. Trying to think. I glance at the path, looking for a sign of Dean, but it's completely empty.

He's laughing as I struggle to breathe, genuinely enjoying my fear. And in that moment, I know he's not going to stop until I'm dead.

You sadistic asshole. You want a fight, you've got one.

I slowly rise until I'm standing with the water at waist height. I stand defiantly, glaring down at him. He stops laughing, and reaches his hands to my waist, his eyes on my body … not my eyes … not my hands. Before he has a chance to react, I ball my hand into a fist and punch at his face with all my strength, connecting with his already bruised and battered nose. I feel his nose crunch beneath my fist and hear a crack as it breaks.

He screams in pain, letting go of me to cover his face with his hands. I dive toward the rocks where we entered the pool, where our clothes are … where his gun is, desperate to get there before he can react and stop me. I reach the rocks and begin to climb out. I don't need to look behind me. I already know he's coming.

Come on, come on, come on, this is your only chance.

I will my muscles to move faster as I scramble over the rocks and stumble to my feet. Rhys grabs my ankle as he lunges from the pool and I slip on the icy rocks, hitting the ground hard. I begin to crawl as he loosens his grip while he climbs out of the water, knowing he still has a chance to stop me. His gun is right in front of me, just beyond my reach. I grab at his clothes and pull them toward me, carrying the gun on top of them, and I've got it. *I've got it!* I roll onto my back intending to fire, but his body slams into me, his hands grabbing at the gun.

For him, this is some kind of sick game. For me, it is pure desperation. I know that if I lose, I will die. I try to hold the gun out of his reach, gripping onto it as tightly as I can, but he grabs my wrist, pulling my arm closer. I scream in anger, expecting to hear a terrifying war cry, and instead, hear nothing more than a pitiful croak as he tries to pry the gun from my fingers.

I realise I'm not going to be able to stop him from taking it, so I pull the trigger and it fires away from us into the trees. I fire again and again and again, trying to use up all the bullets. I keep pulling the trigger until it clicks, the chamber finally empty, and let go of the gun, letting him have it.

He relaxes for only a second, but it's all I need. I roll away from him along the ground to my pile of clothes. He doesn't react, doesn't think he needs to, happy to let me get away so he can play his cat-and-mouse game again. The predator and the prey.

I feel for the knife hidden under my clothes. *There it is.* I stand, keeping my back to him, removing the knife from its sheath as I hold it in front of me where he can't see it, and begin to cry. I don't have to fake the tears—they come easily, I'm truly terrified—but I also want him to think I've given up, that he's won. I hear him stand and wait until I can feel him right behind me. His hand reaches up, winding into my hair again. As he pulls my head back, I spin, taking him off guard, striking him with the knife.

He doesn't react, not even a flinch. I don't think he actually realises I've stabbed him. I watch as blood begins to run out of the wound on his neck and then I see a flicker of realisation on his face. He lets go of my hair and moves his hand to his neck, his eyes revealing his shock as he touches the knife and knows what I've done.

"Don't pull it out," I say to him. "You know you'll bleed out if you do."

His eyes widen in fear, and I wonder if I've gone too far. *Maybe this hadn't been necessary? Maybe he wouldn't have killed me?*

"I'm sorry," I say. "I thought you were going to kill me."

He bellows a noise of pure frustration, realising the hopelessness of his situation. "You know what? I still am."

I watch in horror as he pulls out the knife and lunges at me. I grab his hand in both of mine, but it's almost impossible to hold on. I'm amazed at how strong he still is, and I don't know how much longer I'll be able to hold him off.

Blood pours from the wound in his neck. He doesn't have long. I can feel him beginning to weaken. He falls to his knees, releasing his grasp on the knife, then collapses back onto the snowy ground behind him.

I stand motionless over him and watch his blood spread onto the white carpet, turning it crimson, as Rhys desperately tries to stem the flow from his neck. An act of futility, and he knows it too.

He begins to shiver. He knows what it means. Fear turns to anger, and he sneers at me. "You're all going to die, you know. They're going to kill every one of you."

His attempt to make me afraid one last time erases the remnants of guilt I have that I've gone too far. Now all I feel is relief. Relief that I've survived, and relief that he will never terrorise anyone again.

CHAPTER 42

I watch as Rhys's breathing becomes more and more shallow, until he takes his final breath. He looks almost peaceful, lying there surrounded by red snow, his skin pale, lips blue. And I feel nothing.

I realise I'm shivering. I look down at my hands; they're covered in blood, as is the rest of my body.

Come on, Jess, get it together. This isn't over yet.

I step into the steaming pool, my feet burning, my skin icy after standing in the snow for so long. The contrast in temperature feels like fire on my skin, but once I rinse off the blood and emerge from the water, I see it isn't just the temperature difference that's making it sting. My skin is covered in scratches and abrasions from clambering over the rocks at the edge of the pool and hidden beneath the snow.

I don't waste any more time than I need to, getting dressed as fast as I can. I need to get to Dean, and we need to get to the bunker. I wash the knife and place it in the sheath, tucking it into the band at the back of my trousers, then pick up the empty gun lying discarded on the ground.

As I turn toward the path leading back to the cabin, I see a figure running in the shadows of the trees within. *Dean?* I squint, trying to make out who it is. *It's Dean!* I try to call out, but all I can do is croak, so I begin to run toward him.

"Jess!" Dean yells out as he sees me. "Oh, thank god! I was so worried. I couldn't get free." He hugs me. I hear footsteps behind him and see Johnny running down the track. Without thinking, I push Dean to the side and raise the gun, pointing it at Johnny. He stops as soon as he sees me holding the gun and raises his hands, lifting them away from the rifle hanging at his side.

"It's okay, Jess. Johnny helped me. He came back to help us. That's how I got untied." Dean places his hand on my arm, forcing me to lower the gun. "If he hadn't helped me, I'd still be in the cabin tied to that bloody table."

I look suspiciously at Johnny. Not sure I believe what I'm hearing.

"Really?" My voice croaks. I shake my head. This doesn't add up. I raise the gun again. "What did Sarge think about you coming back to help us?" I try to speak as loudly as I can, but it just seems to make it sound worse.

"What's the matter with your voice?" Dean reaches out to move the collar of my jacket, exposing my throat. "Jesus, what did he do to you?"

I shrug his hand away, ignoring him as I focus on Johnny. "Answer me!"

"Yeah, well, I don't think he's going to be exactly pleased about it," Johnny replies.

"So, you just decided to leave them and come back to help us?" I narrow my eyes at him, still keeping the gun trained on him.

"We heard the gun shots and Sarge wanted me to come back and check that Rhys had everything under control. I'm supposed to catch up with them. I went to the cabin and found Dean trying to bite through duct tape." He raises his eyebrows at Dean.

"What? I was getting desperate. I needed to get free so I could help Jess." Dean looks at me. "I couldn't bloody break the tape like in that video, Jess. Rhys must've used more layers or something. When I couldn't break it apart, I didn't know what else to do."

"Why are you helping us?" I whisper hoarsely. "Why would you betray your friends to help us?"

"I told you yesterday, they aren't my friends. I also told you Rhys was dangerous and I would try to protect you from him if I could. I couldn't just leave you here with him, knowing what he's like."

"You *also* told me Maria and KJ were with you at that

farmhouse." I strain my voice so he can hear me. "But you lied. They weren't there. You made that whole story up to scare me into telling you where the bunker is."

Johnny shakes his head and sighs. "You're right. I did lie about Maria and KJ being there, but the rest of the story was true. What Rhys and Sarge did was true. I didn't lie about that."

"Why would you lie about Maria and KJ being there, then?"

Johnny pauses, taking a deep breath. "Because it didn't sound as bad if they were there."

"What are you talking about? Your story was horrendous and you wanted it to scare me. Why would you try to make it sound better than it was … Unless you were a part of it?" I raise the gun, the truth dawning on me. "What are you hiding? What did you do?"

"I didn't do anything, that's what!" Johnny's mouth turns down in disgust. "I stood by and let it happen. I pretended I didn't know what Rhys was going to do, that maybe it would be okay … but I knew it wouldn't … and I didn't even try to stop him."

"How could you do that? How could you just stand by and do nothing to stop him?"

"I was scared." His face contorts, paining him to admit it. "I know it sounds pathetic, but it's the truth. I was terrified of Rhys, and I thought if I tried to stop him, he'd kill me. I didn't think I had a choice. I thought I had to go along with whatever they did if I wanted to stay with them. I wasn't going to survive out there on my own without them." He takes a deep breath, his eyes silently pleading with me to understand. "I'm not sure how I'm going to live with what I've done. I know I can't make up for it, but I also know I can't make the same mistake and stand by and do nothing again. When Sarge told us his plan to take the bunker, I knew I couldn't let it happen. I couldn't live with myself if someone else died and I didn't try to stop it. I *did* lie to you, Jess, but I'm telling you the truth now. I came back to help you. KJ doesn't want them to do it either. She'll try to help Priya, but I need to get back to them if we're going to stop them."

I keep my gun trained on Johnny. I want to believe him. It feels like he's telling the truth, but I thought that last time too, and my instincts have failed me every step of the way since we were captured. *How can I trust him when I can't even trust myself?*

"Come on, Jess, put the gun down," Dean implores. "We need to get to the bunker before Sarge and the others do. Why would he untie me if he didn't want to help us? He would've just left me where he found me if he was planning to help Rhys."

I look at Dean. He seems so sure Johnny is telling the truth. *Come on, make a decision, Jess. Dean's right, we need to go now.*

Slowly, I lower the gun and put on the safety.

"There's not really any need for the safety when the gun isn't loaded." Johnny gives me a small smile.

I raise my eyebrows at him.

"Unless you've reloaded … which I doubt you've had the chance to do. I counted the number of shots that were fired, and this is the only gun we left behind."

I shrug and put the gun in my pocket.

"But the question I don't know the answer to is … where's Rhys?" Johnny asks.

I turn, gesturing for them to follow, and lead them back to the pool.

Dean lets out a long whistle as he sees Rhys lying on the ground surrounded by blood-soaked snow. "Holy crap, Jess. What the hell happened here?"

Johnny walks over to Rhys's body. He doesn't touch him. There's no need to check for a pulse. He's clearly dead. He picks up the jacket lying on the ground and spreads it over Rhys's face and torso.

"We'll take care of him later. We need to go now if we're going to catch Sarge and the others before they get to the bunker." Johnny rummages in his backpack and holds a box out to me. "You should reload."

We leave as soon as I finish reloading the gun. We hurry back through the trees and then cut across the clearing to join the tracks Sarge and the others had made when they left to find the bunker. Johnny leads the way, taking large strides through the deep snow. I follow behind, trying to use his footprints, and Dean brings up the rear. We move much faster once we reach the other footprints, Johnny's pace picking up now that he no longer has to break a trail.

"How far ahead do you think they are?" Dean asks as we walk through the trees.

"Maybe half an hour, give or take," Johnny calls back, not slowing to talk. "But they're not moving very fast. Priya kept complaining that she needed us to slow down. Hadn't picked her for such a whinger, actually."

Dean snorts behind me. I turn my head and smile at him. Priya is definitely not the type to complain. In fact, she never complains about anything. He nods, knowing what I'm thinking. "That's my girl," he says proudly.

Our suspicion that Priya is trying to buy us time to catch up is confirmed when we reach the river and see their tracks have followed it, rather than taking the faster route directly up the plateau. I look back at Dean as Johnny starts to follow the tracks, and point up the plateau.

"Hey, Johnny. This way's faster." Dean points across the river and straight up the valley.

Johnny stops to look across the field of pristine snow. "How much faster? Because cutting a fresh track through this snow is going to be a lot slower than following the trail they've already made. It won't just slow us down. It'll tire us out faster too."

"When there's no snow, maybe an hour," I say in a loud whisper, deciding this is the least painful and most effective way of speaking.

Johnny hesitates, weighing the two options. "We're going to need to take turns breaking the trail so we can keep our speed up without getting exhausted."

"No problem," Dean replies, and I nod.

As soon as we enter the untouched snow on the other side of the river, Johnny leads the way, bearing the brunt of the hard work to break a trail in front of us. Dean follows behind him, his footsteps continuing to clear the path, and I reap the benefit of their effort as I follow at the back, easily keeping up at little more than a strolling pace.

After about five minutes, Johnny steps to the side and lets Dean take the lead, and I move up to second place. I'm surprised at how heavily Johnny is breathing as I pass him, as though he's been running. He falls into place behind me.

Although our pace quickens initially once Dean takes the lead, he slows after a few minutes. I also find I'm having to put more effort into each step, my feet sinking further in the snow than before, continuing to pack the trail more firmly as I go.

Another couple of minutes and Dean steps to the side, and it's my turn to take the lead. My feet sink to my knees with each step. I lift my leg higher than normal to try and avoid the weight of the snow as I step through it, the effort beginning to take its toll quickly. My heart rate increases and I hear myself puffing. I push myself to move faster, not wanting to be the weak link in our chain. Not wanting to let them down. Finally, I know I need to step aside. No longer able to keep up a fast pace, I let Johnny take the lead again.

We continue like this for an hour. The leader falling to the back of the line when they can no longer keep up a steady pace, using their time at the back to recover for when it's their turn to break the trail again.

We stop only briefly to have a drink of water that Johnny hands us from his pack.

"I assume they'll be going slower than this?" I ask Johnny.

"Yeah, but not by much. Sarge is a big guy. He's pretty good at breaking a trail."

In reality, we have no idea whether we're managing to catch up or not. We just have to keep going and hope that we'll get there before them.

We've been walking another half hour when I hear a voice call out. Dean stops suddenly in front of me and I have to step to the side of him to see what he's looking at. I make out two figures running toward us in the distance. I lift my hand to shield my eyes from the glare and recognise them.

"It's Ethan and Lily," Dean exclaims.

"I take it they're your friends?" Johnny asks as he stands beside us.

Dean begins to move forward, almost at a run, moving much faster than we'd been going previously. I fall in behind, running to keep up. After a few minutes, he steps aside and I take over, continuing to run. I can see Ethan clearly now, Lily following behind him.

"Jess!" Ethan calls out. I lift my hand and wave in response.

I'm puffing hard, but I don't want to fall back and let Johnny take the lead. I want to reach them first. Not only because I want to get to Ethan, but also because I'm not sure how they'll react if they see Johnny running toward them.

It isn't long before we close the gap. I smile when I see the huge grin on Ethan's face as he runs toward me, and laugh as he holds out his arms. I run straight into his arms, and reach out to hug Lily too as she catches up. Dean grabs us all from behind, and we cling to each other as we try to catch our breath, puffing heavily.

Finally, we release each other and Ethan looks suspiciously at Johnny, keeping his arm around my shoulder.

"This is Johnny," Dean says. "Johnny, this is Ethan and Lily."

Ethan and Lily nod, eyeing Johnny warily.

"We've got a lot to tell you. We don't have much time," I croak. "Dean, you tell them." It's too hard to talk.

Dean quickly fills them in on everything from being found by the soldiers to Sarge taking Priya and his plan to get into the bunker. Finally, explaining that Johnny and KJ want to help stop Sarge, and how Johnny had come back to help us get away from Rhys.

"So, we need to get to the bunker before they get there with Priya," Dean finishes.

"Did you change the security code?" I ask hoarsely.

"Yeah, we did it as soon as we knew you were missing," Lily replies.

"Good." I nod, relieved they've followed the protocol.

"What's the matter with your voice?" Ethan asks.

"Long story." I hold my hand up to my throat as I try to speak. "I'll tell you later."

"So, how many of them are there?" Ethan asks.

"There are three soldiers with Priya," Dean replies. "Sarge, Maria, and KJ. Sarge is the biggest threat. He's in charge, and it's his plan to take the bunker by force once they get in."

"But KJ will help us," Johnny adds.

"What about the other one, Maria?" Lily asks. "Will she help us?"

Dean and I look at Johnny for the answer. We want to know too.

"I'm not sure." Johnny shakes his head. "I don't think she's happy with the plan. It's not how she would do things. But she's sleeping with Sarge, so I can't be sure what she'll do."

"And what about the other guy? The one who was guarding you two?" Ethan asks.

"We don't need to worry about him. Jess took care of him," Dean answers for us.

"What do you mean, *took care of him?*" Ethan sounds annoyed. "Is he tied up? Is there a chance he'll get free and join up with the rest of them?"

"No, not like that. He's dead. He's definitely not going to be a problem anymore," Dean replies quickly.

Ethan's eyebrows lift in surprise and Lily's mouth drops open as they both stare at me.

"I didn't have a choice," I croak and unzip my jacket collar to reveal my neck, which I assume is looking quite bruised from Dean's earlier reaction. "Self-defence."

Lily gasps when she sees my neck. "Oh my god. That explains your voice then."

"What the hell!?" Ethan draws back in shock. Then, realising how he's reacted, he reaches out, pulling me protectively into his arms.

"I was tied up," Dean says quietly, shaking his head. "I couldn't stop him. I couldn't do anything to help." His voice cracks as he finishes.

"I came back as fast as I could when I heard the gunshots," Johnny adds. "But I didn't get back until it was already over."

"You shot him?" Lily asks.

"No." I pull away from Ethan's arms. "I … I stabbed him." I shake my head, horrified as I say the words.

Lily's eyes widen.

"We need to make a plan." Dean breaks the stunned silence. "Are we going straight to the bunker or stopping them before they get there?"

"Well, we know they can't get in. We changed the code," Lily says.

"How are they planning to get in?" Ethan asks.

"They're going to use Priya to ask your friends to open the door and let them in," Johnny replies.

"Priya wouldn't help them." Lily stiffens at the suggestion.

"She thinks Rhys will kill Dean and Jess if she can't get them to talk to Sarge," Johnny explains. "And she doesn't know that Sarge is planning to take the bunker by force once they're in."

"And if Priya doesn't do it?" Ethan asks. "What will they do to her?"

"KJ will do her best to protect her. But we need to get there before it comes to that. We need to keep moving." Johnny begins walking, not waiting for anyone to follow, calling behind him, "We should be able to make better time now we don't have to break a trail anymore."

Johnny walks so fast we almost have to jog to keep up. Dean follows behind Johnny, then Lily, with me next and Ethan bringing up the rear.

"Do you trust him?" Ethan asks quietly from behind me after a couple of minutes.

I don't stop walking, but turn my head so he can hear me. My voice barely able to be heard as it is anyway.

"Yeah, I do. He doesn't want Sarge to do this. He came back to help us when he didn't need to. He could've just left us there with Rhys."

"Maybe he was planning to help Rhys, but switched sides when he found out he was dead?"

"No, that wasn't it." I slow down to make some distance between us and the others, making sure they don't overhear. "He untied Dean before he even knew Rhys was dead. He'd tried to warn us that Rhys was dangerous, and he didn't need to do that. I believe him when he says he came back to help us get away from him."

"Jess, stop for a minute." Ethan grabs hold of my arm.

"We need to keep going." I shake my head and turn to keep walking. "We can talk later."

"We'll catch up," he insists, not letting go, forcing me to stop. I turn and face him. He reaches up and brushes some hair from my face. "That guy, Rhys, he did this?" His eyes flick down to my throat and then back up.

"Yes." My voice is barely above a whisper.

I'm surprised at the expression on Ethan's face. I haven't seen him look like this before. His features are serious, his eyes reflecting the depth of his concern. I don't want him to worry.

"I just want to know if you're okay?" he asks gently.

"I'm okay. Really." I smile to reassure him. "Just a bit sore, but I'll be fine. I promise I'll tell you more if you want to know later, but right now, we need to focus on getting to the bunker before they do."

He nods, knowing there's no point in pushing this any further. "Okay, we'll talk later then."

I set off at a jog, wanting to catch up with the others as quickly as possible. I hear Ethan's footsteps behind as he follows. We catch up after a few minutes. Johnny is now at the back of the group and Dean is leading. We continue to follow Ethan and Lily's track to the small clump of trees at the end of the plateau and then out again on the other side.

We've been going for nearly three hours when we finally spot Priya and the others in the distance. I feel relieved when we see them. They're still following the stream, and even though they've nearly reached the forest surrounding the bunker, we'll reach the bunker first if we continue our direct route.

Johnny stops as soon as he sees them and crouches, indicating for us to do the same.

"It'll probably take them another twenty minutes to reach the hot spring island, and then it's another ten through the forest to the bunker," Ethan says. "I figure we should be able to make the bunker in thirty minutes or less from here. Once they disappear behind those trees, we should run straight for the bunker."

"I should cut across and catch up with them," Johnny says. "They're expecting me to return after I've made sure everything's okay at the cabin."

"They'll want to know what happened," I say hoarsely. "Tell them Rhys had everything under control and that he was firing the gun to scare us, like some kind of sick game or something. They'd believe Rhys would do that, wouldn't they?"

"Yeah, I don't think Sarge would be too surprised."

"We need to make them think everything is going to plan, okay?" I cough, the 'okay' catching in my throat. "We need to take him by surprise. But be ready, because as soon as he sees us, he'll know that you've been lying."

"And then what?" Dean asks. "What's our plan then? Do we fight them?"

"No. It's too risky. We don't want anyone to get hurt." I cough again. "Johnny, you need to get Priya away from them as soon as they see us. Once Priya is safe, Sarge and Maria will realise there's no point in continuing with their plan. We'll make them give up their weapons, tie them up, and take them to the bunker. We can work out the rest from there."

"What about KJ?" Dean asks.

"KJ will be fine," Johnny replies. "Sarge and Maria won't suspect her. She'll know what to do."

"Who's going to go to the bunker to warn them?" I say to Lily and Ethan.

"I'll do it," Lily says.

"Can I have your gun?" Dean asks. "I'm going to need something when we confront them."

Lily takes the rifle from her shoulder and hands it to him.

"Alright, they're out of sight," Ethan says. "Let's go."

He begins to jog along the trail in the snow in front of us, leading directly toward the hillside concealing the bunker at the edge of the forest. We follow behind him, taking turns to lead to keep up our pace. About half way across the plateau, Johnny veers off diagonally from the group, cutting a new trail through the unmarked snow. He says nothing as he leaves, only a quick wave to those of us who'd been following behind him. There's no need to say anything. We all know what we need to do.

We reach the edge of the forest in only twenty minutes. We've pushed hard to keep going, none of us wanting to let our friends down, and the urgency of the situation driving us forward. I'm out of breath, puffing hard, and I'm not the only one. We're all breathing heavily from the exertion.

When we reach the edge of the clearing in front of the bunker, Lily wishes us good luck before heading directly to the bunker door.

"How long has it been since we saw them?" I ask Ethan when I notice him check his watch.

"About thirty minutes," he whispers in reply. "They could come through here any time now."

I remove the gun from my pocket, comforted by its weight in my hands. Grateful for the lessons Ethan has given me over the last few weeks in preparation for a hypothetical situation that has now become a reality.

We stay hidden in the trees, using them to conceal us as we circumnavigate the clearing toward the path that leads to the river, knowing that will be the direction they will come. I look back at the bunker and see that Lily has disappeared through the door. *At least we've stopped them from getting into the bunker. No matter what happens next, we've at least done that.*

We position ourselves a few metres back from the track, taking care to make sure we're hidden from sight. We wait in silence, listening for any sound that might indicate the others are approaching. I find it difficult to hear over the blood pounding in my ears. I'm sure my heart is beating even harder now than it was when we were running.

Finally, we hear a noise in the distance. Slowly it gets louder and I recognise Priya's voice. "It's not much further now. You'll see it as soon as we reach the clearing," she calls out loudly.

And then I see them. Shadowy figures appearing and disappearing amongst the trees. Sarge is in front, his rifle held in preparation in case he needs it, but not aggressively as though he's expecting a fight. Maria follows behind, then Priya is in the middle with KJ and Johnny following her. He's not taking any chances that she'll try to escape.

Sarge stops as he reaches the edge of the forest and looks out into the clearing, staying hidden in the trees.

"There it is," Priya says loudly from behind. "I told you we were nearly there."

Sarge stiffens at her words, unhappy at how much noise she's making when he's obviously trying to be covert.

He steps to the side of the path and gestures for Maria to stand on the other side, then waves his hand at Priya to move forward. "We'll walk together," he tells Priya as she stands in between them.

Shit. We should have intercepted them on the path. How the hell is Johnny going to get Priya away from them now?

I glance at Dean and see he's as concerned as I am. We have no idea what we're doing and how we're going to do this.

As Sarge, Priya, and Maria walk into the clearing, Dean moves at astonishing speed to reach the edge of the path beside Johnny. Johnny isn't surprised to see him. He's been watching for us and nods in acknowledgement at his presence. Johnny puts his hand on KJ's shoulder as she begins to walk, stopping her. When she turns to look at him, he places his finger to his lips and points at Dean standing silently in the trees. Her eyes widen in surprise and then she nods in understanding. I step out from behind the tree where I've been hiding so she can see me too, and our eyes connect briefly.

Then everything begins to happen fast. Johnny steps past KJ and quickly closes the gap behind Sarge, Priya, and Maria. KJ is right behind him and Dean follows too. As soon as we see Dean following,

Ethan and I step out of the trees as well, raising our guns. My hands shake as I take the safety off.

Johnny runs the last couple of steps and grabs Priya by the arm. She lets out a scream as he pulls her away from Sarge and Maria.

"Run!" Johnny yells as he lets go of her and stands his ground, pointing his rifle at Sarge's back. KJ takes position beside him with her gun trained on Maria.

Priya stumbles in confusion as she turns, barely staying upright, then her face breaks into a smile when she sees us behind her. Sarge and Maria spin around to the sight of Johnny and KJ, training their guns on each of them.

"You traitor!" Sarge roars at Johnny as Priya runs to us. He lifts his rifle, taking a couple of threatening steps toward Johnny, who quickly steps back, keeping his gun raised.

"Don't do it, Sarge," Johnny warns. "Put your rifle down." I'm amazed at how calm he sounds. I'm terrified for him.

"You too, Maria," KJ says steadily. "I know you don't want this. There is another way."

Maria's eyes flick from KJ to Johnny, then back to me, Dean and Priya. Her gaze pauses on Ethan as she realises there's a new face in the mix. Finally, she looks at Sarge, who's glowering in rage at Johnny. What she chooses to do will determine the outcome. She has the power to defuse the situation or ignite it.

I exhale slowly as Maria places her gun on the ground and steps back, lifting her arms in surrender. KJ moves forward and picks up the gun.

"I'm sorry, Troy. You've got to see this is pointless," Maria pleads as Sarge's glare moves to her. "Please don't do this. Just put your rifle down."

Sarge's face has turned scarlet. I've never seen anyone so angry. His knuckles are white as he grips his gun, trying to control his rage. Johnny doesn't back down, he doesn't move. KJ steps away from Maria and points her gun at Sarge. "You'll only get one shot, Sarge. You can't take down both of us."

Sarge takes a deep breath and lets out an enraged howl of frustration, throwing his gun on the ground. Johnny quickly steps forward and kicks the weapon away from Sarge before picking it up, keeping his own rifle trained on Sarge the whole time.

"I'm so happy to see you guys." Priya hugs Dean. "I was so worried something had happened to you when we heard those shots."

I look back at the others and KJ is tying Maria's hands behind her back with a cable tie from her pack.

"What did you do with Rhys?" Sarge asks Johnny. "Is he alive?"

"He's at the cabin." Johnny stiffens as he replies, but keeps his rifle pointed at Sarge.

"That's not what I asked you," Sarge growls.

Johnny ignores him, not wanting to risk enraging him further. KJ gestures for us to come closer, wanting us to take over guarding Maria so she can tie up Sarge. Dean nods and raises his gun as we move closer. Priya and Ethan follow, but continue to stay behind us.

KJ walks to Sarge and pulls his arm behind his back while Johnny keeps his gun trained on him.

"Why aren't you answering me?" Sarge says coldly to Johnny. "Did you do it?"

"I didn't kill him, if that's what you're asking," Johnny says flatly.

Sarge grits his teeth. "But he *is* dead, isn't he?" He closes his eyes and tilts his face to the sky as KJ takes his other hand, pulling it behind him.

Sarge's head snaps forward, directing his focus at Dean. "So, it was one of *you* then."

I glare back, refusing to be intimidated by the vicious look on his face.

Without warning, Sarge yanks his hands away from KJ and turns, tearing the rifle slung over her shoulder from her side. The violent motion pulls KJ off balance and he steps away from her, holding her gun in his hands.

"Don't do it, Sarge," Johnny yells, taking a step toward him.

"Which one of you killed my brother?" He screams as he points the gun at Dean and then me.

Dean swings his rifle toward Sarge as I continue to point my gun at Maria. And then Sarge fires. I tense, waiting to feel the impact of the bullet, but feel nothing. There's only the sound of a second shot immediately following the first. Sarge falls to the ground and I look at Dean, worried that he'd been hit instead of me. He looks at me at the same time, his face mirroring my relief as we realise the shot missed us.

"Priya's been hit!" Ethan yells.

I spin around to see Priya lying on the ground only a couple of metres behind us, Ethan kneeling over her. Dean drops to his knees beside her and I run to her other side. She looks okay. Her eyes are open. I look for a wound but can't see one. She doesn't make any sound; she doesn't move, her eyes empty. Dean opens her jacket, revealing the bullet hole and blood is spreading over her chest beneath.

Dean places his hands over the wound and presses down. "We need Skye! SOMEONE. GET. SKYE!" he screams when none of us move.

I already know the answer, but feel for a pulse anyway. I can't find it. I try again, moving my fingers along the side of her neck, desperate to find it, desperately hoping I'm wrong. I feel a tightness in my chest, not wanting to say the words as I place my hand on top of Dean's while he continues to press on the wound on Priya's chest.

"She's gone, Dean," I say quietly, barely more than a whisper.

My throat constricts as Dean lets out a strangled sob. "No … no, she's not. She can't be." Dean's shoulders slump in defeat.

I walk around Priya and kneel behind Dean, wrapping my arms around him as he continues to press on her chest.

"I'm so sorry." I cry into his shoulder as I hold him.

He moves his hands beneath her head, tears dripping onto her face, and I hear a sound so pitifully sad, a moan rising from deep inside him. His shoulders shake as he lifts her to cradle her head on his lap until his whole body is shaking with each sob.

I cover my face with my hands, tears streaming down my cheeks. Arms wrap around me. I don't need to look to know who it is. He doesn't speak, just holds me and strokes my hair as I cry silently into my hands.

How did this go so terribly wrong? She was safe, we all were. Priya hadn't hurt anyone. I was the one who killed his brother. It should have been me!

Anger surges through me as I push away Ethan's arms and storm over to where Sarge is lying on the ground with Johnny and KJ kneeling over him. Maria is sitting by his head, her hands still tied behind her back.

His eyes are open, but he isn't dead. His expression shifts from pain to a sneer when he sees me stand over him. I glare at him, wishing my eyes could stab holes in his face. I feel nothing but hatred toward him. Johnny lifts his hand from Sarge's shoulder to allow KJ to place some gauze underneath. She then wraps a bandage around his shoulder.

"Priya, is she—" Johnny looks up at me.

"Dead?" I finish for him. "Yes. She's dead." I turn my glare to Sarge. "You missed us and hit Priya, you psycho son of a bitch. You're just as bad as your brother."

"You think I missed?" he scoffs. "I never miss."

His dismissive tone sends a shiver down my spine. "Why would you shoot Priya? Priya didn't hurt anyone!"

"An eye for an eye, baby." He smirks at me. "He killed my brother. I killed his girlfriend. Now we're even."

The shiver turns into uncontrollable shaking as his words hit me. The realisation that he'd deliberately chosen Priya to avenge his brother.

"You—"

"Jess, don't," Johnny cuts me off, standing to make a physical barrier between me and Sarge. He shakes his head. "Don't say anything more. Let's go for a walk, get some space for a bit." He takes my arm and tries to lead me away.

I jerk my arm out of his hand. I'm not going anywhere. I don't need to get some space. I *need* to make this man feel pain.

"Dean didn't kill your brother," I say hoarsely, straining my voice to make it louder as I step closer to Sarge, until I'm standing directly above him. And now it's my turn to smile. "That pleasure was all mine."

His smug face turns to fury in an instant. Ignoring the pain in his shoulder, he lunges for me, grabbing my foot. Instead of trying to pull away, I kick out with my other foot as hard as I can, smashing it into his injured shoulder. He screams and lets go, falling back onto the ground, panting as blood spreads through the bandage on his shoulder.

"Jess, stop." KJ stands as Johnny grabs my arms from behind, preventing me from doing any more damage.

"Hey! Let go of her!" Ethan yells from where he's kneeling beside

Priya.

"Ethan?" KJ looks at Ethan, who is now storming toward us, intent on making Johnny let me go.

Ethan's steps falter, unsure who is speaking to him. Then a look of recognition crosses his face as he gets close enough to see KJ's features under her cap.

"Katie?"

CHAPTER 43

Johnny lets go of my arm as KJ pushes past us and runs to Ethan, throwing herself into his arms.

"I can't believe it's you." KJ hugs him. "I wasn't sure, but I hoped. After I heard about Emily, I thought maybe there was a chance you were here, too. God, you're a sight for sore eyes."

Ethan looks over KJ's head at me as he hugs her and swallows uncomfortably as I stare at them. "I need to let the others know about Priya," Ethan says, letting go of KJ. "Skye's inside the bunker."

"Skye's here too?" KJ says, standing back.

"I'll get her. You guys need to keep an eye on them." Ethan points at Sarge and Maria as he walks past us to the bunker.

He enters the code and opens the bunker door. Figures are on the other side waiting in position with weapons in hand in case someone manages to force their way in. A few seconds later, Skye comes running out, going straight to Priya.

"Jess!" Matt runs toward me, his features a mixture of concern and relief. He grabs me as soon as he reaches me and pulls me into his arms, hugging me so tightly I can barely breathe. "Thank god you're okay. I've been so worried."

He loosens his hold, moving back to look at me, and before I have a chance to say anything, he kisses me. Although it isn't for long, it's long enough that when we part, Ethan is staring at us. My stomach sinks. I want to go to him, to explain and apologise, to take away the hurt in his eyes. But as Matt pulls me in for another hug, I realise anything I say now would just make it worse. And all I can do is watch as Ethan turns and walks away.

****

There are tears and hugs as Dean and I reunite with our friends, and they learn about Priya. Eventually, Dean carries Priya into the bunker and down to a table that Kai set up for her in the basement. Maria and Sarge are placed on chairs in the corner of the living room. Their hands remain tied and two people guard them at all times.

Johnny and KJ are introduced to the group. KJ, it turns out, is short for Kathryn Jane, also known to her childhood friends as Katie. They tell everyone about what happened to them since the outbreak began, about the refugee centre and the events that led to them ending up here.

Skye and Ethan and the rest of our friends then take turns filling them in on our tale and how we found the bunker.

After listening for a while, I quietly leave the room. I want a shower, desperately needing to wash the blood and violence from my body.

The hot water stings my skin, but I don't care. In a way, the pain brings relief, externalising the ache from a wound I fear may never properly heal.

After dressing in clean clothes, I open the bathroom door and hesitate. I stare at the living room door, trying to decide whether to go back in and join the others, or go to bed. Although I'm exhausted, I'm not sure I'll be able to sleep, but I can't bear the thought of going back into that room with everyone else either.

I head up the stairs, my legs making the decision for me. As I reach the top, Dean opens the door to the upstairs bathroom, also freshly showered and in clean clothes. I walk straight to him and put my arms around him and we stand there in silence, holding each other.

After a couple of minutes, he lets go. "I'm going to hit the hay. I'm feeling pretty beat."

"Me too. I don't really feel like being sociable tonight."

"Yeah. Well, goodnight," he says quietly and turns toward the bedroom he shared with Priya.

I hesitate as I turn toward the bunkroom and call after him, "Dean, do you want me to stay with you for a bit? I can stay until you go to sleep if you like?"

"That's really kind of you." He smiles. "But I think I just need to be alone."

"Yeah, of course. But if you need to talk, I'm here, okay?"

"I know. Night." He walks into his room, closing the door behind him.

I climb into my bed and pull the sheet protectively up to my chin. It's hard to believe that only two nights ago I'd gone to sleep in this very bed, blissfully ignorant of the events that were about to end with the death of my best friend.

I close my eyes and my head instantly fills with images of dead vacant eyes—Priya's expressionless face, and Rhys as he took his last breath. I open my eyes, hoping to stop the images, but the room is pitch black and it just makes it worse.

Pain builds in my throat as I try to suppress the urge to cry. I'm afraid that if I start, I won't be able to stop, unleashing a floodgate. I close my eyes again and this time I see Rhys's grinning face as he strangles me, the pain in my throat growing worse and worse until a sob bursts from me, unable to contain it any longer. I gulp deep breaths, trying to calm myself, and sit up, pushing my back against the wall, my knees bent up to my chest in front of me.

I jump as the door opens, the light from the passage silhouetting the figure standing in the doorway. I try to quieten my crying, not wanting whoever it is to know that I'm upset, taking deep breaths to regain control.

"Jess? Are you awake?" Ethan whispers from the doorway.

Oh god. He'll want to know what's going on between me and Matt. Not now. I can't handle this right now.

I hesitate, wondering if I can feign sleep, but realise he'll be able to see me sitting at the end of the bed once his eyes adjust. "Yeah, I'm awake."

"Can I come in? I just want to make sure you're okay."

"Sure." I pat the bed.

He sits next to me and reaches out to take my hand, giving it a squeeze. "I know I can't even begin to understand what you and Dean have just been through, but from what I can piece together, it's been pretty frightening. I just want you to know I'm here for you. You know that, right?"

"Yeah, I know."

"I don't know what that guy Rhys did to you, but I know he hurt you, and I know you must've been really scared to have done what you did." He takes a deep breath. "I'm just really sorry. I'm sorry you had to go through this, that he hurt you, that he scared you. I wish I'd been there so I could have stopped him."

His kindness takes me completely by surprise. I'd been expecting him to be angry at me. But instead, he's ignoring his own hurt, the hurt that *I'd* caused him, only showing concern for me instead. I wasn't expecting this at all. I try to speak, but only make a strange strangled noise as my throat constricts and tears begin to fall. His compassion is so unexpected … Not because I don't think he cares— I know he does. But because he seems to care more deeply than I'd realised.

I cover my mouth with my hand as grief threatens to burst from my chest. I don't want him to see me upset. But I can't hold it in and the sob escapes with such intensity that it shocks me, my whole body shaking as it fights its way out. It hurts so much. The pain washes over me in waves, each larger than the one before, and I can barely breathe, certain I'm going to drown under the weight of it.

I'm vaguely aware of Ethan speaking to me, trying to soothe me, and then his hands reach under me, lifting me onto his lap. He holds me in his arms as I bury my face into his chest. His hand rhythmically stroking my back, over and over, until eventually the sobbing subsides and I take long, deep shuddery breaths as I slowly regain control of my body. Until I can breathe again.

I climb off his lap and lie on the bed, exhausted from the release of emotions as well as the physical toll of the last couple of days. Ethan lies behind me, his arms wrapped protectively around me.

"Just let yourself go to sleep," he whispers. "I'm not going anywhere."

CHAPTER 44

After breakfast, Ethan and Matt head out with Dean to choose a location to bury Priya, taking shovels with the intention of digging a grave. They return a couple of hours later and tell us the site is ready. Skye and I have prepared Priya's body in the basement, wrapping her in a white sheet from the hall cupboard. We leave when Dean arrives, letting him have some time with her alone.

Jackson and Kai volunteer to guard Sarge and Maria while the rest of us go to the burial site. Dean, Matt, Ollie, and Ethan carry Priya's shrouded body on the stretcher. The rest of us follow in silence until we reach a cluster of trees on a small hill further up the valley. There, we bury Priya's body; we hold each other and cry. Dean doesn't speak, but a few of the others recall memories of Priya and special moments they shared. We then carry stones from the river bed and place them around the grave, marking its location.

"I know this isn't really an appropriate time, but we need to make some decisions about our new visitors, and there isn't really anywhere private to talk in the bunker," Marley says. "I've spoken to each of you individually this morning, and we're all in agreement that KJ and Johnny are welcome to join us and make the bunker their home. That is, if you would like to join us?" He turns to them.

"Thank you. I'd like that very much." KJ's relief is plain to see.

"I would too. Thank you, truly." Johnny nods, glancing at me and Dean.

I feel everyone's eyes turn to look at us, wondering whether we're really in agreement after everything we've been through. I know I need to do something so they can see I'm okay with them joining us and step forward and give Johnny and KJ a hug, saying "Welcome to the family" loudly enough for everyone to hear. Dean shakes Johnny's hand and pats him on the back, ending any speculation, making sure our position is clear.

KJ walks to Ethan and embraces him. He smiles and puts his arm around her, relieved he doesn't have to worry about her not being allowed to stay.

"That was the easy part," Marley continues after the hugs and congratulations subside. "However, there wasn't the same consensus for Maria and Troy, and now that Johnny and KJ are a part of our group, they get a vote as well. They know them better than we do and may be able to provide more insight into how we should deal with them." He looks around the group, waiting for someone to object. No one does. "Okay, how about we start with Maria? Should Maria be invited to join us?" He looks directly at Johnny, then at KJ. "Can she be trusted?"

Johnny hesitates, watching KJ as if trying to read her thoughts, then he looks back at Marley. "Maria wasn't happy with Sarge's plan to take the bunker. You have to understand that Maria is a soldier. Troy was her Sergeant before this whole situation kicked off, and to her, he's still her commander … but she isn't a bad person. She doesn't want to hurt people if there are other options available. That's why she gave up her rifle so quickly."

"You don't think she gave up her weapon because she could see she was outnumbered?" Ethan asks.

"No, I think she needed an out," KJ answers. "She was stuck in a situation she didn't know how to get out of."

"You two didn't seem to have any trouble getting out of the situation," I say. "You both chose to help us. You didn't wait until your hand was forced."

"It was different for us. Johnny and I weren't under his direct command at the refugee centre. We joined up with them after the centre fell. But Maria *was*, and as Johnny said, Troy was her Sergeant." She looks directly at me. She knows that it's Dean and me she needs to convince. If we agree, the rest will take our lead. "You heard the way she talked about the reason why people were being brought into the refugee centre. She hated that they were being attacked, that they weren't safe in their homes. She wanted to protect them."

"So, you think we should let her stay?" I ask.

"Yes, I do."

"And what about you, Johnny? What do you think? Can she be trusted?" I look at him.

"I think so. I think she'll see that she has other options now, and she'll make the right choice."

"Alright then, let's put it to a vote," Marley says. "Raise your hand if you think Maria should be allowed to join our community."

We all look around the group as each of us raises our hands. KJ mouths "thank you" to me and Dean as we raise ours. I nod in reply.

"Alright, that's three down. One to go." Marley furtively glances at Dean and me as we stand together by Priya's grave. "What are we going to do about Troy?"

He doesn't even bother suggesting that Sarge be given the chance to join our group. I'm sure Dean and I weren't the only ones who'd shot that idea down as soon as Marley approached us this morning. I feel everyone's eyes turn toward us, waiting for us to speak again, and take Dean's hand in mine.

"Obviously we're not going to let him stay." Dean's voice is calm, measured. "But we can't exactly let him go either, can we? And there aren't any jails we can send him to." He shrugs his shoulders. "So as far as I can see, there's really only one possible solution."

His pragmatism surprises me. He's not driven by anger, or grief, he isn't looking for revenge. He's looking at this from the point of view of what is practical.

"You can't be serious?" Matt blurts. "We can't go around killing people because we don't want them to join us!"

"Why not?" Dean fires back. "What other option is there? If we let him go, what's to stop him from attacking us again in the future?"

"Well … we could …" Matt flounders, looking for a solution.

"We could build a jail," Marley offers. "We may not have anywhere suitable to lock him up, but we could build something to hold him."

"Where?" I reply. "He'd freeze to death in anything we build outside the bunker, and there's no room inside."

"What about in the cave? We could build a cell in the cave, couldn't we?" Matt suggests.

"What? So, he can just escape and kill us in our sleep?" I reply. "Why would we waste our food and resources on someone who will eventually try to kill us if he gets the opportunity? I don't think it's worth the risk."

"People can change, can't they?" Ollie says, looking at KJ and Johnny. "I mean, look at Maria. You're saying she will choose to be a part of our community and that we can trust her. Who's to say Troy won't too?"

"Because he killed our friend!" I shout. "Maria didn't hurt anyone, but Sarge *chose* to shoot Priya. He did it to hurt Dean, to hurt us, not because he was defending himself. He did it because he *wanted* to!"

"We can't risk him having access to the cave." Ethan shakes his head. "The generator is in there, the water pump, the air filtration system. Everything that's essential for the bunker to operate is in that cave. We can't risk him getting out and sabotaging it. You can't hold him in the cave."

I exhale loudly, relieved that Ethan has vetoed the cave. I don't want Sarge anywhere near us. I know he would destroy us if we kept him captive and he ever got out. It would be far worse than just letting him go.

"What about the cabin?" Marley suggests. "What if we banish him to it? Tell him he has to stay there?"

"What makes you think he'd stay there?" I frown.

"He wouldn't have a choice. He couldn't survive anywhere else up here," Marley replies.

"I don't mean that. I mean, what would stop him from coming back here?"

"We'd put security in place to make sure he doesn't. We'd work it out, Jess." Marley anticipates my next question.

I look at Johnny and KJ. "You know him best. His brother was a psychopath, and Sarge killed people to protect him … to *avenge* him. Do *you* think he's going to just go back to the cabin and live a quiet life and leave us alone? 'Cos it seems pretty bloody unlikely to me."

"Sarge isn't the same as his brother," Johnny says. "He doesn't hurt people for fun the way Rhys did. I think he does what he thinks he needs to do to protect the people he cares about … or feels responsible for.”

“I agree with Johnny.” KJ nods. “He did something terrible yesterday, and he can never be forgiven for that. But Rhys is dead and Sarge retaliated, and we can’t undo what’s been done. I don’t think he’ll look for trouble. I think if we let him go, he’ll stay away.”

I shake my head, my gut telling me it would be a decision we’d later regret. I saw the way he looked at me yesterday when I told him I was the one that killed Rhys. He won’t leave it. I need to make them understand.

“We can’t just let him go,” I say. “You didn’t see how he reacted yesterday. The hate in his eyes when he found out it was me that killed Rhys. If we let him go, he’s going to come back. He might not kill any of you, but he’s going to try to kill *me*.”

“So, what are you suggesting?” Marley challenges. “That we kill him? Because if that *is* what you’re suggesting, who do you think should have to do it? Would you do it? Or would you expect someone else to have to live with that?”

“I guess—”

“I’ll do it.” Dean cuts me off. “I agree with Jess. We can’t let him go. I’m not prepared to take the risk that he might come back. He’s already killed Priya. I don’t think we wait until he’s killed another of us before we realise we’ve made a mistake.”

“We can’t just go killing people because we’re worried that they might decide to hurt us one day,” Matt says.

“Really? Because that’s exactly what Sarge would do!” Dean retorts. “And *that* is who we’re dealing with.”

Matt shakes his head in disbelief. “If we decide it’s okay to do this to him, what’s stopping us from doing that to each other? This is not who we are!” His voice rises in anger. “It’s definitely not who *I* am, and I won’t be a part of it. I will not vote to kill him and there’s nothing you can say that’ll change my mind.”

“Matt’s right,” Marley says. “The decision we make today will determine what sort of community we become. We need to decide how we want to live together … our moral code that will guide our interactions with each other and with outsiders. If we decide to protect ourselves at the expense of all others, how does that make us any different than Troy? Is that how we want to live?”

"But it's all pointless if we end up dead because of it," Ethan replies. "Morals are a luxury for the living. As far as I'm aware, the dead don't get to have them. Shouldn't our priority be ensuring our survival?"

"But not at the expense of others!" Skye shakes her head in shock at Ethan.

"I'm not suggesting we kill *every* outsider who comes along," Ethan replies. "I'm saying that we need to assess the risk here, and if there's a risk that he could come back and hunt us in retaliation, it's not a risk worth taking. We can't protect against that. We won't be able to leave the bunker without worrying about whether he's out there waiting to ambush us."

"We won't let him take any weapons," Matt argues. "And we'll make sure we always go out in groups."

"Look, obviously we aren't going to be unanimous on this. It's going to have to be a majority vote that decides," Marley says. "Let's go back to the bunker. We'll need to get Jackson and Kai's votes too."

"I'm going to stay here a bit longer," Dean says. "You know what my vote is. And I'm prepared to be the one to do it."

"Okay, thanks, Dean." Marley nods as everyone turns to leave. I give Dean a hug before following.

"It's probably best if you do the voting out here," I say when we reach the bunker door. "You know where I stand. My vote is with Dean. I'll take over guard duty and send Kai and Jackson out to join you so they can vote too."

"I'll come with you," Matt says to me, then looks back at the others. "Just to be clear, I'm voting to let him go."

Matt gives me an apologetic smile. I sigh quietly to myself and nod. I'm not thrilled about it, but what did I really expect? Matt would never vote to kill Sarge. He won't even kill an animal to eat.

As I punch the code into the combination lock, I hear Ollie say under his breath, "Do you really think it's a good idea that Jess is on guard duty?"

"Funny you should say that," Ethan replies. "I was just thinking the same thing about the vegetarian pacifist."

CHAPTER 45

Matt and I sit in the seats vacated by Jackson and Kai. I hold the pistol in both hands, letting it drop toward the floor between my knees. Sarge and Maria sit on chairs with their hands tied, resting them on their laps. Skye has tended to Sarge's shoulder, checking the wound and replacing his bandages. She said there was an exit wound at the back; the bullet had gone straight through.

Maria looks drawn and tired. They know we're debating what to do with them and she's worried … As she should be. I feel sorry for her, wishing I could tell her she'll be allowed to stay. I wonder if she's worried for Troy too, whether she cares for him or not. But how could she possibly still care for him after everything he's done?

'One man's terrorist is another man's freedom fighter.' I hear my mum's voice so clearly in my head I nearly turn to look for her. 'There are always two sides to a story, Jess. Never forget that. Nothing is ever black and white.'

I sigh and narrow my eyes at Sarge. *What would I have done if someone had killed my brother? Would I have done the same?*

Sarge sits stony faced, staring at some invisible spot on the wall above my head as I glare at him.

You're a monster for killing my friend … but I killed your brother. So what does that make me?

His eyes suddenly lock with mine and I straighten, refusing to be intimidated by his stare.

I need to know what he's thinking. I need to know if we're deciding the fate of a monster or a man.

"They're going to let you stay, Maria, if you want to." I give her a small smile as she nods, clearly relieved at the news.

Matt's head jerks toward me. I don't need to see his face to know he's surprised that I'm telling them.

"And you." I look at Sarge, shaking my head in disbelief. "They're going to let you go. You get to just walk away." I say it quietly, calmly.

His chin lifts, the news giving him courage, and I see the glimmer of a sneer at the edges of his mouth.

"They're going to let you live in that cabin," I continue. "Shouldn't be too hard for you there on your own. You're resourceful." I let the information sink in.

"You keep saying *they*." Sarge's head tilts to the side. "I take it *you're* not one of them?"

"We're taking a vote. It's not up to just one person," Matt replies.

"But *you* haven't voted to let me go, though, have you?" Sarge's lips turn up a little more at the edges. "And you definitely wouldn't have voted to let me stay. So, what did you vote for then, Jessica? To kill me? Really, Jess? Killing one brother wasn't enough for you?"

I take a deep breath to steady myself and lean forward, resting my elbows on my knees. He doesn't take his eyes from mine as he watches me shift position.

"Rhys's body is by the hot pool. Thought you'd want to know so you can bury him."

Sarge stiffens at the mention of Rhys's name and he shifts uncomfortably.

Are you a monster or a man?

"Johnny covered him with his jacket before we left. Guess he didn't want him to get cold."

Sarge's expression turns to a sneer, baring his teeth at me. "I hope he had some fun before he died." He looks pleased with his attempt to hurt me.

"Your brother had a pretty sick idea of fun."

Sarge lets out a sharp bark of laughter. "Sounds like Rhys."

I can feel Matt's eyes on me, but I don't look away from Sarge. Sarge may not be a sadist like his brother, but I sense he likes a bit of fight too.

"Yeah, well, I did the world a favour. One less psychopath to hurt people." I sneer back at him. And there it is, like a switch being turned on. I literally see the change in his eyes as his pupils dilate, his blue eyes turning black.

"You smug little bitch." He leans forward, his voice shaking with malice. "You have no idea what you've started. You think Rhys enjoyed hurting you? You'll wish I was Rhys before I've finished with you."

I try to hide the shiver that runs down my spine at the intensity of his hatred.

"You killed our friend!" The words explode out of me.

"You killed my brother!" he spits back. "You killed the one person I cared about in this world! So, I'm going to take away everything that you care about. You think I'm going to hurt you? I'm not even going to touch you!" He's screaming now. "But I'm going to kill every … single … one … of your friends, one by one, and I'll save the one you care about most for last and make you watch."

I hadn't noticed Matt leave his seat, until he steps in front of me and smacks duct tape over Sarge's mouth, taking both of us by surprise. As Sarge tries to reach up with his bound hands to remove the tape, Matt pushes his hands down and binds them to his legs so he can't lift them. Sarge continues to try to scream at me through his sealed lips.

"This is for your own good," Matt tells him.

Matt looks back at me, his eyes wide with shock. He's breathing hard, and I realise I am too. He doesn't say anything, but he doesn't need to. I can see he understands the threat now.

The door from the decontamination room opens and Dean walks in. Matt doesn't hesitate, walking straight over to Dean and whispering in his ear, then leaves through the door Dean just entered. Dean ignores us, doesn't even acknowledge our presence. He goes to the kitchen, fills a cup with water, then walks over to sit in Matt's seat beside me.

"That's new." He nods his head at Sarge's taped mouth.

"I think Matt was worried I might shoot him if he didn't shut up."

"I'd quite like to see that." Dean smirks at Sarge. "Maybe I should take it off. How you doing, Maria?"

"Getting a bit sore, actually." She shifts uncomfortably in her seat. "Do you think they're going to be much longer? I'd really like to get this off." She looks down at her cable tied hands.

Dean gives me a sideways look.

"I told her we'd voted to let her stay."

Dean shrugs his shoulders. "I think they're just finishing up now. I wasn't really listening. I'd already made my vote." He smiles at Sarge.

We hear voices as the door opens and the rest of our friends begin to flow into the room. Some going straight to the kitchen to make drinks, others leaving through the opposite door to head to the toilets and bedrooms. Marley walks over to stand next to Dean. He raises his eyebrows when he sees the duct tape over Sarge's mouth, but says nothing. I see Matt looking at us from the kitchen and our eyes connect. He shakes his head in response to my silent question.

Marley takes his knife from the sheath attached to his belt and leans over Maria, cutting the cable tie binding her wrists. He stands back and smiles at her. "Maria, we've unanimously voted to let you join us and remain here at the bunker if you choose to."

"Thank you." She smiles at Marley as she stands, rubbing her wrists and then stretching her back and shoulders, but doesn't leave. She wants to hear Sarge's fate.

Marley looks at Sarge for a second and reaches forward as if to take the tape off his mouth, but thinks better of it.

"Troy, we've spent a lot of time deliberating over what to do with you. I'm sure you've already realised that we won't be offering you a home here with us. But we *have* decided to let you go. We will not imprison you or hold you here against your will. You will be allowed to leave, but you are *not* welcome here. You'll be escorted to the river just north of the forest surrounding the cabin, and that will be our boundary. The cabin will be yours to use and we'll give you food to ensure your survival over the winter, but you'll not be permitted weapons other than a single hunting knife. And if you cross the boundary north of the river, you'll be shot on sight. You leave in the morning."

He steps forward and rips the tape from Sarge's mouth. Sarge grimaces as it tears at his whiskers and he nods. "I understand."

"Good," Marley replies, then walks away.

There are tears in Maria's eyes as she smiles at Sarge, relieved that he'll be allowed to go. He looks up at her and nods. His eyes have lost the edge they had earlier. He does seem to care for her after all.

I watch Maria walk to the kitchen, where she joins Johnny and KJ, then turn my attention back to Sarge. He's already watching me, and as soon as I look at him, a triumphant grin spreads across his face.

CHAPTER 46

I have no idea what time it is when I wake, and I don't know why I've woken. The bunkroom is still completely dark and silent. After a few minutes, I realise there's no chance I'll fall back to sleep, so I make my way down the stairs to the living room.

Skye and Ollie's heads turn in my direction as soon as I enter the room. I wave in greeting and they both raise their hands in acknowledgement. Sarge is lying on his side on a mattress on the floor, eyes closed. I assume he's asleep.

"I can take over from one of you if you want. I can't sleep."

Skye and Oliver look at each other to see who's going to volunteer to stay.

"You go," Skye offers to Ollie. "I'm not tired."

"Are you sure?"

"Yeah, absolutely, you go," Skye replies.

"Thanks, guys. See you in the morning." Ollie stands and holds out the gun to me.

"No problem. Goodnight." I take his seat and look at Skye. "Do you know what time it is?"

She glances at her watch. "Quarter to four."

Sarge stirs in his sleep and she puts her finger to her lips. I roll my eyes, but nod. Skye goes back to reading the book on her lap and I sit and stare at Sarge sleeping in front of us.

I play out scenarios in my head of how he'll try to get to us and the things we could do to protect ourselves. *If we always stay in a group, we'd be safe, wouldn't we? How could he possibly overpower us if we have guns and he doesn't?* The memory of how easily he overpowered KJ to take her gun from her yesterday flashes in my mind. *That's how.*

This is a mistake. We shouldn't be letting him go. I take a deep breath, trying to push away the feeling of dread, turning the gun over in my hand as I watch him lying there. It would be so easy to just shoot him, right here and now, to end this and not have to worry about what he will do to us later. I look at Skye, still reading her book. Her eyes flick up to me and then to my hands, raising her eyebrows.

I look down and realise the gun is pointing at Sarge and quickly lower it toward the floor, giving Skye an embarrassed half smile.

I sit for hours, thinking and watching, saying nothing, until finally the door opens from the hallway and Jackson, Marley, and Johnny walk in. Sarge stirs as they say good morning and begin banging around in the kitchen, making drinks and breakfast. Dean, Matt, and Ethan emerge soon after, followed by the girls.

Johnny and Lily offer to take over guard duty so Skye and I can join the others for breakfast. I accept a cup of coffee from Ethan and take an empty seat beside Dean at the table. I don't feel like eating, even the smell of food is nauseating. Lack of sleep mixed with anxiety is making me feel sick and on edge. My hands begin to shake and I realise the coffee probably hadn't been such a good idea, either.

It's agreed that Ethan, Marley, and Johnny will escort Sarge to the river boundary, where he will be given a backpack of food and other supplies he'll need to survive the winter. Maria will bring him more in a month's time, but other than that, he'll be on his own.

KJ and Maria leave with Skye to pack provisions for Sarge. I give up trying to drink my coffee and go over to Johnny to relieve him from guard duty so he can get ready to leave.

It isn't long before they're ready to go, and Maria comes over and hugs Sarge. Although she's relieved that he's being allowed to go, I can see that she's finding it hard to say goodbye. I heard she'd contemplated going with him, but KJ convinced her to stay.

As they lead him to the door, Sarge casually leans toward me. "I'll be seeing you," he whispers.

My eyes dart toward the others to see if they heard what he said, but no-one seems to have noticed. My heart skips a beat. Yesterday's threat could have been dismissed as an angry outburst made in the heat of the moment. But today, his words provide chilling certainty it wasn't just an empty threat.

I follow them into the hallway that separates the living area from the decontamination room and grab my jacket from the hook by the door, shoving my feet into my boots. I'm surprised to see Dean has just finished putting his on. He waits for me while I tie up my laces. He doesn't ask where I'm going. I don't ask him either.

We catch up with Marley and the others as they're heading out the bunker door. Ethan looks surprised when he sees us, but gives me a smile. "You coming with us?"

"Probably not the whole way," I reply. "I just want to make sure he doesn't have any problems leaving."

"You guys coming to see me off?" Sarge calls over his shoulder as he begins walking. "Aren't you sweet."

"Something like that," Dean says.

We walk in silence along the trail we'd followed back from the cabin, cutting through the trees to the plateau beyond. The snow has begun to melt after the sun of the last two days, patches of brown grassy earth now visible between the deeper drifts. It will be gone in another day or two if the weather remains clear.

We're part way across the plateau when Sarge stumbles and nearly falls. Ethan and Johnny decide we're far enough away from the bunker now to untie Sarge's hands, so Johnny takes out his knife and cuts the cable tie binding them. Sarge rubs his wrists gratefully and stretches his neck. As he rolls his head from side to side, he glances back at me, subtle but deliberate. The hint of a smile on his face.

The memory of Rhys's face leaps into my mind. My hand protectively raises to my throat, a subconscious response I'm not even aware of until I've done it.

I look at Ethan and wonder if Sarge knows he is one of the people I care most about. *Will he kill him first or save him for last like he said he would?* Bile rises in my throat. *This is a mistake. We're making a terrible mistake.*

I feel panicked and look at Dean, his eyes still focused on Sarge. He doesn't trust him either. *Does he think Sarge will try something* too?

Johnny holds out a water bottle to Sarge, taking care not to get within arm's reach. Sarge opens the bottle and tips his head back, taking a long drink. And there it is again. The briefest of glances and this time, even though the bottle is covering his mouth, there's definitely a smile. *He* is *going to try something.*

I raise my shaking hand to my forehead, scratching beneath my hat. My other hand wraps around the gun in my pocket. Watching, ready.

He places the lid back on the bottle and holds it out to Johnny. Johnny reaches for it, holding back the rifle slung over his shoulder to prevent it swinging forward.

My eyes don't move from Sarge, watching, waiting, no longer aware of any sound except my pulse thumping in my ears and my breath as I exhale loudly, trying to stay calm. Everything inside of me screaming a warning that he can't be trusted, that he will kill … every … single … one of us.

As Johnny reaches for the water bottle, it slips from Sarge's hand. Johnny bends to pick it up, and I see Sarge's eyes flick to me again. I know what he's going to do, and I watch in horror as his hand jerks toward Johnny's gun.

I feel a jolt and startle as I hear a shot ring out and Sarge drops to the ground. Ethan and Johnny spin around, guns raised, searching for the source of the gunshot. My mouth drops open in shock. I turn my head toward Dean, certain he must have done it, but he isn't holding a gun. His face turns to me, revealing only the merest hint of surprise.

"What the hell have you done?" Marley yells. I watch in a kind of daze as his hand wraps over the top of mine. I look down and see my hands are raised in front of me. I let out a deep breath and let him unwrap my fingers, removing the gun from my hand.

Johnny kneels next to Sarge's unmoving body, checks for a pulse, then looks up at Ethan and shakes his head. Ethan immediately strides toward us, as though he thinks he might need to intervene between Marley and me.

"You killed him, Jess!" Marley's words snap me out of my daze.

"He's dead?" I know the answer but want to hear it again. "Are you sure?"

Johnny nods at me.

"What the hell, Jess!" Marley explodes. "You shot an unarmed man."

I shake my head. "No. He was going to take Johnny's gun, I could tell. I could see what he was going to do. He was going to do it again, just like he did when he shot Priya." I can see Marley isn't convinced. "You weren't there, Marley. You didn't see it. He was going to do it again! Except this time, he was going to kill everybody!"

"You don't know that." Marley lowers his voice.

"I do know! You saw it, didn't you?" I turn to Dean. "That look he gave us? He was gloating, as though he'd already done it. You saw it, didn't you?"

"Yeah, I saw it." Dean exhales slowly, nodding. "If Jess hadn't done it, I would've."

Marley shakes his head in disbelief, in frustration. "Goddam it, Jess. Can't you see that it doesn't matter what you *thought* he might do? You can't go around shooting unarmed people because you *think* they might do something to hurt you. That's murder."

"I did it to stop him from killing YOU … and Ethan … and Dean, and Johnny … and yes, *me*, but he wasn't going to kill *me* next. He was going to make me watch him kill every single one of you first. He *told* me that was what he was going to do. That's *what* he was about to do!"

"God, this is a bloody mess." Marley rubs his forehead. "I know you thought you were doing the right thing." He holds his hand up to stop me interrupting. "But we voted to let him go. You made it clear to everyone that you thought we shouldn't let him go. So, this is going to look like you've taken the law into your own hands and executed him. They're going to think you've just ignored the decision made by our community and done what you wanted to do anyway."

"I did it to protect our group," I say quietly, shaking my head. "Do you really think I *wanted* to kill someone? I didn't do this out of revenge or because I wanted him dead. I did this because he told me he would come back and kill all of you. And it wasn't an empty threat, Marley. He *was* going to do it! I just stopped him before he could."

"I know … I know." Marley sighs. His response surprises me. I wasn't expecting him to understand, and I can see that he genuinely cares. He puts his arms around me and hugs me, and it reminds me of when my dad hugged me after I crashed the car trying to avoid hitting a cat.

"The road to hell is paved with good intentions." I repeat my dad's words under my breath.

"Indeed." Marley nods sadly.

****

I can't bring myself to make eye contact with anyone when we enter the bunker. Dean and Ethan stay close to me, my personal bodyguards protecting me from the reaction of the others as Marley explains what happened.

I'd expected them to be shocked and disapproving. And I should have expected the anger, especially from Maria, but it does take me a little by surprise. Johnny has to hold her back as she screams at me from across the room, calling me a murderer and telling me I'm no better than Rhys if I thought I could kill someone because I felt like it. KJ doesn't yell at me, but I can see she's angry, as though I've betrayed her trust. It was the same feeling I got from Johnny after he'd gotten over the initial shock of me shooting Sarge, unable to hide his disappointment. I'd let him down.

I understand their sense of betrayal. They'd chosen me and my friends over Rhys and Troy. They'd chosen us because they thought we'd choose peace and kindness over violence and the 'survival by any means' necessary approach they'd witnessed since the outbreak. But as I now realise, terrible deeds are often done for the greater good, and this deed is now *my* burden to bear.

Most of the others sit dumbfounded, shaking their heads in disbelief, but it's Matt's reaction that's the hardest for me to take … because he doesn't react at all. And not knowing what he's thinking is worse than knowing the others are angry. He heard Sarge's threat to me yesterday. He knew it was real. But to him, even killing an animal is completely unacceptable, so killing a person is beyond comprehension.

I know they need to talk, to decide how to deal with me, so I offer to go up to my bedroom to let them talk without me present. As soon as I close the door behind me, I hear voices rise in anger and Marley's rising above them as he tries to get them to listen. I don't want to hear what they have to say and am relieved that I can't once I'm in the bunkroom with the door shut.

I lie down on my bed. Close my eyes. And wait.

CHAPTER 47

I wake to the sound of someone knocking gently on the bedroom door and immediately call out, "Come in," as I sit up on the edge of the bed.

"Hi," Marley says as he enters the room, shutting the door behind him.

He gives me a reassuring smile in response to my worried expression, then reaches out and takes my hand and sits beside me … which only makes me feel more worried.

"Obviously you aren't going to execute me," I blurt. "Because we've already ruled out the death penalty as a punishment. So, what's it going to be? Imprisonment in the cave? Cleaning duty for the next five years?"

Marley takes a deep breath, his smile disappearing. "We've voted to exile you for one month." He pauses, waiting for his words to sink in.

"You're kicking me out?"

"Yes, but only for one month."

"I'm supposed to go to the cabin?" I ask slowly.

Marley nods. "You'll be given provisions, same as Troy was going to get, but you'll be allowed to take a gun and ammunition for hunting."

I swallow, willing myself not to cry. "It's nearly winter." I shake my head, remembering how cold it was there.

"That's why it's only for a month. Some of the others wanted it to be longer, but we settled on a month."

"Did everyone vote for this?"

"No, it was a majority vote. Dean, Ethan, and Matt are angry that you're even being punished at all and said they'd go with you if the group voted for you to leave."

I sigh with relief, almost euphoric at the knowledge that they're not angry with me. On the contrary, they actually support me. "So, they're coming with me?"

Marley shakes his head. "Some of the others got pretty upset and demanded that the exile is done in isolation otherwise it wouldn't be enough of a punishment. It got pretty heated when the boys said they would go with you anyway, whether we wanted them to or not." Marley's forehead furrows. "In the end we had to insist they didn't, and we had to establish our first law as a community to stop them. From now on, anyone who goes against a majority ruling will be permanently banished from the bunker."

My mouth drops open. I can't believe it has come to this.

"We can't allow members of our group to go against the decisions of the community," Marley continues. "If we make a decision as a group, everyone needs to follow it. It's the way it has to be, and if someone doesn't like it … they can leave."

I swallow uncomfortably. I never meant to go against the decision of our community. I never meant to betray them. I did it to protect them because I care about them! And now at least half of them either view me as a traitor or a criminal, or worse, for what I've done.

How am I ever going to fix this? How will they ever trust me again?

"And you?" I ask quietly. "What did you vote for?"

Marley hesitates and looks down at his hands, nervously picking at his thumbnail. Finally, he makes eye contact. "I supported the month of isolation. It was my suggestion actually." He reaches out to take my hand again, seeing the hurt in my eyes. "I was trying to find a middle ground. You have to understand that this couldn't go unpunished. We *have* to have rules if it's going to work for us to live together up here, and we all need to follow those rules, no matter how good our intentions. No one can be above them, otherwise what's the point? And then anyone would be free to do whatever they want, to whoever they want. We have to be held to account for our actions or it'll lead to anarchy."

"And after the exile? What then? Do I just come back and things go back to normal?"

"That's the intention." Marley nods. "And that's why I suggested the time in isolation. It'll give the others a chance to cool down and hopefully we'll be able to move past this so there aren't any issues when you come back. They need to see that some sort of justice is served for what has happened. You see that too, don't you?"

"Yeah, I get it … I do." I nod. "Doesn't mean I have to like it though."

"No, you don't. But let me put it this way. If we weren't stuck up here in the middle of nowhere, you would've been arrested and tried for murder for what you've done, and sent to jail for a very long time. You still might be, when we get out of here."

My hands begin to shake as the truth of his words sink in.

Marley pats my hand. "I'm not trying to scare you. I'm just trying to get you to understand how serious this is, and that a month in isolation is really nothing in comparison to what you'd get in the real world." I nod at his concerned face. "Look, I better go. Matt's waiting outside. I'll let you guys talk alone." He gives my hand a squeeze and then walks over to the door.

I see Matt in the hallway as Marley opens the door. They speak briefly, then Matt walks in and closes the door behind him. I stand and turn to face him. *Don't cry.* He walks over and puts his arms around me as I bury my face into his chest. *Don't cry.* I take deep breaths as he strokes my hair, and when I'm sure I've got my emotions under control, I step back and force myself to smile.

"I hear you wanted to come with me."

"Yeah. I thought it might be kinda nice, just the two of us living in that cabin together all alone for a month … but then Dean and Ethan insisted on coming too."

I let out a quiet laugh. "Thanks, Matt. You always seem to know how to make me feel better."

"Did Marley tell you they want you to do this on your own, though?"

"Let me guess, 'they' is Maria?"

"Yeah, and Katie."

"Who else?"

"Kai and Skye are pretty angry too, and Ollie keeps muttering about giving people the opportunity for redemption."

"And what about the others?"

"They were fairly quiet. I think Jackson is kind of glad in a way that you did it. You know how he's always worried about security and the threat of outsiders, so I think he figures you did us a favour in the long run. But he also understands that we can't just let it go because some of the others are so angry. I think that's where Lily's at too."

"And Johnny?"

"I honestly don't know where Johnny's at. He's not really saying anything. I don't know if he's worried about upsetting Katie and Maria or whether he just doesn't have an opinion. But Maria and Katie wanted you banished permanently, and he voted for the single month, so I guess that gives you a bit of an idea."

"They wanted to banish me for good?"

"They said you should get the same punishment Troy was getting. They said you committed the same crime, so you should be given the same punishment."

How could they think that? Yes, I killed someone, but I did it to protect everyone. It wasn't the same as what Troy did. Was it?

"What about you? Do you think I'm like Troy? Am I some kind of monster?" I'm terrified to say the word out loud, to make it true.

"No!" Matt's eyes widen as he shakes his head. "Of course, I don't think that. You and Dean tried to warn us. *I* even tried to warn them after he threatened you, but they wouldn't listen. You may have pulled the trigger, but we all forced you to do it. Dean actually said we should be thanking you, not punishing you. That we were too afraid of getting our conscience dirty to make the hard call. He said he would've shot Troy if you hadn't, so if you're guilty, then so is he, and that's why he should go with you."

I can't help but smile, knowing that I haven't been disowned by all my friends. That Dean and Ethan and Matt still have my back … like they have every step of this nightmarish journey. I feel overwhelmed with gratitude and love for these boys, and I'm going to miss them terribly.

"So, when do I have to leave?"

"As soon as we're ready. Dean and Ethan are sorting a few last things, and then we'll head off." He puts his arms around my waist. "Everything is going to be fine, Jess, I promise."

He pulls me closer, smiling down at me, then slowly bends his head until our lips meet.

Matt sighs as a loud knock startles us from our kiss. "Impeccable timing." He shakes his head and then calls out, "Come in."

The door opens and Ethan pokes his head through the crack. "Hi." He smiles at me, then looks at Matt. "We're ready. Let's get this show on the road before someone works out we're not coming back."

"What?" I look from Ethan to Matt and back to Ethan, then see Dean standing behind him in the hallway. "What are you talking about, not coming back? Get in here." I pull the door wide open and wait for Ethan and Dean to enter the room, then shut it behind them. "What's going on?"

"We're coming with you," Ethan replies matter-of-factly as Matt and Dean nod.

"Damn right," Dean says. "There's no way I'm letting you do this on your own. We've been in this together from the start and I'm not going to leave you to finish it on your own now."

"I thought you understood we're going to go with you?" Matt looks as confused as I feel.

"No." I shake my head. "Well, yes, Marley told me that you wanted to come with me, but he also told me that you would all be banished permanently if you did."

"There's no way they'll do that." Ethan shakes his head. "They were just having a tantrum yesterday when they realised they couldn't stop us. They'll get over it by the time we come back in a month."

"They can't just throw us out because we don't agree," Matt says.

I shake my head, stunned that they're prepared to do this for me. "But what if they don't let us back in?"

"They will," Dean replies. "They just need time to cool down and then it'll all be fine."

"You don't know that. Maybe we could've taken the risk before Maria and the others joined the group, but I don't think we can trust that they'll get over this anytime soon. Especially not Maria."

"They'll have to let *you* back in, even if they don't let the rest of us," Ethan says. "It's only the three of us that would be banished."

"How does that make it any better?" I say, shaking my head. "Would you really be okay with being exiled if it comes to it?" I look from face to face. "Because I wouldn't."

"If it comes to it, which I don't think it will," Dean replies. "Then yeah, I'm okay with it. I don't think I'd want to be part of this community if it would throw someone out for disagreeing with them."

"There's no way we could survive out there without the food from the bunker." My chest tightens. "I know you and Ethan are good hunters, but it's going to be winter soon and we could starve to death before it's over."

"We'll be fine," Ethan says.

"You don't know that. I won't take the risk with your lives. I can't be responsible for your deaths too." My voice breaks.

"It's our risk to take, not yours," Matt says.

"This is all my fault, all of it." I swallow hard. "Dean, I know you *think* you're as guilty as me because you were prepared to kill Sarge, but that's just not true. *I* killed Rhys, that was all *my* doing, and if I hadn't killed him, none of this would've happened."

"What the hell are you going on about, Jess?" Dean looks incredulously at me. "You can't seriously be saying it would've been better if you'd died instead of Rhys? He would've killed you if you hadn't killed him. How would that have stopped all this? Because then I *definitely* would've been the one who'd shot Sarge if you hadn't been there to do it."

"There weren't any bullets left and Rhys didn't even know about the knife," I reply. "You and Johnny arrived so soon after. If I'd just held him off a little longer, you would've got to us in time. I know you would have, and then I wouldn't have needed to kill Rhys. If I hadn't killed Rhys, Sarge wouldn't have shot Priya. I may not have pulled the trigger, but her death is still on my hands. She would still be here if I hadn't killed Rhys … and so would Sarge." My hands shake as I try to fight back tears. "Somehow I've got to find a way to live with what I've done, and if being exiled to the cabin for a month on my own is a step toward doing that, I'll gladly do it. Because I honestly feel like I deserve so much worse than what I'm getting. I'm responsible for the deaths of three people! I killed two unarmed men, and Priya is dead because of my actions." Tears spill over my cheeks. "Maybe I *can* find a way to redeem myself for what I've done, but I could never forgive myself if anything happened to the three of you because of me. I can't be responsible for your deaths too. I can't!"

I can see that my words have gotten through to them, their looks of stubborn resolve softening as they consider what I'm saying.

"Thank you so much for wanting to come with me, for offering to make this sacrifice for me. You have no idea how much this means … How much *you all* mean to me." I smile through my tears at each of them. "But you can't come with me. This is something I need to do on my own. I didn't feel like I had a choice when I did those other things, but I know I have a choice this time. And I have to make the right one. I can't be responsible for your lives, for fracturing our family. Because until we can get home, this is the only one we've got."

****

I look around the living room as everyone gathers to say goodbye and notice straight away that Maria, KJ, and Skye are missing. I wasn't expecting Maria to be there anyway, and I can understand why KJ isn't. But knowing Skye is still too angry to even come and say goodbye makes the knot in my stomach tighten further.

I feel apprehensive as Kai walks over to me, knowing she'd been angry too, but she takes me by surprise by being the first to hug me and wishes me well. Then Jackson steps forward, his eyes a mixture of warmth and concern. He's holding a book in his hands. I glance down at the title: *Robinson Crusoe*.

"It was on Kalen's list." He holds it out to me. "I found it on the bookshelf and thought you might want to take it with you."

I take the book and stare at the cover for a few seconds, then hug it to my chest, fighting the urge to cry. "Thanks, Jacks. I'd really like that." I reach up on my tiptoes to give him a peck on the cheek.

Marley is next, hugging me tightly as he tells me to be strong and that I'll be back here with everyone soon, and then Johnny approaches and awkwardly gives me a hug.

"I didn't get the chance to thank you for helping us," I say as he lets me go. "I know you probably wish you hadn't, after what I did. You chose to help us to stop anyone being killed and I'm really sorry I let you down. I hope one day you'll be able to forgive me."

"I know you did it for the right reasons," he says quietly. "It's better to do something wrong for the right reasons than nothing for the wrong ones. Trust me, I know."

I nod. "I guess we've both got to find a way to forgive ourselves. But you've started on that path at least. Now it's my turn."

Ollie is waiting beside him, and as I turn to face him, he takes me by the shoulders, holding me at arm's length. "I may not agree with what you did … You know I'm a sucker for the redemption storyline. But I guess that just means I'm rooting for you now. I'm going to miss you, Jess."

"At least that means you think there's hope for me too then, right?" I say as he pulls me in for a hug. "I'm going to miss you too, you big goof."

Lily is last. As I go to hug her, she puts her hand up to stop me. "I'm terrible at goodbyes, so I'm just going to come with you guys."

"Okay." I turn to my escorts, waiting for me beside the door. "I guess we better get going."

"I put in two sleeping bags," Dean says as he hands me my backpack. "It was bloody cold there the other night."

"Yeah. It was." I give him a small smile. "Thanks, Dean."

I'm just about to swing the pack over my shoulder when Skye bursts through the door, pausing as she scans the room. Her face floods with relief when she sees me. "I thought I might've been too late."

I bite my bottom lip as it starts to tremble and lower my head as the tears begin to fall. I don't even notice her cross the room until she grabs me in a hug. "It'll be okay," she says.

"I know," I mumble, wiping my eyes.

"We'll come and check on you in a week or so." Skye looks at Marley, who nods in reply.

"It's not being on my own that's making me upset. I just feel ashamed, I guess, like I've let everyone down."

"Don't say that." Her eyebrows pull together in a frown. "You shouldn't feel ashamed for wanting to protect the people you care about, Jess. Never feel ashamed about that."

I nod, wiping the remaining tears from my cheeks with both hands. "Thanks, Skye."

I swing my pack onto my back and square my shoulders, readying myself, before turning to face the others waiting by the door. "Let's go."

An icy blast hits me as I open the outer door and step outside onto the packed snow. I pause to take a deep breath, filling my lungs with the crisp air, and begin to walk.

I don't wait for the others to join me. I don't look back.

FORTUNE FALLS BOOK 2: NOVAS

Struggling in the aftermath of the devastating attack on the Fortune Falls community, Jess fears history will repeat itself when a new group of survivors arrive. With supplies stretched thin, their only hope is to send an expedition far from the safety of the plateau.

Jess joins a team on a perilous journey to find out if other communities have survived. Determined to go with her, Matt and Ethan have to find a way to put aside their growing rivalry, adding further tension to an already volatile situation.

Can the group find the supplies their community needs? Or will the success of their mission be the least of their worries?

FREE BONUS MATERIAL

Subscribers to Lou Vane's newsletter receive free bonus material, including *Fortune Falls Deleted Scenes* and *Ethan and Skye*—a side-story novella that tells the story of what happens to Ethan and Skye while they're separated from the rest of the Fortune Falls crew.

To receive your free bonus material, subscribe to Lou Vane's newsletter at www.louvane.com/contact

ACKNOWLEDGEMENTS

Thank you to my wonderful family for their unwavering support. Your love, advice and encouragement have meant more to me than you'll ever know.

Mum, Bob, Heidi, Harrison, and Rach, you have been my amazing team of beta readers, providing invaluable feedback while keeping faithful to the story that I wanted to tell. Thank you so much.

To my partner, David, and sons, Harrison and Benjamin, thank you for encouraging my creativity and supporting me in my desire to write this story. Without it, I would never have found the courage to do this. You are the lights of my life.

To Dad, thank you for hauling me up all those mountains and opening my eyes to the natural beauty of our world. My memories of those remarkable places have helped form the backdrop for this story.

Finally, I would like to thank my extraordinary sister, Heidi, my editor-in-chief, who always found the time within her incredibly busy life to read and give feedback on each and every draft. I couldn't have done this without you. This is the best story it can be because of you. Thanks, sis!

ABOUT THE AUTHOR

Originally from the South Island of New Zealand, Lou Vane now lives in Adelaide, Australia with her partner and two young sons, where she's a full-time mum and writer.

Growing up in NZ, Lou spent many weekends hiking in mountainous areas filled with hidden hot springs, waterfalls, and lakes, and then later visited the geothermal wonderland of Iceland on her overseas travels.

Lou's memories of these remarkable places form the backdrop for *Fortune Falls*, and her love of post-apocalyptic tales provided the creative spark that inspired her to write this story.

Fortune Falls is Lou Vane's first novel.

****

Lou loves hearing from her readers, so if you would like to get in touch, you can contact Lou via her:

- Website: www.louvane.com
- Facebook: www.facebook.com/Louvane.Author
- Instagram: www.instagram.com/louvaneauthor
- TikTok: www.tiktok.com/@louvaneauthor
- Or email: lou@louvane.com